DAW=sf
BOOKS

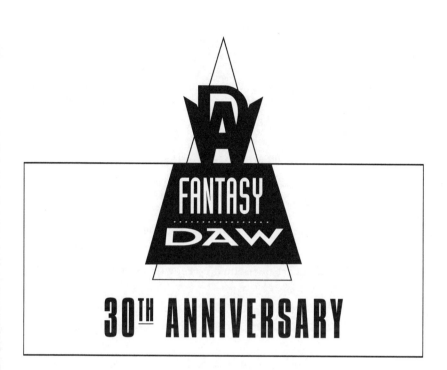

30ᵀᴴ ANNIVERSARY

Edited by

ELIZABETH R. WOLLHEIM

and

SHEILA E. GILBERT

DAW BOOKS, INC.

DONALD A. WOLLHEIM, FOUNDER

375 Hudson Street, New York, NY 10014

ELIZABETH R. WOLLHEIM
SHEILA E. GILBERT
PUBLISHERS

http://www.dawbooks.com

Jacket art by G-Force Design

Text design by Stanley S. Drate / Folio Graphics Co. Inc.

DAW Books Collectors No. 1222.

DAW Books are distributed by Penguin Putnam Inc.

With special thanks to the folks
at Tekno Books for their help in
seeing this project to fruition.

First Printing, May 2002
1   2   3   4   5   6   7   8   9   10

*We dedicate these volumes
in loving memory of our founders,
Donald A. Wollheim
and
Elsie B. Wollheim,
and of our resident curmudgeon,
Mike Gilbert.*

————————

And for all DAW authors, past, present and future.

Acknowledgments

SOW'S EAR—SILK PURSE ©2002 by Andre Norton

THE REBUKE ©2002 by Michael Shea

PERSIAN EYES ©2002 by Tanith Lee

CORONACH OF THE BELL ©2002 by Christopher Stasheff

ENDING AND BEGINNING ©2002 by Jennifer Roberson

AFTER MIDNIGHT ©2002 by Mercedes R. Lackey

NIGHTFALL'S PROMISE ©2002 by Miriam S. Zucker

WE TWO MAY MEET ©2002 by Tanya Huff

THE SACRIFICE ©2002 by Melanie Rawn

HEART-HEALER ©2002 by Deborah J. Ross

A PERFECT DAY IN VALDEMAR ©2002 by Larry Dixon

DRACONIS EX MACHINA ©2002 by Phyllis Irene Radford Karr

THE HAMLET ©2002 by Marjorie B. Kellogg

MOONLOVER AND THE FOUNTAIN OF BLOOD ©2002 by Jane S. Fancher

THE MEMORY OF STONE ©2002 by Michelle West

THE HUNTSMAN ©2002 by Fiona Patton

LINKED, ON THE LAKE OF SOULS ©2002 by Kristen Britain

IT'S ABOUT SQUIRRELS . . . ©2002 by Lynn Abbey

Introduction

MY father never told me that he was planning to leave his job at Ace Books. It was 1971, and I was in college. I can only assume that he didn't want to distract me from my studies—that he wanted to shelter me for as long as he could. So I found out after the fact, with the rest of the science fiction world. It was as much of a shock to me as it was to anyone else. Actually it was *more* of a shock to me than to anyone else—for my dad, the most responsible and loyal man I knew, had just picked up and walked away from his job! It was simply unimaginable but it had happened, and it rattled my world down to its deepest foundations.

Don had been continually employed in editorial positions since 1941 when he had his first (unpaid) job editing pulp magazines. He continued to edit magazines, compiled numerous anthologies, worked in editorial positions at some of the very first paperback book lines ever produced, and in 1952, convinced A. A. Wyn, owner of Ace Publications, to let him initiate a line of paperback books for Ace.

The one thing he *hadn't* been in thirty years was unemployed.

My dad took his responsibility to our family very seriously. He also took his work very seriously. But something monumental had begun to happen to the publishing industry. Publishing was becoming "big business" and was no longer the intimate, eccentric, personality-driven industry it had once been. Don, who had been present during the birth of the paperback book, didn't like what was happening. He was Editor-in-Chief of Ace Books for nineteen and a half years and eventually became the Vice President as well. He considered Ace *his* list, *his* creation, and for most of our field at the time, the name Donald A. Wollheim was synonymous with Ace Books. But Ace wasn't really Don's company, and with the death of A. A. Wyn in 1968 that became glaringly obvious.

As Ace became more and more "corporate," passing from the hands of one owner to another, the situation became less and less tolerable for Don. By 1971, he had come to the end of his rope—so he did the unthinkable. With no concrete prospects for the future, and no warning to his employers, he left his office at Ace Books, never to return.

It was a very tense time for our family, for although Elsie, my mom, had been a professional woman before my birth, my father had been the sole support of our household since 1951. Don wasn't entirely sure what to do. What he *was* sure of was this: he would never again work for years building an editorial list only to lose it. There was only one way to avoid that: by founding his own publishing company. But how could he? As a long-term employee of a notoriously frugal publisher, he had never been able to amass the money necessary for such an enterprise. All Don had was his reputation.

Luckily, it proved to be enough.

In the fall of 1971, Don met with Herb Schnall, one of the chief executives of New American Library. After several brief meetings, Herb made a statement which would change publishing history: he told Don that New American Library would take him "any way [he wanted] to come." Don could write his own ticket.

It was an offer Don couldn't refuse.

Elated, Don came home to think about his options. My dad, my mom, and I sat at the table in our narrow galley kitchen in Queens, and tried to define Don's dream. He wanted the strong national distribution which only a big company could offer— hence his meeting with NAL—but unlike most independently distributed lines, he also wanted the professional production and promotion facilities of a big publishing company. He wanted his company's list to be sold aggressively with the strength of a big corporate imprint, yet he wanted total artistic freedom, not only inside his books but in relation to the cover art and design as well, and he did not want to share the ownership of his company. Basically, he wanted to form a private corporation and enter into a contractual arrangement with New American Library to provide the services that he needed.

But corporate parameters were not Don's only concern.

For thirty years Don had edited all types of fiction. He had edited not only literary books but most of the genres—from westerns to crime to thrillers to mysteries to detective and horror novels. He had put the light into the window of the ever present mansion on the cover of the Gothic romance, had published William Burroughs' first work, and had introduced J.R.R. Tolkien's *The Lord of the Rings* to the American paperback audience. He even edited nurse novels and cookbooks. But since the age of eleven he had had only one real love—science fiction. He had waited a lifetime for this opportunity, and he decided to dedicate his new company to the books he loved the most. He wanted to found the first publishing company devoted exclusively to science fiction and fantasy.

In November of 1971, NAL agreed to Don's proposal, and DAW Books, Inc. was born.

My father had signed a contract, but he was still a long way from fulfilling his dream. As we sat in the kitchen—our traditional spot for family discussions—and Don thought aloud about possible employees to help him in his new venture, I noticed my mom, Elsie, becoming more and more agitated. Finally, she exploded: "Don, what about ME?" My dad looked quite stupefied. It was clear that he had never even considered that his wife would join him in this enterprise, but Elsie was the logical choice: she had legal experience, and had run her father's company. The obvious solution was staring him straight in the face.

Bringing Elsie into the company may very well have been Don's shrewdest business decision. Elsie embraced her new position as Corporate Secretary-Treasurer of DAW with all the fervor of a mother grizzly defending her young. Every aspect of DAW and all DAW authors were sheltered under her huge protective wing. And for a petite woman, she had enormous wings indeed! Marion Zimmer Bradley once said, "Elsie has the spirit of a lion in the body of a sparrow." And it was never more true than when she took up her position as Champion-Of-All-Things-DAW.

The next six months were a nightmare.

With liftoff scheduled for April 1972, Don was under the gun to purchase, edit, and package six months' worth of titles in thirty days to catch up with NAL's production schedule. Elsie had to set up accounts payable, accounts receivable, royalty reports, bookkeeping, and an entire subsidiary rights department. Together, they wrote the first DAW boilerplate contract. For my father, himself a published author with eighteen books and numerous short stories to his credit, it was important to formulate a writer-friendly contract.

My parents were nervous wrecks. Don couldn't sleep or eat—I remember more than one occasion when Elsie or I had to run to the kitchen to get Don something sweet because he was feeling light-headed. Don and Elsie were exhausted, but it was with the excited exhaustion of new parents. It was a frightening and exhilarating time.

The following spring, the first DAW books were due to debut at the 1972 Lunacon, but the night before the convention started, they still hadn't left the warehouse in New Jersey. Elsie and Don were up the entire night collecting their very first DAW books and hand delivering them to the dealers at New York's local convention. Lunacon was thereafter a very special time for my folks.

As for me, I went back to college and graduated with a degree in English Lit, while serving a simultaneous four-year stint in art school. My parents had kept me apprised of the goings-on at DAW, and sent me occasional manuscripts to read and comment on, particularly when Don had discovered someone he felt was noteworthy. I especially remember Don's excitement in 1974 when he sent me *Gate of Ivrel*, C. J. Cherryh's first novel, and *The Birthgrave*, Tanith Lee's first full-length fantasy novel.

Although I was Corporate Vice President of DAW from the get go, and had always been involved on a certain level, Don never pressured me to come home to New York right after graduation. He thought it would be healthier for me to find my own sea legs in the business world. With my experience working as a freelance copyeditor for Ace Books (under my father's stern tutelage) during high school, I landed a job in one of the last hot-type printing houses in Cambridge, Massachusetts as a proofreader, then later, a dual position as proofreader and darkroom technician for one of the very first computerized printing houses in the industry. What a disaster! For every mistake corrected, the printing computer (which took up most of a good-sized wall) would generate numerous new ones. Whole chapters would suddenly become italicized. Thankfully, computers have improved enormously since those days. My two years working for printers have proved invaluable to me as a publisher.

Finally, in 1975, I came home and took up a position as Don's general assistant and Associate Editor. By this time DAW was an established, successful line, and Don and Elsie were a recognized corporate couple. However, it is never easy working with your parents, and Don and Elsie were no exception. One of the saving graces of my situation was the presence of my old friend Sheila Gilbert, who was working as a copywriter for NAL. Sheila and I had known each other since we were thirteen and eleven, respectively, and had bonded through various embarrassing fan activities, such as the Galaxy of Fashion Show at the 1967 NYcon, where I was the "Bride of the Future," and Sheila and her oldest sister Marsha were "The Gemini Twins." Numerous were the times I sought refuge in my old friend's office, and as the years passed, Sheila was promoted to head up the Signet science fiction list, and I wrested more and more editorial and art direction control from the unyielding hands of my father. Sheila and I became close friends.

Neither of us realized just how important that friendship would prove to be.

In April 1985, when I had been working with my parents for ten years, catastrophe struck. Don went into the hospital with a complicated critical illness, and remained there on the brink of death for seven brutal months. We were just about to launch the fledgling DAW hardcover list, which was my exclusive domain, with a novel from our most important writer, C. J. Cherryh, as well as a first novel from a very promising newcomer, Tad Williams. Elsie bravely insisted that I attend the American Booksellers Association Convention in San Francisco, where the DAW hardcover list was being debuted with special bound galleys, and where I was planning to meet Tad for the first time. I left New York not knowing if I would ever see my father alive again.

Well, Don survived, but it didn't take me long to discover what had made him so sick. At fourteen years of age, the health of DAW Books had begun to flag. The science fiction and fantasy industry had gone through some fundamental changes, and our company was desperately in need of renovation. During those terrible months, Elsie and I fought not only to keep Don alive, but to save the life of DAW as well.

Meanwhile, Sheila had been considering leaving her job at Signet. Elsie and I realized that she would be the perfect person to join us: she had editorial experience, knew our list, and was practically part of the family already. With no guarantee that we would be able to pull the company out of its slump, she agreed.

1985 was a difficult year, but Don survived and so did DAW. During Don's long illness and recovery—it was a year before he would return to the office—Sheila and I, with the loving support of Elsie, took over the company.

Don would never again be well enough to lead DAW.

Now, thirty years and more than twelve hundred titles since its founding, Don and Elsie are gone, but the essence of DAW remains the same: a small, personal business owned exclusively by me and Sheila. Sheila and I were startled to realize, as we were writing these introductions, that we have now been running the company longer than Don did. Like Don and Elsie before us, we are committed to keeping a "family" spirit at DAW—something we feel (as Don did) is all too rare in today's world of international conglomerate publishing. If anything, DAW is even more family-oriented now than it was in the beginning. Sheila and I brought our husbands, Mike Gilbert and Peter Stampfel, into the business. Our Business Manager Amy Fodera introduced us to her husband, Sean Fodera, who is now our Director of Subsidiary Rights, Contracts, and Electronic Publishing. Our Managing Editor Debra Euler is single, but we've told her that when she does marry, her husband will have a job waiting for him at DAW! (Or conversely, she has first right of refusal if we hire another employee.) Even our wonderful free-lance cover designer has been with us for nearly a dozen years.

With just six hardy employees (sadly, we lost Mike in August 2000), DAW Books manages to stay afloat in a sea of ocean liners. But our true family extends far beyond the DAW corporate offices. This real family includes the many wonderful authors who publish with us, the artists who grace the covers of our books with their beautiful paintings, and you, the readers who have loyally supported our little company for thirty years. We couldn't have done it without you—and we plan to keep giving you the finest in science fiction and fantasy for decades to come.

BETSY WOLLHEIM

I REMEMBER the day DAW was born. I remember it because the events which led up to DAW's birth had a definite impact on my own life, and though I didn't know it at the time, the creation of DAW Books, Inc. in the fall of 1971 would eventually affect my future both personally and professionally.

Of course, my relationship with the Wollheim family began long before DAW was even the glimmering of an idea in Don Wollheim's imagination. I first met Don, Elsie, and Betsy at a Lunacon in Manhattan in the spring of 1963. I was thirteen years old and it was my first science fiction convention. And among the many interesting people I had a chance to meet (some of whose works filled the bookcases of my own science fiction and fantasy reading family) were the Wollheims. My memory is that they were quite patient with and welcoming to an enthusiastic teen at her first convention. Perhaps the fact that Betsy was eleven at the time had something to do with it. Perhaps it merely foreshadowed the days when we would begin referring to Elsie as our "corporate Mom," a title any DAW author who was fortune enough to become part of our DAW family while Elsie was still alive would certainly understand.

Over the following seven years, I continued to run into the Wollheims at conventions and parties, and when I graduated college and started looking for a job in publishing I sent Don, who at the time was the Editor-in-Chief at Ace Books, a letter of inquiry about a job. Fortune smiled upon me, because the day after I had accepted—but not yet started—a job at another publishing company, I received a phone call from Don. He had a junior editorial position to fill, and he wanted me to come in for an interview. The idea of being paid to read and work on the books I would have been reading anyway seemed like a dream come true.

I started working for Don at Ace Thanksgiving week of 1970, and life was good. Then, one day in the fall of 1971, Don walked into my office to say good-bye. He was leaving the company that very day. I was totally stunned by the news.

Later, I heard that Don was starting his own company, DAW Books, Inc., which would be distributed by New American Library. Perhaps a month after that, I had a phone call from Ruth Haberstroh, a friend who had once shared an office with me at Ace and who was working at New American Library. She told me that before calling me she had asked Don if he was going to hire me. He responded that he wasn't going to be hiring anyone for a while, and so Ruth offered me a job at NAL. So in January 1972, I left Ace and joined NAL. One of the benefits of this move was that I could now frequently see Don and Elsie—and Betsy, as well, once she joined her parents in the family business.

In 1978, I took over the Signet science fiction line, which, in theory, might have put me in competition with DAW, but in reality it did nothing of the kind. Our lists were extremely compatible.

In 1985, Don became critically ill and Betsy had to take on the full responsibility for running DAW. She and Elsie asked me to join them, and after the July Fourth weekend, that was exactly what I did. And, of course, I've been here ever since. In the ensuing years, various members of my family—my husband Mike, and my sisters Marsha and Paula—began working with us in a freelance capacity, with Mike eventually becoming our resident curmudgeon until his untimely death in August of 2000.

We've always said that we consider DAW and everyone associated with it as one big extended family. And that is truly the way we feel about our own terrific staff and all the people we work closely with at Penguin Putnam, Inc., about our stalwart freelancers who never let us down, the artists who create such eye-catching images for us, and, of course, our authors, who, over the years we've worked with them, have become our close friends as well as our valued colleagues.

As thirty is a fairly momentous birthday in human terms (rest assured, however, that you will still be able to trust DAW to provide you with the kind of reading experiences you've come to expect), we wanted to celebrate this coming of age in a special way. And, we reasoned, what could be more appropriate than a book of stories written by the authors who have been such an important part of DAW over the last three decades. As we looked down our impressively large list of names, though, we realized that the only way this project could be accomplished without becoming completely unwieldy would be to divide the stories into two volumes by category. Thus, the books you now see before you: *DAW 30th Anniversary: Science Fiction* and *DAW 30th Anniversary: Fantasy*.

Of course, thirty years is a long time, and as we went through our list we were saddened by the knowledge that a number of the authors we would have loved to have stories from were no longer around to provide them. Despite that, we are very pleased with the number of authors who were kind enough to join us in our thirtieth birthday celebration by creating the wonderful tales you'll find included here. Some of the contributors wrote stories which take place in the universes in which their popular DAW series are set, others have chosen to explore entirely new territory, and yet others have given us a glimpse of the worlds and characters from novels which will see publication in the upcoming years.

When DAW Books was founded, the original logo used on all our books read: DAW = sf, a corporate emblem designed by well-known science fiction artist Jack Gaughan. At that time the logo was extremely appropriate. We were the first company devoted exclusively to the publication of science fiction and fantasy, and as far more science fiction was being published (certainly this was true for DAW in those days) the genre hadn't been broken down into two distinct categories. But over the course of the 1970s, '80s, and '90s, as more writers came into the field from the social sciences and humanities rather than the hard sciences, both styles and subject matter began to change. And as technological leaps began to transform science fiction into science fact, creating believable yet innovative science-based fiction became far more difficult. At the same time, the ever-increasing changes wrought by technology in both the working place and our own homes led more people to read fantasy, probably as a means to escape the stresses and demands of the "real" world.

In recognition of these changes, the very look of DAW Books, as well as the contents, began its own evolutionary process, one that continues to this very day. Our logo went from DAW = sf to a design which incorporated the three letters in our name, and also labeled the particular book it appeared on as either science fiction or fantasy. Of course, this led to a bit of a dilemma when a novel or series didn't fall fully into one category or the other but actually melded elements of both.

What you now hold in your hands is your invitation to join our 30th anniversary celebration. The stories in each volume appear in chronological order, based on the first time the author was published by DAW. Thus our fantasy volume begins with Andre Norton, whose *Spell of the Witchworld* was the very first DAW book to see print in April 1972. The first story in the science fiction volume is by Brian Stableford, whose *To Challenge Chaos* was published in May 1972.

We hope that you will find these anthologies as enjoyable as we have, and that it will offer you a chance to read some new work by old favorites, or perhaps afford you the pleasure of discovering some of our authors for the very first time. Thank you for helping to make our first thirty years as memorable as they have been, and we look forward to sharing many more years of good books with all of you.

SHEILA GILBERT

Contents

Andre Norton

One of the finest qualities of Don Wollheim was his interest in new authors. I always found it a pleasure to work with him, even when I was a near-unknown, for he understood very well the labor that writers endure in creating their books and gave even aspiring wordsmiths both credit and approval.

When he was still an editor at Ace, I met him and Elsie at a country picnic. Both of them were most friendly—a behavior that impressed me, to whom editors were VIPs of the highest rank. At that time, I mentioned my idea for the first *Witch World* book, and Don asked to have the manuscript sent to him for a reading. Since no one else up till then had been interested in a book-length adult fantasy, I was surprised by his encouragement. It was directly through Mr. Wollheim's interest that Estcarp and the rest of that alternate world were brought to readers' attention.

When Don was about to leave Ace and informed me of that fact, I asked him to take with him, if he thought it measured up, the collection of *Witch World* stories I had just brought in. I was greatly honored that *Spell of the Witchworld* became the first work published by the newly-incorporated DAW Books—and I still am. Don Wollheim was both a professional associate and a personal friend, and I, and the genre of fantasy, will always owe him a great deal.

—AN

SOW'S EAR—SILK PURSE
Andre Norton

*I*T *is an accepted fact that, if a maiden is to prosper in this world, she must possess the gift of beauty. If she can claim that blessing, then fortune, fame, and illustrious marriage will surely follow in due time. This "fact," however, is seldom true.*

And if a young lady is not born with a mien of exceptional comeliness—a treasure more precious than the silver-spoon-in-the-mouth of proverb—then ways exist, albeit laborious ones, whereby she may acquire at least a modicum of the desired appearance. No one turns willingly away from the chance to show a radiant face. Or does she?

In the fifteenth year of the reign of King Karl the Sluggard, the town of Yerd boasted several families whose wealth was considerable enough to make them the equals of minor gentry. These prosperous folk were fully aware of the importance of their standing: the Sorens, the Wassers, the Rhinebecks, and the Berdmans had hats doffed and curtsies made to them whenever they chose to go abroad.

Marsitta Wasser had recently made a most fortunate marriage with a knight who held a position (albeit very minor) at court. That he was both threadbare of cloak and empty of pocket mattered not in the slightest when his shield bore the quarterings of four noble families. The young woman's dowry would soon repair any lack in her fiancé's fashions and fortune, and, in any event, the title "my lady" discreetly covered such embarrassments.

Some weeks after this world-altering event, Master and Dame Soren were returning from a visit to the home of the knight and his new bride. Not only had the Wassers still been very full of the wedding—they were now projecting a visit to Court. The Sorens felt thoroughly out of sorts and made their way home in silence and dark thought. Not until the maid, Jennie, had opened the door and Master Soren had stepped inside the hall did he speak.

"You have a daughter—" he barked.

Ingrada Soren bristled and caught him by the sleeve to pull him into the parlor, away from listening ears.

"WE have a daughter!" She spoke with the firmness born of many years' peacemaking in small family wars.

Margus Soren made a sound close to a grunt. "We have a milk-water miss with a body as skinny as a *darem* bush when the leaves are gone, a face as freckled as if one of the carriage team had blown bran at her, and a fat-pudding brain so dull it cannot tell madras from silk!"

Dame Soren was stung by this sorry litany. Certainly Feliciana was no great beauty, but she was biddable and deft with her needle —both desirable traits in a wife—and one lone mistake in the cloth-mart did not mean she was lacking in wit. True, she had to be watched lest she dawdle away hours with those books the rector's wife had lent her. Perhaps it would be best to see soon to breaking off that particular friendship.

With a shrug of his shoulders, her husband moved to one of the long windows that fronted the square. Sweeping the heavy drape to one side, he glanced out as the thunder of the iron-shod wheels of a traveling coach abruptly drowned out the usual street noise.

"The Boroughmaster's nephew must be in trouble again." Margus continued to watch the activity below and did not turn to his wife as he spoke. "Here he comes once more, to wait time out until Rhinebeck mends matters with Lord Gargene."

The arrival of Yerd's most notorious—but well-connected— rascal was hardly of great consequence. Such was Dame Soren's first thought, but it was swiftly followed by another. All knew that Hilda Rhinebeck had chafed at the amount of attention paid to the Wassers' wedding, being always eager to promote her nephew—no matter his reputation as a good-for-naught. Of course, he *was* grandson to a baron, and he *did* rub shoulders with the noble youths—the ones fond of gaming, at least—at the court. (Dame Rhinebeck reveled in the bits of scandal he reported and would arrange her entertaining accordingly.)

" 'Tis near the beginning of the hunting season," Ingrada said slowly.

"Aye," replied her husband, his voice still gruff, "and then half the lay-lazies of the shire will roister in our streets! Rhinebeck will be well out of pocket paying extra constables before the end of the month. That gangrel of a nephew will have to be watched, for has he money or no, depend upon it, a flock of fools will crowd about him to bet their sires' silver—money already owed to honest guildsmen. We could do without that!"

Dame Soren made no answer; her mind was already busied adding this new information to its picture of Feliciana's future, like a thread of gold added suddenly to a drab weaving. Men, she reflected, never really understood the finer points of marrying off a daughter to be a credit to her family.

Ingrada began listing the names of a few prospects as she headed for her chamber upstairs to lay aside her visiting finery—elegant clothing donned all too rarely, as Yerd was sadly lacking in festive occasions. She continued to be thus absorbed as she passed the closed door of the chamber where the object of her musings sat sewing, but the heel-clicks of her best shoes gave her away.

Feliciana's head jerked up. Swiftly she made sure that the letter she had been reading was safely stowed in her workbox. As she heard the door of her mother's chamber open, then close, she gave a sigh of relief—no visit, with the inevitable scrutiny of her limited charms, seemed likely now.

The girl rubbed her eyes tiredly, wishing that she might as easily escape from the mocking memories that had been with her ever since Marsitta's wedding. Ingrada, she knew, would be spurred on by that social slave-auctioning to market her own daughter. Feliciana had no hope of escaping more of those nightmarish, shaming hours of sitting uncomfortably to one side of a ballroom, waiting until one of the "gentlemen" present was drunk enough to ask to partner her in a dance. At such times, she invariably either stumbled or committed some equally-unpardonable offense that she would hear about for days afterward.

She gulped, feeling physically ill with such remembrances, but she forced herself to set another stitch in the linen stretched over the frame before her. In the distance a door opened. Her mother *was* coming, after all! It had been too much to hope that she would not come in—she had been at the Wassers' that morning, and what she had probably heard there would not be such news as to leave her in a good mood.

As Dame Soren entered the sewing room, Feliciana rose awkwardly to curtsy, but Ingrada waved her impatiently back to her seat. She herself remained standing, the better to view her daughter from head to foot, then back again.

The girl, she observed, was dressed well enough, her gown of that rather odd hue of red that was neither copper nor rust but a shade between, and one that truly suited her. There was no denying that she was plain, for her angular body lacked womanly curves; however, at least her eyes were stronger than those of the Berdman maid's and, for all her foolish preoccupation with books, she did not squint. But her hair had always been straighter than a string—

"You have not used the curl-rags!"

With a guilty gesture, Feliciana pulled at a typical lock of lank, dull-brown hair. "The knots hurt so I cannot sleep," she said miserably, "and when I comb it in the morning, it all just goes straight again."

Ingrada set her lips. "Then Jennie must bring the iron."

Feliciana forced herself not to shrink back. *Jennie* and *iron* meant *burned ends* and *nasty smell*—and, again, curls that did not last long.

Dame Soren strode toward a large chest set to one side of the chamber and opened the coffer with such force that the lid banged against the wall. She began to pull out lengths of linen, satin, and patterned silk—the finest such stuffs to be found on the shelves of the Soren shop. As she held up each in turn for inspection, Ingrada glanced from the cloth to her daughter with no lightening of countenance.

"We shall have Dame Roslyn in—and we had best see to that at once, as her work will be in demand."

Then, closing the chest, she was gone.

No—no—and *no!* The denial Feliciana dared not utter aloud rang in her head. She clasped her hands together until her fingers cramped. They would dress her in milk-and-water colors, as became a maid, choosing a modest style of gown, as suited the daughter of a Guildsman of the Council. But, as ever, she would be the object of smirks and titters.

Resolutely, she forced herself to concentrate on her needlework. Sometimes when she bent her mind wholly to her labor, she could, for a time all too brief, forget what lay ahead.

Jennie arrived, bearing not the curling iron but rather a tray of food; Feliciana was, then, to eat her noon meal in private. There was a plate heaped with gluttonous servings of several dishes; beside it stood a tall mug of milk and an after-sweet of rich cakes. This was her regular fare in double portion! So her mother was going to try to stuff her in the hope of producing curves where Nature had shaped her form with a miserly hand.

"Th' Rogue do be back." Jennie had put down the tray, but she was lingering.

"Is he?" Feliciana had little concern for this development; everyone in Yerd was used to Master Rogar's comings and goings.

"There's goin' t'be mighty merrymakin'," the maid continued, ignoring her mistress's lack of enthusiasm in her own excitement. "Dame Rhinebeck—she's been lookin' to outshine th' Wassers. An' th' hunters'll be comin' soon!"

When Feliciana still showed no interest, Jennie smoothed the edge of the tablecloth with elaborate care. Plainly, there was more she wanted to say.

The girl indicated the cakes. "Take one, Jennie," she urged. "I'll never eat so many, but I'll hear about it if they are not all gone."

"Thank ye, miss." The servant bobbed her version of a curtsy and picked up a sweet but showed no sign of leaving. At last she burst out:

"Th' Mistress—she's a-makin' plans again!"

To this ominous statement Feliciana said nothing. Jennie, however, took her silence for encouragement. Dropping her voice to a dramatic whisper, she revealed, "That Wasser girl, 'tis said she went to the *Green Hag* and got her luck there."

Now Feliciana did take notice. "Why would Marsitta need to do that?" she mused, bitterness edging her voice. "She was born with all the bounties."

The maid frowned with the effort of unaccustomed thought. "Sometimes one wants t' make sure," she said slowly. "Maybe she just wanted to make *real* sure. Though I'm a-thinkin' maybe she'll find as how she didn't do so well for herself—that knight o' hers, he had him a mean-lookin' mouth."

"*I don't want to get married!*" The protest wrenched itself from Feliciana, strident as a battle cry.

"Maybe not," said Jennie sadly. Then she shrugged in resignation and repeated, "But th' Mistress—she's got plans."

Feliciana drew a deep breath. Too true, but—*no!* She set down her fork, feeling the familiar wave of nausea at the idea of being exposed yet again to humiliation. In fine clothes that made her thin, awkward body look even more clumsy . . . with hair curled by force but too soon straggling down raggedly . . . powdered . . . painted. . . . She would feel a perfect fool, yet to some man, the girl knew, she would still be acceptable. The only way to escape would be to become so utterly ugly that no buyer would offer a beggar's bit for her in the marriage mart.

Feliciana tensed. Ugly—grotesquely hideous. Could she bring herself to such a fate? She glanced toward her sewing box, in which rested the leaflet that Dame Kateryn, the rector's wife, had given her.

Places existed, the broadside told, where an unsightly or crookshanked maid could find refuge out of sight of the family to whom she was a source of shame. There she could do fine needlework, learn herbcraft for cooking and healing, or freely read and write. The women who lived in the haven of which Dame Kateryn knew taught the daughters of even the high nobility.

"The Green Hag," said Feliciana suddenly. "Tell me about her, Jennie."

Pleased at being invited to such an intimate confidence, the serving girl leaned close and spoke in a hushed voice. "They say as how she comes with th' full moon, an' she'll give ear to the maid or man what takes her a gift she fancies. Them as is brave enough can seek her out near the Ghost Trees—"

Feliciana forced a laugh. "I fear *I* would never be so bold," she said with careful indifference. "But thank you, Jennie." Reaching out to draw her embroidery frame closer, she turned away from the barely tasted meal—and from her recent confidante. The servant hesitated a moment longer, then ducked a curtsy and left.

At the full of the moon—that was only two days hence. As she resumed her needlework, the young woman considered the perilous path of invoking the Wild Magic and the dire fate that might befall one who did so. It would be easy enough afterward—always supposing the tales were true—to say that she had fallen afoul of the Hag and thus had been undone. Feliciana did not like to think of the pity and scorn she now endured being multiplied a hundredfold if she were given a repulsive appearance, but—she stabbed at the fabric viciously—*nothing* could be worse than to have her mother try yet again to marry her off.

So far had she speculated when a sharp knock sounded on the door. A moment later, her father tramped in to plant himself before her with only the needle frame between them.

"Got news for you, girl."

Feliciana scrambled up and curtsied. "Yes, sir?"

"Received an offer for you—most respectable one." Margus Soren cocked his head to one side in a gesture of triumph and waited for his daughter's reaction.

Suddenly the girl was truly afraid. She cast her eyes down, as was modest and fitting, and asked no questions, but her father was watching her closely, and she was sure he could see the pounding of her heart beneath the bodice of her gown. *Who . . . ?*

"Big a surprise as I ever had, mind you," Master Soren went

on expansively. "The Boroughmaster himself sent the offer. He would have you wed with his nephew—the grandson of a baron, no less! True, that House has had a run of bad luck—lost most of their holdings, they did—but naught can take away their standing.

"Yes," the guildsman concluded with satisfaction, "Fortune has certainly smiled upon us. Be getting at your bride clothes now, for it's a soon wedding they want. Marsitta Wasser can be a lady, but you'll be a greater one—your dowry will be the Panfrey estate as came to me for debts five years agone. They'll do well by you, girl, and so will we."

Feliciana's father was smiling benevolently at her, but his eyes were narrowed as he waited for her reaction. The young woman forced a shaky smile. "You have done all a daughter could wish, sir," she said. That reply was the only one she could manage, but it was the truth by the standards of Yerd.

He nodded, satisfied, and left. The bride-to-be sank once more into her seat before the embroidery frame and stared at it, unseeing. The Rogue! His conduct had ever been ill, and many lurid stories were told of his exploits. He was rumored to consort with the red-wigged women on the north side of the town, and he was known to be a gambler, a liar, and a taker of pleasure in the evil plight of others.

The girl wanted to scream. Now the only hope left was to acquire an ugliness so appalling that it would outweigh the promised dowry.

For the next two days, Feliciana somehow bore the burden of her parents' joy and the congratulations from members of the household and friends. In a hand that she forced not to shake, she signed the marriage contract under her father's boldly written name. As yet, her betrothed had not made his appearance, and to that fortunate fact she clung, for if he saw her with her present homely-but-not-unwholesome face, any change would be laid to the meddling of Master and Mistress Soren.

For the next two evenings, the Rogue's unwilling fiancée endured the twisting of her hair in the ritual of torture with the curling iron. But if by night the torture was inflicted with fire, by day it was performed with water, or at least an unending flow of speech from her mother, mixing instruction and admonition. There was also a sticking with pins, as though she were a curse-poppet, though this pain was not intentional: it was the byproduct of long sessions of gown fittings. The girl felt added guilt at the cost of these rich garments that would never be used.

At last the night she awaited came. Wearied by the tryings (and tryings-on) of the day, but more than ever determined *not* to enter the life her parents envisioned for her, Feliciana crawled into bed. Jennie drew the curtains, shutting her off from the unwanted world.

When she was sure the maid had gone, the girl pushed off the covers and sat up. She feared to close her eyes, not only because she must not sleep but because her dreams had become nightmares that showed a death dance of ghastly faces. Finally, she could wait no longer.

Wriggling off the tall bed, Feliciana moved once more into the room. By the feeble light of its night-lamp, she dressed in the simplest gown and the oldest cloak she owned. Before Master Soren had risen in the Mercers' Guild and prospered in the world, the family had lived with far less show, and she knew the town well from walking a number of its cobbled streets.

Yerd had not been threatened for many generations; in consequence, the city gate had stood open for so long that perhaps now it could no longer be closed. A constable was supposed to be on duty after dark, but he seldom stirred out of his shelter.

Keeping to the shadows, Feliciana slipped into the outer world. The Green Hag, she had learned, held rule not far from the ruins of the old Illet Abbey in a pocket-sized wood, the remains of a once-great forest. The way to the forsaken holy place was nearly grown over. She pulled her cloak about her as closely as she could, but every few feet she walked it was caught by a thorny claw from the walling brush.

Too soon, however, she reached the open ground about the abbey ruins. There the moon shone very bright. The girl felt for the small bag held in the breast of her chemise. She had no way of knowing what the Wild Witch would want in payment, but she had brought the only treasure that was truly hers: the pearl necklet given by her godmother at her christening.

It was so quiet. Instinctively, Feliciana went at a slower pace, even though the way was open. To the left, extending from the edge of a crumbling wall of stone, stretched the wood. At one time its growth of trees had been more close set, but now a tall upright stone could be seen, the first sentinel of an ancient shrine. To follow those stones would lead a seeker to where the Green Hag sheltered.

Feliciana passed the first of the towering markers. The silence continued; no cry came from owl or other night-hunter, no rustle of wind brushed leaves. She began to hurry a little, wariness rising in her. Would it be wiser to retreat?

Abruptly the girl stepped into a second open space, a smaller one. Here the moonlight fairly blazed, a fire not of red-gold but of silver. The shrine was open, and One stood in the doorway.

A woman, her white body striped with living vines. Beneath that scanty covering lay nothing but skin, shaped in lush curves that any woman would envy. About her shoulders hung thicker twists of the growing stuff—but none hid her face. That showed a pig's snout, a gaping mouth from which green slime dribbled, eyes that lacked either lashes or brows save for a dried lichenlike crusting. The body of a goddess; the face of a demon.

Feliciana did not hesitate but continued forward; she had the feeling that she was being tested in some fashion. At last she paused at a little distance from the One who stood as still as a statue.

Fear had stolen the girl's speech but not her wits. The being before her might be of no mortal kind, but one could never go wrong in offering courtesy. This she did, gathering cloak and skirts into both hands and dipping graciously as she would have to any of her parents' friends.

Those eyes, which had been dull and unfocused a moment earlier, now centered on the young woman. A purplish tongue flicked out over protruding lips.

"You come as a seeker?" In yet another mad contradiction, the voice that spoke from that monstrous face had the musical lilt of a bard's.

Feliciana summoned her courage, which was already threatening to desert her.

"I—I do, Lady."

The Hag made no immediate reply. After a moment, the girl pushed back the head-folds of her cloak.

"So," came the response then. "You human females are all too easy to read. A fair face, a well-shaped body—those gifts, you believe, will make all your dreams real. You have no doubts of that, ever—"

The Wild Witch paused. Though the nightmare visage showed no change of expression, the singing tone now held a sting of disdain.

"No!" the girl said hurriedly. "I do not want beauty, I wish to be ugly—"

"Now *that* I have never heard!" The Hag laughed, and the sound was no cackle but a noise of honest amusement. "You must be hard-pressed indeed to crave such an ill boon. Why do you wish to change yourself?"

"I—" The seeker hesitated, then hastened on before she could think further of the bargain she sought to strike. "My father has signed my betrothal contract, I do not care to wed. I would be free."

"Is your swain, then, so foul of person or habits?"

The girl shook her head. "His world is not mine. If I am forced to enter it, I shall fail, over and over again, at all I should be expected to do."

Now Feliciana brought her hand into the moonlight. The pearls of her christening necklet shimmered, not with the hard glitter of diamonds, but with a muted beauty that rivaled the moon's own.

"I have only these," she said, feeling compelled to explain the modesty of her offering. "My father is but Mercer Guildsman."

"Be this your dowry?"

"Nay." Now Feliciana could speak without shame. "That is to be the Manor of Panfrey."

"Your mercer father is most generous. One might guess that the groom is of fairly high estate?"

Why did the Green Woman keep her talking? Feliciana wondered. She seemed to be probing for a certain piece of information.

"He is the nephew of the Boroughmaster," the young woman answered, "and his grandfather is a baron."

"Ah—the Rogue is to be wed willy-nilly, is he?" Again that silvery laughter rippled forth, but it changed swiftly to the sober tolling of a warning bell. "You are indeed stupid, girl. There is often far more to life than what humans call 'love.' Consider: you will be mistress at Panfrey! And think also on this: my gifts, once given, can never be undone. Would you truly be an ugling all your days?"

Feliciana swallowed but stood firm. What did one's outer person matter? Veils could shield the unlovely. As for the great manor, she had no rights in her dowry; and the Rogue, who knew well the beauties of the court, might wed her, but he would surely cast her aside as soon as he could.

Bitter though it was, the girl forced herself to pursue the thought to its end. Better that rejection should come now than after they were bonded for life, for there would be none to whom she could even appeal. However, should she be cursed—and the families might well name her fate such—then they would wish to be rid of her, and waiting was that retreat of which Dame Kateryn had spoken. No, she would not be bound to a round of duties she would shrink from more each day. Between the two fates, she would choose this.

"Such is my desire, Lady." Feliciana was proud that she could speak so steadily.

That monstrous head shook, setting the green vines a-rustle. Again came a liquid trill of laughter. "A little threat will be good for the Rogue," the Wild One murmured, as though speaking to herself. "He is entirely too certain that life owes him his every good thing. I am minded to send a message—"

The girl was surprised at this speech. Did the Hag *know* the Boroughmaster's nephew—and, if so, how?

The Green Woman was speaking once more to the supplicant before her, and her tone was grave again. "Remember, human youngling, you cannot come crying for my aid a second time. But if you are heart-set on this course, give me that trinket of yours, and hold up your head—then we shall see what we shall see."

Feliciana stepped closer and dropped the pearls into the waiting hand. The Rogue's betrothed was sure that Witch would not take kindly to any wavering of resolve now. She hoped that the transformation was not to be a painful one—a possibility she had not considered—but no. No hurt of body could equal the searing of soul she had undergone so often. With that thought, her resolution was set.

The Hag twined the necklet about her wrist, then beckoned her seeker even closer. Now she lifted both hands to frame the girl's face. Feliciana felt a soft touch that started at her forehead and slipped slowly down to her throat. Three times thus did the Wild One serve her.

To her great relief, the young woman felt no wrenching of bone or skin, as she had half expected. When the Green Woman withdrew a little, eyeing her critically, she dared to raise her own hands to touch cheek and chin, but she could feel no change.

"I am no different!" she burst out.

"Nay!" retorted the Hag sharply. "Sight and touch are not the same. Never in your own eyes will there be any change you may behold—only by others may your transforming be seen. Mind you—" She paused, holding Feliciana's face in her gaze for a long moment—and doing more, the girl knew, than viewing her own handiwork. "You must live with what has been given. It is for you from henceforth to make the most of the boon you asked."

The moonlight seemed to flow about the Green Witch like a mist, veiling her completely. A moment Feliciana stood transfixed; then she came to herself, sighed, and sought the path of the pillars that would bring her out into the world again.

The bargainer with the Wild Magic found it as easy to return to her bed as it had been to leave the chamber. However, she did not seek sleep under the thick quilt; rather she sat upright, still patting and stroking her face. All she could think of was how she would appear to her parents and the rest of the household at the coming of day.

Before dawn, though, the girl slipped into restless slumber, threaded by dreams that brought great distress. In them, she wandered endlessly through rooms thronged by women of great beauty and well-favored men. On sighting her, they drew back in revulsion, pointing fingers and mouthing cries. She could not make out the words, but it was plain that she was held in horror, a figure to be shunned.

"Feliciana!" That voice she could hear, and it brought her out of the last of those contemptuous crowds: her mother was standing outside the curtains of the bed. As in the hour she struck her bargain with the Hag, the girl steeled her resolve. She had done what she had done, and there could be no more delay; the "gift" must now be shown.

The young woman lifted the bed-drape and waited for the storm to break. Ingrada Soren wore an expression of astonishment, yes, but the look was overlaid not with disgust but with—*delight?*

"What—what—" The woman put out a hand as if to touch her daughter's cheek.

Feliciana called upon all her courage. "I went to the Green Hag that I might be a pride to you. But I angered her, and she cursed me with this—" The girl gestured hopelessly at her face.

"*This!*" The joy in Mistress Soren's own face was now beyond denying. She snatched up the small mirror that hung from the chatelaine at her belt. With a rough pull, she freed the polished disk and held it out.

"What do you mean you are 'cursed,' girl?" she demanded.

Completely mystified, Feliciana took the mirror and gazed at herself. What she saw was the image that had always greeted her; but her familiar appearance was what the Wild Witch had told her she would see, while all others would perceive her as loathsome.

The Hag had played with her, then; as had the folk of human society, the Green Woman had made her a laughingstock. But in what way? Taking a steadying breath, she said, "To me, Mother, I seem to be as I ever have. What do you see?"

By now she was shivering. Had the previous night been a dream? Yet it was apparent that *some* change had been wrought.

"Has the transforming turned your wits, you foolish child? Cursed? You should ever praise the Green Lady for such a bane! What do I *see!*" Ingrada paused, breathless from both speech and excitement.

"I see such fairness as is seldom granted a maid: a face of ivory with the faintest touch of color on the cheeks, brows soft and winged, eyes blue as summer pools. I see a lush fall of black curls, lips that are luminous—"

Feliciana could stand no more of this catalog of her charms. Her "luminous lips" shaped an anguished cry. Indeed she was accursed, undone—and she alone would ever know! Too well she remembered the warning of the Hag before this sorry trick had been played.

Her mother's smile opened into laughter. "La, Feliciana, but they will gasp and roll their eyes when you appear! Master Roger should be grateful all his days that his uncle was so thoughtful for his future. Now get you dressed in haste—your father is fortunately late in leaving for the Guildhall. He will be as thankful for this miracle as am I!"

When Mistress Soren had whisked away to share the wondrous news, Feliciana gave her feelings free rein. Weeping, she stumbled to her dressing table, and in its mirror she beheld again the plain, lank-locked self she had always known—and would always know. Taking up her silver-backed hairbrush, she slammed its heavy head against the surface until the old glass splintered. The world was mad, and she could not put it right again.

She sank down onto the bench before the cracked mirror and began the painful business of preparing her hair. At first she could not understand what was wrong. Finally she pulled a long side section around to the front where she could see why it felt so odd. It was a curl, right enough, but it did yield now to her painful tweaking. Again she remembered the Green Woman's foretelling that she would never behold any of the changes in herself.

Huddling miserably, she wiped the tears from her "color-tinged cheeks." One of the sayings she used to be set to copy when she practiced writing as a child seemed to imprint itself on the air before her: *"Beware what you wish for, lest it be given you."*

And so it had, in its way. She had wanted a change—and the Wild Witch had found amusing the act of altering her life thus. Feliciana sat up straight.

"No one," she vowed in a grim whisper, "will find me a thing to scorn or pity again. I shall learn to play their silly games, but I shall always know who and what I am."

*I*t was said in later years that the Baroness Gargene, for all her great and long-lasting beauty, was strong of character and keen of wit beyond most noblewomen. She drew her lord away from court follies and made a man of him; and never did any plain maids sit unhappily in her hall while their more comely sisters enjoyed themselves but she would welcome them into any merry-making. In spite of much urging, she never permitted her portrait to be limned; and that this was no show of false modesty was proved by a most curious act. Beneath an empty picture frame, holding a blank canvas, she caused this motto to be set:

"Maledicta sum"—"I am accursed."

Michael Shea

Don Wollheim couldn't have been the editor and publisher he was if he hadn't been the writer he was. He had that critical mass of imagination, that hot core of creative energy that makes literature *matter* to someone. I was reminded of this fact about Don when I realized, after my fourth viewing of a favorite sci-fi horror film of mine—*Mimic*—that Don had written the story on which it was based.

I think it was his passion for the speculative side of literature as a whole that moved him, relatively early on, to devote his energies to its furtherance on the larger, editorial/publication level—to make the speculative genres a respected and received part of the world of letters, a status it enjoys today, to our delight. And if any one man can claim a major role in bringing about that acceptance (Acceptance? Hell—Sci-fi and fantasy *rule* the media today!) then Don Wollheim was that man.

I met him face-to-face only once, when I was in New York in hopes of a Nebula I didn't win. I'd drowned my sorrows (I drank back in those thankfully distant days) and came in somewhat hungover to discuss a project in hand. I was, in truth, rather intimidated by the multistoried building on the Avenue of the Americas. I come from a poor background, and felt ill-at-ease in the polished hallways and futuristic elevators. But when I faced Don across that desk, I was at ease in moments, looking into a tough, real face, with shrewd, no-bullshit eyes. And when he opened his mouth, out came wonderful unvarnished words that went straight to the heart of my rough draft, and, in mere minutes, gave me the gist of the story's strengths and weaknesses.

Don Wollheim was the real thing—we'll not soon see his like again.

—MS

THE REBUKE
Michael Shea

I

HACKLE the Smaller, by the spring of his fifty-first year, saw his death almost every day. It was a Death-by-Disease, and like most of this class, was a communicative sort that liked to get acquainted with its clients. The two of them would sit at dusk on Hackle's crumbling porch, talking quietly or pausing in their talk, their eyes musing on the hilly city of Hrabb, just across the Tumble River.

Hackle viewed that city of Hrabb with a stoic bitterness which flared into invective whenever he had a coughing fit. First, of course—whenever he coughed—he shot a questioning look at his death, which had always quietly shaken its head, so far at least. Then, when Hackle had finished the deep, sick labor, and spat out the clot of infection, he would shake his fist toward Hrabb and growl—his voice low to spare his lungs—"Smite and smash you, Hrabb, O Whore among cities! Oh that the blow might fall on you!"

His death understood the reference, which was to a fantasy of Hackle's. The prosperous main body of Hrabb, a clutch of marble-studded knolls, was overloomed by a crag—a tall, ragged eruption of naked rock from the riverside hills. In the cross-river slums where Hackle now resided, there was an old saying about this crag: "If the prayers of the poor could push stone, the Jut would have fallen on Nabob Hill a hundred years ago." Hackle's wish would go this proverb one better.

He had been, before the decay of his fortunes, a Statuarius, Master Grade, and one of his fortes and special loves had always been hands. Bodge of the Central Statuarium had been wont to say, when they sat with their colleagues in the refectory: "Now

Hackle here, God bless him, friends—Hackle here cuts fingers as articulate, as eloquent as tongues. Hackle's hands speak, and they speak not prose, but balanced stanzas. Have we not seen him convey whole epics with the faintest crooking of a left thumb?"

So that now, on half-pension and dying from the toxic rock dust of the quarries, too poor to inhabit the city where once his profession had been dined and eulogized at the tables of the great—now in his ruin Hackle impotently longed to do a masterwork, a stupendous clenched fist of stone poised to annihilate the city under it.

Sometimes Hackle would start running on about this project, which always distressed his death. Averting its small, starved face—usually so sympathetic—it would tactfully encourage him to resignation.

"Ah, well, my dear Hackle! But then, as you know, many of my colleagues have clients here, retired Statuarii. No suffering is unique, after all."

But, in fact, Hackle was no longer really angry at his city. It was half in jest that he pictured his fist as literally falling, for its mere sculpting would suffice him, a colossal proclamation of his contempt for all that was venal, facile, and corrupt in the values of his wealthier countrymen. But how could he really hate something as diffuse and masterless as that circus of follies, the Culture Market? The public purse has always fed or starved the arts according to its whim. In truth, he had better cause for anger at his own Guild. If sculpture in Hrabb, after its long supremacy, was now so displaced by other arts, so unattended, who but the Statuarium itself was to blame? In its infallible lust for immediate profit the Guild had energetically recapitulated whatever sold well, and tirelessly boycotted, blocked, and otherwise muffled every one of those stylistic radicals who might have infused new life into its art. Need anyone wonder that music, haute cuisine, and even literature currently engrossed the well-to-do—and their purses? Once the Guild had given steady birth to a marmoreal populace which took up residence in the gardens and grottos of the rich, the lamaseries and monkeries of the hills, the municipal prayer booths and public parks. Now the market was glutted.

Ships plied the Tumble laden with stony refugees, all bound for sale at discounts far away, where their history was unknown, and they were oddities. Oh, yes, the Statuarium could be said to have achieved what it had so blockheadedly worked for!

Yet, even for the Guild, Hackle felt little more than the remnants of anger. It did still cause him a twinge to recall the zeal with which the Guild's Directors had lobbied for city subsidies to open the pellucite quarry. How greedily they'd embraced this boon of bright, abundant, easy-working stone! But then they had at least all shared the unlucky outcome of its use, the tainted lungs and shortness of life. What else was to be expected, after all, of any human institution? All were heir to misfunction, self-damage, eventual entropy. Witness the Guild's concluding fiasco —the investment of its long-term assets in western blood-oysters, wherein said assets sank without a bubble. This left Hackle and his fellows hunched in the cross-river slums drawing stipends too small to buy more than one meal a day. What a perfect finishing touch, in a way! Guilds and their like are but men, after all, and men are fools.

And so, late one afternoon as they watched the sun wester behind hilly Hrabb, and his death was gently upbraiding him for some of his typical large talk, Hackle made a sudden gesture—as of surrender—and interrupted his companion.

"Please, my friend. After all, you know, it's really little more than a game of mine to carry on about the city, or the Statuarium. The fist—I'd like to carve it, yes. One last great orgy of expression, my concluding judgment on men and their world fairly thundered out, writ huge! But after all, everyone's world is a trap, a course of obstacles and pitfalls. The game has *always* been to outsmart your world—to excel, to accomplish good work in spite of it. Your colleagues must have told you how some of my retired coworkers rant and repine. 'Oh, but for this evil man or that stroke of bad luck, I'd be a wealthy and healthy success today!' And that's childish, after all, isn't it? To cry foul and swear you've been cheated? Far better to accept responsibility. It's a state of mind that leaves you readier for action."

His death sat hunched attentively, its elbows on its stark-knobbed knees. In their shadowy, bruise-colored sockets its eyes were vague and meditative glints. It seemed—while politely engrossed—to be hearing some faint, contradictory undertone in Hackle's words. Absently, it screwed a fingertip into its tattered ear and dislodged a wriggling maggot which, musingly, it flicked away.

"You speak now, my dear Hackle, like the excellent man I know you to be, though perhaps a readiness for action is not the most appropriate state of mind to cultivate in your present, ah, circumstances. Still your gameness does you credit, as does your manly acceptance of responsibility. But, you know, strangely enough, in spite of your assurances, I feel that there *is* some great anger in you, some vengeful fire. There is some deep matter wherein you *do* cast blame."

"Oh, yes, indeed. Nor is it anything I make a secret of. Have I not spoken to you of Haffkraff?"

"Your Guild-sponsor."

"The same. Guide and governor of the first ten years of my education. Oh, brilliant, self-indulgent Haffkraff! How you betrayed me, week in, week out, through the long irrevocable seasons of my first development!"

"I think I have noted some grudge in you against this man. Yet your references to him are elliptical, oblique."

"Have I not said enough in saying that he educated me? Why, after all, did I *not* rise above the Guild? Why *did* I spend my life chained to it, and to Hrabb? Obviously due to a failure of talent—not lack of talent, but failure to master it, to give it the force and focus to accomplish something lasting. Were other worlds ever lacking, had my art been robust and confident enough to put at risk abroad? Why not go free-hammer in one of the south-coast cities, or hang out my shingle as *magus lapidarius* in some city of the Barbarian League, where a theorist of style might try—and get away with—anything?"

"My friend, I see you embrace the very fallacy you just now denounced. You're crying foul, and swearing you've been cheated."

Hackle gave his head a firm shake. "I'm sorry, my friend. That is logically true, no doubt. But this matter of education—it constitutes an exception, I believe. For, in every life's budding phase, where is responsibility for its growth if not with its teachers— with those who nurse its development? How, after all, can it nurse its own? The bitter thing is how *able* Haffkraff was to have done right by me. He had the talent, and my devotion! Any youngster would have burned to be like that lean, crankish man, who could make any solemn matter dance in the quick flame of his mockery, and with one laconic flicker of his scorn—a mere phrase—could reduce the most earnest pretension to ash! His chisel was as articulate—and as irresponsible—as his tongue. There was the key to his cowardice, you see—he lived off what he scorned, and shamelessly carved in stone, for gold, every cliché or fatuity he had ever mocked. Yet he would have bridled at a charge of hypocrisy—he believed his mockery absolved him of sin. For he was one of those satiric sorts whose prime concern was, by invalidating all around them, to remain free. Such men are their own audience, but will also use a pupil for audience, careless of his education. I learned his accuracy, his flexible invention—his comic skills. But I also swallowed whole his facile misanthropy and nihilism and—with these—his primary rationalization for doing pointless work."

"Can any teacher be omnicompetent?" his death asked delicately. "Surely the student's budding powers of judgment must be invoked at some point to assess his teacher's limits."

"But how? How could I have guessed the truths that this errant jack-of-all styles concealed from me? That great work is done only by those who risk seriousness—who stake off a ground of Truth and take a stand on it? Had I known these things in time, I might have imbibed the necessary ardor to forge my talent into something rare! I will tell you how I have come to understand —to visualize Haffkraff's crime against me. The teacher must regard a student as a work in progress. Each stroke, each pressure on his mind, must be deliberate, intended. The teacher's talent may be mediocre, but the mind he shapes will have learned at least of method, care, and purpose—learned the gravity of art.

But to heedless, hedonistic Haffkraff I was no work in progress. I was a practice-stone—such cheap chalkstone as stands in apprentices' halls to study technique on, or chop out a quick study of some theme. He practiced his notions on me—whatever they might be at a given time. There's his crime in essence, for which I never will forgive the damned old mountebank! And there, my friend, you have my history—what made me a jack-of-all-styles myself, a patchy talent, brilliant only in fits and starts—fit, in short, to spend my career, and my life, in the Guild."

After a brief silence, Hackle's death shivered. "Getting cold," it muttered. Leaning forward, and plugging one ragged nose hole with a black-nailed thumb, it blew a maggot from the other hole, and crushed it carefully under the ball of its stark-tendoned foot. "I do hate to hear clients recriminating like this," the death breathed sadly. "Rage is so useless for the business we have at hand."

Sighing, Hackle shrugged. The sigh had concession in it. The shrug was somehow mulish and unappeased.

II

Not many days after this conversation, Hackle and his death took an afternoon stroll by the river, along the slum shore's crumbling quays and rotting wharves. They talked, with many lackadaisical pauses, about mankind's love of life.

"An intractable paradox," the death said at length. "People will, on the weakest pretexts, waste vast amounts of time on aimless and valueless activities. They will do this to avoid fruitful and productive activities—even when these activities are not difficult. It is enough that they be 'work' to make them shunned. And yet no man or woman I have known would give away one week of his life, even if it purchased some rare thing."

Hackle was greatly surprised. "Can this be true?"

The death gave a deprecatory wave of one gaunt hand. "Granting two conditions—that they are aware their deaths are somewhere close at hand, and that they are not in any extreme bodily agony. With these provisos I can swear to you that I have met no one who would willingly trade a week for anything I could offer."

"But this is quite astonishing!"

"Well, not *that* astonishing, surely. There is always the chance that one's fated time of death is less than a week away, and in that case one loses both life's remnant and the reward he sold it for."

"Certainly, but you misunderstood me. What I found astonishing was primarily the fact that you made such offers in the first place!"

The death showed some discomfort. It stayed Hackle, glanced left and right, and spoke in a lowered voice. "You must understand. These little bargains are in the nature of a personal interest of mine. They are not, ah, sanctioned, or even countenanced, by my superiors. Quite the reverse, in fact."

Hackle nodded sympathetically and kept his own voice low:

"I understand. What do you offer in exchange for this week of life?"

"Anything within my power to manage," the death said with quiet emphasis. A tentative smile tautened the yellow skin of its lean jaw. "The only reservation is that your wish involve or aid no evasion of your expiration date. And you *do* understand that this date is immutable, regardless if it supervene before or at any time during your enjoyment of your wish?"

"I do, indeed. And, without wishing to insult you, I must ask you if you mean this offer seriously. For I tell you frankly, I am most seriously minded to take you up on it."

The death's smile grew wry. "Forgive me if I am skeptical in my turn. The offer is seriously made, be sure, but, as I have pointed out, I have yet to meet the person who dared to take it up."

"Be comforted. You have just met him."

"Indeed? And what is your price for this week of your life?"

"An interview with Haffkraff, wherever in death he may lie."

"I must ask your purpose."

"To do myself justice. I intend to rebuke him, who was more my father than my father was. I mean to accuse him to his face, I who loved and honored him to my ruin. If I have any life left after doing this, I will be able to live it with peace of mind."

Still faintly smiling, the death gazed at him a moment.

"You ask much, good Hackle. I can implement it, but you must accomplish it. The map, the procedure, and gold I can give you. The going and the doing must all be yours, and it will be arduous."

"Give me the how of it and give me gold. Sweet gold! Gold will serve me for strength through the hardest territories! Give me much gold and then only my Closing Date, by coming too soon, can stop me! But thus, of course, has it stood throughout my life."

"Aye, had you but believed it," replied his death. After a pause it added: "Haffkraff's death was Death-by-Winter, a very great death. Death-by-Winter's fastness is in the Titanleg Basalts in Bythoggia Major. You must climb into the Titanlegs and solicit the aid of one of the Death's gatekeepers. I recommend Man-of-Blizzards, for he was Haffkraff's conveyor to Death-by-Winter. I will tell you how to invite his aid. But first, with your permission, I will take the week from your life. There's no point in wasting my breath on explanations if you're not going to survive the gamble, is there?" The death smiled a faintly sadistic smile.

"True enough," said Hackle, squaring his shoulders. "All right, then, take it."

III

Had Hackle known how long his rebuke's preparation would take, he would have shunned the gamble from disbelief that sufficient life was left him. He had thought, with a week of his time, to purchase one daring but relatively brief exploit, after which he was reconciled to a speedy embrace by his death.

But simply to reach the threshold of that exploit took three months, and the mere standing upon that threshold was a feat of endurance. The snow-toothed winds chewed on his sunken cheeks, and each breath stabbed his sick lungs with air as thin and sharp as knives. As he rested briefly from his work, he did not even try to pry his aching fingers from the handles of his ice-saw.

He gazed downslope where Squamp, the drayman he had hired, flogged his team uphill with yet another sledful of dead wood, and marveled at his own continuing vitality. Perhaps, if death were not so strictly fated as most thought, he had actually delayed his own by undertaking this rebuke, for a vengeful spirit seemed a tonic to both mind and body.

A tonic had, in any case, been called for, since the invocationary acts required to summon Man-of-Blizzards were so toilsome. He must be summoned here, near a mile above timberline. He must be summoned with a fire blazing four times a man's height. And both the preparation and the lighting of the fire must be done strictly during times of snowfall.

Nonetheless, the toil had suited his mood, for as he cut and laid each ice block in the curving wind-wall he was making, his mind was reviewing his past—trimming, dressing and ordering the charges to be laid against his old preceptor. And, as Squamp brought up each load of wood and Hackle laid the dead limbs on the fuel heap, his sculptor's eye saw in each one some cryptic, fragmentary gesture of remonstration and reproof, all soon to combine in one blaze of accusation against Haffkraff.

The load Squamp now dumped before him was, they had concurred, the last one needed. Hackle unclamped his hands from his saw, unpocketed and tendered the burly drayman a voucher for the withdrawal of funds from a bank in Bythoggia's capital. The man accepted this somberly.

"I must say, Master Hackle, that I'm still affronted by the distrust implied by this arrangement."

"But how can you be, Master Squamp? I am old and ill and already near my time. I've brought you far from the sight of men. If I'd carried the cash, who would *not* have been tempted?"

"I would never have dreamed of committing a crime on the person of a lunatic like yourself, sir. It's bad luck to harm the daft. And, if I may intrude my unwelcome opinion of the matter one last time, I still think you ought to leave the old man alone. I mean, this kind of vindictiveness is really outrageous, you know!"

"Thank you, good Squamp, for sharing your views with me yet again. It saddens me that we must now part ways."

The drayman smiled dourly. "It gladdens me to leave this cold. This storm will surely hold—you should have snow enough to do your summoning." He climbed on his sled and whipped up his team, then slanted leisurely away downslope.

Hackle watched the dark shape's zigzag disappearance into white silence. The air hit a snag in his lungs, and he hugged himself to hold in a coughing fit. It racked him—convinced him for a moment that it would not end. He spat up the clot of infection it worked loose, reelingly inspected it against the snow. Still only veined and freckled with red.

"Oh, splendid," he said sneeringly to the mountain peaks—to his fate at large. "For this stay of execution I humbly render thanks!"

Unsteadily, he marched back to the glacial knoll where he quarried his ice blocks, and took up wedge and maul again. His pain had anesthetized an obscure pang, a cryptic qualm that the sight of Squamp's departure had caused him. He settled to work, a sense of triumph dawning on him as he considered the nearness of his goal. The wind-wall towered fifteen feet already. A block at a time, he laid the penultimate tier, his numb, boot-bulky feet slogging up and down his ladders of spliced boughs. Donning gauntlets, he wrapped in chain-mail coals from the flaming brazier already sheltered by the wall, and mortared the row in place with melt refrozen by the wind.

In his rage to be done he found himself pushing his lungs too hard, so by way of rest he laid the last of the wood in its place on the huge, crooked mountain of tented limbs. He returned to the wall, trying all the harder to slow his pace because now a dread of what he was so near doing began in its turn to dawn on him. Perversely, the last tier of blocks seemed to leap from the quarry and spring to their places in the wall, while he himself swam easily through the work of it. Shortly, he found that his moment had come.

The wind had risen, raking the wall with crystal claws. The sky—or rather, the enveloping white swarm—was graying, the

light draining from it with what seemed a terrible haste. Hackle
stared at the unkindled bonfire as if it were the very essence of
his accusation, that grievance he meant to carry to Haffkraff in
his death. As if in perfect doubt of it—as if it were the fire-to-be
of someone else's outrage—he kicked over the brazier, spilling its
embers onto the heap, gaping to learn if they would catch or not.
Flames, like fugitive spies, spread with fitful stealth through the
mazed limbs. The main assault followed. Increasingly fierce, it
forked up in thickening legions which, with a roar and a rush,
were finally snatched by the gusts at the rim of the barrier, and
hoisted high into the blizzard above, orange sabers, tusks and
tines which even the blizzard—though it bent them—could not
break. Hackle cringed against his wall from the heat, his eyes
hunting the snowspume over the flame crests for a revelation.
Abrupt as blinking, it appeared. The flame tips tickled the Man-
of-Blizzards' boot soles, seemed to hold aloft his ogre's hugeness
with these feathery licks of energy. His shaggy tunic and nude
(but also shaggy) arms and legs were sugared with snowflakes.
His scalp, beard, and brows, formed wholly of brambled ice, ac-
cented and parenthesized a somber-eyed, big-jawed face that was
both forbidding and fractionally amused.

"So," the Man-of-Blizzards said, "your wish?" His voice—
conversationally pitched—seemed to occur in a miraculous little
zone of silence localized around Hackle's ears. Against the wind's
howl Hackle pitched his own voice at a shout:

"I . . . WISH . . . TO . . . BE—"

"Please!" With a pained expression the Man-of-Blizzards
raised a palm. "Do not bellow."

"Forgive me. I wish to be taken to Haffkraff, former Statuarius
of Hrapp. Death-by-Winter, your lord, has him in keeping."
Hackle could feel his voice as a thrumming within his ribs, but
could hear no sound of it, which was utterly erased from his lips
by the gale. This disoriented and obscurely frightened him. He
had thought of this declaration of his as ringing out, a bold, reso-
nant hammering against the door of Haffkraff's deathly retreat.

"I must ask your purpose," the Man-of-Blizzards answered.

"It is to rebuke him. He was my sponsor. I wish to upbraid

him with his failure of me, and with the flaws in himself that made him fail."

"Mmmm. I remember Haffkraff. He was part of a caravan of adventurers that I enrolled—in a freak spring storm—at Ragged Pass in the Phystian Gnarlies. I remember my surprise at his age—the oldest in the party. The recruits for such foolish causes run young as a rule."

Hackle nodded, smiling disgustedly. "A caravan of privateers, or so I heard. Bound for honor and booty in the Holy Wars in the Isles of the Northern Splash, was he not, O Man-of-Blizzards?"

"Just so, but a front in fact. A ploy by one of the slave-magnates of these mountains. Unknowingly, Haffkraff was en route to a Death-in-Chains when I took him."

"He was in dotage then, believing his own lifelong affectations of freedom and daring. Are you going to take me to him?"

"Yes." As if he stood on something solid, the Man-of-Blizzards leaped with a firm launch down to the glacier. Huge as a hill-troll, he scarcely made the impact of an alley cat. "Climb upon my shoulders," he said, kneeling with his back to Hackle. The sculptor, with an horripilation of either loathing or awe, mounted the giant and grasped his thorny neck. The Man-of-Blizzards sprang straight up into the storm.

IV

Now the blizzard utterly sealed Hackle's eyes and ears. Blind, up-surgent, for an unmeasurable time he was borne numbly aloft.

Then he was on his legs again, his bearer beside him. They stood on a snowy plain where—close enough, two miles away, to blot half the sky—a tremendous figure lay.

The Behemoth slept on his back. His frosty hair and beard were bound with the ice on that populous, knolled, and gullied plain. Streams of icy melt leaked from his ears and nose and slack, snor-ing mouth, thawing grottos from the wilderness of his hair. The sky was a skim-milk opacity without feature. The figures that thronged the plain, grottoed most thickly in his hair and choking the gullies like anemones, were the unmoving dead. Hackle's guide indicated the Behemoth.

"Death-by-Winter, insofar as he does not *notice*, will not *mind* your stealing an interview with Haffkraff. You follow me?"

"Perfectly."

"To ensure that he does *not* notice, look that you exchange nothing but views with Haffkraff. Neither take nor give anything but words. Haffkraff lies just past yon knoll, in his own little hollow. When you have done, return here, and make your own exit." The giant pointed at the ground, where a hole gaped. At its bottom, indeterminately deep, a smoky movement could be seen, and a distant whining heard—a storm noise that seemed minute beneath the vast, rumbling sound ceiling of Death-by-Winter's snoring.

"How?" asked Hackle, knowing, but afraid.

"Just jump into it. Oh, yes—where would you issue from it?"

"In the slums cross-river from Hrapp?"

"Done. Good-bye." The Man-of-Blizzards leaped into the hole. His bulky shoulders shrank to a spot, a dot, to nothing before he seemed to reach the storm below. Hackle turned toward the knoll his guide had pointed out.

The dead he passed sat staring stupidly at the ground. Some slowly looked up, to blink at him, and a few knit their brows with the remnants of perplexity, but all returned their gazes to the ground. And just so sat Haffkraff when Hackle, arms akimbo, stood before him, relishing the sight.

The old man's back was half propped by an outcrop of ice. He stared dully at his legs, which were sprawled like a dropped marionette's, and frozen to the ground. He wore the raffish two-peaked hat known as the "corsair's cap." Its snow-powdered prongs, jutting askew above his glassy-eyed face, made him look less like an adventurer than a bumpkin got up for a fair. The spectacle's pitifulness filled Hackle with horror, hinting the same droll futility his own life had come to.

"Haffkraff! Look up! Look here! Do you know me, old man?"

Slowly, the snowblind, milky eyes lifted to his. Haffkraff's lip hung doltishly. It mouthed vaguely, fishlike, bringing out no sound.

"So," mocked Hackle, "you don't know me? But of course I'm sure you never thought of me enough to have imagined how *I* would look as an old man. I am Hackle, your journeyman! Hackle, your pupil of ten years!"

A faint palsy had begun to rock Haffkraff's head. His eyes seemed to thaw at the centers, where two attentive glints grew blacker. Now the sottish lips brought out sound—an all but voiceless gasp.

"Hackle?"

Fury flared in Hackle, a rage to melt this cosmic torpor binding the man he had come, at such risk, to prosecute.

"Yes!" he thundered. "Hackle! Whom you robbed of his true career! You, who should have prepared him for accomplishment!"

Here, somehow, his voice displayed awful power—seemed to roll booming for miles in all directions. The titan's huge snore actually faltered. This, and a tremor of one of Death-by-Winter's eyelids, made Hackle's body rubbery with horror.

"Hackle," said the dead man wonderingly. His voice broke free on the word with a frosty crackle. With measured effort he brought out more words:

"How . . . are . . . you . . . so . . . free?" The old man's eyes moved up and down Hackle's body to indicate his standing, his mobility.

The giant's snoring had resumed. Still shaken, Hackle looked at Haffkraff with a somewhat chastened wrath.

"Free!" he grunted. "In all my life I've been free only in this last act of coming here alive to confront you. As for the rest, and all my work, I have *never* been free from the triviality and futility you bequeathed me."

Haffkraff's head, still faintly palsied, showed a catch in its wobble, as though a suspicion had just wakened in him. His eyes looked fully thawed, but his voice hadn't quite reached that state.

"You still live? . . . And come to death? . . . To confront me?"

"And to rebuke you. Oh, to think how I looked up to you! You slight, slippery man! To think how I—yes—loved you!"

"You have come here to *rebuke* me?" The icy gasp of outrage the old corpse gave the word inflamed Hackle anew. He almost howled again, caught himself, then leaned close to his old teacher, his teeth clenched:

"You mountebank! You jack-of-all-styles! On call to any mass-producer who needed his clichés trimmed and polished. Yet who praised and detailed greatness better than you did in your swaggering extemporizations? You ducked every artistic challenge, every serious devotion to an idea. What else *could* I have become but the adept and addict of that same hollow facility?"

"Curse you, Hackle, you mealy-mouthed whiner!" Haffkraff's voice was now fully his own, with that light, sandpapery, chafing quality—like pumice buffing marble—that had always made the man's diatribes so bright and savory to Hackle's ear. The sound, unheard for twenty-five years, sparked a senseless, automatic warmth in his heart. "Your arrogance astounds me," Haffkraff was saying. "Am I to have no surcease of fools and their follies, not even here?"

"Am I a fool?" choked Hackle. His old master's voice had mixed grief with his rage. He ground his teeth. "If I am, who made me so, who trained me? I did not lack native talent when I came under your care. *Care!* Ha! If I am a fool, what were you—you there in your corsair's cap? Posturing dwarf! Swashbuckling beetle!"

"Of course. But my follies were my own, and I didn't go whining to anyone else with the charge of them. Did your needs not crowd my career enough, that you should crowd me even here and now with your complaints?" Indignation had so limbered the old man's icy innards that even his derelict limbs began to wake, to tremor with the ardor that had melted his lungs and warmed his words to all their ancient resonance. Now, at last, Hackle felt the triumph of accomplishment. His spirit soared above the pallid, death-encumbered plain. He was touching near the heart of his rebuke, and having it felt.

"Crowd your career? What care did you ever take to show me

more than you were expert in? To strut your special tricks, spread your peacock's tail of paltry plumage to an ignorant and worshipful eye—*this* you would do readily enough, and at little labor."

"What? My limitations? Have you come to scold me for these? Blame your own upon them? You're in your dotage, surely, Hackle! Look at this trek you've made to me—it can't have been other than grueling and full of risk! Couldn't you have spent all this tenacity and daring on curing your *own* limits, instead of on carrying blame to a dead man's door?"

"Ah, but one never knows one's weakness till it has toppled him, till he has fallen short of what he aimed at!" He was half-smiling, and almost shouting again, careless of the Titan in the near-ecstasy of speaking the truths delimiting his life. "By the time I knew whether I must move, my soul had stiffened! My eye and ear for inspiration had grown dull by the time I knew what to look and listen for!"

"So! The sum of your folly is that I was to have taught you what I had not mastered?"

"Yes! A truth your sarcasm cannot avert. For you had talent! You knew at least the shape of what you had not achieved! The frontiers of the territory you had not dared to penetrate. If you had *cared* for my life, you could have taken just one step outside your vanity. You could have sketched for me those realms you *had* to know existed beyond the realms of your small-scale expertise and easy superiorities. In such a spirit of love, you could have let me know there are degrees of dedication in art that purchase something lasting, something rare that repays all effort, recompensing everything death takes from us."

His rebuke, Hackle felt in this moment, was delivered. And yet, amazingly, it felt not so much like the transmission of an idea, as the shedding of an entire state of mind. Everything he saw—abruptly—seemed different. Those white miles of tumbled lives around him, all those wrecks in Death's freeze, now filled him with a giant tenderness. Death-by-Winter, blotting half the sky, shimmered, faintly nimbused by auroral lightnings. The rumble of his slumbering breath now purred with a majesty almost musical, like the trumpets and drumrolls of a mighty army mustering.

But foremost of these transformations was Haffkraff's. The cadaver blinked, stared a moment, and was shaken by a laugh. This laugh—albeit but a single bark, and soft—was like a final thawing of the old man's body. For the first time he moved his hands, stiffly presenting them palms-up to his own wry gaze.

"Nothing, my dear Hackle, recompenses everything death takes from us—recompenses *anything* death takes from us." He lifted his look to Hackle. Weasely, his former student had always thought that look, for instance when Haffkraff was peering at a block and ferreting out with his eyes the shape latent in the stone. "As for loving you, I did," the corpse continued. "But with the same lazy and imperfect sort of love I showed myself. For had I been capable of the pure and strictly honest kind you rant about, I might have shown it to myself and *been* the artist you so rightly say I wasn't. And the same goes for you, of course, doesn't it?"

"Of course," smiled Hackle. The easy concession was like shedding weight, ejecting a ballcast of ancient grievance. Indeed, he felt ever more levitational. His sickish lungs felt inflated, engorged with a healing arctic air of unimagined freedom. "How churlish I've been, Haffkraff!" he almost crowed. "What a churlishness has possessed me in these last few years of mine!" He flung his words jubilantly abroad. His echoes, big and distinct, dispersed over the plain. Half calmingly, Haffkraff's hand came up.

"Yes, well, an angry and accusing state of mind is a kind of balm to a hungry spirit, I suppose," he offered. He seemed faintly uneasy at his former student's fire, and cast a glance toward Death-by-Winter.

But Hackle was highly volatile now in his heart's emancipation. He was all fire and air, it seemed, and could not be bothered to tone down his dithyramb.

"Ah, dear old Haffkraff! Bless your patience with my fractious taunts!"

"Well, *here* of course, calm and patience are—"

"Just think, whatever your faults, how unlucky I might have been with a different sponsor! I could have got some square-nosed sober-sides who would have felt duty bound to pinch and sour and buckle down my imagination! You know it's simply not enough, just to thank you. No! For a decade of instruction? Which, whatever its deficiencies, was always patient, friendly, and inventive in its explanatory methods? Not enough by half, oh, no!"

Hackle had begun to pace a fervent little circuit before his recumbent—and now visibly uneasy—former sponsor. Pacing, rubbing his hands together, he spoke in a tone of dawning revelation. "For haven't you carried me, metaphorically speaking, through my student decade, a major passage of my life? Then I should do no less for you, and carry you literally back *to* life. Oh, yes! A major passage that, wouldn't you agree, my dear old teacher?"

The corpse, impossibly, blanched. Blatant fear now caused his legs to palsy with his head, and his shaking blue hands were raised in prevention.

"Madness, Hackle! You are proposing madness! *It is not done!*"

Hackle stood suddenly still, and smiled. Purpose surged through him. "Old teacher!" he trumpeted. "Old friend! When an enormity is to be done it must be done at once, to outrun second thoughts!"

He bent and clamped the dead man's ribs between both palms. He hoisted too hard and almost fell, for Haffkraff was bulkily light, like the skeleton of a big bird. Hackle draped his teacher down his back, clamping the fragile forearms against his chest. He set out striding for the portal he had entered by.

"It is not done, Hackle! It is not done!" Though Haffkraff's lips were at his ear, his voice sounded eerily distant and feeble. His passenger struggled as he spoke, but this protest, too, was strangely weak. His twitches might have been the wind stirring Hackle's pithless, unseen burden. For indeed, a stiff wind had suddenly sprung up, and kicked to life ahead of him, shifty, shrill wind devils of powdered snow. He had scarcely put behind them his teacher's resting place when the vastly overlooming snore of Death-by-Winter came—with a grinding boom—to a pause. Hackle broke into a jog trot.

The wind devils quickened and swelled, came hornet-swarming against him, expunging visibility. Slothfully, the colossus shifted where it lay, and the ice plain under Hackle's feet groaned and faintly tautened. That torque was slight, but dreadful in its scale and Hackle now began to run outright, shouldering fanatically forward through the stinging whiteouts, steering by glimpses of the portal-pit. From this a spumy vortex now towered, as if either this air were draining down it, or the lower air were cycloning out of it. Again the Titan stirred, and awful stresses tensed the icy world-floor. Eyes mad, a war cry on his lips that he himself was deaf to in those gales, Hackle broke into a reckless sprint. His lungs, in this delirium, were restored him, and his feet, unhesitant and firm, found their way on that blind and broken ground. His teacher felt ever lighter—like a banner that he towed, a trophy waving behind him like a flame.

A shift in the devil winds showed him the spuming pit was near, a terrible and ambiguous thing to leap into, were it not for the huger thing visible beyond it. This was the slow opening of one of Death-by-Winter's mammoth, nacreous eyes. The immense, cataracted orb rolled to aim down upon the thieving sculptor. A tidal front of fear swept down against Hackle then. With fierce, unslackening drive, mad Hackle hit the portal-pit at a dead run and dove into that howling, eyeless throat of storm as to some refuge from the meaning in the giant's eye.

There was a fall through miles of storm, a strange, buoyed fall that didn't hasten past a certain speed. The storm opened out, its winds made wilder music and the air tasted richer. Hackle hit a snowbank—solidly, but the drift was deep and soft. He floundered instantly to his feet, for he had felt at impact an absence at his back, though his hand still pressed his teacher's to his chest.

Indeed, Haffkraff was gone. His pithless forearm had snapped bloodlessly in half. It made Hackle smile, after a moment, to reflect that all he'd brought back of his old sponsor was his right hand. He stepped out of the snowdrift, which was a big, bright anomaly in the arid hills behind the slums. Across the river, Hrabb sparkled beneath the Jut's towering, inarticulate mass.

"Home again," he told himself. He looked anew at his knuckly memento of Haffkraff. The fingers were frozen in a partial closure which struck Hackle, the longer he looked at it, as remarkably, mysteriously eloquent. He laid it on the ground to look at it from varied vantages. When, after a time, it turned suddenly to ice, then molded snow, and then was gone, Hackle found he had memorized its gesture.

V

Hackle went home and slept till the following noon. He rose with a determined expression, which looked grim and peaceful in equal parts. He had some breakfast and then strolled out to his front steps, where he expected to find his death sitting, and did. He sat down beside it.

"Welcome home," the death said. "Accept my congratulations. You're a rare and worthy man, I assure you, Hackle. I am most impressed with your tenacity and your daring."

"Thank you. May I impress you further?"

The death's affability just perceptibly froze. Dispassion now qualified its smile. "You suggest a further indiscretion on my part?"

"I do, yes."

"Mmmmm. I don't reject this out of hand. Of course, I shall now be harder to impress, if you see what I mean."

"One month of my life is what I'd pay."

"A month?" The death's voice echoed with a note of lugubrious awe. Its pit-black gaze dwelled wonderingly on Hackle, showing him the vacuum that his gamble risked. A maggot, as if called forth by its host's amazement, shyly poked its snout from its burrow in the cheesy orbit of the death's left eye. The death plucked, balled, and flicked it, then replied:

"I am impressed anew. What services would you require?"

"The help of a Death-by-Lightning for one night."

"We can do business." After a delicate pause, it added: "You wish to yield the month up now?"

"I do."

"I don't mind telling you, by way of warning, you're playing this one very close."

"Thank you, but proceed."

That evening a storm gathered over Hrabb. It fell so furiously and long the citizens cowered awake all night beneath their beds. It seemed to center on the Jut where incessant lightnings played—vast, brief blades of fire that whittled and bit and hewed a steady hail of rubble from the crag. Gravel chittered and rattled on the city's roofs like a second rainfall. At sunrise the Jut stood utterly remade before the timid eyes of townsfolk blinking out at the sudden calm. Its form was that of a raised hand, a thousand feet high. Its gesture was ambiguous, and this ambiguity was to father sects in Hrabb in generations to come. Some held that the hand was poised to grasp the city, others that the hand proclaimed a benediction on it.

Only Hackle, who survived by almost a day the carving of it, and spent the time admiring it till he died—he alone knew the identity of that gesture: that of a sculptor's hand that is pausing to weigh a concluding stroke upon some labor of love.

Tanith Lee

When I think of Tanith Lee, I think of nighttime. I remember the hot summer nights when we ran around Manhattan, full of the exuberance of youth. But I also remember sitting alone in the dark empty office reading manuscripts long after closing time. Tanith's manuscripts were the only ones that we never took home. Typed on fragile onionskin, (to save in postage from the U.K.) they had to be hand copied, page by laborious page. Tanith's actual originals were written in longhand. The typescript that we received was painstakingly transcribed, first by Tanith's mother, herself a writer, and in later years by Tanith herself. I'll never forget the one time I saw Tanith writing—she was like a person possessed.

And when a Tanith Lee manuscript came into the DAW offices, *we* were like people possessed. Don always read it first, and the frustration of waiting for him to be finished was nearly unbearable. When it was my turn, nothing could interrupt me. I stayed in the office until I was finished, often not returning home until the wee hours of the morning. Leaving our dark and eerily deserted office near dawn, I used to feel like Tanith's heroine from *The Birthgrave,* her first DAW book: a girl emerging from a volcano into a strange and alien land.

—BW

I

THE Roman stood looking at his slave. She was one of many, in the fine house on Palace Hill. They came and went barely noticed, across his vision, like shifting columns of sunlight, or the diurnal shadows that changed shape over the floors. But something, now, had made him see this one.

"Come here," he called. Not harshly, he was not a cruel man to his slaves, did not believe in it unless it were needed—and then a sound beating usually settled the offender. The female slaves especially he did not like to chastise unduly. Like flowers, or animals, they looked better, and were a nicer ornament to his house, if well kept.

The slave came across the garden toward him. It was the fifth hour,* late in the morning, and the sun gilded the little fountain, and the marble statue of Apollo with his lion. The slave, too, was polished a moment with light gold. And then she was in front of Livius, her head lowered.

She had black hair, plaited back and held with a thong. She wore the coarse linen tunic of her status, but of a pleasant soft cream in color. It made her honey skin look darker. She was about sixteen years old, or probably younger, for like most slaves, she would tend to appear older than her years.

Livius regarded the slave carefully. Had his wife said something about this girl? He thought so—what had it been? That she, his wife, had bought her privately, a favor to some rich friend— Claudia Metella perhaps, or Terentia. . . . *Why* as a favor?

There was nothing wrong with the girl that he could see. And

*About 11 A.M.

if there had been, his fastidious Fulvia would hardly have wanted her, nor would he.

"Look up," he said.

The slave looked up. For a second, a flash of her face, small and Eastern, triangular in form, the nose long and lips full. The eyes—

She had glanced down again.

"No, I told you to look up."

A slightly longer flash of face then, but not much. Obviously, she was frightened of him, the Master, thought she had done something wrong and would be punished. Maybe she had been badly treated elsewhere.

"I'm not angry. Where were you going?" This was the voice he used for a young nervous horse.

She whispered some words, his slave, which did not sound like the Imperial Tongue. Not even like the argot of the lower orders. Some Eastern muttering. But she had known enough Latin, of course, to understand his orders, if not to reply to them.

"All right. Go along, then."

She dipped her body before him, graceful, mindless, then turned and walked away across the garden.

A strange creature. Like having a tamed but shackled leopard in the house.

Livius smiled at his idea, and returned into the cool of his library.

"She has strange eyes, that slave," said Livilla to her mother.

Fulvia took no notice.

They had been having their hair dressed in the summer court-yard that opened from Fulvia's summer bedroom. Fulvia's hair, bleached by quince juice, was ornately curled and crimpled; Livilla's dark hair had been dressed more simply, as became a maiden. The slaves who had seen to this were now gone, and none of them had been the slave to whom Livilla referred.

She tried again, "Mother, that new slave—where did she come from?"

"Which slave? What? What are you talking about? Why should slaves interest you?"

"They don't. Or only this one. The one with green eyes."

"Yes," said Fulvia. She sipped her wine, mixed with the liquified pulp of roses. She looked thoughtful, considering. But said nothing else.

Livilla would not be put off.

"Mother, the other slaves dislike her. You know it can cause trouble when they get upset. They get careless. Look at how Lodia nearly burned you with the tongs—"

"Yes, yes. But I hit her with the mirror. She won't do it again."

"She was nervous, Mother. Unsettled."

"Livilla, that shade of yellow doesn't suit you. I've thought so for a long while."

Diverted, disconcerted, Livilla looked down in outrage at her yellow stola, figured with anemones. And forgot to say any more about slaves.

Fulvia, bored with the Livillan torrent of insecurities now released, in the matter of dress, hair, and skin, sat with apparent patience, offering calming words. Fulvia was used to being bored. It was her life.

Of course, she wanted for nothing, and she did not wish to change this. She did not really *wish* for anything.

Birds sang. She thought about the slave.

It had only been ten days ago that Terentia Austus had sought Fulvia out, arriving in person that morning, sitting frowning and hard among Fulvia's pretty things.

"I want," Terentia had finally announced, "you to take a creature off my hands."

Fulvia had raised her brows. Terentia was several years older, and looked it, her makeup much too heavy and her gray hair covered by an auburn wig, of a color known as *Flame*. Terentia was also powerful, the wife of an electoral candidate sure to do well, a rich woman securely fastened in a prestigious marriage. What did she want? One could doubtless not say No, whatever it was.

"A creature, dear Terentia. What kind of creature?"

The Austus family kept a menagerie, as Fulvia knew. She

suspected a snappish wolf or porcupine was about to be unloaded on her.

"A slave," had said Terentia.

Fulvia was almost relieved.

"A slave. I see."

"There's nothing unsuitable about her. She's biddable and not work-shy. I'll be frank with you, Fulvia. My husband pays her too much attention."

Fulvia waited behind her polite mask. She thought that if every married woman worried about her husband's activities with *slaves*, the gods knew what would become of them all.

However, "Yes, it sounds absurd," said Terentia, seeming even more aggravated. "Why should I care? I have my sons, and besides Austus is still most attentive to me. I've no complaints. Also he keeps a woman near the Circus Gorbus. I've never had any concerns about *her*."

"Then . . ." prompted Fulvia, sensing a prompt was expected.

"This slave came to me from my sister Junia's household. She begged me to take her, wouldn't say why, or only some rubbish about the slave's being disruptive. And of course, her husband's a drunk, so one never knows."

"No."

"Then I take the wretch into our house. She does her work perfectly adequately. And then Austus—becomes obsessed with her."

"Obsessed—"

"Yes. I choose the word with care. Perhaps it's his disappointment last year in the election—"

"Oh, but, *this* year—"

"Exactly. And he must concentrate on that. So she goes. Will you accept her? A gift. I won't ask a sesterce for her. It would be unlucky."

"Well, but, Terentia—couldn't you merely—"

"No. I can't explain. Are you willing, that's all I'm waiting to hear." Terentia had risen abruptly from her seat in a flare of costly garments and clash of pearls. The severing of valuable connections twanged in the air. Fulvia did what she must. Terentia nodded. "I'll send her to you before the dinner hour."

And so the slave arrived. Looking her over, Fulvia thought her nothing much, simply an inferior from an Eastern country, which Terentia had actually said was most likely Persis. She had wondered, too, what Terentia would say to the obsessive husband, and if he would presently storm across Palace Hill after his property. This did not happen.

The girl seemed to sink into the household with very few ripples. The slaves were not notably antipathetic to her. In Fulvia's experience, they often took a dislike to newcomers, particularly females.

Her eyes were a little odd. That glassy gray-green, unusually clear in the dark skin, between the black lashes.

But there.

(Livilla had stopped lamenting, and was instead admiring herself in the silver mirror.)

Fulvia had mentioned the new slave to Livius, naturally. He had been quite uninterested, as one would predict.

They ate the evening meal in the garden, then lingered there. From beyond the house came the low rumble of heavy-wheeled traffic on cobbles, the occasional shouts of some party or other revel. Above, the sky deepened until, undimmed by the uncountable lamps of Rome, the stars were put on.

"The snails were good," said Jovus.

"No, too sticky. Cibo still doesn't know how to cook them," added Parvus, the connoisseur.

Livius listened to his two sons, neither yet a full-grown man. He had been reading, and had fallen asleep in the thick heat of afternoon, like some old grandfather. Now, leaning here, he felt curiously alert, as if expecting something. But nothing, nothing at all was expected.

A girl had brought more wine and was pouring it into his cup. Her.

He wanted to say again, *Look up.* But the eyes were downcast, she might not have had any eyes—

Outside a wild raw shout blew up. Palace Hill was a select area, but it got noisier by the night. Perhaps he should buy a farm, move out into the country among the olives and vineyards, vegetate. . . . But there was Jovus, the eldest, to secure first in a worthy career. And Livilla to marry suitably, to someone or other.

None of this, his duties, caught his attention greatly tonight. But there, the lamp was being lit by Apollo, and she was standing straight again, and the flame splintered in her eyes. How green they were. Fig-leaf green, yet cooling, like marble.

He glanced at Fulvia. She had been watching him.

"Did you like the pork liver?" she asked, solicitous, as a good wife should be. And he sensed her boredom, both with ordering the liver and its cooking, and now asking. His answer, his approval, also bored with those, as *he* was with all of it, including his children, his house, the noises of the city, the city, the night. . . .

"Delicious, Fulvia. How clever you were to think of it. Aren't the stars fine?"

Fulvia lay sleepless on her bed. It had been made in Egypt, and sloped a little, keeping her head higher than her feet, and tonight this gave her a peculiar feeling of weightless drifting, as if she might float up and out of the door, and over the high walls into the city.

What would she see? The lit porches of festive houses not her own, hung with garlands. The seven arched spines of Rome, crowded with their temples, gardens, mansions, and the dark valleys between, where the markets, dens, brothels, and slums lay twitching and surging, also sleeplessly.

Fulvia turned on to her side. At this ninth hour of the night,* it was very quiet on Palace Hill. There was only the faint stir of the plane tree in her private courtyard beyond the curtain. It sounded like the moving coils of a snake.

*About 3 A.M.

She had thought her husband might sleep with her here to-night. Generally she knew the signs—little attentions, a kind of heat which came from his body. She had been anticipating the visit, had taken down her hair and freshened her perfume. She no longer thrilled to his sexual attentions—all that had left her with the birth of Jovus, the first son. As if sexual pleasure (as she had) had done its duty, and so now she need no longer experience any. She had been sorry at first, then philosophical. These things happened. And she still enjoyed his arousal. The manifestation of his continuing desire, however infrequent, was a compliment.

Why had he not come in, then?

Perhaps he was tired. He had eaten a large meal, and taken a little too much wine. And it was, though the summer was so young, a hot night.

I must sleep, Fulvia commanded herself. She listened to the tree rustling, and glimpsed inside her mind a silvery snake winding through leaves, in the instant before she fell from consciousness.

Livius woke with a start.

What had disturbed him? (He listened, hearing nothing, even the noisy neighbors were silent now.) And—where was he?

Ruffled, he got to his feet. He had come back to the library and stretched out on the couch here to read for an hour before going to Fulvia. She would have realized, and he always gave her time to prepare. But again—he had slept. Now he could tell from the feel of the house, it was only an hour or so from sunrise.

Far too late to disrupt Fulvia's slumbers. He was a considerate man. It had been different, of course, when they were young. They had shared a bed every night, and kept busy.

The lamp was guttering on the desk. He trimmed the wick and took the lamp with him along the corridor. When he reached his garden, he paused between the pillars. The stars were dull now. The garden was moonless, ghostly, and the fountain shivered like a piece of silk.

As he turned into his own room, the light of the small lamp flared fierce as a torch against furniture and hangings. Livius winced at the heavy gold, the bright inlay of ivory, the blast of scarlet curtain. How much had he drunk? Too much, it seemed. He blew out the lamp and undressed in blackness.

I'm not old, he thought, lying there. His vision seemed a little disturbed, and in the blackness, weird faces leered and smoked at him from near the ceiling. The wine, or even the pork—*I wish the gods would make me young again,* he resentfully mused. *Even five years younger.*

He thought of fig trees—he did not know why—their shade, the glow of their leaves filtering the summer sun.

We should be like that. Sleep for a while in winter, and then grow strong and new again, like leaves.

Livius smiled now at his own foolishness. He slept.

The slaves of Livius curled in their tiny cubicles tucked deep and windowless within the house. Most had a bed; that was their Master's kindness. Now and then one would creep to the privy, a dirty, stinking place, without the fitments of the rich man's easements, let alone of the lavish thermal bathroom with its sheltered terrace facing south.

Cibo met Lodia in the dark, between the privy and her cubicle. As the house cook, he had somewhat better quarters behind the kitchen, and also some power in the slave-world.

"Well, Lodia. Like a moment with me tonight?"

Lodia grinned. It was her way of saying she knew she had no choice.

Cibo guided her, and when they reached the corridor with the lamp burning, he saw the bruise on her arm. The Mistress had struck her today with the polished silver hand mirror, for carelessness. Now he joked about it, telling Lodia she was an idiot and had better watch out, or Master would sell her off to the mines.

Lodia was used to his foreplay. She said nothing. Cibo led her into the kitchen, past the man-tall pots and burned-charcoal smelling oven. He gave her a piece of bread, a leftover, smeared with pork fat. In a corner, his two assistants lay on the stone floor, snoring.

Cibo took Lodia against the wall, in a hot rush and snuffling almost-silence. He finished quickly, scowling. "All right, you can be off now. You're not so juicy as you were. Next time I'll take that new girl. The Persian."

Lodia said, "If you do, don't look in her eyes."

"Eh? What does that mean? Lodia was once more dumb. Cibo said, "It's not her eyes that would fascinate me, Lodia. Go on back to your pit."

Jovus dreamed he was a man, and wore the Man's Toga. An augur had been taken and it foretold great things for him—though what, he was unsure. Even so, he was making a speech in the Forum, and older men nodded, and the crowd was all applause.

Then a girl walked through the crowd. She moved like a breeze through a cornfield, and the human figures swayed away from her, and back again when she had passed, but took no notice of her otherwise.

Jovus, however, lost the thread of his oration. He stopped speaking entirely, and an enormous quiet filled the Forum, and in the blue-scorched sky, another color came, as if an awning had been erected, as they did it at the circuses.

Beyond the wall, Parvus, nine years old, dreamed he was swimming in a deep green pool. He was rather anxious, for he knew that he was tiring, and the sides looked sheer.

Livilla, on her own bed across the corridor, was sobbing in her dream because she could not bear the saffron color of her stolas, and they were all like that, every one, even those she was brought that began as pink woven-air muslin, or delicate white silk—and none of them therefore suited her. She looked blotchy and too fat, unmarriageable, so she wept.

II

As he gazed about him, the Artifex Iudo was puzzled. But then, his clients often puzzled him with their requests—a perfectly serviceable pillar to be removed and replaced by a carved prop that made the room into a stage set; a wall with charming nymphs changed to a bacchanal of the wine god, lewd female companions, and goats.

This, though. This did intrigue him slightly.

"Yes, sir. Certainly it can be done. I have a new color that has come from the Libanus region. They call it *Sea-Wave*. Or, then, from Egypt—"

Livius said, "The color of this perfume pot, like this."

Iudo accepted the pot with its hint of nard. One of the lady wife Fulvia's, probably. It was a deep, nacreous green. He thought perhaps he would not be able to match it at all. Green was a color which so often turned, like milk. One painted it on, and as it dried, something in the plaster made it too shallow, or too strong. Which normally might not matter. But now, with this insistent instruction—

"And the subject? As I have it here?"

"Trees," said Livius absently. "Leaves. Pools. Green things."

Of course, more unusual than all the rest, (than the commission for the artifex and his assistants to paint the two dining rooms, the library, and the rich man's bedroom, all in greens and variations of green) was the straw hat, such as a farmer might put on, clamped down on Livius' noble head, even here in the shade. And beneath the hat, a band of thin cotton, itself dullish green in color, perhaps to catch sweat from the forehead?

Livius' eyes were watering in the sun. They looked inflamed.

Iudo had noticed the elder of the two young sons also had this problem with his eyes, although not so badly, nor had he put on a hat against the sun.

The boy was there, now, out in the garden court, sitting on a bench, brooding the way they did at that age, whether patrician or citizenry. (Supposedly the plebian poor, in their sties, did not have time to brood in youth. They were already out pimping, whoring, stealing, cutting throats, or training in the gladiator schools. Or at the very least, standing in line for the free food the city offered.)

"Well, then. You may do it."

"Thank you, sir. We shall try our best."

"Begin today."

"Ah—very well. That may be somewhat—"

"Take this." The bag clanked heavy as a legionary's full campaign armor.

Livius sighed. He hooded his lids.

Iudo, hurrying off to organize his men and paint, did not see the rich man pull the green cloth right down over his eyes.

In the garden, Jovus *did* see this.

He stood up, nervous, his inner, nonphysical body attenuated, like the eyes of a slug standing on stalks.

Jovus picked a way across the sunny court, as if avoiding invisible obstacles, between the beds of roses and late iris, whose reds and purples seemed to be on fire.

"Father?"

Livius did not answer.

Was he asleep again? He had fallen asleep at dinner yesterday.

"*Father,*" said Jovus, more loudly, and then his father's face turned toward him, and Jovus saw his father's open black eyes staring at him through the band of thin Egyptian cotton.

For some reason—every reason—this frightened Jovus. He was fifteen, almost a man, but he was afraid.

"Sir—"

"What is it?" The voice was weary, dismissive. Jovus knew that really all his father ever was to him now, at best, was courteous. The happy man who had played with him as a child, the grieved man who beat him when he skimped his lessons, who took pride in every achievement—that man was gone. But where?

"Which rooms are to be painted?"

Weary, short, Livius told him.

Jovus went away and slouched through the house into his own rich boy's bedroom, with its carved garment chest and bed of ebony and pine. The crimson panels painted on the walls offended him, but he stared at them until his eyes ached.

Past the doorway, then, she went.

It was just like that. As if there were no other in the house, it was all vacant but for himself, and then for her. Jovus watched her.

She *slid* along the corridor, vanishing suddenly at the turn, as if merely to turn a corner were supernatural.

He had seen his sister Livilla earlier throw a cut piece of her own hair into the flame before the household guardians in the larger dining room. But then, too, he had heard her whining about wanting to make an offering to Juno Viriplaca, to ensure her marriage.

Jovus thought the gods would not be concerned with this. They never offered help, even his family ancestors did not. Rather like Livius, they had lost—in their case with immortality or death—all involvement in the human world, save where they could be harsh in it.

The house of Junia Lallia, Terentia Austus' sister, stood behind the Gardens of Fortuna, screened by the massive poplars and ilexes. Fulvia approached uneasily and in full panoply, in the closed litter with curtains of Indian silk, with her bodyguard and two attendants.

At first, sitting in the vestibule, on a hard, gold-adorned seat, Fulvia thought that perhaps Junia might not see her, despite the delivered gifts of goose offal in honey, early-ripened peaches from the coast, and spikenard.

But then one of the house slaves conducted Fulvia into Junia's private sitting room, which opened on a courtyard garden depressing in its glory of trees, a terraced water course, tame doves, monkeys, and a peacock marred only by its rusty shrieks.

Junia was a youngish woman who scorned to bleach her hair. Her clothes and jewelry said all there was to say on such matters.

"It's most kind of you to see me," murmured Fulvia.

"Such lovely presents," replied Junia coldly. "Is this about the elections?"

"No—no, dear Junia Lallia—I wouldn't think of bothering you, but—"

"Then it is," said Junia, staring now into space, "the slave."

"Oh," said Fulvia.

"Yes," said Junia. "The Persian woman," she added. "Her

name—did anyone tell you? Roxara. Or so they called her in the market at Ostia—or again, so I understand." She paused. Then she clapped her hands. A girl came in with wine and cinnamon-water and little cakes. After the girl had served these and gone, Junia said, "It had to be faced. Of course you would come here. Terentia told me what she did. But I think she didn't tell you what *I* had done, or why."

Fulvia gave over caution. "Tell me."

Junia lifted her brows, that was all. Then she told.

"My eldest son, who as you know lived here in my husband's house when not away in Gaul, bought this slave, as men do, on a whim. He presented her to his wife, a poor virtuous little ninny with the wits of a pigeon. I suppose he liked the looks of the slave, and meant to sample her, and the poor little ninny wouldn't even have noticed, very likely. However. My son didn't sample the slave called Roxara. Instead, Fulvia, he went mad."

Fulvia felt herself whiten. She felt the blanched and rosy makeup standing out on her skin like a *separate* skin, and herself, all horror, glaring through.

Junia Lallia said frigidly, her eyes on nothing at all, "Firstly he wouldn't return to Gaul. My husband covered this up by saying our son was ill. All sorts of devices then had to be resorted to, in order to avoid disgrace. I won't tax you with those. Meanwhile physicians came and went. And my son—my beautiful son—" shocking Fulvia once more, this abrupt break into emotion, as swiftly mastered, "—lay raving in a darkened room, unable to bear the light, or any bright color, wanting the girl—not for any proper reason, but simply to *look at her*."

"To—look at her?"

"He couldn't keep his eyes from her. She had to sit in the room with him. I witnessed it day after day. She sat and looked at the ground, and then he would go to her—groveling along the floor like a dog—staring up into her face—" All at once, Junia sneezed. Having done this, she made a sign against the bad omen. She said, "We tried to keep her from him. He would cry for her. I mean he would *scream* for her as if he were in agony. Oh, then, I called priests to the house, from various temples, and other persons. Because it was sorcery, what else?''

"What else," gasped Fulvia, shuddering.

"They had some effect—mostly through drugging him to insensibility. But then they told us we must send the woman away.''

"But surely—if she's a sorceress—you should have killed her—your husband, excuse me, but really, he should have killed her at once.''

"He didn't dare to," said Junia. "Another strong man brought to his knees. We were afraid . . . And so—I sent Roxara to my sister, a very reasonable and sensible woman, who assured me it was all nonsense, and she would put all to rights. But, as you know, in the end my sensible sister, who fears nothing, and will walk through a cemetery on nights when the ghosts hover in the moonlight, she, too, became fearful, and she sent this evil being away to *you*. Forgive us, Fulvia. We are in your debt forever.''

Fulvia thought, *So you are, but how will that help now?*

She, too, controlled herself. She said, "And your son?''

Junia turned her head, but not before Fulvia saw why she had sneezed—her eyes were bursting with tears she did not permit to fall. Junia said, "He's gone.''

"To . . . Gaul?''

"No, not to Gaul.''

"Then—can he be *dead*?''

"I don't know if he is dead.''

Fulvia blurted "But you must know—''

"He vanished. My son vanished. When Terentia's slaves came to fetch Roxara, he was already gone, and we knew nothing. Each of us thought he had wandered to some other part of the house. Then that he was in the city. Searches were made. It was discreet. Then less so. He hasn't been found. If you have heard no rumors, that is due to my husband's connection to the Flavians.''

Among the forgotten cakes, Fulvia was panting, but Junia now sat icy, stone still.

"Perhaps he will come back," Fulvia faltered at last.

"Do you think so? Now you sound like his dolt of a little

wifelet. Of course he can never come back. She cast a spell on him, and it took him somewhere he can never escape and never be found, out of this world."

Junia rose.

Fulvia staggered to her feet.

"I'm in your debt," said Junia. "If I can assist in any way at all, I will do so. What will you do?"

Fulvia drew in her lips. She said, "There's only one way."

"Yes, perhaps. If you're brave enough."

The litter raced over the hills, the bearers running, the body-guard thrusting lower citizens from its path.

At the portico of Livius' house, they came to a halt. The door was knocked upon. The doorkeeper opened it.

Fulvia got out of the litter. She was trembling, it was true, but she had crossed this threshold many hundreds of times, only once carried over it as a bride. Now, as she moved forward into the familiar house, her foot caught in the tile of a second step, *which was not there*. She felt herself falling and watched surprised as she flew out on to the mosaic floor. She heard the crack of her head against its ungiving surface, from some way off. And then nothing.

It was the Greeks and Egyptians who had thought everyone but themselves to be barbarians, as alike in their limitation as sheep. Romans, though, were also inclined to this idea—the barbarity of other races . . . the Egyptians and Greeks by now not always unincluded.

So, she was a barbarian then, from Persis, that land Great Alexander had subdued, a country of crags and brown dust and lions, of green gardens mysterious under an alien moon . . .

Livius looked about him slowly. The walls of the library were pale and painted over by green, green fruits, green leaves, green figures that danced or swam in a distance of green waves and

green dolphins. The artifex and his men had worked swiftly, perhaps with not as much agility as speed. A curtain, (green) hung
at the yard door. The summer sun was always too bright. He
found lamps were better. And sometimes he shut one eye and
looked, through the spyglass of flawed emerald, at their green
flames.

This amused him. But he was waiting. He knew that he was.

Once, a child, a boy, had come to the inner doorway.

"Father—the physician says—"

Something unimportant.

Who was this child, addressing him as *Father?* One of the
slaves? Perhaps. In certain patrician homes, the Master was called
Father.

This child-slave had been distressed, wet-eyed, and snotty. Parvus, he was called. A nickname.

Someone had told Livius his wife Fulvia (he thought they
called her Fulvia) had hurt herself. He had gone to see, starting at
the loud colors—raucous red, orange—in her room. He did not
recognize the woman stretched out on the bed, over whom the
physician bent. The smell of medicinal resins turned Livius'
stomach. He did not stay there long, thinking maybe he had made
a mistake, and come to look at the wrong woman.

The door curtain moved. Who would it be now?

It was her, of course, the barbarian Persian. She came in with
a wine jug. She was pouring the wine. Seen through the emerald,
the wine was black-green.

Livius waited for the Persian girl to raise her eyes so that he
could look into them. But she would not do it.

"Sit," he said, "sit over there." She moved so adeptly, as if
alive. But really he did not think she was. None of them were,
nor he himself. This girl, however, although unliving, was *moved*
by something live *within* her.

She sat down on the couch.

"Look up."

She raised her eyes, lowered them.

How could he ever have thought her afraid or nervous? She

had no feelings or emotions, and probably no brain inside her skull, under its covering of amber skin and coarse rich hair.

"No, let me see your eyes."

A look. Gone.

He wondered if he should have her whipped for insolence. If that happened, or if he cut her with the little knife he kept here, for breaking the edges of wax seals, would she bleed green, like the sap of a plant?

Livius got up and went over and sat on the stool, gazing up into her face, and so into the lowered, half-obscured depths of her eyes.

The flames of the lamps were there in the green irises. It was like looking into a hall under the sea, lit by torches.

"Where do you come from? From Ocean? Or out of a tree—a tree nymph or a water nymph?" Her lids drooped lower. "Don't close your eyes. Obey me."

Her face—expressionless, mindless. All slaves were of this kind, unless singled out and made pets of. Would she change now, since he favored her? Livius thought she would not.

He did not want to touch her, let alone take her to him in the sexual act. He found it restful—and yet curiously exciting— simply to sit here like a boy, and stare up at her, trying to see in at the tiny glinting cracks between her eyelids.

When Fulvia opened her eyes, the room was a rippling dimness smeared by lights.

She said, alarmed yet imperious, "I can't see—"

"It will pass, madam. An effect of the drug I've had to give you. You banged your head when you fell. Your cranium is bruised but whole. And I've bled you. All's well."

"Did I fall? Where? I don't remember . . ."

"At the house door. You entered in a hurry."

"Did I? I don't remember . . ."

"You'd been visiting the lady Junia Lallia." (The physician—a know-all.)

"I don't remember . . ."

Livilla had appeared, white and terrified. She ran to the bed and made a grab for Fulvia's hand. "Mother—Mother—"

"Gently, child," barked the physician, annoyed at seeing his handiwork disarranged.

But Fulvia said quietly, "Where is Livius?"

The physician turned and busied himself at a table loaded with his salves and infusions. The air smelled of burned beetles, mint, and Greek incense.

"This doctor is Idas," said Livilla, trying to be adult, "he is the doctor Claudia Metella recommends for all things to do with the head—"

"Yes. Where is your father?"

"In his library," said Livilla. "He came in once. Then he went away."

"He mustn't be troubled," said Fulvia. She felt bitter at his lack of care for her, and resigned, because this was only what she would anticipate. Virtuously and grimly, she put him first, and did not know how thin her lips had become. But she was also sleepy from the bleeding, and the potions. "Make sure," she said to Livilla, "your father eats a good dinner."

As she slipped back into sleep, Fulvia thought, *This isn't right. I should get up and go and see to something. I know it was to be done—that was why I was in such a hurry coming in, and so I fell.* But her head ached. She thought of the thing she could not remember. *Never mind it.*

Parvus was standing behind Jovus just outside.

"Don't go in," instructed Livilla. "She's asleep."

"She's slept for days," said Jovus.

"I know," said Livilla. "But Idas says she's in no danger, and must rest."

"He's a Greek," said Parvus, a red-eyed racist, "and he may be useless, too."

Jovus put his hand on his brother's shoulder. "Hush. The Metellas sent him. He's all right."

Livilla said, "I have to go and see to the kitchen, since Mother can't."

When she had stalked off, dismayed at her (temporary) position, Parvus said, "What's Father doing?"

"What he was doing before."

They had seen him. Both had peered around the edge of the green curtain. Seen Livius, their father, a man, sitting at the feet of the Persian woman in the green darkness.

"Is she a witch?" whispered Parvus, "like the sorceress Medea?"

"It's nothing to worry about," said Jovus. He lied, wanting to be alone. "A man—does these things with his house-women. It's just some fancy of his."

Livilla entered the kitchen, and saw that it was empty, and although the day was advancing, nothing much had been done toward the main meal. Oil, onions, and herbs lay about, and some fish—one of which the cat had got hold of, dragged under a bench, and was now eating.

The girl clapped her hands, and no one came, and Livilla had a strange horrible sudden fear that all the house was as empty as the kitchen seemed to be, but for herself and the cat. Everyone was gone, the slaves, her brothers, her father, and Fulvia, too, borne off into the air.

The urge to cry ripped through Livilla, but she tried not to, for she would soon be a woman and married, and she must not let go of her dignity.

Then Lodia crept in.

Her slave's face was pale and deranged, an almost exact match for Livilla's own.

"Cibo choked," said Lodia.

"What—do you mean?"

"The cook—he choked on something. Look—he's there, by the ovens."

Livilla turned and saw Cibo's fat, impossible-to-miss body sprawled in a shadow that had somehow hidden him, and now did not. His face was turned away, and Livilla was glad.

Lodia stood swaying, holding herself in her arms. In a sort of chant she announced, "He must have tried to have her. He must have tried to." Then she sank to her knees and cowered, wondering if one of her masters would come to kill her.

But when Lodia looked up again, the Mistress-daughter had run away.

"I was glad to leave that house," said Idas the Greek. (Rather as Iudo the artifex had felt, if Idas had only known.) "Something goes on there. A great house, and full of people and slaves, and workmen, and so *silent*. And you know how now and then I see things other men are unaware of." His acquaintances in the tavern, attracted by the wine he had bought them, nodded. "Well, then, in the walls of that place—oh, at first it was aswarm with artisans painting everything green, yes, even panels in the tables and chests—I never saw the like, such a dingy, leaden color. But then, as I came from the sick lady's chamber and was passing one of these rooms, now all green-painted—and so badly—" the acquaintances waited, to see what the old romancer would bring out now, "—I saw faces in the walls, among the painted leaves. They watched me. Oh, not *painted* faces—they moved—not human faces either. The gods know what they were. Not animals—not quite that—perhaps like the faces one sees in the trunks of trees, or leaves clustered together, or in weeds under a pond . . ."

The greened house lay silent about its green courtyards. Green shadows dappled Apollo with the panther-skin of Bacchus.

No one went out. And yet it was as if they had *all* gone out. Even if you glimpsed them move there, in the rooms, along the corridors, shifting the sunlight and the hangings, even then, it was as if they were not really there. But if they were not, what was?

For a kind of energy filled all the cells. Time had passed. Some tens of days, thirty, forty. And no one called, not a single trader, and no visitors. Behind the door, in his alcove, the door-slave slept. Yet it was as if he were not there. It was as if the *house* were no longer there, merged into a green shade or green wave. Become one more grove or fountain of the decorated city.

People on Palace Hill, going by the blind outer walls, failed to glance at them, as if—the house of the patrician Livius had vanished.

III

At noon, Jovus went to the kitchen and took some of the olives and figs that lay on the table, and some of the stale bread. A slave—he had forgotten the man's name—had slunk out when Jovus came in, rather as the cat had been used to do, before it ran away. The slave had also scrounged some of the leftover food. Although it spoiled, there still seemed to be enough. And somehow Jovus did not think about when it would all be gone. (He had noted the body of Cibo was no longer there. Someone must have dragged it away. He did not *like* to think of *this*.)

But the house had no Master, so what could you expect of it? Or, it had one, but a Master who stayed in his library and did not move, no, not even to seek the privy or the bath. And the house had a fragile Mistress, who had been sick from a fall, and walked only a short way from her room, and back again.

The hotter colors faded from Jovus' bedroom walls, he thought, as they had faded from the flowers in the garden. Livilla's saffron stolas were now the color of soured cream.

Jovus ate the figs and bread standing in the garden, and he looked up at the sky, which he did not think was blue, not truly, or else something came between him and the sky.

The city was deeply quiet. Occasionally he thought he heard traffic on the roads, or vague cries, but it was perhaps only the rustle of blood behind his own ears.

Moss grew in the mane of Apollo's lion. Jovus was examining this, when he heard his mother's voice from the colonnade.

"Where is your father?"

Fulvia had asked this a great deal, but then she had stopped asking, as the answer was always identical.

"In his library," said Jovus, as always. "Mother, would you like this fig—look, there are raisins, too."

"Never mind," said Fulvia.

She turned, and then she turned back. She said, her voice like pearls which had been crushed, "He isn't there. I looked. He isn't anywhere in this house."

Jovus felt panic spring in him like a tiger.

Fulvia wore no makeup. This made her seem both younger and quite old. Either way she would be no help.

Nevertheless, together they went again through the house, through room after room, into each of the courtyards. They pulled aside drapes and let sunlight into the spaces—was sunlight green? They walked through the three rooms of the bath, steamless and unheated. They searched the cubicles of the slaves. Sometimes they met these slaves, who shied, but seemed deaf and dumb, or who bolted, and this made Fulvia irritated, and so more like her previous self, a remote and pragmatic woman, offering calm words that snapped with repressed rage.

At some point, too, Livilla joined them, crying a little, but stupidly, like a small child who had mislaid what it was upset about. Parvus also appeared. He was quite naked, and very dirty, but none of them reproached him, though Fulvia clicked her tongue.

They did not find Livius.

At last, they were back in the library, where, in the curtain-dusk, the scrolls and wax tablets shone dull in their cubbyholes, like ranks of peculiar skulls.

Fulvia stood there at the room's center. She glanced now and then demandingly at the couch, the chair, then at the stool, which had fallen over. She seemed to think she might still find her husband. She tapped her fingers on her gold bracelet. (The gold was discolored.)

"It's what she told me," said Fulvia, frowning, concentrating. "I remember now. Her son. They disappear. And now Livius has done it."

Livilla sniveled. Parvus picked at a scab on his knee, embarrassed.

Jovus thought, *I don't know them, these people. Who are they?*

Fulvia thought she heard her elder son thinking this, but she did not care. She hated him really, her son Jovus, who had, with his birth, robbed her of sexual pleasure. Even the wretched, time-consuming Livilla had not done that. As for Parvus, what was he, some spawned thing, like a frog—

But there had been something Fulvia meant to do. That was it. This thing had been the reason why she had rushed home from the woman's house—which woman? It did not matter—the one who told her about a son who disappeared, as now Livius had.

What was it Fulvia had meant to do, been so concerned with that she had tripped over an unreal tile loose in a stair that was not there under her feet?

Fulvia turned to Jovus.

"Where is *she?*"

Fulvia wondered if she should go back to her husband's bedroom. She had not looked beneath the bed. Livius would not be there, but *she* might.

"Who?" quavered Jovus, but Fulvia saw the tiger of panic smoldering under his skin.

"The Persian—what was her name—*Roxara.*"

The name sounded in the room incredibly, as though it was actual, and the only thing that could be so.

And after it there followed the most subtle, silky feather of sound, the noise something might make, uncoiling over a bough heavy with leaves.

"Ah," said Fulvia. She moved quite quickly, and pulled the curtain right down from the courtyard door, and then she put her hand on Livius' desk. She took up the little knife he had always kept there. It was only a small knife, but a young woman's neck was usually slender, and the vital vein unmissable.

Yet now Jovus was in her way. Fulvia did not care enough about her son to wish to kill him, and so she only said, "Stand aside from her." Not using his name either since she had forgotten it.

But Jovus went on lumpenly standing there, between Fulvia and the slave called Roxara, who all that while had been, presumably, sitting motionless and invisible in the room's other chair.

Then Fulvia lost patience. She struck the boy across his shoulders, and thrust him aside.

Fulvia herself stood then only inches from the Persian Creature. Fulvia could smell her. She did not smell human, but spicy, like mummia. Her head was not bowed. She was looking back at Fulvia with her opaque serpent-scale eyes, and Fulvia lifted the knife in a steady hand, because this Roxara's snake-neck was very slim, and the vein was plainly to be seen there.

And Jovus screamed, "*No—no—*Mother!" And punched her hand away. And he was strong after all, it felt as if he had broken Fulvia's wrist, there under her green-gold bangle.

"Leave me alone, you fool!" she cried. She was exasperated.

"No—*no*—" shrieked Jovus. "No—Mother—you can't kill her—you *mustn't* kill her. Mother—no—*look in her eyes!*"

Fulvia snarled like a wild beast. But even so, with the Creature's face so near to her, almost inadvertently, she did what he said.

Then she saw the eyes' real greenness, and then she saw through, to *within* their green. She stared. She stared into a limitless hall built of glaucous nothingness, like the depths of a sea. Here and there currents moved in it, like liquid winds, and faint glimmerings, like drowned stars. And there, too, deep down and far away inside it, and in miniature, Livius was wandering—she made him out exactly, his every detail, even to his disheveled hair and filthy toga—her Livius, her husband. Beyond him, were some other smaller figures, farther off. She could not yet quite make them out, although they seemed, as he did, familiar to her.

FANTASY
DAW

Christopher Stasheff

Christopher Stasheff is best known for his *Warlock* series, which now spans more than ten volumes, and his *Wizard in Rhyme* novels, both successful fantasy series with devoted followings. He holds a Ph.D in theater from the University of Nebraska, and has written theater plays, and also edited several anthologies, including *The Enchanter Reborn,* edited with L. Sprague de Camp, and *The Crafters* and *The Crafters 2,* both edited with Bill Fawcett. Recently he has taken up teaching again, overseeing a writer's workshop program at the University of New Mexico. He lives with his wife and children in Champaign, Illinois.

CORONACH OF THE BELL
Christopher Stasheff

THERE is a spruce, a skeleton, that stands above a forest in a
mountain valley, and from its tip, a bell hangs high and lone,
moaning in the wind.

There is a pass into that valley, but the sides are sharp and
jagged—torn and twisted, blackened granite. One slip means
death.

Once a clan lived there, when the spruce was quick with resin
and fields of maize filled half the valley. There was no pass between the mountains then, for a granite bridge once joined them.
But that bridge was hollow, gutted out by adze and pick, honey-
combed into a home for Manninglore.

Manninglore, bald and bearded, hunchbacked, stunted, muscle-
bound, stooping from his years of toil.

Manninglore, born old.

The wrinkles of birth never left his face; hair never grew upon
his scalp. "Changeling!" the children called him. He did not dare
protest, for his bandy legs could scarcely run and his bulging
arms were much too slow for fighting.

So, of course, his bald pate became the target for their mocking
slaps—blows which, as Manninglore learned quickly, he could
but endure. The lesson of his childhood was patience; the companion of his youth was solitude.

So, when he was old enough for numbering among the grown
men of the clan, and his beard (already white) begun, he set the
village at his back and climbed up to the granite bridge between
the mountains. Behind a grove of trees he hewed him out a cave,
hiding his door from village eyes. There, in the leaf-broken sunlight of the cave mouth, Manninglore sat cross-legged and opened
his soul to the totem of his clan, the Wind.

They grew old, the men and women who had been young with Manninglore. Old and wrinkled, stooped and gnarled, they looked up to the mountainside with envy—envy, now, and longing; for those who rose before the dawn saw Manninglore up high upon the granite bridge, leaning on his staff in sunlight, though the village of the clan still lay in shadow. His beard was long, his shoulders stooped—but in all else, he had not changed.

"He is a sorcerer," said some. "He has dark knowledge."

"No," said most. "How could he age, who was ancient at his birth?"

Yet Manninglore had aged, though not in body. The whole of the bridge was hollow now, filled with crucibles and books, with heaps of ore and precious earths. At the back, away from the valley, stood the bellows, anvil, and hearth of a smithy. At the front, two windows, too small to be seen by the clan, looked out toward the village.

When Manninglore's generation were long in their graves, their children's children, old in their turn, looked to the mountain with a curse, for Manninglore stood hale as ever, on the bridge of sunrise.

"Our grandfathers are dust," they muttered, "yet Manninglore lives."

"All that mountain is his home. We will die in huts of mud."

"What have we done with our lives?" they wondered. "We, and our grandfathers before us? Yet how much more has Manninglore gleaned!"

"He has knowledge, dark knowledge to lengthen his life. But will he give of it?"

Then, in their envy and their shame, they would have gone to the mountain and put Manninglore to death, had they dared—but the span of his powers was hidden, their limits unknown. So they kept to their village in fear and cursed the mountain.

Then their anger fermented into bitterness and hatred. They cried to their totem for a sorcerer that they might safely burn. Thus, from their guilt and self-pity, Demouach was born.

The clan gathered round the central fire, muttering, quiet in the night.

Then Demouach was hopping round the flame-pit, grinning and chirping—Demouach, the height of a knee, brittle leather, hairless, with the form and the face of a man, but with parchment between his arms and sides and legs, and claws where a man should have feet. Wordless, with only chirpings or wailings— Demouach, imbecile.

One long moment the clan crouched staring, silent. Then howling broke out, with drumming of feet and brands from the fire whirling at the monster.

Demouach flew, screaming in terror and pain. Still coals struck him; the clan, gleeful, followed.

But they turned away, cursing in fear, when Demouach fell onto the mountainside.

Manninglore, bent over alembics and crucibles, heard the wail at his threshold, stumped bandy-legged to the entryway, hauled back the door.

Burning leather, cries of torture, smoldering parchment writhed in the light from the doorway.

The next generation knew Manninglore chiefly from Demouach, ever about his master's business, sailing over the valley with a leathern sack in his claws, fetching the raw stuffs of magic.

Legend had hidden Manninglore's birth from them. He was their sage, who always had dwelled on the mountain; only this could they know of him. "Our forefathers sinned against him," they said, "but in his mercy, Manninglore spared them." So they lived in awe of the hermit, awe and reverence. "Be diligent," they told their children. "Be steadfast," they told their youth. "Care well for your children," they told those new-come to parentage. "Be industrious, tenacious, generous, loving, and the child of your children's children may be like to Manninglore."

But the sage in his mountain knew nothing of their reverence. High in his granite hall, he thought of wood and stone and metal only, and hearkened to none but the totem of his clan, the Wind.

"Go," he said, putting a leathern pouch in Demouach's claws, "and fetch me clay from the bank of the river, and wax from old hives, for I would hear my totem speak in words."

He took the clay when Demouach returned and squared it into a block, a cubit on each side.

Looking up at Demouach, he frowned. "Be still!"

For Demouach danced, hopping from foot to foot on the window ledge, keening like the birds of dusk.

"Be still!" said Manninglore again, but Demouach sprang from the ledge, catching Manninglore's sleeve in his horny lips, pulling the sage to the window.

Manninglore looked down, down to the village of the clan of Mannin under the noonday sun.

The people wandered thin and haggard, stumbling as they went.

"They starve," said Manninglore. "What is that to me?"

Demouach wailed, dancing on the ledge.

"Their cornfields lie in darkness," said the wizard. "The stalks are pale and flaccid, for they lie in the shadow of the forest pines even at noon. But that is not my care."

Demouach cried in short, lamenting calls, hopping from one foot to the other as though the window ledge burned beneath his claws.

"They revere the forest excessively," said Manninglore. "They will not fell a tree, not even to let the sunlight in upon their crops. They are fools. But their folly is not mine."

Then Demouach chittered, scolding.

The wizard's visage hardened; the ends of his mustache drew down. "Only pain they gave me, Demouach. In the days of my youth they mocked me, striking me when my face was turned away, then running, for I could not follow. I have built my home and gathered knowledge, never asking aid of them. I owe them nothing."

Still Demouach lamented.

"You also, Demouach, have suffered at their hands. They have burned you, Demouach, and hunted you, and cursed you. And would you aid them, now?"

Then Demouach howled, flapping from the ledge to beat his wings about the wizard's head till he raised his arms as a shield and stumbled from the window. "Peace!" he bellowed over Demouach's cries. "Peace, Demouach! I shall heal them, I shall pull down the pines and give them light! Only give me peace, good Demouach, that I may work!"

Then he filled a pouch with seeds and gave it to Demouach. "Scatter these over the forest," he said, "and oak and ash shall spring up 'mongst the giant pines, to bring them down."

Caroling, Demouach gripped the pouch in his claws and tumbled through the window.

"Demouach, hold!" cried Manninglore, and the messenger hovered.

"Spare one spruce," the wizard called, "for I would not have the dark beauty of that tree lost, forever and irrevocably, to the clan of Mannin."

Demouach bobbed his head, then turned to soar away in swirling song. He sped out over the village, over the fields, to the forest.

There he tilted the pouch, spilling out the seeds, spiraling in to the center of the forest till the pouch was empty.

When the sun rose again, the pines had fallen. In their place, but half their height, stood oak and ash, full-grown.

The clan of Mannin stood and stared and marveled, and their corn was green by sunset.

"The wizard has saved us," they murmured, and blessed the name of Manninglore.

But deep in the forest stood one sapling spruce.

Manninglore in his granite hall carved a deep bowl in a cube of clay. He widened the lip, flaring, and carved the name of his clan and its totem, "Mannin—Wind," into the side. Then he made a mold of it in ways that only wizards know, a mold that could hold the heat that would char an enchanter in an instant. At last he kindled coke in his forge and fanned it hot; filled a crucible with copper and tin and swung it over the flames; he donned enchanted garb and helm to protect him from the heat and, when the metal flowed, with gauntlets took up tongs and chains to tilt the crucible and pour the fiery sludge into the mold, then left the chamber.

For days he let it stand until he was sure it held a killing heat no longer, then broke away the inner bowl, flinched from the heat it still gave off—no longer enough to slay, but enough to make a wizard gasp. At last, he filled its form with frozen air and crystal-lized water, and looking in, saw the stars roll past in majesty.

"Now the Wind will speak to me in words," said Manninglore. He broke away the outer clay, chilled and cleaned the metal there, then satisfied that it was no warmer than was he himself, he set it on a tripod, wet his finger on his tongue, and stroked its lip in circles.

A deep tone rose from the bell, then formed itself into words: *"What would you know?"*

"Wind!" cried Manninglore. "Only spirit that I venerate!"

He turned, arms swinging in a circle. "I have hollowed out a mountain for a home. I have filled one wall with books of lore. Tell me, spirit, for I must know—are these things worthy?"

"No," the spirit answered.

Manninglore turned in a temper and took up his pick. Children in the valley grew old and died while Manninglore tore into the bowels of the mountain. Then Manninglore called again to the spirit of the Wind and cried, "A mountain of gold have I amassed! Wealth beyond a world of kings! Tell me, spirit—is it worthy?"

"No," the spirit answered.

Manninglore swore and stamped away. Folk howled in birth, shouted loud in the joy of youth, groaned in the labor of matur-ity, then coughed in death while the wizard labored and his mes-senger passed in weary flight again and again about the world. Then, high in his hall, Manninglore called upon his totem: "Ten thousand books have flowed from my quill! There is no secret of wood or stone or metal that I do not know! Tell me, spirit—is this worthy?"

And, *"No,"* the spirit answered.

"Then is nothing worthy!" cried Manninglore. "Mountains, houses, wealth, and tomes—are none of these things worthy?"

"None," the spirit answered.

"Why?" the wizard stormed.

"Wizard," intoned the spirit, *"look to the valley."*

Slowly, Manninglore turned to the window. He saw the fields barren, his clan staggering, emaciated.

"They die," said Manninglore. "What is that to me?"

"*Sage,*" droned the spirit, "*who will read your books?*"

Manninglore stood frozen.

"*Miser,*" mourned the spirit, "*whom shall you pay?*"

Manninglore's eyes showed white around the rim.

"*Builder,*" the spirit tolled, "*who shall dwell in your halls?*"

In the hour before dawn, when all the world was still, the clan of Mannin shot trembling from their beds as the earth beneath them shook with thunder. Rushing from their doors, they saw a great notch torn between the mountains.

"The ridge is gone," they whispered; and, "The wizard of Mannin is no more! Who shall aid us now?"

Then Manninglore stepped into the village, a pack of magics on his back, a bronze beaker in the crook of his elbow, Demouach upon his twisted shoulder.

He paced through the village that day, gaze probing the folk of the clan, tagging each person and allotting each category, for Manninglore had studied Humanity once, long before, had wrought through the gear-meshing strivings, the escapements of mores, to the tightly-coiled spring of the cravings. Then, when he knew why Man and Woman did what they did and when they would do it, he had given over the study as ephemeral, and therefore unworthy.

Now, though, as he measured the paths with his stride, his eyes sought through flesh and marrow to the souls within, and found them all shrunken, dwindled to gibbering, skeletal monkeys, atrophied. And Manninglore marveled that this dwindling had come to pass within his gaze, but without his notice.

They were dying, all about him, the folk of his clan, those in their prime. The elders still mumbled and moved with some sign of life, with jerkings and tics, and youths still walked, limbs responding slowly, as though they forced their way through some dark and viscous fluid. But the men and women in the fullness of their days sprawled in the doorways, muscles sodden, bones sagging. Here an old one gave his woman-grown daughter water to drink; there a girl nearly grown crooned her parents to their final slumber. Of babes and little children there were none.

Yet kindness was here, and love, in the pitiful efforts of the old and young to ease the slow, sinking deaths of maturity.

Manninglore saw, and shame grew within him.

"O Spirit!" he cried to the Wind, "totem of Mannin! Hear the tale of a life come to naught. My cry has been only, 'For me!' for I labored only to say, 'I have built, I have crafted, I shall always endure in my works!' while here in the valley they have cried only, "For thee! All for thee!"

"It is true," chimed the spirit, "yet but half the truth. They have cried, 'All for thee, my child, that you may someday be like Manninglore!' Wizard, you have served them in your selfishness; you have given them a mark for their striving, and thus have brought them out of greed to giving."

"Yet how little to give!" cried the sage; but Demouach crooned upon his shoulder.

So they came to the fields, the beaker, the hermit, and the bat-wing. There they looked upon the maize standing tall, in buff serried ranks, tasseled heads nodding to make the wind whisper.

Manninglore scowled; words growled low in his throat. "There is corn in the field, there is grain in the bin, there is gruel in the pot. Yet the strength has gone from their bodies. How is this?"

"Go among the people," answered the spirit, "and ask."

There in the village, a man lay flaccid by the door of a cottage. A palsied hand, blue-veined and wrinkled, lifted his head; its mate held a cup to his lips. The man gulped at the porridge, then lolled his head back. The old hand lowered him gently to the earth. "I fed him once from my breast," its owner said, vein pulsing slowly in the stalk of her throat. "He throve, then . . . but my breasts are long dry now, and fallen."

And she turned away to her mortar.

"You have fed him," said Manninglore. "Why then does he fail?"

"Watch," she said then; and "See," and touched the kernels of maize with the pestle. They fell apart into powder.

"Dust," she said, lifting her hand. Flour strewed on the wind and was gone. "There is no substance to it. The kernels have form, but no weight. They are empty."

She turned; the eyes of the man had glazed over. Sighing, she closed the lids gently.

"He was your son," the wizard murmured.

"I had twelve sons," she replied. "Six remain. I had sixteen daughters. Only two still walk."

Her face was thin and shrunken to the skull. But the eyes still were large, the hair a cascade of foam down her back. Manninglore's throat tightened; he put his hand out to her. She did not feel his touch.

Manninglore ordered the corn mown, the stalks plowed under. Then he kindled fire and brewed magic powder. He broadcast it over the fields and planted the maize.

And the old woman moved through the village, tending her children, for the young now were dying.

The corn grew green and tall—but the kernels were small, and crumbled to powder as the husks were stripped off.

It was plowed under, and the wizard brewed waters of power from the saps of trees, then planted the maize.

And the old woman knelt by her last dying daughter. Breath stilled; the old woman stayed by her in silence awhile. Then, stretching out her quivering hand, she closed the eyes of her child. She sighed, and fell limp in the dust.

Manninglore cradled her head in the crook of his arm, holding a steaming cup to her lips. The old eyes opened slowly. "I loved you, wizard," she whispered. "I saw you at dawn on the mountaintop, and I loved you. I could not be content with any man, because my love was you. I bore a child to every man of my generation, twenty-eight children, one for each year I could bear, because of my love for you. No other man would I have; I lived therefore in shame and in scorn. Yet still I love you."

Then her head fell back as her eyes rolled up, and the slow rise and fall of the flattened breasts ceased.

He closed her eyes, pressed her hair to his cheek. "She loved me—I, hunchback and cripple, who swore no woman could look upon me without revulsion. I ruined her life, and she loved me. I gave her nothing, yet for all of her days, she loved me."

He looked up to the old folk crowding about him, bodies of wire and paper under the fiery sun. "Are all the youth dead?" he asked, and they nodded.

He tallied the walking mummies about him and muttered, "These at least shall not die."

Then Manninglore brewed fierce magic, a potion of earth and water long simmered with berries of virtue and bones of creatures dead a hundred thousand years and more. Into the fire beneath he cast powders that flamed in strange colors so that the broth would breathe the powers of their vapors as it drew into itself the flames below and the air above. Long he watched it churn and roil while stars drifted across the sky and the sun rose like a grim coal where once his ridge had stood. Then he set it aside an hour and, when it had cooled, held the beaker in his hands, frowning down upon it, considering at length what he had wrought and what he meant to do, for he knew the potion's power, knew how long it would keep him alive, knew why it would need to—and thereby knew its cost. At last he stood, squaring his shoulders, set the beaker to his lips, and drank the entire brew.

Then did Manninglore strip off all his garb and walk out over the fields, each step a mighty labor, for as the sun rose higher and heat beat down, red drops began to spring from every pore—and the wizard measured the fields with his tread all that day, stooping forward to water the earth with his blood.

But when he leaned, drained, on the trunk of an oak, the blood still stood, thick and heavy, over the furrows. It failed to sink into the earth through all that long night, and the sun, in the morning, baked it to glaze.

"Now, spirit, how is this?" sighed the wizard. "I have given the blood of my life, but the earth will not take it."

"*You have waited too long,*" mourned the spirit. "*Sage, your blood has grown thick with the ages. It will not yield to the earth.''*

Then Manninglore slumped to his knees and leaned to strike, rolling full length in the dust. The old folk of the clan saw the fall of their sage and, moaning, slipped one by one to measure their lengths on the clay under the glare of the sun.

The afternoon light burned red through his eyelids; the last labored breathing ceased near him. Only the rustle of Demouach's wings by his shoulder, and the calling Wind over the lip of the beaker, were left him.

Then, slowly, the red of the light slipped from his sight. A cool breeze touched his cheek. Forcing his eyelids open, Manninglore saw the tip of a spruce standing between his face and the sun.

And there in the shadow, by Manninglore's elbow, a shoot of green corn speared through the glaze.

"Too late," the sage muttered. "Too late."

Then he rose up on his elbow screaming, his free, shaking arm pointing up at the spruce. "Go, Demouach! And hang this sounding bell to the top of that tree, that men may know there was once a clan here!"

And Demouach leaped into air with the beaker, bound it to the top spike of the spruce with a ribbon of corn husk. Crying, then, he swooped to the side of his master and friend.

But the wizard's eyelids were closed, sunken in, the skin of his face become ashen, the last fate-spiting breath expired.

Then Demouach swirled into the air with one last screaming wail, and ceased.

The forest has reclaimed the valley, filling it from hill to hill. But high above the restless green of hickory and oak towers the skeleton of a spruce, bleak against the annealed sky. From its scaling, brittle tip there hangs a bell, a bell of bronze without a clapper, alien in the wind's demesne. And the cataracting gale exacts a tribute from it, a tribute paid in moans, a groaning lament caught from the mouth of the bell and flung out over the forest, to break against the mountains and be funneled down into the mountain pass.

There, in the notch between the peaks, the dirge collects again, feeding in upon itself, slapping into the baffled granite and rebounding, rolling in its torment till it echoes up into a banshee wail, an eternal keening coronach, despair.

And far below, a patch of forest floor is bare, fused into obsidian. At its center stands a mummified cornstalk, paper wrapped around a hollow core, sole testament to the clan of Mannin.

Jennifer Roberson

Jennifer Roberson will always have a special place in my heart. Her first DAW novel, *Shapechangers,* was the first book I bought without my father's approval. Previously, Don and I had discussed every purchase and frequently put our heads together editorially on his projects as well as mine. We enjoyed working together—sitting in his office analyzing the books we were publishing. But Don never read *Shapechangers.* I never asked for his opinion. I simply bought it.

Obviously, my instincts in signing Jennifer were on target. With fifteen DAW books to her credit, as well as several historical romance novels from another publisher, Jennifer has a strong and varied career working in two genres.

A native Arizonan, Jennifer has a way of imbuing the desert with a special kind of life, as one can see in her popular *Sword* books. And, like Marion Zimmer Bradley, she manages to integrate socio-political issues, especially sexual politics, into her books without ever losing entertainment value. Quite the contrary in fact, the arguments and differences her characters have with one another are often highly humorous. But one of my favorite aspects of her writing (although a somewhat quirky minor one) is the way she writes about horses. As a former Miss Rodeo Arizona, Jennifer obviously has extensive experience. Her most famous equine character, simply called "the Stud," is as full of piss and vinegar as any human character I've ever read. The Stud gives his rider, Tiger, almost as much of a run for his money as Jennifer gives her many fans.

The following story debuts the world of Jennifer's new fantasy series *Karavans*. As you read this, she is hard at work on the first volume. The tantalizing glimpse she's given us here has this editor hoping she finishes her first draft early!

—BW

ENDING AND BEGINNING
Jennifer Roberson

FOUR had died. Killed ruthlessly. Uselessly. Three, because they were intended as examples to the others. The fourth, merely because he was alone, and Sancorran. The people of Sancorra province had become fair game for the brutal patrols of Hecari soldiers, men dispatched to ensure the Sancorran insurrection was thoroughly put down.

Insurrection. Ilona wished to spit. She believed it a word of far less weight than *war*, an insufficiency in describing the bitter realities now reshaping the province. *War* was a hard, harsh word, carrying a multiplicity of meanings. Such as death.

Four people, dead. Any one of them might have been her, had fate proved frivolous. She was a hand-reader, a diviner, a woman others sought to give them their fortunes, to tell their futures; and yet even she, remarkably gifted, had learned that fate was inseparably intertwined with caprice. She could read a hand with that hand in front of her, seeing futures, interpreting the fragments for such folk as lacked the gift. But it was also possible fate might alter its path, the track she had parsed as leading to a specific future. Ilona had not seen any such thing as her death at the hands of a Hecari patrol, but it had been possible.

Instead, she had lived. Three strangers, leaving behind a bitter past to begin a sweeter future, had not. And a man with whom she had shared a bed in warmth and affection, if not wild passion, now rode blanket-wrapped in the back of the karavan-master's wagon, cold in place of warm.

The karavan, last of the season under Jorda, her employer, straggled to the edges of the nameless settlement just after sundown. Exhausted from the lengthy journey as well as its tragedies, Ilona climbed down from her wagon, staggered forward, and began to unhitch the team. The horses, too, were tired; the caravan had withstood harrying attacks by Sancorran refugees turned bandits, had given up coin and needed supplies as "road tax" to three different sets of Hecari patrols until the fourth, the final, took payment in blood when told there was no money left with which to pay. When the third patrol had exacted the "tax," Ilona wondered if the karavan-master would suggest to the Hecari soldiers that they might do better to go after the bandits rather than harassing innocent Sancorrans fleeing the aftermath of war. But Jorda had merely clamped his red-bearded jaw closed and paid up. It did not do to suggest anything to the victorious enemy; Ilona had heard tales that they killed anyone who complained, were they not paid the "tax."

Ilona saw it for herself when the fourth patrol arrived.

Her hands went through the motions of unhitching without direction from her mind, still picturing the journey. Poor Sancorra, overrun by the foreigners called Hecari, led by a fearsome warlord, was being steadily stripped of her wealth just as the citizens were being stripped of their holdings. Women were widowed, children left fatherless, farmsteads burned, livestock rounded up and driven to Hecari encampments to feed the enemy soldiers. Karavans that did not originate in Sancorra were allowed passage through the province so long as their masters could prove they came from other provinces—and paid tribute—but that passage was nonetheless a true challenge. Jorda's two scouts early on came across the remains of several karavans that the master knew to be led by foreigners like himself; the Hecari apparently were more than capable of killing anyone they deemed Sancorran refugees, even if they manifestly were not. It was a simple matter to declare anyone an enemy of their warlord.

Ilona was not Sancorran. Neither was Jorda, nor one of the scouts. But the other guide, Tansit, was. And now his body lay in the back of a wagon, waiting for the rites that would send his spirit to the Land of the Dead.

Wearily Ilona finished unhitching the team, pulling harness from the sweat-slicked horses. Pungent, foamy lather dripped from flanks and shoulders. She swapped out headstalls for halters, then led the team along the line of wagons to Janqueril, the horse-master. The aging, balding man and his apprentices would tend the teams while everyone else made their way into the tent-city settlement, looking for release from the tension of the trip.

And, she knew, to find other diviners who might tell a different tale of the future they faced tomorrow, on the edge of unknown lands.

Ilona delivered the horses, thanked Janqueril, then pushed a fractious mass of curling dark hair out of her face. Jorda kept three diviners in his employ, to make sure his karavans got safely to their destinations and to serve any of his clients, but Tansit had always come to her. He said he trusted her to be truthful with him. Hand-readers, though not uncommon, were not native to Sancorra, and Tansit, like others, viewed her readings as more positive than those given by Jorda's other two diviners. Ilona didn't know if that were true; only that she always told her clients the good and the bad, rather than shifting the emphasis wholly to good.

She had seen danger in Tansit's callused hand. That, she had told him. And he had laughed, said the only danger facing him were the vermin holes in the prairie, waiting to trap his horse and take him down as well.

And so a vermin hole *had* trapped his horse, snapping a leg, and Tansit, walking back to the karavan well behind him, was found by the Hecari patrol that paused long enough to kill him, then continue on to richer pickings. By the time the karavan reached the scout, his features were unrecognizable; Ilona knew him by his clothing and the color of his blood-matted hair.

So Tansit had told his own fortune without her assistance, and Ilona lost a man whom she had not truly loved, but liked. Well enough to share his bed when the loneliness of her life sent her to it. Men were attracted to her, but wary of her gift. Few were willing to sleep with a woman who could tell a lover the day of his death.

At the end of journeys, Ilona's habit was to build a fire, lay a rug, set up a table, cushions, and candles, then wait quietly for custom. At the end of a journey clients wished to consult diviners for advice concerning the future in a new place. But this night, at the end of this journey, Ilona forbore. She stood at the back of her wagon, clutching one of the blue-painted spoke wheels, and stared sightlessly into the sunset.

Some little while later, a hand came down upon her shoulder. Large, wide, callused, with spatulate fingers and oft-bruised or broken nails. She smelled the musky astringency of a hard-working man in need of a bath; heard the inhaled, heavy breath; sensed, even without reading that hand, his sorrow and compassion.

"He was a good man," Jorda said.

Ilona nodded jerkily.

"We will hold the rites at dawn."

She nodded again.

"Will you wish to speak?"

She turned. Looked into his face, the broad, bearded, seamed face of the man who employed her, who was himself employed several times a season to lead karavans across the wide plains of Sancorra to the edge of other provinces, where other karavans and their masters took up the task. Jorda could be a hard man, but he was also a good man. In his green eyes she saw grief that he had lost an employee, a valued guide, but also a friend. Tansit had scouted for Jorda more years than she could count. More, certainly, than she had known either of them.

"Yes, of course," she told him.

Jorda nodded, seeking something in her eyes. But Ilona was expert at hiding her feelings. Such things, if uncontrolled, could color the readings, and she had learned long before to mask emotions. "I thank you," the master said. "It would please Tansit."

She thought a brace of tall tankards of foamy ale would please Tansit more. But words would have to do. Words for the dead.

Abruptly she said, "I have to go."

Jorda's ruddy brows ran together. "Alone? Into this place? It's but a scattering of tents, Ilona, not a true settlement. You would do better to come with me, and a few of the others. After what happened on the road, it would be safer."

Safety was not what she craved. Neither was danger, and certainly not death, but she yearned to be elsewhere than with Jorda and the others this night. How better to pay tribute to Tansit than to drink a brace of tall tankards of foamy ale in his place?

Ilona forced a smile. "I'm going to Mikal's wine-tent. He knows me. I'll be safe enough there."

Jorda's face cleared. "So you will. But ask someone to walk you back to your wagon later."

Ilona arched her brows. "It's not so often I must *ask* such a thing, Jorda! Usually they beg to do that duty."

He understood the tone, and the intent. He relaxed fractionally, then presented her with a brief flash of teeth mostly obscured by his curling beard. "Forgive me! I do know better." The grin faded. "I think many of us will buy Tansit ale tonight."

She nodded as the big man turned and faded back into the twilight, returning to such duties as were his at the end of a journey. Which left her duty to Tansit.

Ilona leaned inside her wagon and caught up a deep-dyed, blue-black shawl, swung it around her shoulders, and walked through the ankle-keep dust into the tiny tent-city.

She had seen, in her life, many deaths. It rode the hands of all humans, though few could read it, and fewer still could interpret the conflicting information. Ilona had never *not* been able to see, to read, to interpret; when her family had come to comprehend that such a gift would rule her life and thus their own, they had turned her out. She had been all of twelve summers, shocked by their actions because she had not seen it in her own hand; had she read theirs, she might have understood earlier what lay in store. In the fifteen years since they had turned out their oldest daughter, Ilona had learned to trust no one but herself—though she was given to understand that some people, such as Jorda, were less likely to send a diviner on her way if she could serve their interests. All karavans required diviners if they were to be truly successful; clients undertaking journeys went nowhere without consulting any number of diviners of all persuasions, and a karavan offering readings along the way, rather than depending on itinerant diviners drifting from settlement to settlement, stood to attract more custom. Jorda was no fool; he hired Branca and Melior, and in time he hired her.

The night was cool. Ilona tightened her shawl and ducked her head against the errant breeze teasing at her face. Mikal's wine-tent stood nearly in the center of the cluster of tents that spread like vermin across the plain near the river. A year before there had been half as many; next year, she did not doubt, the population would increase yet again. Sancorra province was in utter disarray, thanks to the depredations of the Hecari; few would wish to stay, who had the means to depart. It would provide Jorda with work as well as his hired diviners. But she wished war were not the reason.

Mikal's wine-tent was one of many, but he had arrived early when the settlement had first sprung up, a place near sweet water and good grazing, and not far from the border of the neighboring province. It was a good place for karavans to halt overnight, and within weeks it had become more than merely that. Now merchants put up tents, set down roots, and served a populace that shifted shape nightly, trading familiar faces for those of strangers. Mikal's face was one of the most familiar, and his tent a welcome distraction from the duties of the road.

Ilona took the path she knew best through the winding skeins of tracks and paused only briefly in the spill of light from the tied-back door flap of Mikal's wine-tent. She smelled the familiar odors of ale and wine, the tang of urine from men who sought relief rather too close to the tent, the thick fug of male bodies far more interested in liquor than wash water. Only rarely did women frequent Mikal's wine-tent; the female couriers, who were toughened by experience on the province roads and thus able to deal with anything, and such women as herself: unavailable for hire, but seeking the solace found in liquor-laced camaraderie. Ilona had learned early on to appreciate ale and wine, and the value of the company of others no more rooted than she was. Tansit had always spent his coin at Mikal's. Tonight, she would spend hers in Tansit's name.

Ilona entered, pushing the shawl back from her head and shoulders. As always, conversation paused as her presence was noted; then Mikal called out a cheery welcome, as did two or three others who knew her. It was enough to warn off any man who might wish to proposition her, establishing her right to remain unmolested. This night, she appreciated it more than usual.

She sought and found a small table near a back corner, arranging skirts deftly as she settled upon a stool. Within a matter of moments Mikal arrived, bearing a guttering candle in a pierced-tin lantern. He set it down upon the table, then waited.

Ilona drew in a breath. "Ale," she said, relieved when her voice didn't waver. "Two tankards, if it please you. Your best."

"Tansit?" he asked in his deep, slow voice.

It was not a question regarding a man's death, but his anticipated arrival. Ilona discovered she could not, as yet, speak of the former, and thus relied upon the latter. She nodded confirmation, meeting his dark blue eyes without hesitation. Mikal nodded also, then took his bulk away to tend the order.

She found herself plaiting the fringes of her shawl, over and over again. Irritated, Ilona forcibly stopped herself from continuing the nervous habit. When Mikal brought the tankards, she lifted her own in both hands, downed several generous swallows, then carefully fingered away the foam left to linger upon her upper lip. Two tankards upon the table. One: her own. The other was Tansit's. When done with her ale, she would leave coin enough for two tankards, but one would remain untouched. And then the truth would be known. The tale spread. But she would be required to say nothing, to no one.

Ah, but he had been a good man. She had not wished to wed him, though he had asked; she had not expected to bury him either.

At dawn, she would attend the rites. Would speak of his life, and of his death.

Tansit had never been one known for his attention to time. But he was not a man given to passing up ale when it was waiting. Ilona drank down her tankard slowly and deliberately, avoiding the glances, the stares, and knew well enough when whispers began of Tansit's tardiness in joining her.

There were two explanations: they had quarreled, or one of them was dead. But their quarrels never accompanied them into a wine-tent.

She drank her ale, clearly not dead, while Tansit's tankard remained undrunk. Those who were not strangers understood. At tables other than hers, in the sudden, sharp silence of comprehension, fresh tankards were ordered. Were left untouched. Tribute to the man so many of them had known.

Tansit would have appreciated how many tankards were ordered. Though he also would have claimed it a waste of good ale that no one drank.

Ilona smiled, imagining his words. Seeing his expression.

She swallowed the last of her ale and rose, thinking ahead to the bed in her wagon. But then a body blocked her way, altering the fall of smoky light, and she looked into the face of a stranger.

In the ocherous illumination of Mikal's lantern, his face was ruddy-gold. "I'm told the guide is dead."

A stranger indeed, to speak so plainly to the woman who had shared the dead man's bed.

He seemed to realize it. To regret it. A grimace briefly twisted his mouth. "Forgive me. But I am badly in need of work."

Ilona gathered the folds of her shawl even as she gathered patience. "The season is ended. And I am not the one to whom you should apply. Jorda is the karavan-master."

"I'm told he is the best."

"Jorda is—Jorda." She settled the shawl over the crown of her head, shrouding untamed ringlets. "Excuse me."

He turned only slightly, giving way. "Will you speak to him for me?"

Ilona paused, then swung back. "Why? I know nothing of you."

His smile was charming, his gesture self-deprecating. "Of course. But I could acquaint you."

A foreigner, she saw. Not Sancorran, but neither was he Hercari. In candlelight his hair was a dark, oiled copper, bound back in a multiplicity of braids. She saw the glint of beads in those braids, gold and silver; heard the faint chime and clatter of ornamentation. He wore leather tunic and breeches, and from the outer seams of sleeves and leggings dangled shell- and bead-weighted fringe. Indeed, a stranger, to wear what others, in time of war, might construe as wealth.

"No need to waste your voice," she said. "Let me see your hand."

It startled him. Arched brows rose. "My hand?"

She matched his expression. "Did they not also tell you what I am?"

"The dead guide's woman."

The pain was abrupt and sharp, then faded as quickly as it had come. *The dead guide's woman.* True, that. But much more. And it might be enough to buy her release from a stranger. "Diviner," she said. "There is no need to tell me anything of yourself, when I can read it in your hand."

She sensed startlement and withdrawal, despite that the stranger remained before her, very still. His eyes were dark in the frenzied play of guttering shadows. The hand she could see, loose at his side, abruptly closed. Sealed itself against her. Refusal. Denial. Self-preservation.

"It is a requirement," she told him, "of anyone who wishes to hire on with Jorda."

His face tightened. Something flickered deep in his eyes. She thought she saw a hint of red.

"You'll understand," Ilona hid amusement behind a business-like tone, "that Jorda must be careful. He can't afford to hire just anyone. His clients trust him to guard their safety. How is he to know what a stranger intends?"

"Rhuan," he said abruptly.

She heard it otherwise: *Ruin.* "Oh?"

"A stranger who gives his name is no longer a stranger."

"A stranger who brings ruination is an enemy."

"Ah." His grin was swift. He repeated his name more slowly, making clear what it was, and she heard the faint undertone of an accent.

She echoed it. "Rhuan."

"I need the work."

Ilona eyed him. Tall, but not a giant. Much of his strength, she thought, resided beneath his clothing, coiled quietly away. Not old, not young, but somewhere in the middle, indistinguishable. Oddly alien in the light of a dozen lanterns, for all his smooth features were arranged in a manner women undoubtedly found pleasing. On another night, *she* might; but Tansit was newly dead, and this stranger—Rhuan—kept her from her wagon, where she might grieve in private.

"Have you guided before?"

"Not here. Elsewhere."

"It is a requirement than you know the land."

"I do know it."

"Here?"

"Sancorra. I know it." He lifted one shoulder in an eloquent shrug. "On a known road, guiding is less a requirement than protection. That, I can do very well."

Something about him suggested it was less a boast than the simple truth.

"And does anyone know *you*?"

He turned slightly, glancing toward the plank set upon barrels where Mikal held sovereignty, and she saw Mikal watching them.

She saw also the slight lifting of big shoulders, a smoothing of his features into a noncommittal expression. Mikal told her silently there was nothing of the stranger he knew that meant danger, but nothing much else either.

"The season is ended," Ilona repeated. "Speak to Jorda of the next one, if you wish, but there is no work for you now."

"In the midst of war," Rhuan said, "I believe there is. Others will wish to leave. Your master would do better to extend the season."

Jorda had considered it, she knew. Tansit had spoken of it. And if the master did extend the season, he would require a second guide. Less for guiding than for protection, with Hecari patrols harrying the roads.

Four people, dead.

Ilona glanced briefly at the undrunk tankard. "Apply to Jorda," she said. "It's not for me to say." Something perverse within her flared into life, wanting to wound the man before her who was so vital and alive, when another was not. "But he *will* require you to be read. It needn't be me."

His voice chilled. "Most diviners are charlatans."

Indeed, he was a stranger; no true-born Sancorran would speak so baldly. "Some," she agreed. "There are always those who prey upon the weak of mind. But there are also those who practice an honest art."

"You?"

Ilona affected a shrug every bit as casual as his had been. "Allow me your hand, and then you'll know, won't you?"

Once again he clenched it. "No."

"Then you had best look elsewhere for employment." She had learned to use her body and used it now, sliding past him before he might block her way again. She sensed the stirring in his limbs, the desire to reach out to her, to stop her; sensed also when he decided to let her go.

It began not far from Mikal's wine-tent. Ilona had heard its like before and recognized at once what was happening. The grunt of a man taken unawares, the bitten-off inhalation, the repressed blurt of pain and shock; and the hard, tense breathing of the as-sailants. Such attacks were not unknown in settlements such as this, composed of strangers desperate to escape the depredations of the Hecari. Desperate enough, some of them, to don the brutal-ity of the enemy and wield its weapon.

Ilona stepped more deeply into shadow. She was a woman, and alone. If she interfered, she invited retribution. Jorda had told her to ask for escort on the way to the wagons. In her haste to escape the stranger in Mikal's tent, she had dismissed it from her mind.

Safety lay in secrecy. But Tansit was dead, and at dawn she would attend his rites and say the words. If she did nothing, would another woman grieve? Would another woman speak the words of the rite meant to carry the spirit to the Land of the Dead?

Then she was running toward the noise. "Stop! *Stop!*"

Movement. Men. Bodies. Ilona saw shapes break apart; saw a body fall. Heard the curses meant for her. But she was there, telling them to stop, and for a wonder they did.

And then she realized, as they faded into darkness, that she had thought too long and arrived too late. His wealth was untouched, the beading in the braids and fringe, but his life was taken. She saw the blood staining his throat, the knife standing up from his ribs. Garotte to make him helpless, knife to kill him.

He lay sprawled beneath the stars, limbs awry, eyes open and empty, the comely features slack.

She had seen death before. She recognized his.

Too late. Too late.

She should go fetch Mikal. There had been some talk of establishing a Watch, a group of men to walk the paths and keep what peace there was. Ilona didn't know if a Watch yet existed; but Mikal would come, would help her tend the dead.

A stranger in Sancorra. What rites were his?

Shaking, Ilona knelt. She did not go to fetch Mikal. Instead she sat beside a man whose name she barely knew, whose hand she hadn't read, and grieved for them both. For them all. For the men, young and old, dead in the war.

In the *insurrection.*

But there was yet a way. She had the gift. Beside him, Ilona gathered up one slack hand. His future had ended, but there was yet a past. It faded already, she knew, as the warmth of the body cooled, but if she practiced the art before he was cold, she would learn what she needed to know. And then he also would have the proper rites. She would make certain of it.

Indeed, the hand cooled. Before morning the fingers would stiffen, even as Tansit's had. The spirit, denied a living body, would attenuate, then fade.

There was little light, save for the muddy glow of lanterns within a hundred tents. Ilona would be able to see nothing of the flesh, but she had no need. Instead, she lay her fingers gently upon his palm and closed her eyes, tracing the pathways there, the lines of his life.

Maelstrom.

Gasping, Ilona fell back. His hand slid from hers. Beneath it, beneath the touch of his flesh, the fabric of her skirt took flame.

She beat it with her own hands, then clutched at and heaped powdery earth upon it. The flame quenched itself, the thread of smoke dissipated. But even as it did so, as she realized the fabric was whole, movement startled her.

The stranger's hand, that she had grasped to read, closed around the knife standing up from his ribs. She heard a sharply indrawn breath, and something like a curse, and the faint clattered chime of the beads in his braids. He raised himself up on one elbow and stared at her.

This time, she heard the curse clearly. Recognized the grimace. Knew what he would say: *I wasn't truly dead.*

But he was. Had been.

He pulled the knife from his ribs, inspected the blade a moment, then tossed it aside with an expression of distaste. Ilona's hands, no longer occupied with putting out the flame that had come from his flesh, folded themselves against her skirts. She waited.

He saw her watching him. Assessed her expression. Tried the explanation she anticipated. "I wasn't—"

"You were."

He opened his mouth to try again. Thought better of it. Looked at her hands folded into fabric. "Are you hurt?"

"No. Are *you?*"

His smile was faint. "No."

She touched her own throat. "You're bleeding."

He sat up. Ignored both the slice encircling his neck and the wound in his ribs. His eyes on her were calm, too calm. She saw an odd serenity there, and rueful acceptance that she had seen what, obviously, he wished she hadn't seen.

"I'm Shoia," he said.

No more than that. No more was necessary.

"Those are stories," Ilona told him. "Legends."

He seemed equally amused as he was resigned. "Rooted in truth."

Skepticism showed. "A living Shoia?"

"Now," he agreed, irony in his tone. "A moment ago, dead. But you know that."

"I touched your hand, and it took fire."

His face closed up. Sealed itself against her. His mouth was a grim, unrelenting line.

"Is that a Shoia trait, to burn the flesh a diviner might otherwise read?"

The mouth parted. "It's not for you to do."

Ilona let her own measure of irony seep into her tone. "And well warded, apparently."

"They wanted my bones," he said. "It's happened before."

She understood at once. "Practitioners of the Kantica." Who burned bones for the auguries found in ash and grit. Legend held Shoia bones told truer, clearer futures than anything else. But no one she knew of used *actual* Shoia bones.

He knew what she was thinking. "There are a few of us left," he told her. "But we keep it to ourselves. We would prefer to keep our bones clothed in flesh."

"But I have heard no one murders a Shoia. That anyone foolish enough to do so inherits damnation."

"No one *knowingly* murders a Shoia," he clarified. "But as we apparently are creatures of legend, who would believe I am?"

Nor did it matter. Dead was dead, damnation or no. "These men intended to haul you out to the anthills," Ilona said. Where the flesh would be stripped away, and the bones collected for sale to Kantic diviners. "They couldn't know you are Shoia, could they?"

He gathered braids fallen forward and swept them back. "I doubt it. But it doesn't matter. A charlatan would buy the bones and *claim* them Shoia, thus charging even more for the divinations. Clearer visions, you see."

She did see. There were indeed charlatans, false diviners who victimized the vulnerable and gullible. How better to attract trade than to boast of Shoia bones?

"Are you?" she asked. "Truly?"

Something flickered in his eyes. Flickered red. His voice hardened. "You looked into my hand."

And had seen nothing of his past nor his future save *mael-strom.*

"Madness," she said, not knowing she spoke aloud.

His smile was bitter.

Ilona looked into his eyes as she had looked into his hand. "Are you truly a guide?"

The bitterness faded. "I can be many things. Guide is one of them."

Oddly, it amused her to say it. "Dead man?"

He matched her irony. "That, too. But I would prefer not." He stood up then; somehow, he brought her up with him. She faced him there in the shadows beneath the stars. "It isn't infinite, the resurrection."

"No?"

"Seven times," he said. "The seventh is the true death."

"And how many times was this?"

The stranger showed all his fine white teeth in a wide smile. "That, we never tell."

"Ah." She understood. "Mystery is your salvation."

"Well, yes. Until the seventh time. And then we are as dead as anyone else. Bury us, burn us . . ." He shrugged. "It doesn't matter. Dead is dead. It simply comes more slowly."

Ilona shook out her skirts, shedding dust. "I know what I saw when I looked into your hand. But that was a shield, was it not? A ward against me."

"Against a true diviner, yes."

It startled her; she was accustomed to others accepting her word. "You didn't believe me?"

He said merely, "Charlatans abound."

"But you are safe from charlatans."

He stood still in the darkness and let her arrive at the conclusion.

"But not from me," she said.

"Shoia bones are worth coin to charlatans," he said. "A Kantic diviner could make his fortune by burning my bones. But a *true* Kantic diviner—"

"—could truly read your bones."

He smiled, wryly amused. "And therefore I am priceless."

Ilona considered it. "One would think you'd be more careful. Less easy to kill."

"I was distracted."

"By—?"

"You," he finished. "I came out to persuade you to take me to your master. To make the introduction."

"Ah, then *I* am being blamed for your death."

He grinned. "For this one, yes."

"And I suppose the only reparation I may pay is to introduce you to Jorda."

The grin flashed again. Were it not for the slice upon his neck and the blood staining his leather tunic, no one would suspect this man had been dead only moments before.

Ilona sighed, recalling Tansit. And his absence. "I suppose Jorda might have some use for a guide who can survive death multiple times."

"At least until the seventh," he observed dryly.

"If I read your hand, would I know how many you have left?"

He abruptly thrust both hands behind his back, looking mutinous, reminding her for all the world of a child hiding booty. Ilona laughed.

But she *had* read his hand, if only briefly. And seen in it conflagration.

Rhuan, he had said.

Ruin, she had echoed.

She wondered if she were right.

Mercedes Lackey

Mercedes Lackey came to me from a seemingly unlikely source: the author C. J. Cherryh. I only say unlikely because C.J. is known primarily for her hard science fiction, while Mercedes (Misty) was an aspiring fantasy writer. C.J. and Misty are both native Oklahomans, and had met in fan circles. Misty, an active songwriter, had written an impressive song about one of C.J.'s characters. C.J. showed it to me, and I asked if Misty had ever written prose. Shortly thereafter, I had the first rough draft of *Arrows of the Queen* in my hands. The rest is history.

Mercedes Lackey has grown to be not only one of the most prolific writers in the fantasy field, but also one of the best loved. That DAW was the first company to publish her is a source of great pride to us. Sixteen years and nearly thirty books later, Misty and I are even closer editorially and personally than we were back then. Although she publishes with other houses (no one publisher could handle all of her output), DAW publishes more of Mercedes Lackey's work than any other house, and most, if not all, of her solo-byline novels, including all of her Valdemar books. We have a serious, lifelong commitment to her career.

It is one of the greatest rewards of an editor's life to see an author she discovered become a major best-seller. But my pride in Misty's achievements goes way beyond sheer numbers. Her work speaks to the widest and most varied readership I have ever seen: from preteens to straight and gay adults, including the entire staff of a nuclear sub. And Misty takes her responsibility as a best-selling author very seriously. Her books contain subtle moral messages about all sorts of ethical, social, and political issues without ever soap-boxing or lecturing. And since so many of her readers are young, this makes her an especially important writer.

—BW

AFTER MIDNIGHT
Mercedes Lackey

THE Author woke up, knowing that she was not alone.
Simply opening her eyes proved that her instinctive feeling was correct. The bed was enveloped in a seafoam-colored,
glowing mist. Surrounding the bed were dozens of people.

All were costumed more-or-less outlandishly. Some looked irritated, some angry, but none were happy. All were familiar.

"Oh, awake at last, are you?" asked a handsome man with
silver-streaked hair and silver eyes, who just happened to be the
spitting image of actor Michael Praed. "It's about time. We have
a few bones to pick with you."

The Author scooted herself up into the headboard, trying to
get as far away from the mob as possible, and addressed the
speaker. "Um—Vanyel—before you say or do anything rash, I
think you should know that you're probably one of the most popular characters in my books—"

Vanyel snorted. "Popular. Popular! And that's supposed to
make up for what you did to me? It's not enough to give me the
family from Hell, it's not enough to make me gay in a hostile
redneck society—oh, no—you've got to kill off my first love and
make me go an entire trilogy pining after him, like some kind of
medieval soap opera! And then you write me dialogue that
sounds like a Morrissey record!"

Someone in the background snickered, and chanted to the tune
of "London Bridges"—"I'm depressed and so I whine, so I whine,
all the time, I'm depressed and so I whine, my name's Vanyel."

Vanyel spun around and glowered at the offending party, and
another speaker took advantage of the momentary distraction to
step forward.

"Like he's got problems?" said Diana Tregarde, a young woman dressed in jeans and a leotard, whose long, dark hair managed to look as if it had come straight from the hands of an Uberstylist. "You give me a vampire for a boyfriend, you end the third book on a cliffhanger, and then what? You drop me like a hot potato!"

"At least you got a third book," mumbled Jennifer Talldeer, who could easily have been Diana's Native American twin sister.

"Yeah? Well, none of you had to spend a few centuries as a forest," Vanyel countered. "A forest! I ask you! You think athlete's foot is bad, ever tried root rot? Hah!"

"You had Stefen and Yfandes with you," the Author ventured timidly.

"Oh, great, so how, exactly, am I supposed to get it on with my true love when we're both a bunch of trees?" Vanyel snarled.

"Cross-pollinating?" someone offered from the back.

"At least you got a true love—and a whole life," complained Lavan Firestorm. "I get what—a talking horse and a nice tombstone? Thank you so very friggin' much!" His tone turned mocking. "And then you brag about it! 'The Lackey-patented formula for success—make your audience identify with and care deeply for a character and then drop a mountain on him!'"

A tall, blonde woman snorted. "Teenagers! What would you know? I have a perfectly reasonable life as a mercenary—hellfires, I have my own company! It's looking like comfortable retirement city! Then Ms. White-Horsies-On-The-Cover rips it all up and turns me into some kind of do-gooder in a uniform like a walking target and inflicts me with crap that talks in my head! I'm ready for menopause, and she starts with this nonsense!"

"Well, if you're going to start in on that line of thought," interrupted another woman, this one in black armor and silver hair, with a face like an ax-blade. "Let me tell you, it was no picnic being saddled with arthritis and teaching you and your little buddy!"

"And thanks so much for turning me from a heroine into the prime bitch-slut of the millennium!" called a young woman in the rather idealized costume of a Russian czarina, who stood on tiptoe at the back of the room.

"You didn't deserve Ivan anyway," snapped another in a gown

of glowing feathers. "All you ever do in the ballet is stand around and wait for rescue!"

"Speaking of ballet," Prince Siegfried interrupted. "I know you had to do something with the character, but did you have to make me into such a selfish bastard? Selfish, fine, bastard, all right, but both at once? And if you ask me, you really didn't pull off my so-called redemption very convincingly. . . ."

"Nobody asked you," murmured Odile, who earned a glare from Odette.

"Don't tell me you've got a complaint!" the Author exclaimed indignantly. "You got the title and a happy ending! Not bad for someone who's best known for thirty-two fouettes in the last act!"

"But did it have to be Benno?" Odile countered. "The guy who never does anything but lift Odette so the Prince won't put his back out?"

"Hey!" said Siegfried indignantly.

The Author glanced quickly around. "I don't see Maya or Peter Scott," she murmured with relief.

"Oh, I say!" Lord Peter Almsley waved from the back of the crowd. "You still haven't planned a book for me! You just can't leave me dangling as a hanger-on—"

"She left me dangling after three books!" countered Diana Tregarde.

"Look, it's not her fault that some nutcases decided you were real!"

"My knee hurts. Whose dream sequence is this, anyway? My knee shouldn't hurt in my own dream sequence. Shar?" said Tannim plaintively.

A graying, indomitable figure in Herald's Whites stepped forward, and the rest of the group stepped back a pace as she placed herself between the author and the mob. She put her hands on her hips and took a deep breath to begin an oration.

"Uh-oh," Kerowyn groaned. "I know that look."

"Have any of you ever bothered to think about an author's responsibilities?" asked Herald-Chronicler Myste. "They aren't just to you, the characters—face it, if that were the case, every one of you would have wonderful lives full of adventures that never got you into trouble . . ."

A black gryphon in the back put up a talon and rumbled, "Yes, please. I'd like that."

Myste glared at the offending party. ". . . and ended so happily that people would gag! Right?"

There arose a murmur from the crowd, tones that sounded to the Author's ears like grudging agreement.

"Furthermore," Myste continued, "if that was what she wrote, nobody would ever bother to read it!"

A tiny woman with curly chestnut hair, also in Herald's Whites, nodded agreement. "I hate to say this, folks, but Myste is right. I started out that way—and if that was the way I'd stayed, none of us would ever have been published." She spared a slightly sour glance for the Author. "I could have done without the crushed feet, though."

"Oh, sure, crushed feet. That's a limp through the park compared to root rot," Vanyel murmured indignantly. "I'm not even going to start on how Japanese beetles and Dutch Elm Disease feel."

The Author winced. "Sorry, Talia. I'd just read this book on medieval tortures . . . and you were in my first book. I hadn't figured out where to stop with the research yet."

"All right, all right—" Myste interrupted, before anyone else could start lodging complaints again. "That'll do. The point is, the author hasn't got much in the way of responsibility toward you, the characters, except to make you interesting enough that people will want to read about you. Her responsibility is always toward the audience, the readers."

"I would have preferred—"the black gryphon began to rumble.

"All of you would have preferred something else," Myste said, cutting him off. "Think about this, while you're preferring. Look at the kind of job she's got in front of her. She's got to juggle real-life problems, some of them just as grim as the ones she put you through, somehow manage to get books written and turned in on time—"

"Mostly on time," interrupted a blue dragon from beside the black gryphon.

"All right, mostly. And she's got to figure out how to do things with you that she hasn't done before, so the readers don't get bored! Now do you think any of you could do that?" Myste crossed her arms over her chest and glared at them. "And give you happy endings as well?"

"Mostly," said Lavan Firestorm, but without much anger.

"Tragedy," Myste countered, with great dignity, "is generally considered to be more compelling than any other dramatic force."

"I could have done with being a little less compelling," several male leads said in unison, then looked at each other.

"Oh?" Lavan replied. "Is 'compelling' supposed to make up for getting dead before I ever got laid?"

"Teenagers," Myste and the Author mumbled together, and exchanged a knowing glance.

"And do you think she doesn't suffer as much as you do in all of this?" Myste continued. "The amount of facial tissue this woman goes through—not to mention cola—! The long nights, the frenzied sessions at the keyboard? Van, she didn't have a life when she was writing you—you were her life! Everything you people feel, she feels! Oh, maybe not the physical torture—"

"I did work for American Airlines," the Author murmured.

"—but she goes through the same emotions, or she couldn't write all of yours so well! Did you ever think of that?"

"Yeah, but—" Lavan started another objection, then looked around. But the rest of the crowd seemed to be talking it over among themselves, and even Vanyel tapped Lavan on the shoulder and drew him into a four-way colloquy with Stefen and Talia. A line of limping, scorched, arrow-pincushioned, or just plain exhausted blue-eyed white horses merely sighed from the sidelines. The Author began to relax, as one by one, the characters turned away from the bed and its contents, and wandered off into the green haze. Eventually, there was no one left but Myste and the Author.

The Author heaved an enormous sigh of relief. "My God, you

saved my ass," she said, sincerely, but rather without the grace she usually showed in her prose.

"Well, I am you," Myste shrugged. "Lucky for me, they haven't caught on yet. On the whole, you've done rather well at not putting yourself in your books, though. That's pretty admirable."

The Author shrugged and blushed a little. "Is there anything I can do to thank you?" she asked.

Myste raised one eyebrow, an expression cloned straight from the author's own face. "Well . . . I don't suppose I could get a walk-on in the next book, could I?" she asked.

The Author considered it. "I don't see why not," she said cautiously. "There's room. But I'd have to figure out why you're permanently at the Collegium."

"Not another missing leg in the Tedrel Wars," Myste snapped. "You've done that. Twice."

"Er," replied the Author guiltily, because she'd been considering it. Then she brightened. "I know! And every fan-kid in glasses would love it! You're myopic!"

"Nearsighted? Can't that be Healed?" Myste asked dubiously.

The Author shook her head in triumph. "Nope. Established canon. Healers can't Heal genetic defects; they work on the existing pattern of the DNA and—"

"Enough!" Myste interrupted, holding up her head. "That's the stuff the readers don't need to know. But you've got the Artificers; surely they'd have come up with glasses by now. You've got good optics established canonically."

"In the Field?" the Author countered.

"Well . . . they'd probably have to have big wooden frames and straps that went around the back of the head . . . they'd look like dorky sports-goggles, but they'd work."

The Author frowned. "True enough." Then her expression changed to one of glee. "But not after you went into bifocals, my dear!"

"Eh?" Myste said, puzzled. "Benjamin Franklin had them, and you're into steam-tech by now—"

"Oh, no—you're me, remember? That's why I had laser-correction, bifocals made me dizzy." The Author sat back with an air of triumph.

"Point taken. Can't have dizzy Heralds, at least not in the Field." Myste nodded her satisfaction with the solution. "One other thing, though—think you could get me a boyfriend, too?"

"A love interest?" the Author asked.

"Whatever."

She frowned. "I'm not sure I want to bring in too many incidental characters. You know how they try and take over a book. Look at Almsley!"

"Oi!" objected a voice from deep in the haze.

"Use an existing one," Myste suggested.

The Author looked thoughtful. "How about Alberich?"

"Alberich?" Myste considered that. "Good body. Facial scars aren't that bad a handicap. Sexy, in a Bruce Campbell's Evil Twin sort of way. Yeah. Kind of monofocused, though, isn't he?"

"Aren't you all?" the Author countered. "That kind of goes with the white suit."

"Along with the periodic severe bodily injuries. Point taken." Myste nodded. "Cool. Alberich it is." She frowned as a thought occurred to her. "Don't go giving me the hobby of raising fancy chickens, though."

"But I like fancy chickens," the Author said weakly.

"I know, and so will everyone else if you put it in," Myste replied. She walked off into the green haze herself, which began to close in around her. "Most excellent! I get a walk-on, a fleshing-out, and a boyfriend!"

"Love interest!"

"Whatever."

The green haze closed down to a pinpoint, and vanished. *And once I make her really likable, I can drop a mountain on her. . . .*

Mickey Zucker Reichert

I first met Mickey Zucker Reichert, child prodigy, when I was still at NAL, running the Signet science fiction line. She was introduced to me by one of my authors there, Joel Rosenberg. Joel also made it a point to give Mickey all sorts of advice about what to do when she came to see me at the office and we went out to lunch. I'm not going to say he set her up, but Joel does have a unique sense of humor. Despite his advice, Mickey and I had a great afternoon, and not only have both our friendship and our working relationship continued to this day, but all three of my cats were born at Mickey's Iowa homestead.

When I referred to Mickey as a prodigy I was not exaggerating. Even while she was doing her residency before becoming a pediatrician, Mickey was busy writing novels. I have no idea where she found the time. But I do know that she had more than one novel in progress back then because after looking at the first novel she submitted to me, a story that would eventually grow into the *Renshai* series, I told her that I felt it still needed work and asked if she had anything else she could show me. She did indeed! The story was *Godslayer*, and it was a perfect book with which to launch her writing career. *Godslayer* became the first novel in what would grow into a five-book series, *The Bifrost Guardians*. Since that first book was published by DAW in August 1987, Mickey has continued to create wonderful tales for her many fans. And I know that readers of her work will be delighted to once again encounter one of her most popular protagonists in "Nightfall's Promise."

—SG

NIGHTFALL'S PROMISE
Mickey Zucker Reichert

I N the western quarter of the country of Schiz, a fire danced in
the hearth of the He-Ain't-Here tavern, casting scarlet and
amber patterns over the diners. Nightfall sat in the corner chair
of a corner table, beside King Edward Nargol of Alyndar. Guards
ate and drank around the periphery, their presences ironically un-
necessary. On his last visit, the eighteen-year-old monarch, then
an impetuous idealistic prince, had survived with only Nightfall
for protection and company despite dangerous naïveté and a pur-
suing sorcerer hell-bent on slaughter.

Arrayed in Alyndar's purple and silver and its crest, a powerful
fist clutching a hammer, they all cut dashing figures; but the
young monarch put the rest of them to shame. Brilliant golden
hair offset a round, handsome face. His tall, muscle-packed frame
exceeded even his guards', but his friendly blue eyes gave him an
air of approachability despite his imposing size. Of all the men at
the table, he overshadowed Nightfall most of all. Of average
height at best, slender and sinewy, the assassin-turned-king's-
adviser sported short mahogany-brown hair and blue-black eyes
that still held a glint of evil. Once a master of disguise living as
seven different men, Nightfall had spent months adjusting to his
given name, Sudian, and the one appearance he had never used:
his own.

Commoners and travelers swarmed the nearby tables, keeping
the help in constant motion. Nonetheless, a barmaid or busboy
remained always by the royal table, prepared to wipe up any spill,
to relay their least request.

When not cooking or cleaning, the pudgy proprietor stood in
the doorway between kitchen and common room, wringing his
hands. He was not accustomed to royalty in his simply furnished

red-stone building. The upper class normally took lodging in the south-end inn that Nightfall had gotten to know well in his persona of Balshaz the merchant. As the polio-stricken odd-jobber, Frihiat, however, he had grown familiar with the He-Ain't-Here's few rooms, now booked solid. He took some guilty pleasure in the usually unflappable proprietor's discomfort.

In the best position for surveying the entire room, Nightfall noticed two men approaching, before any of the guards so much as rolled a gaze in their direction. In his mid-twenties, the younger one sported an overlarge head topped with muddy curls, a crooked nose, and broad lips. The other appeared middle-aged, tall and thin with a mop of sandy hair and a scar that ran from the outer corner of his right eye to his chin. Nightfall recognized both. The first was Brandon Magebane, a gifted man with the most dangerous career Nightfall could imagine: hunting sorcerers. The second, Gatiwan, had accompanied Brandon on some of his forays, risking his life to rid the world of its greatest evil. Sorcerers gained their magical abilities only by slaying those rare people born with a "talent," and their method required tortuous ritual slaughter and taking possession of the victim's soul.

Quick as a cat, Nightfall rose and held out his hands in greeting. "Brandon. Gatiwan. Good to see you both again."

Guards' hands went to hilts, but the exuberant greeting of the king's adviser kept them from standing or making any overt sign of threat.

Brandon bowed appreciatively to the king, then addressed Nightfall. "Sudian. How wonderful to see you again. I presume you've come to fulfill your promise?" It was a ludicrous assumption. No king would travel halfway around the continent merely to escort a servant. As fast as the thought arose, Nightfall quashed it. *King Edward would.*

Edward turned a beetle-browed look on his adviser. To most of the world, Sudian had sprung from nowhere, the next in line to replace the thirty-six previous stewards who had abandoned the job of protecting and educating the brash young prince. Then, bound to him by magic, Nightfall had had little choice but to keep Edward safe and his best interests always in mind; and he did that by pretending to admire the boy to the point of slavish toadyism. For these men of Schiz to know Nightfall as Sudian, they had to have become acquainted with him while he traveled with Edward; yet the king had never seen them.

In fact, Nightfall had met Gatiwan in a tavern while Edward slept, and the older man had referred him to the younger. Nightfall had met with Brandon in secret, seeking one of the magical stones the Magebane created with his natal talent, which could thwart a sorcerer's magic for a single spell. Brandon had given Nightfall the stone with the promise that, one day, Nightfall would assist the magehunters on one of their projects.

Nightfall smiled. Born with the ability to adjust his own weight across a vast spectrum, he appreciated what the Magebane and his rotation of volunteer followers did. Nightfall had also finally found a happy life, friends, and a woman he loved, and had no interest in becoming part of a suicide mission. "Not today, Brandon. But thanks for the offer."

Looking around, Nightfall found King Edward staring at him and knew what had to follow.

"Did you make this man a promise, Sudian?" In Edward's tone, Nightfall heard the same damnable nobility that had caused the king's late father to bind the boy to an assassin despised as an otherworld demon.

"Well, yes, Sire," Nightfall admitted. "But just as a general 'maybe someday' type of—"

Edward would hear none of it. "If you promised . . ."

"Ned . . ." Nightfall warned, knowing the king had no way of knowing to what dangers he was about to commit his adviser. He used the name Edward preferred from people he considered friends, also trying to remind the boy-king that his companion, at thirty-four, was nearly old enough to be his father: older, wiser, and far more experienced.

Edward ignored the unspoken advice. "A man of honor holds dear even the least of his vows."

Nightfall crooked a brow. No words were necessary. Of all the men present, Edward alone knew his previous guise as the night-stalking demon of legend, anything but a man of honor.

King Edward's blue eyes held that fiery gleam of a personal crusade, a look that brooked no compromise. For whatever reason, he believed his adviser's actions reflected on him and on the esteem of Alyndar itself.

Nightfall sighed, then turned his gaze back to a smiling Brandon Magebane. "I'd love to help you," he said, with clearly feigned enthusiasm. "What would you like me to do?"

The healer's one-room cabin smelled of myriad herbs, some as sweet and pungent as nutmeg, others as overwhelmingly bitter as onion. Nightfall glanced around the windowless space at the four dingy chinked-log walls and the thatch ceiling. An eight-year-old boy lay on piled straw, his small pale body enveloped in a patchwork of bandages. One circled his forehead, encasing his ears in salve-smeared, bloodstained cloth. A fringe of fine, page-cut sandy hair surrounded a heart-shaped face, and large brown eyes peered back at Nightfall. The room's only piece of furniture, a small table, held a basin filled with medical supplies.

"Sudian," Brandon said, "I'd like you to meet Byroth."

The child continued to stare at Nightfall, managing a weak smile.

Nightfall nodded cordially, heart rate quickening. "What happened?" Though he intended the question for anyone, he continued to look at Byroth.

Apparently believing himself the target of Nightfall's inquiry, Byroth responded, "I don't remember." Looking at Nightfall's livery, he added, "Sire."

Having played many parts, Nightfall remained unrattled by the label of respect, though he did correct it. "I'm just a servant, son. No need for titles."

Byroth nodded. "I keep trying to think what happened, but I can't remember much. Someone grabbed me; I know that. Then, a lot of pain." He stiffened, then grimaced at the discomfort that small movement caused him. "Then my father hugging me, my mother screaming. Lots of blood." He shrugged. "That's it."

"Thank you." Nightfall looked askance at the Magebane and

his assistant. He despised sorcerers at least as much as anyone, had spent much of his life dodging them and had nearly fallen victim to two. He particularly hated those who targeted children, though nearly all of them did. Simpler prey, they were also more likely to accidentally or innocently reveal themselves as one of the natally gifted.

Brandon avoided Nightfall's questioning gaze to address Byroth. "Would you mind if Sudian examined your wounds?"

Byroth gestured assent. "So long as you don't hurt me."

Not wishing to cause the boy further anxiety or pain, Nightfall declined the invitation. "I don't need to see them. Thank you."

Brandon Magebane glanced from man to child and back, then waved toward the door. "Why don't you try to sleep, Byroth. We'll come back in a little while."

Byroth's young face turned stricken. "You won't leave me alone, will you?"

"We'll be right outside," Gatiwan promised.

Nodding, Byroth closed his eyes as the men filed from the room.

As soon as the door clicked closed, Brandon rounded on Nightfall. "What do you think?"

Nightfall glanced around at the familiar city bathed in twilight. His alter ego, Frihiat, had often come out to earn drinks in the tavern with stories. Crickets screed their high-pitched song while the people scurried about finishing their work before sunset. Seeing and feeling no one near enough to overhear them, Nightfall turned his attention to Brandon's question, which held many possibilities. "What do I think about what?"

"The wounds." Gatiwan took over impatiently. "Do you think a sorcerer could have inflicted them?"

Nightfall blinked, missing some of the information and the intention of his companions dragging him to visit a wounded child. "Does Byroth have a birth gift?"

"Not that he's admitted," Gatiwan said. "But we haven't pushed that hard."

"What do the wounds look like?"

Brandon's scrutiny grew more intense. "You just gave up the chance to see them."

Nightfall shrugged. "You didn't give me a reason to." Not wishing to disturb the boy any more now than then, he added, "What does the healer think they are?"

"Stab wounds." Brandon also searched the gray-lit streets. "Simple stab wounds, she thinks, from a regular old knife."

"Nothing weird and magical-looking? No burns or oddly shaped bruises?"

Brandon shook his head. "They look like stab wounds to me, too. But you never know."

"No." Nightfall admitted. "You never do know with magic." He had once faced a sorcerer who could freeze a man's head, then shatter it like the ice it had become. Another had opened an agonizing gash from his hipbone to his buttocks with only a distant motion. At a man's throat, that same spell might prove immediately fatal. The natal talents spanned skills beyond his imagination. The so-called "gifted" each harbored only one special ability, but the sorcerers could juggle an assortment, limited only by the number and type of talent-cursed souls they could obtain. They especially enjoyed hunting down one another, as the ritual slaughter of one of their own meant gaining all the harnessed souls of the loser. That last was the Magebane's salvation. It meant the sorcerers dared not reveal themselves or band together, even to destroy such an obvious and self-proclaimed threat.

Nightfall continued, "Besides, it doesn't matter what means the sorcerer uses to create panic and suffering in their victims. Any type of severe emotional distress together with excruciating pain brings the soul and its talent to the surface."

Brandon and Gatiwan stared at Nightfall, who suddenly wished he had not said anything. "What?" he demanded.

"You speak," Brandon said, barely above a whisper, "like a man with firsthand experience."

Nightfall did not like the Magebane's implications. He had spent all of his life hiding his talent, telling his secret to only one person. When Alyndar had captured him in other guise, he had believed her his betrayer, an assumption he had later discovered was wrong. Even King Edward knew only that Nightfall had some sort of birth gift sorcerers wanted. Nightfall would not reveal himself to two men he hardly knew. "Are you accusing me of having a natal gift? Or of being a sorcerer?"

Brandon's homely features opened questioningly. "You tell us which."

"Neither," Nightfall lied, then added, "but if either were the case, you know I'd have to give you the same answer."

"So just tell the truth," Gatiwan suggested.

Nightfall noted the serious expressions on the men's faces and mentally tracked the locations of his throwing knives. "How do you know I'm not?"

Brandon kept his voice steady and intense, though low. "Because when you came to me, you needed something to help you fight a sorcerer who had attacked you and your master."

Gatiwan took over, the somberness of his expression highlighting the scar across his face. "If King Edward the Enthusiastic had a natal talent, he'd have displayed it for the world in the excitement of righting some injustice."

Nightfall tried to divert the conversation. "He prefers King Edward the *Just*."

Brandon managed a smile. "When he's old enough to temper some of that zeal with wisdom, he'll probably earn the nickname he wants. Until then—" Apparently recognizing Nightfall's successful tactic, Brandon returned to the matter at hand. ". . . are you a sorcerer or gifted?"

Nightfall did not bother to deny both again. "I'm not a sorcerer."

"If you were a sorcerer, you'd say the same." Gatiwan reminded Nightfall in his own words.

"If I were a sorcerer," Nightfall corrected, "I'd kill my damned, disgusting, slimy, hideous self."

Brandon laughed. "Believe it or not, I actually met a sorcerer with the self-control to never act on his birthright. And I didn't kill him." As if to catch Nightfall unaware, he asked quickly, "So what's your talent?"

"Even if I had one, I . . ." Nightfall started.

They finished in unison, ". . . would have to deny it."

With clear reluctance, Gatiwan returned to the case. "Byroth's the fourth child in a year."

That caught Nightfall's attention. As rare as the natal gifts were, it seemed highly unlikely that Schiz could harbor four children with them. Of course, since those with the talents hid them for their own safety, no one really knew exactly how frequently they occurred. "Tell me about the others."

Brandon ran a hand through his dark curls. "First one happened a year or so ago. Playmate of Byroth's, seven years old, drowned in the creek."

Though tragic, it seemed fairly commonplace. "What makes you think a sorcerer was involved?"

"I didn't at the time." The Magebane continued to finger comb his hair, dislodging bits of bark and sand. "In hindsight, I noted a couple of suspicious things. He had a nasty head wound. The healer thought it might have happened after, when the current drove him into a rock, but they found an awful lot of blood on the bank for it to have come from a corpse already dead. He had many bruises, but the ones around his neck seemed impossible for jutting rocks to have caused."

Nightfall was impressed. "You really delve into the details, don't you?"

Brandon's fingers stilled. "I do this for a living, remember? And these happened on my own home territory."

"And the second one?" Nightfall ran a hand through his own hair, cut short and plastered in Alyndar's style. He did not miss the wild, filthy tangles he had worn in his original Nightfall guise.

"An infant." Gatiwan cringed, and his face screwed up as if he might cry. "Stolen from its crib in the night and found mangled nearby the next day."

Brandon lowered his head.

Nightfall examined the facts critically. He had suffered and inflicted too much evil to feel anything for a baby he knew only in the abstract. "Did it have a talent?"

Brandon raised his shoulders. "We don't know for sure. Proud parents. First baby after years of trying. They took him to a lot of gatherings. They think he must have done something in front of someone—could have been anyone. An uncle believes the baby might have made him trip over nothing, and an aunt says he could have caused a flash of light." Brandon let his shoulders drop. "All after the fact, of course, so it's hard to know if they really remember these things or are just searching for some logic to a hateful act."

"Or telling us what they think we want to hear," Gatiwan added. "Wouldn't be the first time."

Brandon nodded. "They just want to help."

"Some help." Nightfall wondered how many ignorant people would prefer to believe a loved one died for the wicked desires of a sorcerer rather than without any cause at all. They had no way of knowing how the sorcerers bound the souls to their bidding, how the natally gifted suffered even after death until the sorcerer either died or the soul "burned out" and the sorcerer lost that particular talent. "And the third one?"

"Eleven-year-old girl." Gatiwan fully regained his composure. "Had a knack for getting her little brothers and sisters to sleep." He added suggestively, "An inhuman knack."

"A clear talent," Nightfall guessed.

"It's a wonder she made it to eleven." Brandon removed his hand from his hair, the curls popping back into disarray. "Though sorcerers tend to avoid coming this close to where I live."

"Except the really stupid ones." Gatiwan gave Nightfall another searching look, as if to remind him that they had not yet ascertained whether or not he might be one.

Nightfall ignored the insinuation "Was she stabbed, too?"

"Stoned, apparently." Brandon shifted from foot to foot. "Found her wedged in a ravine covered with bruises and surrounded by rocks."

"Brutal," Nightfall said. In all his days as the demon, he had never murdered a child and no one in such a cruel fashion. "But there's only way to know whether these killings might be related."

When the other two men just stared, Nightfall finished.

"Find out if Byroth has a talent. If at least two of the children did, that's a pretty clear sign."

"He won't tell us," Gatiwan reminded.

"Then," Nightfall said. "We might want to start with his parents."

Though tidy and sparsely furnished, the main room of Byroth's family cottage felt dangerously closed in to Nightfall. He had let Brandon take the most secure position, a stool pressed against one wood-and-thatch wall that granted him a full view of the fireplace, both windows, and the door. Nightfall understood the Magebane's need to see any danger before it struck and did not want to seem similarly hunted. Consequently, he found himself peering out the window at his back at intervals, unable to grant the parents his full attention. Gatiwan had chosen to sit on a storage chest between one of the windows and the door, while the mother hunkered on a rickety stepladder that led to an overhead loft. In two places, the main room opened onto the children's bedrooms. Byroth's five sisters slept in one. The other still held the bloody straw pallet that had served as his bed.

Byroth's father had chosen a seat on the floor where he rocked himself like a fearful toddler. A large man with work-callused hands and strong arms, he now looked more like a lost child. His wiry hair lay wildly snarled, and he had not shaved in several days.

The mother had clearly made more effort to appear presentable in front of important company. Her black hair lay neatly pressed, braided, and twisted on top of her head; and she wore a clean, if simple, shift. Her hands twisted in her lap, never still. "What can I tell you men?" she asked hopefully. Though she had relived the terror more than once, she obviously hoped these professionals might find answers where others had failed.

Gatiwan's usually gruff manner softened. "We know this is hard for you, madam. We're just hoping you could tell us what happened three nights ago."

The woman looked at her husband, who continued to weave

back and forth, eyes unfocused. "Jawar's not taking this well," she explained. "Five daughters and only one stillborn son till Byroth came."

Nightfall nodded encouragingly. To a manual laborer, having strong assistants was important, and none came cheaper than one's own male offspring.

"He doted on the boy. Best friends, they did almost everything but sleep together."

Jawar murmured to no one in particular. "Nothing, nothing on this fair earth is precisely as it seems . . ."

All eyes jerked to the father.

Byroth's mother apologized. "He's been babbling since the attack."

". . . the placid plow horse, the deadly mosquito growing on crystal pond . . ."

Politely, the visitors ignored the father's ramblings while the mother returned to the unanswered question. "We had gone out that night, as we often do, to the docks. That's where would-be storytellers, poets, and philosophers try out their material."

It was a long-standing tradition, Nightfall knew. As Frihiat, he had gone there often, and bartenders frequently attended, hoping to discover new talent. Occasionally, they did find someone worth paying, in coin or board, to entertain their customers. Frihiat had never made the cut, though Nightfall had used the persona to tell good enough stories to earn drinks from fellow patrons.

". . . the children were all fine on our return. All peacefully asleep." The mother gestured at the two rooms leading off from the one they now occupied. "We went up to bed." She made a sweeping upward motion to indicate climbing the ladder on which she now perched. "Later that night, Jawar said he heard something outside and went to investigate. I had fallen back to sleep when I heard Byroth scream. I was scared, so I waited for Jawar to handle it. But when the screaming continued, I sneaked down to see." She swallowed hard, and tears obscured her eyes. "I saw — I saw . . . oh, Byroth—" She folded her face into her hands, the rest of her description muffled. "I heard a scuffle, a shout. By the time I dared to tear aside the doorway covering, Jawar had chased the assassin out the window and was cradling our little boy. Both covered in blood. On the walls, the straw, the floor. More on the window ledge, and I thought I saw a man's shadow disappearing into the night."

"You're sure it was a man?" Brandon interjected, their only clue thus far to the identity of the sorcerer.

"It could have been a large boy or woman. A trick of shadow." The mother heaved a heavy sigh. "I was too focused on my loved ones to pay much attention." Finally, she looked up. Moisture still blurred her eyes, but they held a deep hardness, a glint of hatred. "Whoever did this must be caught and punished." She turned her attention to her husband, and her look softened. "I believe Jawar saw the man who tried to kill our son, maybe even wrestled with him. But he's too distressed to talk."

Apparently believing himself addressed, Jawar muttered, "The bond between man and daughter is sacred; but the son, the son, is his true reflection."

"To talk *coherently*," she corrected.

Gatiwan directed his gaze fully upon Byroth's mother. "So he's not making sense to you either?"

She sucked in another lungful of air. "Not since the . . . incident. He just sits there, quoting the poets and philosophers from the docks." She added, clearly to provoke her husband to anger if not reason, "I had always believed him a strong man who could handle terrible things better than me."

Brandon Magebane swooped to the father's rescue. "It may not be his fault. The sorcerer might have inflicted some sort of spell on him."

The mother stiffened. "Sorcerer," she said weakly. "You think it might have been—?"

"We don't know." Gatiwan stretched his legs out in front of him. "We're here to try to figure that out."

Brandon added, "Do you know if Byroth had a talent?"

"Many." The mother gave her husband another glance. He had reason to know the boy better than she did. "But nothing magical. Not that I ever noticed." She shook her head. "No. No, I'm sorry. Byroth didn't have . . . a birth gift. Nothing a sorcerer would . . ." She trailed off, her head rocking harder, as if to convince the world of her certainty.

The father babbled, ". . . the placid plow horse, the deadly mosquito, the crystal pond." He glanced at Nightfall with vacant, hollow eyes. "The bond, the bond."

The woman waved at Byroth's bedroom. "I haven't gone in there since. Haven't touched anything. The knife's still there; he just dropped it. You're welcome to look."

"Look, look," Jawar echoed. "But why? That most obvious is hardest to see."

Liking this case less and less, doubting they could gather enough information to find the sorerer if, in fact, one was even involved, Nightfall followed Gatiwan and Brandon to the bloody bedroom.

The scene yielded no useful clues, at least to Nightfall. The unadorned knife, well-used and sharpened many times, could belong to anyone. The only bloody footprints could have belonged to either parent as easily as the attacker, and the scattered straw revealed nothing but an understandable struggle. The frowns scoring his companions' faces told Nightfall they found nothing more significant than he had. So they had returned to the healer's cabin and dismissed its guard, needing to confront the victim one more time.

Byroth seemed stronger to Nightfall this time, a testament to children's ability to bounce back from the worst trauma. He handled nearly getting mauled to death better than either of his parents. "I knew you'd come back," he said.

Brandon sat on the edge of the bed. "Byroth, we're trying to help you, and your family, too."

"My father's gone insane," Byroth pronounced with the forthrightness only a child would dare.

"Not insane," Gatiwan corrected. "Just very distraught. We believe it will pass."

It was essential truth. Uncertain if shock, loss, or magic had unhinged the man, they could only guess whether time would cure him. The natal talents spanned such a gamut, Nightfall could only wonder if such a spell would last for days, weeks, or forever. If the sorcerer had such a power, he had not used it against Byroth. Further consideration brought an answer for that. Driven from his rational mind, Byroth might not react logically to inflicted pain; and the sorcerer might lose his soul. Nightfall shook off the thought, not yet even convinced a sorcerer had attacked Byroth.

"But to help them and you," Brandon continued, "I need the answer to a question I already asked. Don't be frightened. We're here to help you and others like you, to keep you safe."

Byroth looked from man to man. He looked longest at Nightfall. "You want to know if I have a birth gift."

Brandon nodded. "Because, if you do, you'll need our protection. Perhaps forever."

Nightfall wondered just how many people Brandon warded and how he managed to keep them all safe.

Byroth said nothing, gaze still straying between them. Finally, he pursed his lips and nodded. "I . . . can tell . . ." He seemed to be measuring their responses as he spoke each word. ". . . if someone else . . . has . . . a birth gift."

Brandon and Gatiwan exchanged looks. "You can?" Brandon pressed, laboring not to strangle his words.

Even Nightfall, the master of role-playing, could not stop his nostrils from flaring. To a sorcerer, it might prove the ultimate talent, the one he would risk everything to get.

"Like," Byroth continued. "I know you have a talent." He met Brandon's gaze. "But he doesn't." He gestured at Gatiwan, then turned his attention to Nightfall. "And you've got one, too."

Exposed, Nightfall kept his features a blank mask, ignoring the triumphant smile spreading across Gatiwan's lips.

"Do you," Brandon started, then paused to swallow hard. "Do you know what those talents are?"

"No. It just tells me you have them."

Now, Nightfall would not have given up the mission for anything. He had little choice but to commit himself fully to Byroth's safety. If a sorcerer got hold of that power, the talented, including himself, had no place to hide. One by one, the spell would expose them and the sorcerer would feast upon them.

"Thank you," Brandon said. "I know that was hard, and I'm going to tell you something ultimately important, then we will never mention this again. *Do not, under any circumstances, ever tell anyone else that you, or anyone you sense, has a birth gift.* Yours is a powerful talent, and there's not a sorcerer in any part of the world who wouldn't give his own . . . favorite body part to have it."

"Oh," Byroth said, dark eyes growing round as coins. Nightfall could feel his gaze on all of them as they exited. And, though he knew the boy as much a victim of his natal talent as the rest of them, he could not help feeling like prey.

For the first shift, the Magebane assigned Nightfall to stay with the boy, Gatiwan to sleep, while he patrolled the outside. That suited Nightfall well enough. He could not have slept yet, not with Byroth's revelation hanging over him. The sentry position seemed better suited to him, given his background; but he had no intention of giving away another of his deep dark secrets. So, he accepted the assignment Brandon gave him, pausing only to leave word of his whereabouts with King Edward before settling in with Byroth.

The power of Brandon's words clearly had a daunting effect on Byroth as well. As the room plunged into a darkness the windowless room only enhanced, he rolled and pitched on his pallet, sleepless.

Hunkered near the door, Nightfall understood the boy's restlessness. He fiddled with the stone in his pocket, one of Brandon's spell-breakers. It took the Magebane months to place his natal ability into an inanimate object, and it only worked once. Since he had not preplanned this particular hunt, he had only made two since his last outing and had given one to each of his companions. "Are you all right?"

Byroth's voice floated out of the pitch. "Just scared, I guess. I . . . don't want . . . to suffer like that again. You understand?"

"I understand." Nightfall sought movement, a shadow amidst the darkness, a wariness awakened by something he could not quite sense. "I understand. No one wants to suffer." Preferring quiet, he added, "Try to sleep. You need as much as you can get."

Byroth stopped talking, but he continued to flop around on the pallet. "Maybe if you sang to me?"

Nightfall rolled his eyes and shook his head, both movements the boy could not discern. His prostitute mother had never softened the night with lullabies, and the bawdy bar songs he knew did not seem appropriate. "I don't sing."

"Oh." Byroth slumped into a new position on the ticking. "Would you mind if I did it, then?"

Nightfall shrugged, still trying to make out objects through the gloom. He wanted it dark enough that any sorcerer who got past Brandon would not notice him, but he would need his own vision well adjusted. "Go ahead, if you think it'll help."

"Thanks." Byroth's thin, reedy voice floated into the cold, night air. "Hush, my darling, my sweetest babe—"

Nightfall ignored the boy, thinking of his encounter with Byroth's parents. They had seemed so broken, so utterly devastated by the near-loss of their son; they both clearly loved him fiercely. Nightfall had not lamented his own empty upbringing for many years: the mother who had alternately beaten and cried for him, the men who came and went, the father who could have been any one or none of them. *The bond between man and daughter is sacred; but the son, the son, is his true reflection.* Nightfall was once the true reflection of the men to whom his mother had sold her body, including the one who had battered her to death. Now, he had found a way beyond the poet/philosopher's claim. *How much better have Byroth and his father fared?*

It was a question that needed no answer. Nightfall found himself trapped in recollection, the world fading into a dark void around him. His watchfulness withered, replaced by a mental world where word and sound came only from within. *Nothing, nothing on this fair earth is precisely as it seems. The placid plow horse, the deadly mosquito growing on crystal pond.* In the world of the dreamer, nonsense can become a statement of vivid brilliance. *Nothing is what it seems.*

Suddenly, Nightfall understood. He closed his hand over the stone Brandon had given him. His fingers tightened with awkward slowness, seeking the laxity of sleep. He felt his head sagging, heavy as lead; and the welcoming darkness of sleep erased the significance from all but his dream-world thoughts. But those anchored him well enough. A wholly mental pursuit, he called on his talent to overcome the heavy inertia magical-fatigue forced upon him, driving down his weight to a sliver of normal. Lighter than feathers, his fingers obeyed him. He drew out the stone, which now seemed more like a boulder, and hurled it toward the boy.

The singing broke off in a high-pitched squeak, and Nightfall's senses returned in an overwhelming rush. He scuttled aside, and something sharp jabbed into his thigh instead of his privates. Restoring his mass, he kicked at his attacker, rolling as he moved. His attack also missed, and he dropped to a crouch, realigning, waiting for the other to reveal himself. It all made sense now. He knew who had attacked Byroth, and he also knew why.

A shadow lunged toward Nightfall, and a knife glinted in the slivers of light leaking through cracks in the construction. Concentrating fully on the weapon, Nightfall sprang for his attacker. He caught the thin wrist, twisting viciously. The knife thumped to the floor. The boy screamed, pain mixed with frustration. His arms and legs lashed violently, wildly toward Nightfall. Several blows landed with bruising force, but Nightfall bullied through the pain. He dropped his mass again and hurled himself at Byroth. The instant he felt the boy beneath him, he drove his weight to its heaviest. Air hissed out of Byroth's mouth, in a crushed and muted screech.

Expertly, Nightfall sorted limbs and parts until he had Byroth fully pinned and one of his own hands free. He flipped a dagger from one of his wrist sheaths and planted it at Byroth's throat.

"Wh—" the boy started, forcing words around the tremendous burden crushing him to the ground. "What are you going

. . . to do to me?" The voice sounded soft, pitiful, the plea of a confused eight-year-old.

Nightfall bit his lip. Even in his most savage days, he had never enjoyed killing. He could afford to choose his victims with care, and he based it upon his own judgment of their worthiness. He had never murdered a child, yet this was no regular child. Byroth was a sorcerer, one who had already shown a cruel streak far beyond his years. The first talent he had stolen, from a seven-year-old friend, had given him the means to detect the gifted from birth. He had callously slaughtered an infant, probably for the ability to heal more quickly or to make the huge leaps he had taken to attack Nightfall. He knew some people who could kill an eight-year-old without compunction, but most could never conceive of such a thing. *Brutal at eight; merciless by twenty.* Nightfall took solace from Jawar's words: *Nothing on this earth is precisely what it seems. Byroth is no child; he's truly the demon so many named me.*

"What are you going to do with me?" Byroth whispered again.

"I'm going," Nightfall said coldly, "to finish the job your father began."

By the time Brandon Magebane and Gatiwan arrived, Nightfall had completed the deed. The two men stared at the little body on the floor, the rumpled sheets, the peaceful look on the corpse's face.

"I couldn't save him," Nightfall said, crouched beside Byroth. He let grief touch his voice, not wholly feigned. Though the others would misinterpret, his words were grim truth.

Brandon crouched beside Nightfall. "Don't blame yourself. The sorcerer got by me, too. I'm not sure how."

Gatiwan grunted. "Some sort of teleportation spell, I'd warrant."

Nightfall lowered his head. Lying came easily to him, though not always for so noble a reason. No one but him ever needed to know that Jawar had tried to kill his own son. If the boy's father could eventually forgive himself, at least he would avoid the condemnation of his wife and neighbors. He had done the right thing, and Nightfall planned to tell him that.

Brandon's hand dropped to Nightfall's shoulder. "At least you managed to prevent the ritual. The talent died with Byroth, and he doesn't have to suffer the limbo of a harnessed soul."

Nightfall nodded philosophically. The ability to become a sorcerer was as innate as the gifts. That curse had destroyed Byroth's soul long before Nightfall had dispatched it to whatever afterlife it warranted. In the process, so many innocents had been saved.

Gatiwan sighed heavily. "Let's go report this death to the authorities."

Nightfall and Brandon rose together. "I think," the Magebane said, "that the King of Alyndar will forgive us."

Tanya Huff

Tanya Huff is an amazing writer. She is the author all of our other authors love to read. Her books are also a perfect way to lure your non-fantasy reading friends and relatives into giving the genre a try. They may not see the error of their ways but they will at least continue to ask for all of Tanya's books. That said, I hasten to add that Tanya is indeed writing fantasy and, more recently, science fiction as well. No one would dispute that her first novel, *Child of the Grove*, or its sequel, *The Last Wizard*, is fantasy. Nor could anyone deny that *The Better Part of Valor* and *Valor's Choice* are science fiction novels. But Tanya's sense of plot, place, character, and dialogue are so strong and clear that her work strikes a universal chord even with people who swear that they'll never read the genre.

Tanya also has a very good sense of humor. And although she swears she'll never write another humorous work after she finishes one, sometimes she just can't help herself. Her novels *Summon the Keeper* and *The Second Summoning* are perfect examples of just how well she handles humor. And the story you are about to read, "We Two May Meet," is another example of Tanya at her humorous best.

—SG

WE TWO MAY MEET
Tanya Huff

MAGDELENE was beside herself when she woke that first morning home from Venitcia—which wasn't really surprising as she'd never been much of a morning person. If truth be told, she was more of a midafternoon, heading into cocktail hour kind of a person.

What *was* surprising was that the self she was beside appeared to be snoring.

"**M**istress?" Kali's red eyes widened as two wizards walked into the kitchen—identical but for the fact that one had her thick chestnut hair pulled back into a tight bun and seemed to be wearing an outfit in which all the items not only complemented each other but covered her from neck to knees. The demon housekeeper turned to the other wizard, whose hair fell in the usual messy cascade and who was wearing a vest and skirt in virulently opposing shades of green. "Mistress, there are two of you."

"No." The first Magdelene crossed the kitchen and pulled a mug embossed with the words *The most powerful wizard in the world* off the shelf. "There's still only one of me. I just seem to have gone to pieces."

Kali sighed, but said, as was expected, "Well, pull yourself together."

"Not without a cup of coffee."

"Very funny," the second Magdelene snorted. "But neither misplaced humor nor your unseemly addiction to that beverage is getting us any closer to solving our problem!"

"We've managed to determine that she's my unfun bits," Magdelene-one informed the demon, sinking into a chair and reaching for a muffin.

"I hope you're not having butter on that!"

"Also my nagging, uptight bits."

"Mistress, how did this happen?"

Magdelene-one shrugged, spreading butter liberally on the muffin. "Beats the heck out of me. She was there when I woke up; large as life and twice as tidy."

"And I can't seem to get her to care," growled Magdalene-two through clenched teeth. "We must find out who did this to us and why."

"It's too hot to care." One stuck her foot out into a patch of sunlight and grinned down at the shadow of her bare toes on the tile floor.

"Mistress, if there is a wizard powerful enough to do this . . ."

"What difference does it make? I mean, really? It's been done."

"You see? You see what I've had to put up with?" Two glared down at her double. "Well, fine. I don't need you—I was only including you in the process to be thorough. I can get the answers on my own." Pivoting on one well-shod heel, she stomped out of the room, the door slamming behind her.

"What a bitch," One snorted.

"Mistress, if she is a part of you . . ."

"Then I'm well rid of her."

The door swung open hard enough to crash against the wall. "What have you done to my house!"

Magdelene-one sighed, reaching for another muffin. "What do you mean, your house? Try, my house."

"The tower is *missing*!"

"Is not."

Shaking her head, Kali went out into the hall. Not only was the tower missing but two of the hall's four doors opened into the garden and the door that should have returned her to the kitchen led sequentially to the sitting room, the bathing room, Joah's old room, and a room the demon didn't recognize although, from the piles of debris, it appeared to be a storeroom of sorts. A half-grown calico cat meowed indignantly down at her from a stack of crates.

"I have no idea," she said, closing the door again. If the house was causing the cats problems, things were even more serious than they appeared.

A fifth attempt finally took her back to the kitchen. Magdelene-one was licking the jam spoon while Magdelene-two made notes on Kali's recipe slate.

"The house," she announced, "is out of control."

"That's just so unlikely," Magdelene-one scoffed stickily.

"Nevertheless, Mistress, it is the case."

Sighing heavily, Magdelene-one heaved herself up out of the chair and sauntered over to the door, Magdelene-two following close behind, arms folded and lips pressed into a thin line. They walked out of the kitchen and stood in a square hall, warmly lit by the large skylight overhead.

"Sitting room, bathroom, stairs to the Netherhells . . ." The doors opened and closed showing the rooms behind them as they were named. ". . . stairs to the tower." Magdelene-one rolled her eyes and headed back to the kitchen. "You guys make such a fuss over nothing."

As the door closed behind her, the house shifted and the green-and-gold lizard who had moments before been sunning himself in the garden stared up at Magdelene-two in shock.

"You're right," she told it. "The situation is completely unacceptable. Fortunately, a reasoned analysis finds a simple solution." Opening a door, she reached into the kitchen, grabbed her other self by the back of the vest and hauled her into the hall. The lizard disappeared, the doors returned. "Clearly, we must stay together in order to maintain the house."

"Clearly," Magdelene-one mocked. "Why?"

"Let me think . . ."

"Oh, you're thinking. I can smell the smoke."

Magdelene-two ignored her. "As you observed previously, there is still only one of us, we have merely been separated into pieces. It's therefore logical to assume that our power has been equally divided between us. Together, we remain the most powerful wizard in the world. Separate, we are merely powerful—and not powerful enough to mindlessly support old magics."

"That sort of sucks."

"Indeed. We need answers." Clutching her other self's elbow, Magdelene-two threw open a door and marched them both up the steps to the cupola on the top of the tower.

"Stairs; what was I thinking?"

From the outside, the turquoise house on the headland seemed to be only one story tall. From the cupola, the two wizards had an uninterrupted view of the surrounding countryside from fifty feet in the air.

Magdelene-one gazed down at the cove and the fishing village that hugged the shore. "Nothing much happening there. Wait a minute, that's Miguel working on his boat. Would you look at the shoulders on the man. And the ass—you could bounce clams off that ass." Leaning forward, she whispered something as if in Miguel's ear. The fisherman turned and waved. Even at such a distance, they could see his broad smile.

"What did you say to him?" Magdelene-two demanded suspiciously.

One giggled. "I told him that if the kaylie weren't running I knew something else he could spend the morning spearing."

"Have you no concern for your dignity? And if not," she continued, before her double could reply, "have you no concern for mine? We are the most powerful wizard in the world and we have position to maintain!"

"Prude."

"Slut."

Magdelene-one stuck out her tongue, flickered once, and glared across the room. "You stopped me! How dare you stop me!"

Hands on her hips, Two returned the glare. "Have you forgotten why we came up here?" A half turn and a sharp wave toward the large oval mirror in the rosewood stand. "We must discover who did this to us!"

"Why?"

"So that we can undo it."

"Why?" One asked again, dropping down onto the huge pile of multicolored cushions that filled most of the floor space. "Personally, I think I'm better off without you dragging me down."

"Me dragging *you* down?" the other Magdelene snorted, turning to the mirror. "Oh, that's a laugh."

The mirror—an expensive replacement after a wizard wannabe had broken her original trying to use the demon trapped inside—showed nothing but a reflection of both Magdelenes.

"You've broken it!"

"I haven't done anything."

"Oh, you never *do* do anything, do you?"

"At least I know how to enjoy myself," Magdelene-one pointed out. She flashed her double a sunny smile and vanished.

"At least *I* won't end up with sand in unmentionable places," Two sneered to an empty room.

"Where . . . ?"

"The village. She is such an embarrassment, Kali." Lowering herself into a chair, legs crossed at the ankles, Magdelene-two quivered with apprehension. "I shudder just thinking of how she's perceived."

"The villagers have always treated her—you—with respect, Mistress."

"But she's so . . ." Manicured nails beat out a staccato beat against the polished wood of the table as she searched for a description that managed to be both accurate and polite and managed only: ". . . enthusiastically athletic."

"From what I have heard, they respect that as well, and I have received the impression on a number of occasions that some are rather in awe." Kali set a lightly steaming cup of tea on the table by the wizard. "Did you discover who is responsible for this division?"

Magdelene-two took a ladylike sip of tea and sighed. "I'm afraid not. The mirror is nonfunctional and showed only our reflections. Whoever divided us in two must have disabled it in order to cover their tracks."

The demon nodded thoughtfully.

"What's this?" Magdelene-one blinked down at the lightly steamed vegetables and the poached fish on her plate.

Kali placed a pitcher of water and a glass on the table. "Lunch, Mistress. High in fiber, low in fat. Your double ordered it."

"Then why isn't my double here eating it?"

"She remains in the workshop, delving in eldritch realms to discover the cause of your affliction."

"Hey, it's nothing a little salve won't cure. Oh, *our* affliction. Right. Well, she's going to get us into trouble with that whole eldritch realms thing. It's likely to bring on an angry crowd of villagers with torches and pitchforks. And, hang on, I don't have a workshop."

"She has added one on, Mistress."

"And you just let her?"

"I am her housekeeper as much as yours, Mistress. If you are unhappy with her decision, perhaps you should confront her yourself."

"Yeah, probably, but I don't really feel much like doing it now. Maybe later." A lazy flick of a knifepoint teased apart two translucent flakes of white flesh. "Any chance of getting some tartar sauce with this?"

"**W**hat are you doing?"

"What does it look like I'm doing?" Magdelene-two demanded. She tossed a cushion onto the ground, dropped to her knees on the cushion, and began inscribing runes in the fresh earth. "I'm laying out protective wards around the house."

"Didn't there used to be cat mint there?"

"Do you *want* what happened last night to happen again?" Magdelene-two sniffed, ignoring the actual question.

Magdelene-one settled back down in the hammock and scratched at her bare stomach. "Don't see how it can. We're already in two pieces."

"And what would you say to four pieces?"

"Five card draw, monkey's wild, it'll cost you a caravan to open."

Magdelene-two sniffed again. "You're making absolutely no sense."

"With four," her double sighed, "we'd have enough for poker."

"You think you're very funny, don't you? You're just lucky you have me to take care of things."

A tanned hand waved languidly in the hot afternoon air. "Whatever makes you happy, sister."

"Don't call me that!" Two protested, vehemently tucking an escaped strand of hair back behind her ear. "I'm not your *sister*, I'm you!"

"Then I really need a nap. I'm not usually this cranky."

"**K**ali, what is this?"

"Supper, Mistress." Thankful that the kitchen was one of the more anchored rooms, Kali put down the plate of spiced prawns in garlic butter. "Your double ordered it." When faced with the inevitable, she felt she might as well just say the lines assigned.

Magdelene-two's lip curled. "Then why isn't my double here eating it?"

"There was a delivery from the village this afternoon."

"A delivery of what?"

"I do not know. He never reached the house."

"Why not?"

Kali opened her mouth to answer, but a raised hand and a scarlet flush on the wizard's cheeks cut her off.

"Never mind. How can she take a chance like that? He might not be a mere delivery boy, he could easily be our enemy attempting to take us unawares. He could be the wizard who divided us, arriving to check on our weakened condition." Magdelene-two leaped to her feet. "He could have weapons designed to destroy us!"

The demon placed her hand on the wizard's shoulder and pushed her back down into the chair. "I believe he was searched quite thoroughly," she said.

Magdelene-two looked up from placing her folded clothing neatly into a chest and clutched at her voluminous nightshirt. "What do you think you're doing here?"

"It's *my* bedroom."

"Excuse me, I believe that it's my bedroom."

"Whatever." Magdelene-one shrugged. "It's a big bed." She began to work at the laces on her vest.

"I am not sharing this bed with you."

"You're not my first choice either but . . ." The vest hit the floor, quickly followed by the skirt. ". . . so what. It's late. I'm sleepy. And this is *my* bed."

"You can sleep in one of the spare rooms."

"I don't want to." She kicked her crumpled clothes into a corner. "Besides, I have dibs. I'm clearly the original."

"And how do you figure that?"

"I have all the dominant character traits."

"You're a lazy, lecherous slob!"

"I rest my case." Triumphant, she dropped onto the bed. "And you're only angry because you know I'm ri . . . HEY!"

Releasing her double's ankle, Magdelene-two stepped back and pointed toward the door. "Out. Now."

Magdelene-one scrambled up off the floor. "You shouldn't have done that."

"Really? What were you planning to d . . . AWK!" Pressed up against the back wall, she struggled to get an arm free.

"I plan to get some sleep if you'd just shu . . . OW!

For every offense, an equal defense. For every spell, a counterspell. For every pillow slammed into a face or across the back of a head, there was a pillow slammed in return. The pillows were, by far, getting the worst of it.

The villagers stared up at the lights and noises coming from the house of the most powerful wizard in the world and they wondered. Some wondered what fell enchantments were afoot. Most wondered why they hadn't been invited to the party. One wondered why the ground seemed to be shaking slightly. . . .

The impact shook the house and knocked both Magdelenes to their knees, hands buried in each other's hair.

"*Now* what have you done," Magdelene-two demanded, eyes wild.

"Wasn't me," her double denied hurriedly. "It must have been you."

"Well, it wasn't. Unlike some people, I maintain perfect control at all times."

"So, if I didn't do it and you're maintaining perfect control," Magdelene-one mocked. "Who's doing all the bang . . ."

The second impact was more violent than the first.

The wizards' eyes widened simultaneously and together they raced for the hall.

Unencumbered by the tangled ruin of a nightshirt, Magdelene-one reached the door first and threw it open, peering down the long, long flight of stairs that led to the Netherhells. Swinging free, the door began to tremble.

"DUCK!"

After the impact the two wizards lifted their heads to peer wide-eyed at the object embedded in the wall. It was a large bone, almost five feet long and a hands' span in diameter. Crude sigils had been carved around the curve of the visible end.

"That can't be good," Magdelene-one observed, standing.

Gaining her feet a moment later, Magdelene-two crossed to the bone. "It appears that one of the demon princes is attempting to breach the door. This sigil here is the sign of Ter'Poe, and this the sign of conquest, and this . . ." She tapped her finger lightly against another. "This is what appears to be a corrupted version of my name with certain Midworld influences apparently creeping into the actual lines and curves."

The other wizard gave an exaggerated yawn. "Even facing potential disaster you're boring."

"Potential disaster, Mistresses?"

They turned together to face the housekeeper.

"You don't think an invasion by the Netherhells where we all end up murdered in our beds and all manner of evils like sloth and gluttony . . ." Magdelene-two paused long enough to glare at her double. ". . . run loose in the world is a disaster?"

"I merely question your use of the word 'potential,' Mistress.

If their missile was able to reach the house, they are already through the door."

On cue: the distant sound of pounding footsteps rose from below.

Magdelene-one scratched thoughtfully. "At the risk of repeating myself, that can't be good."

"You idiot!" Magdelene-two charged across to the open door and lifted both hands to shoulder height, palms out, fingers spread. "*And while the darkness from the deep doth into this world try to creep, I raise my powers from their sleep . . .*"

"What are you doing?"

"Stopping an invasion by the Netherhells!"

"With bad poetry?" Accepting a dressing gown from Kali, Magdelene-one belted it on then pointed down the stairs. "Go home."

"Ow!" The exclamation was distant but unmistakable. The footsteps paused.

And then they began again.

"That can't be . . ."

"Yes, we all know. That can't be good. Stop repeating yourself and start throwing things at them before we're horribly killed and responsible for the deaths of thousands."

"I don't think . . ."

"Fortunately for the world, *I* do."

"I can think of *someone's* death I'd like to be responsible for," Magdelene-one muttered.

"That . . . was close," Magdelene-two gasped, sagging back against the now closed door.

"Too . . . close," Magdelene-one agreed from where she lay panting on the floor.

"As long as your power remains divided, I very much doubt you could stop a second assault," Kali pointed out. "And there will be a second assault, Mistresses. You may count on that as a certainty."

"She has . . . a point."

"Two. They're horns."

"She has a point about the two of us not being able to defeat the demonkind a second time," Magdelene-two ground out through clenched teeth. "We have to do something before we're all destroyed. Before we're chopped into pieces and devoured. I'll return to the workshop and attempt to find the strongest spells we can perform with our reduced power."

"Good on you. I'll have a nap."

"No," Kali sighed. "You will both come with me to the tower."

"Kali, lest you forget I . . ."

"We," amended Magdelene-one.

". . . are mistress here."

Kali ignored them both and started up the stairs. After a moment, they exchanged identical expressions of confusion, and followed.

"The mirror is not functioning properly," Magdelene-two reminded the demon.

"Yes, Mistress, it is. Ask it other than who divided you from yourself."

After a moment spent working out demonic syntax, and another moment spent jockeying for position, the wizards took turns asking questions to which they already knew the answers. The mirror performed flawlessly.

"Now," prodded the demon, "ask it who is responsible for this division."

Magdelene-one shrugged, leaned past her double and asked.

The mirror continued to show only the reflection of the two Magdelenes.

"See? It's busted."

"No." Kali shook her head. "It is not. Think, both of you, who is strong enough to do this to the most powerful wizard in the world? You did it to yourself," she confirmed as understanding began to dawn. "The mirror has been giving you the correct answer from the beginning."

"We did this to ourselves?"

"Bummer."

"How? When?"

"When? It happened in the night as you slept. How?" Scaled shoulders rose and fell. "I do not know. Only you know."

"I don't know." Magdelene-one flopped down on the pillows. "Do you know?"

Magdelene-two pushed back a straying strand of chestnut hair and shook her head. "I'm forced to admit that I have no memory of doing any such thing."

"But clearly, it was done. And it must be undone before the world is overrun with others of my kind who are less . . . nice." Kali folded her arms. "For reasons only you can know you have brought this division upon yourself. Only you are powerful enough to undo what you have done."

"Granted, but we don't *know* what we've done."

"It is in your heads, Mistresses. It must come out."

"Eww." One's lip curled. "Look, I have an idea, let's just stay like we are."

"I want you back as a part of me as little as you want me in you," Two snorted, "but we have a responsibility to everyone in the world. We must save them from the encroachment of the Netherhells."

"Why? We've been saving them from that encroachment for a very long time. I say let someone else take the responsibility so I can have some fun."

"You've *been* having fun!" Magdelene-two reminded her sharply, arms folded over the ruins of her nightshirt. "In fact, you've been having everyone who's come within twenty feet of this house and it's GOT. TO. STOP."

"Bitch."

"Tramp."

"Mistresses, enough. You must pull yourselves together before disaster overcomes us all! There is a man," Kali continued, shooting a warning glare toward Magdelene-one, "a Doctor Bineeni, in Harmon, a town three days' travel inland. I have heard he attends to problems of the mind."

"Heard from who?"

"The baker's husband has a nephew whose friend had very good things to say about the man."

"The baker's husband's nephew's friend?" One shook her head in disbelief. "Oh, yeah, that's a valid recommendation."

"Do you have a better idea?" Two demanded.

"Sure. I leave and the demon princes do what they want to you."

"Fine. Two can play at that game."

"It is not a game and no one is playing." Kali's crimson eyes glittered. "If you have no consideration for the peoples of this world, then consider this: the demon princes have vowed vengeance for the death of their brother. They will not care how many pieces you are in when they begin, but I guarantee you will both be in many more pieces when they finish. You may continue arguing and die, or go to Harmon and live."

The only sound in the tower was the soft shunk, shunk, shunk of Magdelene-one stroking a silk tassel.

"Live?" she said at last, glancing up at her double.

"Live," Magdelene-two agreed.

"We have to walk?"

Kali rolled her eyes, white showing all around the red. "You have never been to Harmon, Mistress. You cannot go by magic to a place you have never seen."

"What about borrowing Frenin's donkey and cart?"

"You may not be seen in the village like this. It will cause them great distress."

Magdelene-two looked pointedly at her companion who was wearing wide-legged purple trousers, an orange vest, and yellow sandals. "I can fully understand why."

"Ice queen."

"Sleaze."

Kali stared up at the huge wrought-iron gate overfilling the break in the coral wall and sighed. Deep and weary exhalations weren't something demons indulged in as a rule, but over the last day she'd become quite accomplished. Had she ever stopped to anticipate their current situation, she might have expected two Magdelenes would be twice as much trouble as one. She would have been wrong. *Twice* as much trouble was a distinct underestimate.

"What in the Netherhells have you got in that thing?" Magdelene-one drawled, poking a finger at her companion's carpet bag.

"Clean handkerchiefs, water purification potion, bug repellent, extra sandal straps, desiccated dragon liver, a comb, one complete change of clothes, soap, a talisman for stomach problems . . . What?" Two demanded, the list having raised not one, but both eyebrows to the hairline of her listener.

"You do remember you're a wizard?"

"Your point?"

Magdelene-one held up a small belt pouch. "I have everything I need in here."

"And if we're unable to use our powers?" Two demanded.

"I still have everything I need."

"There's not enough room in there for a pair of clean underwear."

Rubbing at a rivulet of sweat, Magdelene-one grinned. "Good think I don't wear them, then. I still don't see why we can't take the carpet," she complained to Kali before her double could respond.

"With your powers divided, it would take both of you working in concert to keep the carpet aloft," the demon explained again. "Should your attention wander, even for a moment, it could be fatal."

"Three days on the road with Ms. Nettles-in-her-britches here could be fatal, too."

"No one ever died of boredom, Mistress. Or embarrassment," she added as the second Magdelene caught her eye. "And the sooner you begin, the sooner we can put all this behind us. Remember what is at stake." She all but pushed the wizards through the gate and onto the path. As they rounded the first turn, already squabbling, she sighed again and closed her eyes.

Which was how she missed the black shadows slinking around the corner behind them.

soon soon
at their weakest
away from home
away from help
soon soon

Harmon was a largish town, four, maybe five times the size of the fishing village nestled under Magdelene's headland. It boasted a permanent market square, three competing inns, two town wells, a large mill, four temples, a dozen shrines, and one small theater that had just been torched by the local Duc who'd objected to having his name and likeness appear in a recent satirical production.

In its particular corner of the world, Harmon was about as cosmopolitan as it got.

Which could have been why no one gave the two identical wizards a second glance—although it was more likely they passed unnoted because no one knew they were wizards and they weren't, after three days' travel, particularly identical.

The shifting shadows of early evening hid the bits of darkness that entered the town on their heels.

soon

"Excuse me, we'd like a room."

"Two rooms," Magdelene-one corrected. "A dark, narrow uncomfortable room for her." She nodded toward her companion. "And a big, bright, comfortable room for me." Smiling her best smile, she leaned toward the barman. "With a big, bright comfortable bed."

Totally oblivious to the beer pouring over his hand, the barman swallowed. Hard.

Magdelene-two gestured the tap closed. "One room," she repeated, her tone acting on him with much the same effect as a bucket of cold water. "The one at the end of the hall with the two beds will do and we will not," a pointed look at her sulking double, "be sharing it with any other travelers." As four coins of varying sizes hit the counter, she swept the common room with an expression icy enough to frost mugs and drop curious gazes down to the tabletops. "First night's payment plus payment for use of the bathing room. I want the water hot and clean linens— clean, mind you, not just turned clean side out. And don't bother telling me you never do that," she cautioned, spearing the barman with a disdainful snort. "I *know* that you do."

"How?"

"We're the most powerful wizard in the world," Magdelene-one told him brightly while being dragged toward the stairs. A shower of coins hit the bar. "I'll get the first rou . . . OW!"

Maintaining her grip, Magdelene-two leaned in close to what should have been a familiar ear. *Except that one never sees one's own ear from that angle,* she reflected, momentarily nonplussed. "Don't you think we should be keeping a low profile?" she asked quietly, dropping her voice below the sudden noise of fourteen people charging toward the bar, tankards held out. "We shouldn't be letting the whole world know we're at half strength. That's just asking for trouble!"

"You worry too much." Rolling her eyes, Magdelene-one pulled her arm free. "Look, you have the first bath while I hang out here. I'll be fine." She sighed at the narrowed eyes and thin lips. "What? You don't trust yourself?"

"You are not the parts of myself that I trust!"

". . . so he said, *Are you waiting to see the whites of his eyes?* and I said, *Not exactly!*" Magdalene's gesture made it very clear just what, exactly, she'd been waiting to see. As the crowd roared its approval of the story, she upended her tankard and finished the last three inches of beer.

Before she could lower it, a hush fell over the room.

By the time she set the tankard on the table, the hush had become anticipation.

"Rumor has it you're a wizard."

A quick inspection proved her tankard was definitely empty. Since no one seemed inclined to fill it, she sighed and turned. There were three of them. Big guys, bare arms; attitude. Since this particular tavern didn't cater to the "big guys with bare arms and attitude" crowd, they'd clearly dropped by to make trouble.

"You don't look like a wizard," the leader sneered. "You don't act like a wizard." He leaned forward, nostrils flaring over the dangling ends of a mustache adorned with blue beads. "You don't smell like a wizard."

His companions grunted agreement.

"We wanted to see a wizard and we get pissed right off when we don't get what we want." A booted foot kicked the end of a bench; two people toppled to the floor.

Magdelene knew how to deal with this sort. One way or another she'd been dealing with these kinds of idiots her entire life. Unfortunately, she couldn't remember what she usually did. And the bicolored codpiece worn by the man on the right wasn't helping.

The bath was helping. Deep, hot water to soak away the road and the indignities. How could she even consider becoming one again with that low-minded, badly dressed hussy?

On the other hand, how could she consider allowing the Netherhells to visit death and destruction on the Midworld?

Vigorously exfoliating an elbow, Magdelene wondered how she'd got herself into a situation with no viable alternatives.

The sound of raised voices caught her attention. One of the voices sounded familiar, although the language left much to be desired and nothing at all to the imagination.

"Oh, for the love of . . ." The water sluiced off skin and hair as Magdelene climbed from the tub, and by the time she reached her neat pile of clean clothes, she was completely dry. Dressing quickly as the noise level rose, she opened the bathing room door, stepped out into the hall, paused, and returned to hang the mat neatly over the side of the tub. There were some things a wizard had to do to retain her self-respect.

She wasn't surprised to see herself as the center of attention in the common room. After pushing through the crowd, she *was* a bit surprised to see that the man who had her double by the vest was standing on chicken legs under the multicolored arc of a rather magnificent tail. There were two others, also half-man half-chicken and a couple of dozen onlookers who seemed uncertain if they should be amused or appalled. Whatever her other half had done, it had only half worked.

In the midst of being shaken, Magdelene-one caught her double's eye and croaked, "Little help here?"

Two rolled her eyes. "Were you going up the scale, or down?" she asked, pitching her voice under the roars of the chicken-man.

"D . . . d . . . down."

The three roosters, the largest marked with blue dots on the ends of its wattles, made a run for the door and the wizards found themselves alone in the center of the room. The noise building in the surrounding crowd began to sound like an angry sea.

In Magdelene's experience, crowds became mobs very quickly. Familiar fingers interlocked, left hand to right.

One voice from two mouths murmured, "Forget."

"**W**hy roosters?" Two asked as they climbed the stairs.

One rubbed at a beer stain on her trousers. "Well, all three were acting like pricks and pricks are another word for co . . ."

"I get it. You have to be more careful. Just because it's on your body, doesn't mean I want some overmuscled idiot rearranging my face. The world can be a nasty, brutal place and you must be prepared for that at all times."

"I don't think I want to live in your world," One snorted, pushing open the door to their room and slouching inside.

Two glared down at the handprint on her double's right cheek. "I *know* I don't want to live in yours." Closing the door with more force than was necessary, she walked over to the window and reached out for one of the shutters. Frowning, she stared down into the inn yard. "The shadows are roiling."

"Yeah, whatever *that* means."

"They're excited about something."

Magdelene-one dropped onto the nearest bed and belched. "Probably not about the beer."

together
not now
not when together
when apart

"You Doctor Bineeni?"

The elderly man slumped over the scroll jerked erect so quickly his glasses slid down to the end of his nose. Half turning, he glared at the chestnut-haired woman standing in the door to his inner sanctum. "Here now, you can't just barge in unannounced!"

A second woman joined the first. "That's what I said, but she never listens to me."

Magdelene-one jerked a finger toward her companion. "Thinks she's my better half. What a laugh, eh?"

Pushing his glasses back into position, Doctor Bineeni stared. "Twins? But at your age even identical twins would be less than identical as differing experiences would write differing histories on the face."

"At our age?" Two bristled.

"You look . . ." He frowned. "But you're not young."

One sighed. "You don't know the half of it, sweet cheeks. We're the most powerful wizard in the world."

His eyes widened, strengthening his resemblance to a startled lizard. "You're Magdelene?"

Waving a bundle of dried herbs onto the top of the tottering pile across the room, One dropped into a chair. "He's heard of us."

"That should make this easier," Two agreed. She ran her finger along the edge of a shelf and clucked her tongue at the accumulated dust.

"But . . . you're a legend. You don't really exist."

"Oh, I exist. You can touch me if you like. Ow!" Shooting a steaming look at Two, she muttered. "I meant he could touch my hand."

"Sure you did."

Wide-eyed the doctor looked from one to the other. "*You* are the most powerful wizard in the world?"

"Yes."

"Both of you?"

"That's correct."

"There should only be one of you."

"Also correct." Two dusted off her hands, tucking them into the sleeves of her robe. "It appears that in the split, we both got half the power . . ."

"And she got the really shitty bits of the personality."

". . . and we need you to put us back together before the Netherhells make another try for the stairs."

"The stairs?" Dr. Bineeni asked, looking from one to the other.

"Yes, the flight of stairs in my house that descends into the Netherhells."

He smiled and raised an ink-stained finger, shaking it in their general direction. "Almost, you had me, ladies. I can help with your delusion, but you'll need to make an appointment."

"Under other circumstances, I'd be more than willing to follow protocol, but we need to see you now."

"Ladies, I'm sorry . . ."

"Not as sorry as you will be if Ter'Poe gets up those stairs," One snorted. "We're not leaving until you help us."

The smile gone, Dr. Bineeni turned toward a back door. "Evan. Petre."

Two burly young men pushed their way into the room past the piles of books.

"Not bad." Magdelene-one fluffed out her hair and undid the top fastener on her vest. "One each."

Two stared at her in disbelief. "Is that *all* you ever think about?"

"No!" One's brows dipped in. "Well . . ."

"Slattern!"

"Anal-retentive!"

Evan, or possible Petre, reached for Magdelene-two's arm.

"Oh, go to sleep!" she snapped.

Both men fell to the ground.

"Horizontal. Very nice."

"Slut!"

"Ha! You're repeating yourself."

Two gestured. One countered. Power sizzled against power in the center of the room.

now

Darkness rose out of the shadows, divided an infinite number of times, took form and substance.

"Imps?" Two stared at the swarm of tiny figures scuttling toward her. "They dare to send imps against *me?*"

"Whatever." One didn't bother standing. She waved a languid hand and several imps imploded. The rest kept coming. Chestnut brows drew in. "That can't be good."

"Would you quit saying that!" Two shrieked as the first imps reached her.

They climbed into mouths and ears and noses. They tangled in hair. They tried to fit themselves into every bleeding wound they made. And for every dozen Magdelene destroyed, another dozen rose from the shadows.

Driven out of the chair, Magdelene-one staggered around the room, flailing power at her attackers. Stumbling over a muscular body, she began to fall and grabbed hold of the closest solid object: Magdelene-two's hand. As their fingers tightened, the wizard looked herself in the eye and smiled.

An instant later the only sign that a battle had been fought and nearly lost was the tangled mess of Two's hair.

"I can't believe they'd send imps after us," she growled, her hair rearranging itself back into a tight bun.

"I can't believe the imps almost kicked ass," One added.

A whimper turned them to face Dr. Bineeni, who was kneeling on the floor, staring up through the bars of his stool.

"You're actually her!"

Yawning, One dropped back into the chair. "Yeah, we actually are."

"And we need your help. You saw what happens when we try to fight the darkness as two separate wizards."

"Yes. I saw." Drawing in a long, shuddering breath, the doctor seemed to come to a decision as he slowly stood. "Who did this to you?"

"Well, it's like, uh . . ."

"Are you blushing?" Two demanded, taking a disbelieving step toward her double. "I wouldn't have thought you still knew *how* to blush!"

"Up yours."

"You know what your problem is? You're not willing to face reality." Straightening her robe, Two speared Dr. Bineeni with an irritated glare. "We did it to ourself. Ourselves."

"And you want me to . . . ?"

"Put us back together."

Bushy gray brows rose above the rims of the glasses. "You *want* to be back together?"

"It doesn't matter what we want," Two explained over One's gagging noises. "We have a responsibility to the world to be back together before the Netherhells attack again."

"Not to mention a responsibility to not be personally sliced and diced."

"I see. You held hands to defeat the smaller darkness," he added thoughtfully.

"We can't keep doing that."

"Why not?"

"We can't stand each other."

"Again, why not?" He spread his hands. "Are you not both you? Do you dislike yourself so?"

"I like myself just fine," One broke in before Two could answer. "It's *her* I can't stand. Bossy, uptight, neat freak!"

"Lazy, lascivious—you don't care about anything but yourself!"

"Lady Wizards, please." Stepping over a sleeping bodyguard to stand between them, the doctor looked from one to the other and sighed. "What happened to make you dislike yourself so?"

Dr. Bineeni's consultation room was as full of books and scrolls and candles and jars as his inner sanctum, but it also held a wide chaise lounge. Magdelene-two created a second and the wizards—wearing identical apprehensive expressions—lay down.

"All right." Settling himself in the room's only chair, the doctor picked up a slate and a piece of chalk. "Let's start with some stream of consciousness. I'll begin a phrase and you will finish it with the first thing that comes into your head. You," a finger pointed toward Magdelene-one, "will respond first and then you will alternate responses. Are you ready?"

"Sure. I guess."

"With great power comes great . . . ?"

"Booty!"

Her chaise lounge collapsed.

"Hey! It was the first word that came into my head!"

"No surprise!"

"Lady Wizards! Please. Let's try something else. What is the last thing you remember before this happened."

"I went to bed."

"Alone?"

"Yes. I'd just got back from Venitcia and I was tired."

"Venitcia?"

"A city." Two frowned, trying to remember.

"And you were there because?"

"I don't know."

The doctor turned to One, who shrugged. "You got me, Doc."

"This is important." Dr. Bineeni pushed his glasses up his

nose. "I will begin the thought, I want you to finish it. I went to Venitcia because . . . ?"

"Someone asked for my help."

"Our help."

Right hand gripping the rail with white-knuckled fingers, Magdelene straightened and wiped her mouth on the back of her left. "Did I happen to mention how much I hate boats?"

"You did." Trying not to smile, Antonio handed her a waterskin. "And then you called a wind to speed our passage, and then, if I'm not mistaken, you mentioned it again." He waited until she drank, then reached out and gently caressed her cheek. "Did I happen to mention how grateful I am that you would not allow this hatred to keep you from helping my people?"

"You did." Leaning into his touch, Magdelene all but purred. Not even the constant churning of her stomach could dull her appreciation of a beautiful, dark-eyed man. She liked to think that she'd have agreed to help regardless of who the Venitcia town council had sent to petition her, but she was just as glad that they'd hedged their bets by playing to her known weakness.

Until he'd climbed the path to the turquoise house on the hill, Antonio had thought he'd been sent on a fool's errand—that the most powerful wizard in the world was a legend, a story told by wandering bards. Told *enthusiastically* by bards who'd wandered in the right direction. Magdelene had always been partial to men who made music.

And to those who actually made an effort to seek her out.

"My village was built many, many years ago on the slopes of an ancient volcano, a volcano that has recently begun to stir. My people cannot leave a place that has been home to them for generations."

"Cannot?"

"Will not," Antonio had admitted, smiling, and Magdelene *was lost.*

"We're close," he told her, tucking her safely in the curve of his arm as the boat rolled. "That is the smoke of the volcano. When we round this headland, we'll see Venitcia. . . .

When they rounded the headland, they saw steam rising off the water in a billowing cloud as a single lava stream continued to make its way to the sea. There was no town. No terraced orchards. No temples. No wharves. No livestock. No people.

The captain took his vessel as close as he dared, then Magdelene and Antonio took the small boat to shore. It took them a while to find a safe place to land and then a while longer to walk back to the town. Antonio said nothing the entire time.

Magdelene laid her palm on the warm ground, on the new ground, so much higher than it had been. "It happened just days after you left. Long before you found me. It was fast—ash began to fall and then the rim of the crater collapsed. The town was buried."

"How . . . ?"

"The lava told me." It had been bragging actually. She left that part out.

Antonio walked to the edge of the crust and stared down into the last river of molten rock. "Is everyone dead?"

"Yes."

He sighed, brushed a fall of dark hair back off his face, and half turned; just far enough to smile sadly at her. "It wasn't your fault," he said.

Before Magdelene could stop him, he fell gracefully forward and joined his people in death.

Until that moment, she hadn't even considered that it might be her fault.

"I didn't take it seriously enough."

"I should have hurried."

"You called a wind to fill the sails of the boat," Dr. Bineeni reminded them gently.

"That was for my comfort," Two said bitterly. "Not for Venitcia."

Sitting with her back against the wall, legs tucked up against her chest, One wiped her cheeks on her knees. "I was too late."

The doctor shook his head. "It wasn't your fault. Antonio was right."

"Antonio is dead."

"Yes. But he made his choice. You have to let that go." Looking from one to the other, he spread his hands. "You can't raise the dead."

"Actually, I can."

Dr. Bineeni blinked. Then he remembered to breathe. "You can?"

"If the flesh is still in a condition for the spirit to wear it," Two amended.

"Although I sort of promised Death I'd stop," One sighted. "It screws up her accounting."

"So, given the manner of his death, you couldn't bring Antonio back."

"No."

"Nor any of his people."

"No."

"But if I'd known," Two insisted, "I could have stopped it."

"So many things I could stop if I knew," One agreed.

"But I don't know. Because all I do is lie in the sun and have a good time."

The doctor's brows rose. "All *you* do?"

"All I *did*." Two's lips were pressed into a thin disapproving line as she nodded toward her double. "All *she* does. I recognize my responsibilities."

"But without her, you can't fulfill them." He rubbed his upper lip with a chalk-stained finger as he studied his slate. "I have one final question."

One scooted forward to the edge of the lounge. "then you can fix us?"

"No. Then you can fix yourself."

"If I'm going to fix myself," One muttered, "why'd I have to come see you."

Dr. Bineeni ignored her. "You have to learn to like yourself again."

"Myself, yes. Her . . ."

". . . no," Two finished, lip curled.

"We'll see." He sat back, glanced from one to the other, and said quietly, "You have, in your house, a flight of stairs that descends to the Netherhells. Why?"

One snorted. "It's convenient."

"Convenient? To have demons emerge out of your basement?"

"Well, it's more of a subbasement, but yeah."

"Why?"

"So that I know where they are," Two interjected before One could answer. "The demon princes gain power by slaughter. You don't want them running around the world unopposed."

"No, I don't." As the silence lengthened, he added, "Legends say there were once six demon princes, but the most powerful wizard in the world stood between the mighty Kan'Kon and the slaughter he craved, and now there are five. Mourn for Antonio, mourn for his people, but do not define the rest of your life by his loss."

Although she had the boiling oil ready at the top of the stairs, Kali stepped gratefully aside as a single pop of displaced air heralded the return of her mistress. The clothing suggested that only Magdelene-one had returned, but then she noted the purposeful stride and the light of battle in the wizard's eyes and the demon-housekeeper gave a heavy sigh of relief.

Even given that the light of battle was more accurately a light of extreme annoyance.

"Mistress, they are very close."

"I can see that," Magdelene noted as the bone spearhead came through the door. Grasping the handle, she flung it open and smiled at the demon attempting to free his weapon. "Hi. I'm back."

It froze. Those members of the demonic horde pushing up the

stairs behind it who were within the sound of her voice, froze as well.

From deep within the bowels of the Earth, a fell voice snarled, "What's the holdup!"

"She's back."

Silence. One moment. Two. Then: "Oh, crap."

The demon at the top of the stairs curled a lipless mouth into what might have been a conciliatory smile.

"It it's any consolation," Magdelene told it, raising a hand, "you'll be at the top of the pile."

A moment later, the stairs were clear, although the bouncing continued for some time. Magdelene waited until the moaning and the swearing and the recriminations died down, then she leaned out over the threshold. "Don't make me come down there."

The lower door slammed emphatically shut, the vibration rocking her back on her heels.

"Temper, temper," she muttered, stepping back into the hall.

"I am pleased you are yourself again, Mistress." Lifting the vat of oil, Kali carried it into the kitchen. "I am happy the doctor was able to heal you."

"He got me moving forward again," Magdelene allowed, following her housekeeper. "Although I *am* the most powerful wizard in the world and I probably could have figured it out eventually on my own."

"We had time for neither probably or eventually, Mistress."

"True. I guess I needed someone to get into my head."

Kali stared at the wizard for a long moment, then surrendered to temptation. "That's a change," she said.

Melanie Rawn

Once you've put in some time as an editor, you develop an instinct for who can and can't write, even when you are reading a manuscript that, good as it is, would not be the best way in which to launch a talented newcomer's career. So when Sharon Jarvis—a longtime friend who had abandoned her editorial desk to become an agent—sent me a manuscript by an unpublished author she was pretty excited about, I was eager to read it. Sharon was right. This unknown, whose name just happened to be Melanie Rawn, was a terrific writer. But the subject matter of this novel was very tricky. I knew that it would be a mistake to start Mel's career with this book. So, naturally, I asked the question: "Does she have anything else?"

What she had was a story that immediately grabbed my attention, and made me forget all the rush projects I had to get through that week. The title of this wonderful novel was, of course, *Dragon Prince*. And the rest, as they say, is history. When *Dragon Prince* hit the book-store shelves in December 1988, it was an immediate best seller. And it was only the beginning. Melanie's fantasy novels have won her a huge following around the world, and I'm sure her many devoted readers will enjoy the fantasy twist on history she offers in "The Sacrifice."

—SG

THE SACRIFICE
Melanie Rawn

May 29–30, 1431
Rouen, France

THE cell was small, about twenty feet in diameter, hexagonal in shape, cold and dark and damp. There was no furniture but a few wooden stools for the guards, and a bed that was nothing more than a hay-filled mat atop a rough wooden pallet. There were two narrow slits in the wall, for ventilation only; they let in no light. He had been told of this, and had brought a large taper from his own stores. Made of fine beeswax, not spluttering tallow, it burned with a peculiar soft brightness, as it would have on the high altar for which it had been made. Now, it showed him not the gold plate and jeweled vessels of the mass, but the prisoner. A girl in men's clothing. She was nineteen years, four months, and twenty-two days old.

Henry Beaufort gestured the guards out of the cell with one gloved hand. "Think you that, chained as she is, she can do us any harm?" he asked the one who frowned an objection. "Leave us."

"Yes, your grace." The guard was not happy about it, nor were the others, but one did not gainsay the Cardinal of England and a son of a Royal Duke to boot.

The door clanked closed. He turned his gaze upon the prisoner, who sat up on her bed.

"I would rise, your grace, and beg to make my respects, but as you see—" She shrugged, and her chains rattled. It was obvious she could not stand.

"*De rien, ma fille,*" he murmured. It was of no consequence. He had more important things to do than allow his ring to be kissed. Before he could say what he had come to say, however, she spoke again, eagerly.

"Please, your grace, have you come to hear my confession? Have you come to celebrate mass for me?"

Leaving aside the absurdity of a Prince of the Church saying the Holy Office for an illiterate French peasant girl, it amused him to find her so continually single-minded. She asked for this again and again and again, and was always denied it. She must know she would be denied now. So he ignored the questions and said instead, "There have been no more incidents, I trust."

"Incidents?" She looked puzzled.

"The guards," he explained gently. Three of them had attacked her in an attempt at rape; she had fought them off so strenuously that they would have scars for life—and it would take a while for clumps of their hair and beards to grow back. Their chagrin would change to pride soon enough, Beaufort knew, and the scars become battle-honored because of who had given them. "They have left you alone?"

Incredibly, she blushed. "Y–yes, your grace."

"*Trés bien.* My lord of Warwick gave specific instructions."

"Not because of any tenderness for me, I think," she replied with a shrewd glance. "He wants a living head to chop off at the neck."

"I am pleased to find you so perceptive." Odd to think that she could still believe she would escape the fire.

Quite unexpectedly, she said, "You speak French well, for a goddam."

Amused again by her use of the nickname for Englishmen, he almost smiled. "I am half French, in truth. My mother was a very beautiful woman from Picardy. Very beautiful," he repeated softly. "Even her tomb mentions how lovely she was. I used to watch the courtiers stare at her—even in the later years, when she was fifty and more, when she was older than I am now." He paused, studying her. "She had power over men. So do you. Yet you're not even pretty."

"No, your grace," she replied quite seriously.

He watched her eyes for a moment—large, fine eyes, remarkable in their clarity and the only claim she had to beauty—then said abruptly, "I have noted that during your trial you spoke of preferring to have your head cut off rather than say something you had no permission to say. Why is that, Joan? You know what the penalty is for heretics: fire. Ah, you see? You blanch even now at the mention of it. It is not death you fear, but the manner of your death. You all but invite your judges to slice off your head, yet the very word 'fire' makes you start like a doe. You are afraid—nay, terrified—of the fire. Why?" Without giving her time to answer, he continued, "Is it because the fire will burn you to ashes, and there will be no blood? Blood must be spoiled, mustn't it, for the sacrifice to be complete."

"Sacrifice, your grace?"

She was brilliant, he reflected, at imitating innocence. "I am a learned man, Joan. I have read and studied since my earliest youth, for that seemed to me to be the only way I could make something of myself in a world that despises bastards—especially royal ones. Having no talent for the sword, not being a man of my hands as my brother John of Somerset was—may God assoil him—I decided I must use my brain. And I have used it well, Joan. I counsel the Holy Father. I have been Chancellor of England—and will be again, I daresay, despite my cousin of Gloucester."

He stopped then, arched a brow at her, and almost smiled. "I know where you come from," he continued softly. "Lorraine, out of which no good can come—as the saying has it. A country rife with witches. I know of your fountain and your faerie tree—the Charmed Tree of the Faerie of Bourlement, where nearby there is an enchanted spring. I know that your mother had dealings with—"

"That is not true!" she cried. "We are good Christian folk! I, too, know what is said of my home, and what the superstitions are, but I do not believe them!"

"And I do not believe you," he told her. "Unlearned and untaught as you are, did you know of the prophecies? Years ago Marie Robine foresaw a maid in armor, and even Merlin, who had much to prophecy about my own house, told of a virgin from the forests of Lorraine who would come to the aid of France. Have you listened to such things, Joan, and decided to use them to your own ends?"

"No!"

"I do not believe you," he said again, still very gently. "How else but by magical arts could you have known about the sword buried beneath the altar at St. Catherine-de-Fierbois?"

The frown cleared from her face; evidently mention of some specific thing, something as real as the sword, gave her ground to stand upon.

"It was God's Will that I find and bear that sword—"

"—God's Will as told to you by your Voices? Or by faerie spirits?"

"It was St. Michael, and St. Catherine, and St. Margaret—"

"My mother's name was Catherine," he commented almost idly.

"*En nom Dieu!*" she exclaimed. "Is it your mother about to die?"

"Perhaps she burns even now, with my father," he mused. "They sinned, you know. As have I. As have I. . . ." He looked straight at her, then away. "My daughter, also named Joan, is only a little older than you."

"Your grace, what has this to do—"

"*Passez outré,*" he interrupted, mocking her with her own phrase repeated so many times during her trial. "Shall I tell you why not one drop of your blood will spill on French soil? Shall I tell you, Joan, why you will burn?"

She paled again, and her chains rattled faintly, as if she shivered. "I—I am tired, your grace, I would sleep, by your leave."

"Soon you will sleep for all eternity. You will die, Joan. Unconfessed, unshriven, and unassoiled by God and His Saints. What is more, you will have failed the pathetic lackwit you call your king. Shall I tell you how you will fail?"

"May I not Confess, your grace, and be Absolved, and hear Mass before I die? I beg it of you, please!"

He started to answer negatively, then considered. "If you do as you have been told—"

"I will not put on women's garments," she warned, "and I will not lie and say my Voices are not from God."

Stubborn, he thought. Then: *But why not? Eh bien, perhaps I should allow her to hear Mass after all. This blood sacrifice is a pagan thing, and if she is meant to be what I think they mean her to be, would not receiving the Body and Blood of Christ make her unacceptable?*

"You have at least the virtue of consistency," he replied at last. "But, come, allow me to explain your life to you—and your death."

Learned as he was, he could not quite fathom his own purpose for telling her of his deductions and inferences, of his research and his reasoning. Perhaps it was because to speak of such things finally, and to their subject, would be a relief to his mind. Especially after so many months of enduring that *canaille* Cauchon. He did not understand himself in this matter, but he spoke to her anyway.

"Prophecy has it that you will save France. In my country, our king *is* England. Thus, to save France, you must save your king. And to do this you must die. Bloodily."

"Your grace?" Bewilderment again. *Bon Dieu,* she did it well.

"Silence," he said. "I will come to that in a moment. Nowhere is it written or sung—"

"I'm sorry, your grace—'sung?' I don't underst—"

"I ask you to be silent, *ma fille.* The ancient bards have much to teach us—and I enjoy music for more than its pleasing sound. No song or story tells of a woman taking a man's place, of a woman taking a *king's* place. Thus you have abandoned women's ways and garb. You ride like a man, war like a man, wield a sword like a man—"

"I never killed! Never!"

"Should there be any further interruptions, Joan, I will gag you with my own glove. When I wish you to speak, I will ask you a question. Is that understood?"

"Y–yes, your grace."

"To continue. You have scorned all that a woman ought rightly to do, refusing even to consider marriage when most girls your age are already mothers. What could this imposture be but an attempt to make yourself into a man?

"As for your Voices—let us examine their identities. St. Michael the warrior Archangel, champion of God's people—surely he is no fit saint for a woman to revere as her patron."

Sparks of defiance lit her eyes, and for a moment he thought she would protest that she could not help who had spoken to her. But her lips stayed stubbornly closed. He admired her self-control.

"Then there is St. Margaret, Virgin and Martyr—they attempted to burn her, yet the flames left her untouched. A cauldron of boiling water was similarly useless. Finally, she was beheaded. Do you consider yourself worthy of a saint's death such as hers? And lastly you claim St. Catherine, also Virgin, also Martyr—condemned to die on the wheel, which at her touch was miraculously destroyed. My mother's name was Catherine. No virgin, she, and no martyr. I have something that belonged to her, I carry it always with me."

And from the folds of his scarlet robes he brought out a small leather purse, soft with age, stippled here and there with the remains of gold tooling. From the purse he drew a ring; it had not belonged to his mother.

"That is mine!" the girl cried. "My parents gave it me!"

"Do you see the Catherine wheels here on this purse, in gold? Is this what you wish, Joan? Anything but the fire?"

"Give me back my ring!"

"Let us not forget that in the end, St. Catherine's head was cut off, and her blood flowed."

"Please, your grace—"

"Would you rather have it than your sword?"

"My sword is broken," she whispered, bending her head.

"Yes. I had heard that. An ancient sword, found in a chapel built by Charles Martel. How did you know it was there? Not, I think, because any person living told you. It was the Voices, was it not, the Voices you claim to be those of saints, who have told you things you should not have known." He ticked off the points on his fingers—long, elegant fingers, like his mother's. "You knew that Sir John Fastolf had defeated the French at Rouvray. You knew you would be captured before Midsummer's Day. You knew you would be wounded at Orléans but not unto death. You knew where the sword would be hidden. And, most amazing of all—for I have heard reports of the Dauphin and he is a poor excuse for a prince—you recognized Charles at once in a roomful of people determined not to reveal his identity. But above all else, you knew you will surely die. You told the Dauphin so, did you not? That he must make the most of you, for you would only last one year?"

"Yes," she said dully. "I told him that. It seemed such a long time, then. . . ."

"You survived that which you should not have survived," he went on, replacing the ring in the leather pouch. "Your wound at Orléans. Your wound at Paris. How is this possible?"

"St. Catherine cured me of the wound I took at Orléans."

"And in less than a fortnight, too," he agreed. "Remarkable, yes? And the wound taken at Paris—five days to cure that one, wasn't it? Miraculous, most would say."

"But—you do not say it, Cardinal."

"No, I do not. You survived a leap from Beaurevoir Tower, a structure fully seventy feet high. How?"

"It was very wrong of me to do that," she said earnestly, looking him in the eye once again. "St. Catherine told me almost every day that I should not do it, and that God would help me—" Her jaw set, and her fine eyes sparked once more. "But I would rather have died than fall into the hands of the English!"

"Why? Because you knew you would burn, with no blood spilled?"

"Blood! Blood!" she exclaimed, exasperated, as if she truly did not know what he meant. "Why do you speak always of blood?"

"Do you remember what day it was that the Dauphin was absurdly crowned in the cathedral at Rheims? Of course you do. Sunday, the seventeenth day of July. There was a full moon that morning." When she looked blank, he snapped, "It was not God who consecrated Charles, but the devil. Your so-called king was ordained by witchcraft, not Holy Scripture."

She looked horrified, and crossed herself. But then the peasant shrewdness returned to her face, and she said, "You have made a study of such things, your grace. You know more about them than ever I did and ever I could. May I ask 'why' of *you?*"

"You dissemble, Joan. You were born in a land of witches, of faerie trees and fountains, of secret rituals and foul heresies. Your actions have betrayed you. I shall give but one example. When you put your armor in the church at St. Denis, you caused candles to be lighted, and said that the melted wax from these candles should fall on the heads of little children, so that they would know happiness." He eyed her disdainfully. "Did you dare ask for black candles, Joan, or was that going too far?"

"That is not true! I have denied that! I never did or said such things!"

"Witnesses say that you did. And you continually assert that all you have done was by the command of God, speaking to you through your Voices! *Alors, ma fille,* as to the nature of these Voices . . . why should saints appear to such as you? Ignorant, unlettered, uneducated, of the commonest common blood—what smallest thing about you is worthy to receive the notice of such holy beings? My answer is this: that these Voices were not saints at all, but manifestations of Satan and his minions, and that you are the tool of a false religion."

"I am not!" she cried. "*Nom Dieu,* I swear that all I have done—"

"But we have not yet explored the meaning of these things," he said, as calm as she was agitated. "I will educate you. Long ago, my ancestor, the great William, Duke of Normandy, claimed England as his right. And the blood of Harald the usurper spilled onto the ground from an arrow through his eye. Years later, William's son, also a king, died—also arrow-shot. They say he bled for miles as they carried him home in a cart. Another king, for whom I am named, ordered that an archbishop be slain most bloodily—though they say he was careful with his words on the subject, was that Henry. A hundred years ago the Scot Wallace was hanged by the neck, cut down whilst still living, and his bloody entrails drawn out of his body as he watched—and The

Bruce had his kingship. The father of my grandfather, also a king, was killed as well—but without a mark upon his body, without a drop of blood. So someone else must naturally be sacrificed in his stead so that his son, the third Edward—"

"Your grace," she interrupted impatiently, "I do not understand this talk of blood and sacrifices. What has this to do with me?"

"*You* are the sacrifice." There, he had said it plain at last, this thing he feared. Not a sign of his turmoil showed outwardly; fifty and more years as a Plantagenet bastard had taught him facial discretion first of all.

Yet her eyes—she saw something, he knew it. Settling himself, he went on, "Why else do you fear the fire so? Your blood must touch the soil of France for your death to have any meaning. That is the ancient belief, is it not? *Alors*, why am I asking you, who have known it all this time? You, who used the prophecies and have the powers of a witch—do you know they called my mother that? Even my own father, or so the chroniclers would have it, named her witch and whore—though I never believed it of him, he loved her too long and too well—"

Very suddenly—as if God's golden finger touched her—the candle in his hand illumined the peasant girl, and she became beautiful. "I see," she breathed. "Oh, yes, now I see."

"See what?" he jeered. "Your so-called saints? Perhaps God Himself?"

"Only the truth, my lord. And it is all so simple."

"Explain yourself, girl!"

"It is only this: Why me, and not you?" Sitting straight up on her cot, eagerness lighting her plain face, she nearly laughed aloud. "Oh, do you not see it? You have everything—lands, titles, wealth, royal blood, power and influence, fame—all but that which you want most." She leaned forward, her hands clasped together, her eyes shining. "What you lack is the certainty of God. You do not think yourself worthy in His Eyes—and you a Cardinal of His Church!"

"No more. I will hear no more."

She spoke on, enraptured with her own understanding. "Only

have faith, your grace. I do not know why I was chosen. I said during my trial that if those who asked for the signs and did not receive them were not worthy of them, then I could not help it. It is not for you or me to decide, your grace. Do you think I asked for my Voices? I was but thirteen when first I heard them, and for three years I tried with all my might *not* to hear them. I do not know why they chose me and not you. I am sorry for you, and I wish with all my heart that you could know the joy I have known."

She dared pity him? *Him?*

"But now it appears that I shall die for my king and for France. God has not deserted me. I am content."

"You *will* die," he rasped, breathing with difficulty, and it took every bit of courage he possessed to meet her translucent gaze. "You will burn until there is nothing left of you but fine gray ash. There will be no blood sacrifice. Your death will go unconsecrated by any power ever known."

He went to the door and called for the guard, then turned back to face her where she sat on her cot—so serene, so certain. "France will become what it was ever meant to be: a province of England, as in the days of Henry FitzEmpress and Eleanor d'Aquitaine. Your worthless Dauphin Charles will never rule here, never. You will fail of your purpose, and fail your failure of a king."

She appeared unmoved. Her voice was soft, compassionate, as she asked, "Had you thought, your grace, that although God has sent me here, to this time and this place, to do this thing for France, perhaps He has also sent *you* here to be the means of my death?"

"Thank me for it," he snapped, "when the flames char the flesh from your bones."

And he left her alone with her Voices.

Well before dawn the next morning—he slept not at all that night—the Cardinal of England summoned a certain man to his apartments.

"Take heed, my son. She is to be burned. Completely and utterly annihilated by fire. Not one drop of her blood shall touch the soil of France. Do you understand us?"

"Yes, m'lord—I mean, y'r grace—y'r worship—"

"Enough. It is enough that you understand. Leave us. Do your work well, and God shall reward you."

A little while later he was looking out upon the square of St. Ouen. Platforms were on either side of the south door of the church; the Bishop of Beauvais and the rest of the clergy occupied one, and the girl stood on the other. Within the cemetery there was ample space for a large crowd to collect on the gently sloping ground facing the south door of the church. There would be plenty of witnesses: noble ones to attest the truth to kings and princes; clerical ones to swear to the Church; common ones to spread word among the people. There would be no mystery here, no magic.

The herald named him for the crowd. He could hear the capital letters.

"The Most Reverend Father in Christ, Henry, by Divine Permission Priest of the Holy Roman Church, the Cardinal of England."

He slipped a hand into a pocket of his robes, closing his fingers around the purse that had been his mother's, containing the ring that had been the girl's. Cauchon had given the ring to him. He would give it to his daughter when he returned to England—and suddenly he longed for England with all his soul.

The Maid was looking at him—he could swear she was staring him straight in the eyes as she called out in a rough, ringing voice, "I ask you, priests of God, to please say a mass for my soul's salvation—"

Cauchon muttered angrily.

"May I have a crucifix, please? Please—on a level with my eyes, so that I may see it—"

Someone—he would never know who—held up a plain wooden crosier, with the Suffering Christ carved on it by a crude and awkward hand. Thus had the greatest King of all died, his blood spilling on the earth. Hers must not.

The faggots were heaped above her knees now. By rights the crowd ought to have been cheering. Oddly enough, he could hear nothing but the quiet measured beat of his own heart. He felt calm, patient, as if waiting for he knew not what—not the smoke and the flames and the stench of seared flesh, but something else. It was the sort of interior stillness he experienced sometimes just before Communion. Just before the miracle and the magic of the wine and bread becoming the Blood and Body of Christ. He heard nothing at those times, and he heard nothing now. He'd always thought that perhaps God stopped up his ears for that little while so that His servant might hear His Words more clearly.

But God had never spoken to him.

She was speaking again, proud and defiant. "My Voices *did* come from God, and everything I have done was by God's order!"

"Silence her!" Cauchon hissed.

It was then that he realized he did not hear the bishop the way he had heard the girl. He had seen the man's lips move, and knew what words he spoke. But he truly heard only Joan.

Or perhaps God, speaking in Joan's voice.

He stared at the small plain face, the short sturdy frame, the hair shaved now where it had been worn in a man's style just above her ears, and to him she appeared well-nigh sexless. Male by appearance and clothing, male in warlike habit—but also female, assuming the guise and greatness of a warrior over the small soft breasts and gently curved hips of a woman. She ought to have borne babies, not arms. But even though he knew her to be female, still with her man's clothes and her unflinching gaze as the pyre was lit, she was to him neither woman nor man.

But certainly more of a man than that puling fool she had seen crowned King of France.

You do not deserve her, Charles, he thought. *And you will not have her, not as you and she intended. There will be no blood to seep into French soil. There will be no Sacrifice.*

He could hear again, but only the hiss and crackle of the flames. She was still staring at him. Nearby, Cauchon leaned eagerly forward, avid as a scavenging crow for carrion. White smoke began to rise, obscuring her from view. He heard her cry out to God.

Smoke draped the roof and walls of the church like white wedding garments. But the smell of the marriage feast was the stink of her own scorched flesh.

At length, she was nothing but ash. He left the platform with his fellow priests, wondering if any of them would heed her final request and say a mass for her soul.

As he walked from the square, he heard them. The voices.

"Did you see it? In the flames—"

"Writ with fire!"

"The name of Jesus, right above her head—"

"And the dove, did you see the dove fly from the pyre?"

"A saint, they have murdered a saint—"

He steeled his jaw and strode away.

He was writing to his daughter, inquiring about the health of his grandson and namesake, when Bedford burst into his apartments.

"You haven't heard?" demanded the duke. "That stupid, *stupid* man! He ruined everything! We'll never be rid of her now!"

"Calm yourself, nephew," he said. This man was his least-favorite relation but for that colossal moron, Gloucester. Bedford invariably ground his teeth when reminded of their kinship—but never dared insult him to his face. Not the Cardinal of England. "I recognize the 'her' of this, for we have been solely concerned with the wretched girl for a very long time. But who is the 'he'?"

"The executioner, that's who!" Bedford flung himself onto the crimson cushions padding a window embrasure, but was just as quickly up again and pacing. "He tried and tried, but he couldn't burn either her heart or her guts! So do you know what he did with them? Threw them into the Seine, that's what!"

Leaning back in his chair, he rested his gaze on his daughter's name—rendered in the French spelling, in his precise cleric's hand, on the finest parchment. *Jehanne.* But it was not his daughter's sweet face he saw, a face so like his long-dead mother's that sometimes his heart caught in his throat on seeing her smile. It was the earnest, unlovely face of a different *Jehanne* that rose up before him.

Her heart bled into the Seine, the great Mother of Waters that bleeds into the soil. From Normandy to Bourgogne her heart blood will mix with the lifeblood of France.

"Her heart! Her guts!" The duke's voice intruded. "By Our Lady, what parts of her could he have picked to better effect? To put heart and guts into the French army and the French king, that's what they'll say when they find out!" Bedford made a few more circuits of the room, then spun round and spat, "Well? What have you to say to this, *Uncle?*"

Beaufort regarded his kinsman with concealed loathing. *Your father, my half brother and late king, would be nauseated by you. You are an idiot and a fool, and a disgrace to the royal blood we share. And you will fail, Nephew, because of what you are. I am neither an idiot nor a fool—yet my failure has been the greater. And my failure has come about because of God, Who allowed her blood to spill as His Son's was spilt. Were it mere symbol, as Bedford believes, still it is the most powerful symbol in the world. Does it mark me heretic, to believe it is more than that?*

"I say," Beaufort murmured, "that dead is dead, and let that end it."

But what he was thinking was, *I say that we had best resign ourselves to a brief and unhappy rule over France. For now she has a true king, crowned and blooded, with the Sacrifice duly made—and there is nothing we can do to change it.*

* * *

Note: Although Cardinal Beaufort's visit to Joan of Arc is of the author's imagining, the details of the prophecies and the events of her life and death are accurate. (She did find the sword at St. Catherine-de-Fierbois; the executioner did find it impossible to burn Joan's heart and entrails, and so threw them into the Seine.) Many years later, Joan's mother appealed to the Vatican to reopen the case, and Joan was exonerated. Canonized in 1920, she is the patron Saint of France.

Beaufort's parents were Katherine de Roet and John of Gaunt,

Duke of Lancaster, son of Edward III. Katherine was John's mistress for many years before a parting of the ways, at which time (according to contemporary chroniclers) he denounced her as a witch. They married in 1397 at Lincoln Cathedral; their four children were legitimated by the Pope and recognized by Richard II. This was the origin of the Wars of the Lancastrian and Yorkist Roses that ended at Bosworth Field in 1485 with the victory of Henry Tudor—a descendant of Katherine de Roet and John of Gaunt through Cardinal Beaufort's brother John, Earl of Somerset.

Deborah J. Ross

Many readers of fantasy and science fiction were brought to the field by reading the works of Marion Zimmer Bradley. Marion's novels about the world of Darkover, first published over forty years ago by my father while he was at Ace, has spawned more fans than almost any fantasy world. Over the decades, many writers have added their own voices to Darkover, but only the most privileged have worked with Marion herself.

Deborah J. Ross, who first published science fiction with DAW under her married name, Deborah Wheeler, is one of those lucky few.

During the last few years of her life, as her health declined, Marion Zimmer Bradley was wise enough to realize that she would no longer be able to continue her writing unaided. It was during this time that she began discussing the *Clingfire* trilogy with her close friend Deborah J. Ross. Now, years after Marion's death, Deborah has made these discussions—saved on hours and hours of tape recordings—a reality by publishing her first Darkover novel, *The Fall of Neskaya,* Book One of The *Clingfire* Trilogy.

It is very important to Deborah that she retain the atmosphere, flavor, politics, and culture of Darkover as closely as possible. Darkover was very important to Marion. She often described it as her "most personal and best-loved work." We have had to say good-bye to Marion, but for those of us who cannot bear to say good-bye to Darkover, Deborah J. Ross carries the torch.

—BW

HEART-HEALER
Deborah J. Ross

AFTERNOON light slanted across the infirmary which occupied most of the ground floor of Heron's cottage. The windows, thick and ancient mullioned glass, had been left half open to admit the freshening breeze. Two iron pots, one for cooking and one for preparing medicines, hung above the patchstone fireplace, and the narrow trestle table which dominated the kitchen corner held distillation apparatus, mortar and pestle for grinding, and scales for measuring. On the bench just inside the door sat an old woman and her two grown daughters, hope and resignation on their faces.

Heron straightened up from listening to the old man's chest. She had conducted her examination as she had been taught in the healers' college at Temple. The stiffness of his limbs and rib cage, the brittle quality of his skin, the wheeze and creak of his lungs, all bespoke a lifetime of unrelenting struggle. Yet he had done well for himself and his family, a kindly man in a land that too often forced men to be harsh.

Were this Temple, or any of the easy southern lands where life followed a far more rational course, Heron's work would be almost done. She would dose him with foxglove, prescribe that his food be prepared without salt, forbid him pickles and sour-cabbage, and order a daily measured amount of wine and gentle walking. He might rally, for the herb had true therapeutic qualities. In all likelihood, the extra care and the easing of his heart would bring some benefit.

But here in the shadow of the Basalt Mountains, men did not fall sick from merely physical causes. Age and hard usage weakened the body and thus allowed the influence of other forces. She already knew his heart was losing its battle with the demands of his aging body. It took no magick to see the swelling in his ankles or feel his thready pulse.

This man before her—this Jem Ryan—would surely die, despite her herbs and advice. Her only hope of saving him was to discover the true nature of his heart.

She went to her cabinet of camphor wood, set with tiny drawers, each one bearing a different symbol. The cabinet had come over the Willow Road from a land so distant she did not know its name.

Heron moistened the fingers of one hand with her tongue and with the other hand slid open the drawer bearing the mark like a running stag, fifth down and third from the right. Inside, in an even smaller box of oak lined with tightly-woven silk, her fingertips met coarse powder, like incompletely burned ash. It was not ash, nor was it one element, and it meant death to any who took more than a pinch of it. She touched her fingers to the underside of her tongue. The familiar bitterness swept through her.

It took only a moment for the powder to take effect. Heron's sense of smell sharpened, changed. She felt as if she were breathing through a long tube. The hairs on her forearms prickled. Then the sensations faded and she turned back to her patient. "I'm going to examine you in a different way," she told him with her best professional smile. "It won't hurt, but it would be better if you not talk until I'm done."

Jem Ryan stared at her, his eyes widening minutely, for he had endured the examination and answered all of her questions in monosyllables or gestures.

Heron settled herself once more on her padded stool and arranged the patient's arms at his sides. The skin on his forearms was deeply tanned, like oiled bronzewood against the milky paleness of his body. The muscles of his chest and shoulders had withered with age, but she could see the traces of the powerful, active man he had once been. She took her first reading, one hand on his left shoulder, the other on the tip of his breastbone, at the angle of the curving ribs. Her hands moved to the second position, two fingers'-width higher and to the left of the breastbone itself, then the hollow between the fourth and fifth ribs.

She lowered her eyes to better concentrate on her inner senses. Her fingertips slid over the old man's skin, finding the anatomical landmarks. His chest rose and fell under her touch.

The pattern began to emerge, built up layer upon layer between her hands. Sometimes she envisioned swirls of colored smoke condensing into a veil calligraphed with the heart's true name. Other times, the heart took the form of a musical phrase or a picture, bright and sudden, in her mind. Jem Ryan—husband and grandfather, a stoic, gentle man who asked no more than to tend his orchards season by season—bore the heart of a wild boar.

Heron smiled as she lifted her hands from his skin. Even knowing him as little as she did, this answer struck her as perfect.

Our bodies are our own, muscles and sinews and nerves, Willet, the old hedge-wizard who had been her final teacher once said, *but not our hearts. We are loaned them for the space of our lives before they return to their true nature. In the south, they know nothing beyond what they can grasp with their own two hands. We of the mountains—*and here he had turned his opalwhite eyes toward the peaks—*we know that only truth can call to truth.*

To call a man back from the edge of death, to heal a dying heart, she must speak to its true nature and form, not the outer shell of the flesh.

Wordlessly, she went back to her cabinet and selected herbs sacred to the spirit of the boar. Murmuring words of praise and power, she mixed them into a cup of apple wine. It was her last bottle, but the resonance was far better, the catalyzing effect upon the herbs more profound, than if she had used ordinary grape wine or even ale. And for a boar spirit, water would be unthinkable.

Boar, O most puissant boar whose eyes are carbuncles in the night and whose feet trample the unworthy! O Boar, symbol of courage and fidelity, abide with this man! Strengthen his human heart, sustain his human dreams. O Boar, remain with us this day! Smiling again, she offered Jem Ryan the cup. His flicker of suspicion vanished as the sweet heady aroma of wine and herbs

reached his nose. Grinning broadly, he lifted the cup in silent sa-
lute—

—not only to her, but to the spirit which now bent its massive
bristled head, tusks gleaming like mother-of-pearl—

—and downed it in a single gulp.

"Well-ah," he said, running his tongue over his lips to catch
the last droplets, "if this is a fair taste of yer medicine, lass, ye'll
hear no argument from me."

Heron laughed and took the empty cup. " 'Tis a different cure
for each, so don't go making promises to anyone else. I'll be sending along a packet of dried herbs now and another in a month or
so, to be mixed with apple wine, or cherry if you have any, and
taken every evening."

"Ah, and won't the wife be loving that?" His eyes twinkled.

"By my orders!" Heron said, laughing again. "Or I will know
the reason why."

The room fell silent after Jem Ryan's family had taken him
away. Heron noted the skepticism in the eyes of the daughters,
the wife's disapproving scowl. But even a blind woman could have
seen the rising color in his cheeks.

Sometimes, the spirit of the heart turned away from her, and
all she had to offer was comfort. Occasionally, the human heart
was too frail to hold its true nature. Sometimes, the end came
blessedly quickly. Sometimes, the family might whisper a plea.

I don't do that, Heron would answer.

A death with dignity, that's all we ask, they would say, tearing
at her with their basalt eyes. *Who is to say it isn't a blessing?*

But not today. Not Jem Ryan. He would live to see another
blossoming of his apple trees, another harvest festival. Well,
Heron thought as she tidied up her workroom, maybe he
wouldn't dance at the festival, but she didn't think he would
mind. She might well discover a barrel of his best apple wine
upon her doorstep on a frosty autumn morning.

Heron poured out the brew which had been cooling in the larger
iron pot into a filtering apparatus and washed her hands in the

basin. It sat, along with scrubbing brushes and a precious bar of honey soap, on a wide, worn shelf in the far corner of her kitchen. Pots of garlic sets, aloe, and false-ginger lined the windowsill. Beyond, in the tiny garden, twilight glimmered on the rows of medicinal herbs.

She wanted nothing more than to sit outside for a few minutes, in the seat one of her patients had carved at the foot of her rowan tree, inhaling the deep green scents. Yet she had several hours of work before she could put away her laboratory and cleanse the kitchen for cooking.

Using a scrap of chamois to insulate her fingers, she reached into her pantry, past the strings of beads and carved bone, and took out a wedge of cheese left over from her morning meal. It would be enough to keep her going, although she was afraid that this evening, like too many others of late, she would finish too tired to do more than crawl up the ladder to her sleeping loft and fall asleep in her clothes.

Heron was yawning and had stopped feeling hungry by the time she finished bottling the last of the feverbane. Unlike willow bark tea, which was simple enough for even a patient to prepare, the feverbane took days of attention to imbue it with not only pharmacological but magickal properties. If she could have done so safely, she would have waited until the morning to finish.

She wondered, not for the first time, if she ought not to look for an apprentice. But there had not been room in her life for another person since Darrin left.

What is it to be—this nonsense or me? he'd stormed.

She had never really had a choice. Healing was all she knew, and once the magick had sung in her bones, she could never have lived anywhere else. Darrin had gone south, along the Willow Road. She thought of him sometimes, on long winter nights when her body ached with exhaustion.

Outside, full night had fallen, and the breeze through the partly opened windows sent shivers along her skin. Oonat, her brindled cat, jumped through the window just as she leaned over to close it. She hoped the cat had caught his own dinner, for all she wanted at the moment was sleep, but then, as Oonat rubbed his sleek length against her legs, purring loudly, she relented. Dinner for both of them, then.

"What would I do without you to take care of me?"

The cat paused in his attentions, tufted ears pricked in the direction of the front door, and one forepaw raised in midstride. "*Meerow?*"

Heron felt the tension in the cat's body. Oonat might not use human speech, but his instincts were infallible. He had woken her a full hour before the earthquake three years ago, batting her face with sheathed claws until she stumbled down the loft ladder and out into the garden.

Heart racing now, she went to the door, placed her palm upon the age-darkened oak. Listened. And heard nothing, not even the coo of a night-dove or the call of a neighbor's child. She held her breath and reached for the latch. A moment passed, and then another. Then, like a storm breaking on the heights, sound returned. She heard the distant bark of a dog, voices muffled by distance, the hum of the village settling down for the night.

She was about to return to her meal preparations when she noticed that Oonat had not relaxed. The hair along his spine stood up in a ridge and his eyes looked twice their normal size. Head lowered, each paw placed precisely in front of the other, he approached the door.

That settled it. Heron grasped the latch and yanked it open. A man, still as death, fell across her feet.

She stood there for a long moment, looking down at him incredulously. Patients came to her or were brought by their families, sometimes literally carried, but inert bodies did not just appear. Surely she would have heard if someone had dragged him here, or if he had crawled on his own.

As best she could tell with her shadow falling across him, he looked to be a strongly built man in his prime, a head or so taller than she and broad in the shoulders. He wore the sort of loose tunic and leggings common in both village and farm. Hair, glinting red-gold where the light from inside her cottage touched it, tumbled over his face, masking his features.

He wasn't dead. She knew that from the warmth of his cheek against her bare ankle. Nor would Oonat have kept up that low, barely audible growl for a corpse. Heron sighed again and bent over, mentally apologizing to her back muscles for how they were going to feel in the morning after dragging this fellow inside. She laid the unconscious man beside the hearth and rolled him on his back.

He was younger than she'd thought, though an odd redness, like sunburn, etched a mask on his face. His pulse, though strong, was slow. She touched skin moist with a fine sheen and fever-hot, lips dry and slack. She rolled back his eyelids to reveal irises the color of the sea. His pupils contracted symmetrically to light. His skull felt intact, his spine supple.

Heron opened the laces of his tunic. Healed, whitened scars marked his upper arms, one on his ribs. Sword cuts, she guessed, touching the calluses on his palms. He wore a pendant, a piece of polished rose quartz, drilled with a hole and looped with a leather cord. She placed her ear against the almost hairless skin of his chest to listen better. Air whispered through the delicate tissues of the lungs. The heart, like distant thunder, beat too slow, too strong.

There was nothing Heron could point to, other than the elevated body heat, no sign by which she might diagnose what was wrong with this man. Yet she knew as surely as she herself breathed, that he was dying.

She turned away, looking back out the kitchen window into the cave of darkness which was her garden. At night, the well-known shapes took on sinister forms; it became a place she did not know, a place in which anything could happen.

She was tired, that was all, and had been on edge all evening, filled with fanciful dark imaginings. She was tempted to wait, to eat something, to rest, before finishing her examination. But the delay might cost her the small measure of determination she now had.

Heron went to the cabinet, touched a fingerful of powder

beneath her tongue, positioned her hands, and closed her eyes. Bitterness washed through her, quickly fading.

As she touched his chest, the sensation of lightless space engulfed her. She fought the rising urge to break off contact, to run away. When she opened her eyes, the coppery glow from the banked embers steadied her. She inhaled and tasted wood fire, the faintly medicinal smells from the kitchen, the lingering sweetness of the apple wine. Oonat flowed across the far corner, shadow upon shadow, eyes like fairy gems.

Heron turned her attention back to the image between her hands, the true nature of this man's heart. Again, she sensed emptiness and dying light. As her fingers sought out the next contact points and layer built upon layer, her inner vision sharpened. The man's own heart wavered like a ghost, a shadow compared to the compelling images. He carried the true nature of a second heart, and the weight of it was killing him.

Walls arched above her head, rising long and graceful like the inside of a cathedral. She saw not in shades of color, hue and tint, but in heat and taste, the metallic tang of blood, the singing silver, the deep rich harmonics of molten gold. With each passing moment, with each new triangulation, the world around her grew more vivid. She found herself moving forward. The ribs, smelling of alabaster and volcanoes, curved above her head. She could almost touch them.

Heron became aware of a pulsation, a rhythmic waning and strengthening, a musical chord just below her hearing, an intensification of color.

Red/gold/ebony/cinnamon . . .

She went on, though now the walls closed in on her and she could clearly see the knobs and interweavings where the ribs joined above her head.

Throb . . . Throb-THROB . . .

She heard it now, not with her human ears, but singing through the marrow of her bones. Sinking down, she felt it in every fiber of the cathedral cave. The alabaster ribs flexed with its rhythm.

Throb . . . Throb-THROB . . . Throb-THRRROBBBB . . .

A shape coalesced before her, emerging from a crimson fog. At first, it appeared to be an animal, one of the familiar forms she sought. But it was shape and not-shape, form and thought, rubies and dreams.

It was the heart of a dragon.

Not a heart with the nature of a totem beast, but the heart of a dragon somehow imprisoned in this human body.

For a long time after she came back to herself, Heron sat looking at the man who bore the heart of a dragon and wondered what she could possibly do to save him. The only one who might know was her old teacher, Willet. For five years, she had studied the true nature of things at his feet, swept his hearth and stirred his brews, and studied his ancient scrolls. From her training at Temple, she knew anatomy and diagnosis, how to observe, listen, probe, and percuss, how to question a patient, how to counsel his family. What she did not know was why the things which worked so well in the southern cities failed in the shadow of the mountains.

Heron forced herself to eat a little and sleep for those few hours until dawn. Oonat curled up in the crook behind her knees, purring softly. She drew as much strength from his presence as from the brief rest.

To her surprise, when she awoke, Heron discovered the man sitting up, gazing into the dying embers. He would not answer her questions, but he followed, willingly if slowly, when she took his hand and led him about the room. Sometimes he seemed like a simpleton, at other times a blind man.

Heron drew out her satchel, the one which had once held all her worldly goods, and packed it with everything she might need—changes of linens and socks, an extra shirt, her warmest sweater, packets of herbs and medicinals, a small sewing kit, her folding knife . . .

She needed a gift for Willet. He would not help her without a gift. Money? Too commonplace. Ale? Too heavy to carry. The stoneware pot with the rainbow glaze? Too feminine.

Ah! She sorted through the drawers of her cabinet until she found a vial of tincture of dragonsblood. It had nothing to do with dragons other than the name, being the crushed seeds of a plant which grew on the other side of the southern deserts. A few drops in a cup of wine brought dreams of unusual clarity and pleasure. It was exotic enough to please even Willet.

From one of her patients, a trader in livestock, Heron borrowed two riding animals. Her jennet was sturdy and quiet, with a black stripe running down her spine, a shaggy coat of soft gray, and dark liquid eyes. The beast trotted on willingly enough, apparently pleased to have a rider so light and so sparing of the whip. The man made no attempt to use either stirrups or reins, but when Heron tugged at the lead line and they started off, his body moved easily with the gait of his sturdy mule.

The days spent traveling to Willet's hideaway passed uneventfully. Heron's purse was considerably lighter from indulging in the hospitality of road-inns. The last two nights there had been none to take shelter in, only a burned-out shell the first night and the scant comfort of a small wooded area the second.

As dusk fell on the last day, rain drizzled fitfully, dampening clothing along with spirits. Heron was wet, cold, and hungry, and the jennet in little better shape. When she remounted after a brief rest, the beast tried to bite her. Only the man seemed unheeding of the weather.

As twilight coalesced into darkness, Heron spotted winking orange lights ahead. The jennet pricked her ears and surged forward. The place looked smaller than Heron remembered, the yard overgrown, the outlying sheds like dark sentinels. The door swung open, streaming firelight and the smell of parsnip and rosemary stew.

"Put the animals in the farthest shed," said a rusty voice, "and get yourselves dry."

Just as she had always done, Heron did as she was told. The man stood dripping inside the door until she pushed him onto a corner stool and toweled him vigorously. Heron offered Willet the dragonsblood, which he set aside. Soon they were all sipping the thick vegetable stew. Even though it was unsalted and pungent with last season's turnips, Heron relished every bite. Warmth flowed along her muscles.

"So you've finally met something you can't handle on your own," Willet said when three empty bowls lay upon the hearth, "and you've come back to your old master for help. I knew you would."

"So you always said."

"Well now, you'd better tell me what this is all about." Willet handed Heron a cup of honey-laced chamomile tea and settled back in the one good chair, stroking his tangled beard, ready to hear her story.

"Ach, I have not heard of such a thing in many an age, not in this one, that's sure," he said when she had finished. "A dragon's heart is not a quest to take on lightly."

He thinks dragons are better left alone, and he is probably right.

Willet examined the man carefully, even as she had done, as he had taught her. Afterward, he was silent for a long time. Slowly, he began to speak, at first in the rusty tones and halting rhythms of an old man too long alone. But soon, his voice gathered strength. He wove a tapestry of images, of the darkness beneath the mountains and things living there too ancient for naming, about the sendings of nightmares and the funeral pyres of dragons in the country beyond the sun. Heron recognized the traditional phrases, bits of ballad and folk story, mixed with vague allusions to terrors better left buried and something more, something which rang of the truth behind the legends. She allowed her mind to wander with his and gradually a pattern emerged.

The Basalt Mountains had once been the abode of creatures stranger than dragons. Mantichordons, born from the unholy union of scorpion and elephant, half-living lithiotropes who ate rock and belched forth ash . . . and men.

Necromancer, sorcerer, warlock. None of the words she knew could name them truly. Perhaps one of them still lived . . . and had summoned a dragon to do his bidding . . . and put the drag-on's magickal heart into this nameless soldier.

Then what had befallen the dragon? Whose heart did it bear?

Heron shuddered with a sudden chill, despite the nearness of the fire. "It's hopeless, isn't it? How could I find one of those creatures, let alone convince him to restore the dragon's heart to its proper place? I have only my medical skills and the little magic I learned from you."

He would have taught her more, had she asked, had she stayed. She saw that now with a pang of regret. Since she had left, she'd grown beyond these thorny confines, these age-stained vellum scrolls, had thrust herself into the very lives of those she served, and she could never go back.

"You have far more, though you have never chosen to develop it. My dear, I guide you on this quest. I am a cantankerous old hedge-wizard, dreaming before his fire. But you are a healer who has held the heart of a dragon, and it has left its mark upon you."

This was not a thing Heron wanted to hear. She brushed aside his words. "Where—how do I start?"

He drew out maps from their leather storage tubes and un-rolled them before her. Then he took the amulet from the sol-dier's neck and, casting it into the fire, chanted invocations in a language Heron had never heard before. When he drew it forth again, the cord was a little singed, and the quartz glowed as if with its own inner light.

"Come back if you can," he said, "and tell me how it all turned out."

Willet took out the dragonsblood and sprinkled a portion in his cup of ale. She sat back, sipping the last of her tea, and waited. Soon his body sagged in the chair, the lines of care and petty fear lifted from his face, and a faint smile played over his thin lips.

Dawn found Heron and her companion on the trail again. She sang tunelessly to the jennet who, with repeated sighs and flicks of her long ears, expressed her disapproval of so early a departure. Fortunately, the rain had stopped and the day promised to be

mild. The mingled smells of damp earth, grasses heavy with rip-
ening seed heads, and late-blooming mountain daisies filled the
air.

They climbed and rested and climbed some more. The bones of
the land jutted out in lumps of misshapen rock unsoftened by
wind or rain. Heron soon realized that for each stone and crag
she could see with her eyes, there was another, a shadow stone, a
phantom crag. When she took out the quartz amulet, their out-
lines grew stronger. She glimpsed colors she had no names for,
and the very taste of the wind shifted.

. . . the metallic tang of blood, the singing silver, the deep rich
harmonics of molten gold . . .

At the end of the jumbled slope, a relatively flat apron circled
the mountain proper. With her newly awakened sight, Heron saw
fissured gaps where only weather-smoothed rock had appeared.
One such opening looked wider and blacker than the others. She
felt a chill, like moon-cast shadow, flowing from it.

Perhaps it was not chill at all, but only the gulf between the
sorcerous world and her own . . .

The man shifted in his saddle, his eyes moving in sharp little
jerks as he scanned the mountains. His breathing quickened and
he opened his mouth as if to speak, but only a low moan came
out. His eyes were as blank as ever, as if focused on that invisible
second world. When Heron touched his hand, she felt his skin
burn even hotter, as if he were being consumed from inside.

Heron left the animals, reins tucked under a stone, easy
enough to pull free. Grasping the man's hand, she stepped inside
the fissure. Daylight cast a slant of brilliance across the floor, fading to black beyond that narrow space. The quartz amulet grew
suddenly light and tugged at its cord.

The fissure narrowed and twisted, but she worked her way
carefully along it, always finding just enough room for them both
to pass. Within a few minutes, the crack opened into a vast echoing space. Daylight faded into a soft golden effulgence. The walls
themselves glowed as if living.

She started across the cavern at a shambling walk, then faster
and yet more smoothly. Her feet skimmed the dust and never

struck a pebble or one of the weird rock formations growing from the cavern floor like arthritic fingers. She heard the man cry out. His hand tore away from hers, but she could not stop to retrieve him.

Something bright and singing danced in her veins, cantatas of molten carnelians, garnets like stars, the ecstatic smell of burning rubies . . .

Is this what it is to be a dragon?

Her human heart wept at beauty too great for flesh to bear.

Heron's soundless cry died down and in its wake, she became aware of a presence. Vaster than vast, more crimson than blood, blacker than jet, yet bounded by a thousand scales, each thinner than a feather and harder than tempered steel. The dragon condensed before her, as mist become carborundum. It breathed upon her. For a terrible moment, she felt her flesh tear away, whipped into ghostly streams, felt her bones turn crisp and shatter. But she had touched the heart of a dragon, and part of its nature had seeped into her. She stood fast within its realm and knew its deadly fire could not touch her.

"You have taken something which does not belong to you," she shouted.

The eyes blazed vitriol. From the great throat there came a bellow of anger, brass and thunder.

Instinct dropped her to a crouch. The flame passed over and through her, for she offered no resistance. Instead, she slipped her pack from her shoulder and plunged her hand inside. Her fingers brushed the packets of oiled paper. They were as she'd placed them, tied with a bit of yarn. The one she sought was under the knot. A twist freed it. She dipped her fingertip into it, felt the familiar gritty powder. Slowly, she lifted her head.

"You must return what you have stolen."

I WILL BLAST YOUR FLESH AND SCATTER THE ASHES OF YOUR BONES.

She recoiled in surprise, for she had not expected her words to have such power over a dragon. Its power was that of volcanoes and of stars. It need not have noticed her at all, let alone answered her.

The dragon leaped forward, pouncing like a cat, one foreleg on either side of her. Extended, its claws gave off a smell like hot metal. She had not realized the creature was so large; it had not seemed so a moment before. The claws grew larger still as they closed around her, elongated now like prison bars. Knocked to her knees, she found herself carried toward the massive chest. The heat of the eyes burned her skin. Every instinct urged her to shrink in upon herself, to bury her face under her arms, to hide. She kept her gaze lowered, but not from fear. It was not the dragon's eyes she sought, but the keel of its breastbone.

The claws opened. Thunder echoed in the back of her mind, or something very like it, some parody of malevolent triumph.

SO YOU THOUGHT TO COMMAND A DRAGON? LOOK NOW UPON THE TRUTH, O MORTAL, AND KNOW YOUR FOLLY!

Heron covered her face with her hands, as if despairing. She slipped her fingers into her mouth, beneath her tongue, welcoming the familiar bitterness.

She slid one hand along the obsidian claw, then lunged forward and slapped the other palm against the dragon's breastbone, as low as she could reach. And held the heart of the dragon between her hands.

The dragon pulled back. Rearing, it drew its forelegs—and its captive—to its chest. Heron shifted her position, pressing her advantage. She could only guess at the anatomical landmarks, for to either side of the midline, armored plates covered the dragon's underside. Surprisingly, these seemed to conduct the images she sought just as well as bare skin. In her mind, the shape and rhythm of this heart took form.

It was the heart of a man. In that moment, she saw him truly, a small, cowardly man, so terrified of his own mortality that his soul had shriveled into a knot of bitterness.

His own body, so decrepit that not even centuries of sorcerous power could sustain it any longer, had disintegrated at last, a pile of dust and splintered bone. Unable to destroy the dragon's heart outright, he had lured a stranger, a man without place or kin, to carry it until both perished.

Once, Heron had summoned the true nature of a man's heart, whether it be hawk or fish or stag. She had called the beast back to life in order to save the man. Now she must reach the man's heart within the dragon.

I swore I would never use my gifts to send a man to his death. The thought rocked her to her marrow. Then she remembered the nameless soldier, enslaved without hope. The man with the heart of a dragon. *Let all things be as they are. Nothing more than this, let dragon be dragon and man be man.* She shrank away from what she must do next, for the nature of this sorcerer's heart was so turned in upon itself that she could not imagine even a small space for joy or love. She heard the rumbling of his thoughts, slow and grinding strange, year upon year of twisted greed, of vengeance nursed and sucked dry like pumice. . . .

He was what he had made of himself, how he had shaped his life, the centuries of spite and fear. Nothing she could offer would change that.

O man, O creature of wonder and of misery, whose eyes penetrate the heavens and whose hands bring forth glory from the earth. You who dwell between the two, depart now to your own place—

A roar of anguish, turbulent as a tidal wave, a desert storm, an avalanche on the heights, answered her. *I WILL NOT! I AM DRAGON NOW!*

You are man! You are kin to the eagle and the tortoise, the mayfly and the whale. But you are not any of these things. As all things of the natural world pass in their season, so you must pass—

I AM DRAGON—DRAGON—DRAGON—

The glare of the dragon's eyes built into an inferno glare. It battered her exposed skin. She dared not shift her position or risk losing her contact. For the first time, she felt its breath—copper and phosphorus. The smell engulfed her. It was so real, so different from that of any natural creature. A dragon's breath from a dragon's body.

I name you man! she cried once more, *and I summon you by that name.*

"Man—I am man—" The words came now from behind her, and across her mind flickered the image of eyes the color of the sea, no longer blank but seething with inner storm. The heart of the dragon even now tore at his soul.

Heron turned her full concentration back to the husk of the man within the dragon. She now knew that she could not compel, she could only call. Her sole weapon was the truth. If she failed, she might survive in some crippled state, but the soldier would surely die and along with him, the heart of the magickal beast. She did not know which would be the greater loss.

The sorcerer, why had he done this thing? She forced herself to think, to gather her next argument.

He so fears his own death that he would do anything, pay any cost, to escape it.

I FEAR NOTHING! I AM DRAGON, IMMORTAL!

In her mind, she held up the images, like silken banners spread upon a gusting wind. Dragons soaring against a sky which had no name . . . mantichordon and sphinx . . . towering trees, mountains raw from the belly of the earth . . . each exultant in its glory, each fading with time. . . .

She had heard it said that for anything new to come into the world—a song, a dream, a baby's first cry—something old must pass away.

The sorcerer had caught her thought. *What remains? What endures? Neither stone nor fire nor the memories of men, that much is certain!*

"Only this," Heron said, shaping the words with infinite sadness. "That each thing which has ever been has had a secret name, a true nature. That in the end, it is this to which we all return."

She released her hold on the heart which bore the nature of a man, encased in the body of a dragon, but she left one hand on its breast. The fine quivering could be felt all through its body. Moments stretched one into the other, time marked only by the slow beating of the dragon's heart, the bellows of its breath. At the edge of her senses, rubies wept their songs, silver shimmered as if lit within by fairy fires.

"You are a man," she whispered into that silence. "And out of all the creatures who have walked upon this world, since time began and the heavens took shape, you alone know what you are."

I have always . . . loved dragons. I thought that if I became one, I would change. But I have not changed. Nothing has changed.

In that moment, she saw beyond the fear of his dying to an even greater fear—of being alone. The fear that once he passed from this life, everything would be as it had been, as he had made it.

She could not change death. Sometimes, she could postpone it for a while. But this she could help. "Tell me your name," Heron said with all the gentleness she had to give, "and I will sing you to sleep."

He did, and she sang. Not the songs of molten silver or red-gold embers, the high sweet harmonies of the stars. She sang of cats curled in the sun, of the smell of herbs after a rain, of the coolness beneath her rowan tree, of the curve of a woman's arm holding a baby to her breast. She sang of the nights of weariness, of the sickness of the soul when she could not help a dying child, of the warmth in her lover's arms, of the kind, dark eyes of her jennet, of chamomile tea, and of the taste of tears.

She never felt the exact moment when he was gone. He slipped away as day slips away, twilight into gloaming, when the first stars appear between the blinking of an eye. For a long moment, she felt only emptiness, the familiar grief when a patient died. She wondered if he had found what he so feared, or only an ending to those fears. Her eyes stung with unexpected tears.

Around her, the cathedral rumbled and shuddered. The soldier cried out as his body thudded to the ground. Pale flames roared from the mouth of the dragon. They did not burn, but each nerve in her skin thrilled on the edge of pain.

Suddenly released from the claws, Heron landed on her feet. The great crimson form reared above her, eyes glowing, wings unfurled. She saw now the old scars lacing its underbelly, the crooked claw, the chipped tooth. The age of the beast, old beyond its kind, shivered through her. The dragon bent its head. Its form, outline and color, wavered in her sight like a heat-born mirage. Something deep and atavistic rushed through Heron, as if its magick stirred in her bones. She stretched out one hand to touch the dragon one more time.

Red/gold/ebony/cinnamon . . .

Heron blinked, startled in the realization it had spoken to her.

Wings spread wide against a sky like fire opals, the taste of burning copper, the crackle of unseen lightning. On the far side of the stars, others of its kind waited . . .

The dragon gathered itself, and in its shadow she glimpsed the fallen soldier. She cried out, wordless, and in that instant she once more held the heart of the dragon. Though its nature made it immortal, a thing of ancient magick and not of flesh, she felt it answer her.

The massive tapered head bent over the body, over the long muscled back and legs. Slit nostrils flared wide, taking in the man's scent . . . remembering. Where it had been, what it had been. The edge of the dragon's breath caught Heron and swept through her, furnace-white. Blinded, she fell to her knees. Her outstretched hands slammed against rock, jagged and laced with pebbles. The impact jarred the breath from her lungs. Tears streamed from her eyes. She could not see, could not breathe, her only thought that the dragon was gone forever.

"Come on," a man's voice said, husky as if from long silence. "This is no place for the likes of us."

At his touch, she turned. The eyes which had been so blank now burned with urgency. They transformed the man's face into one which, if not handsome, was unforgettable. Everything he had witnessed and suffered, the evil he had done and the good he had defended, were etched upon his features.

A cavern of ordinary stone, shaped by volcanic fire and centuries of dripping water, surrounded her. Only the lingering radiance, crimson fading into gray, held any evidence of the dragon's presence.

"The light won't hold," he said, and took her hand. His fingers around hers felt warm, but no longer fever-touched. She felt the callouses on his palm, the strength and gentleness of his grip.

Together they raced through the cavern, tripping over the weird stone shapes which protruded from the floor. By the time they reached the fissure, not a mote of dragon light remained. Darkness enveloped them. They made their way by touch along the rough walls.

As they stumbled into the day, the jennet and the mule looked up from their browsing. Heron grasped the saddle, shaking too hard to mount and afraid that if she fell again, she would not be able to get up. She startled when she felt hands, warm and strong, on her waist.

Turning in the soldier's arms, she saw the spark of wonder in his eyes. He was as surprised as she, as each recognized the echoes of the dragon in the other. Like called to like, truth to truth. She heard his thought, *I can never repay what you have done for me.* And she knew that he heard hers, *I would have done the deed for its own sake*—slipping her hands into his.

But I am glad it was for yours.

Then he put his hands around her waist again and she rested her cheek against his chest. The warmth of his body, now a human warmth, soothed her. His strength held her up. Loneliness melted from her. No matter what happened now, no matter where their separate lives led them, she would always have this perfect moment, as she listened to the beating of his human heart and beyond, that other pulse, slow as a mountain, strong as a dream.

Red/gold/ebony/cinnamon . . .

The heart she had once held between her hands and which now and forever beat as one.

Larry Dixon

When I first met Larry Dixon, he was a skinny teenage boy hanging around Mercedes Lackey at a convention. But inside that narrow, unfinished frame there was much more substance than was immediately visible. For now, more than ten years later—and all grown up—he is Misty's husband, constant companion, illustrator, and collaborator. He has published six novels with DAW, all Valdemar books co-written with his famous wife, beginning with *The Black Gryphon* in January 1994. But Misty has told me numerous times that whether or not he has a co-byline, Larry has helped her with every book she's written since she met him. When Larry decides to write his first solo novel, DAW will be here to publish it.

I wasn't the least bit surprised that Larry's story for this anthology had a military theme and a gritty martial feel. Larry is an army brat, and grew up in a family that was steeped in armed forces history. I also knew it *had* to have a gryphon in it. Larry is the undisputed king of the gryphons.

—BW

A PERFECT DAY IN VALDEMAR

Larry Dixon

SECOND Guard Hallock Stavern fought toward consciousness, only to find that his eyes had been glued shut.

There was a feeling that he knew was pain, but it was of such magnitude that it was not a part of him—instead he was just a bit of flotsam tossed around on its churning flow. Hallock felt only a sickening detachment. His awareness of his body extended about as far as knowing he had limbs—two legs, yes, and arms—two of them. Breathing created a heaving pull of muscle that seemed to roll upward and never recede quite as much in return. Moving his hands was no more productive, because Hallock's body seemed to be restrained by a web of thick syrup. At least that was how it felt, insofar as he could feel anything with certainty. He couldn't move by his own volition, but as best he could tell he was moving. Carried—that must be it. He was being carried.

Hallock moved his head to the left and right, feeling wet webbing restricting the sway of his head and neck. The viscous glue that held his eyes shut cracked, apparently dry at the edges, but then returned to pool in his eyes, dimming what little he saw. His right eyelid reluctantly slit open enough for Hallock to perceive a lurching view of sky and trees. Vertigo made them spin around him.

That wholly unwelcome vision provided enough added disorientation that he gave up on consciousness as a place of residence. For an unknown amount of time, he would only be an occasional visitor there.

Hallock found awareness and memory returning in sporadic fits. There were recollections of the skirmish, the fallback, and the formation for retreat. Then, the peculiar memory of falling to the ground, and watching an arrow fall with him. That much he remembered, as clearly as he remembered his last birthday or his daily sword drills. He was on a dapple-gray stallion named Dughan. Hallock was yelling a break order to his company third, and then he found himself spinning sideways. He hadn't intended to. As the ground came up to meet his face, he remembered seeing a great war arrow dropping along with him. Its bladed tip was as long as his own sword hand, barbed in well-cut triangular serrations, and it was trailing a line of slow-falling blood. He struck the earth, left shoulder first, then rolled to his side and onto his back. He remembered seeing a riderless horse churning the earth to run away. His vision narrowed in from all sides and that was the end of the memory.

There was the vague memory of jostling and trees, and the unsettling vertigo, and being carried. Then—nothing for what could have been weeks.

When Hallock regained awareness of his own being, it was from feeling his eyes being prodded at. There was a voice murmuring a reassurance in Valdemaran. It didn't register just yet what the specific words were. Even though that sensation of tremendous full-body disorientation was still present, he felt annoyance that someone was messing about with his eyes. He hazily realized the clinging goo that had blocked his vision had been congealed blood, and plenty of it. He lifted his right hand to swat away the offending "help," but his arm didn't respond as expected. There was a movement, to be sure, but his hand might have been waving a baton in front of the Company Chorus as far as he could tell.

"Just stay still until I get you cleaned up, sir," the voice insisted, and Hallock felt his arm being put at his side. There, at last, was a point of reference. A nudge of his left hand against his hip confirmed that it was in a similar position. Left leg—kick. Not quite. More of a twitch.

"Sir, you aren't helping," the voice snapped, with clear exasperation.

"Is he giving you trouble, Birce?" another voice called out from afar.

"I've had worse," the voice responded close by Hallock's face. "I've had to patch up Heralds before. They think they're ready for action with two broken legs and a hangover. This one's just twitching right now because he had his bell rung, I think. Could you come over here for a look?"

There was still a surreal element in all of this. Reason told him that he was hurt and being attended by Healers, but, to Hallock, it felt like it was happening to someone else. He was aware he was alive and that things were not right. There was something where pain should have been, pain but it didn't hurt him, as much as it filtered out anything in his mind that made normal sense. Fear, logic, or linear thought were immaterial. Time was just an unneeded detail, discarded in favor of a floaty haze.

Hallock sucked in a deep breath and had an inexplicable sensation that he couldn't exhale as much as he'd drawn in. His forehead felt the size of a horse regiment, and it throbbed like a regiment's hoofbeats with his pulse. The sensation of pressure in his lungs and head was relentless. The Healer attending him held a glass vial to his crusted lips and poured a syrup into his mouth, which seemingly absorbed into his tongue and throat.

Suddenly very much awake, Hallock surged upward with a cry of pain. Full consciousness rushed in. To say that he suddenly "hurt" would be like saying that an ocean was "damp."

His eyes opened abruptly and he found himself on a cot, looking up at stained and patched canvas strung with cord holding dozens of bright oil lamps. Clots of blood were still stuck to his eyelashes, blotting out most details. The dozens of slightly different shadows cast by the individual lamps complicated the view further, mixed with the dazzle from the pain. Hands were pushing him back onto the cot even as he already felt himself falling backward, and the two Healers in attendance were practically screaming at him to calm down. Hallock realized that they were screaming to be heard over his own howls of pain, and pulled himself together enough to lower his utterances to a series of groans.

"Sir . . . sir, I'm going to give you something for your pain," the one apparently named Birce told him as he propped his head up from the cot. "Stavern, right? Second Officer Stavern? I had to get you awake and cleaned up first, I'm sorry. I know that was unpleasant. Things will be better. I'm Senior Healer Birce Bedrin. Drink this." Birce Bedrin, heavyset but clearly strong, was not in the best of shape himself; his own neck and temple had small bandages, and several uncovered abrasions and bruises graced his businesslike midlands features. His accent was upper-class Haven, but this was obviously a man who was unafraid to be in the thick of mud and muck to do a job.

"Just—" Hallock began, then grimaced as a cupful of cold, thick, and lumpy juice laced with something tasting of charred bark was all but poured down his throat. "Just get me an officer in here to report."

"Soon, sir. Sorry about the taste. Devon's going to get someone for you as soon as he can. Devon?" Birce looked around to find the only other man in the spacious tent. "Devon, the Second here needs an officer from his unit."

"Sixteenth Regiment, Third Company," Hallock murmured, and heard it repeated to the other man more loudly. Devon was thinner than Birce by half, with the swarthy skin of a far-southerner, and hair as black as coal. Devon gave Birce a significant look, and the senior Healer excused himself, wiped his blood-caked hands on his Greens, and went to confer further at the tent entry. Devon nodded and left, flipping the tent flap aside with a hint of frustration.

What Hallock saw hanging from the tent flap filled his attention entirely, all pain and misery forgotten in a moment of dread. It was horrible to contemplate. Just last week had found him walking with Genni under trees laden with fragrant white blossoms in the narrow presentation walk in front of the Guard house. Genni, with her lovely light brown eyes, and her dreams of the future and their children, had lovingly taunted him that they would grow old together as great-grandparents before he retired from the Guard.

He had known and trained with enough Healers to recognize

what was tied to the tent's closure tab, and what it meant. It was a loosely knotted yellow ribbon—one knot indicated "one patient."

And yellow, in Healer sorting code, meant "unlikely to survive."

A sullen-looking man in a Guard-blue undershirt and riding pants lurked around the tent's doorway as a light spattering of raindrops tapped on the stretched canvas of the tent. He wore a uniform cap with Support bars, and looked as weary as if a horse had been riding him. He didn't give his name, but related a briefing from four respectful steps away that allowed Hallock to piece together the order of occurrences that had put him here in this isolated tent. The candlemark of steady medicinal fluids had made Hallock lucid enough to realize the impact of the past days' events.

Haven's Sixteenth Guard Regiment had been sent at point, with three companies of light horse and moderate support following a day behind, to reinforce Lord Breon's household troops after reports of a particularly nasty trade dispute. On the way there, the Herald that rode with the Captain warned that the situation was bad enough that there was a possibility of encountering full insurrection around Deedun.

The word was that a former city magistrate named Farragur Elm had been propped up by twenty or more major trade barons and declared "Chancellor of Prosperity," a pompous title at best. He was reportedly already making declarations about a fledgling nation claiming independence from Haven, in the northwest of Valdemar. Secession was not impossible, but this coup was apparently being built upon goods seized from honest tradesmen, expressly for the purpose of staging the secession. The illegality of that action was clear, but what was even clearer—and had brought the troops out—was news from Kelmskeep that entire villages had found their expected income cut out from under them. Entire taxpaying villages of loyal citizens, to be more specific.

When a Herald returned with word from Deedun that a mercenary force under contract to the Crown had been hired out from under Valdemar by this Chancellor, the Guard mobilized. When it was realized that the Herald was a circuit rider evicted from Deedun at swordpoint, the response from Haven took on an entirely different feel. The problem with Hallock Stavern and his fellow Guards being dispatched to assist Lord Breon, though, was that Deedun was between Haven and Lord Breon's hold of Kelmskeep. The Terilee River ran as strong as ever on the eastern side of Deedun and the only main route was the trade road north from Haven. This was, he'd suspected at the time, a testing mission to get a feel for the resolve of the insurrectionists' hired swords when they saw troops of some kind on the move toward them.

The Sixteenth Guard Regiment advanced to the brink of Pawta's Wood and found a double picket of professional mixed cavalry and three lines of war archers barring the road. The flurry of arrows that rained into the Valdemaran ranks confirmed that battlefield diplomacy was not an option. The closing assault that followed left no doubts about the resolve, or skill, of the mercenaries.

Hallock had gotten the retreat call from his Captain, and had been shouting out fallback orders to his Third when the first arrow from the initial volley had creased him across the forehead. That was the memory of the falling arrow.

A second arrow had pierced his left side between the belly muscles and his intestines. His Third had pulled him up onto his horse and led the rest of the company back toward Haven. The Sixteenth's relaying retreat was only barely quicker than the merc cav apparently chose to disrupt. As soon as a rout was apparent, the mercs held their attacks and went defensive in posture, finally pulling back to what their employers had evidently declared was their border. Mercifully for the Sixteenth, the mercs sent no cleanup units to finish off stragglers. Hallock and the other wounded were relegated to travois and stretchers for the remainder of the fallback. Individual Guard units had been scattered into the countryside, and regrouped on the roadside south of the attack, some of them riding for candlemarks. Even now, they continued to straggle into this improvised camp around a riverside mill town.

The clerk rubbed his eyes and begged to be let off for some sleep. The patter of raindrops was increasing in frequency, and he wanted to get to his rack before getting soaked. Hallock was clearer of thought, but hadn't even realized his time perception was so badly altered by the juice he had been fed until he had been asked for dismissal three times. The Healer Birce guided the clerk out once Hallock had grunted an assent, then returned to answer a few questions before another draught. The explanations didn't honestly make him feel any better.

"Healer Birce, isn't it? Mmm. Let me guess. Gut wound. Bleeder."

Birce nodded gently. "Yes, sir. You don't seem like the kind of patient that wants me to make it sound any better than it is."

"I'm a veteran, son. I know what a yellow ribbon is in Healer code. What's keeping me from being fixed?"

Birce rubbed his right hand, hard, and picked at his dark-stained nail beds. He paid a great deal of attention to his hands while finding adequate words. "It isn't that I am not skilled, sir. You've just had some wounds of a type that we don't have the ability to cure under the very best of circumstances. You were hit when you were already down, by another arrow, after the first one had creased your forehead and unhorsed you. In your belly, a couple of fingers' width below your stomach. It wasn't incurable, then, I don't think, because it was mostly in the belly muscle. But when you were dragged off the battlefield, the arrow was still pierced inside you. While you were carried, the serrations of the war point sawed away until . . ."

Birce held his hands apart, letting his explanation end there. "I've sent word with the dispatch rider that a magical Healer is needed, someone with a Gift or spell or maybe some kind of obscure knowledge I just don't have. But whether Haven responds with anyone, or quickly enough, I cannot say." He folded his hands, wringing them twice before letting them be still. "In the meantime, I have drugs that can keep your pain down, your mind in the here-and-now, and keep you asleep when it's best for you."

As optimistic as the Healer tried to be, Hallock knew better than to think he had much of a chance of seeing Haven again. It was one of the worst thoughts to have as the last one before a helpless sleep.

Hallock had much more to return to than just Haven, a point he tried to stress to Birce as he drank his medicine. When Birce turned his back to put the cup away, Hallock mustered up his voice of command. Midway through, he was all too aware of how it weakened and cracked.

"Healer, listen to me. I have a wife. We're going to have a family. I know you probably can't get me well enough for active duty again. I can accept that." Hallock paused for a breath, and there his stoic demeanor broke. "But at least keep me alive for her. At least keep me alive long enough to get back to Haven for Genni. She needs me."

Birce pursed his lips so tightly they turned pink. He resumed picking at his nails and then exhaled gustily. "Sleep now," was his answer. "I should know by the time you wake up how things will go. All right?"

It wasn't all right, but that was how it was. The oil lamps faded, and Hallock was in oblivion before Birce had even left the tent.

Hallock heard a commotion outside, but it was as if it was far distant and heard through a tube of parchment. Peaceful rest was hopeless. His sleep was a storm of memories of rain, uniforms, sunlight, brown eyes, smiles, horsemanship classes, weapons drills, war, falling, Genni, the arrows, spinning trees, and Haven. He wanted to stay in the initial oblivion the Healer's draught had put him in, and couldn't, but the drugs he had been given wouldn't let him be as awake as he wanted either. Now some bastards outside were making more noise than a free beer Festival full of cadets. Shouts and hoofbeats passed around his tent, followed by twice as many and the sound of wagon wheels.

The din was split by an inhuman and impossibly loud shriek, answered by expletives and sounds of breaking wood and bodies falling. He was shocked fully awake, sucking in a deep breath. He couldn't sit up due to the bindings and stitching of his belly wound, but he did manage to edge up on his elbows little by little, only making the tent spin mildly in his vision. He tried to see through the slight gap in the tent flaps.

Birce's voice could be heard, shouting as he passed outside the tent, "No! He cannot be moved to another tent, I strictly forbid it! You, come with me now . . ." And nothing more of that command was discernible to Hallock's thrumming ears.

More lucidity helped him take control of his limbs. He had been warned not to try to use his belly muscles for anything at all, but it was much easier said than done.

He knew that kind of shriek—a piercing, raspy blast from a strained, capacious throat driven by huge lungs. He recognized it—from Haven. From the Collegium.

Hallock heard Birce's voice calling for supplies and lamps, and then there was another bestial shriek that fell away into a rasping gurgle, then silence. A candlemark could have passed, or two, or half of one. It was impossible for Hallock to tell, but when the tent flaps were pulled back, he was still up on his elbows with his chin against his ribs. A throng of Guard regulars burst into the tent, and several of them stared at him for one surprised moment before dashing out yelling for the Healer in charge. The ones remaining in the tent stammered apologies, apparently not realizing they had mud and fresh blood spattered across their uniforms making them look as bad as the bedridden officer they stood before.

Devon pushed past them to get to Hallock and blurted, "Sir, there's something here, it's one of the—" then turned back to yell "I'm asking him now!" to someone outside. "Sir, there's—"

A minor Guard officer appeared at the tent entry to interrupt the Healer, and jabbered something to Devon quicker than the Healer could follow. Surprisingly, Devon smacked the soldier with an open palm on the cheek, and screamed "Pull yourself together! Healer's orders!"

There were two heartbeats of absolute stunned silence from everyone except Devon, who just said, "Tell the Second what happened." The soldier composed himself and explained more slowly, and with significantly less vigor.

"What I was told was that the patrol found merc outriders, an' got spotted, an' the mercs chased 'em down. An' the patrol turned to make a stand, 'cause the mercs was faster. An' when th' mercs was closin' in, this thing jus' came screamin' out o'the sky an' tore inta th'mercs—killed 'em, killed 'em all! Th' mercs kept stabbin' an' hackin' at it, an' it just wouldn't fall! An' when th' patrol came out from hidin', there was heads bit off, an' arms an' legs strewn 'round by th' bodies an' all! An' the thing spoke— spoke Valdemaran! Said it was an ally to the Crown an' then keeled over. Been delirious th' whole way—they jus' got it dragged back here on some farmer's wagon." He turned angry and jabbed a finger at Devon's chest. "Look! It's as may be that it's some weird ally, but I jus' saw the thing tear up the earth like a whirlwind an' slash at people what was tryin' ta help it. Yer Healer Birce wants ta fix it up, that's his say, but I'm tellin' ya! You put the thing where ya' want but nowhere near me an' my Company!"

Annoyed, Hallock raised his voice.

"Healer! Attend now!"

Devon blinked, stopping with his mouth open in his reply to the regular, and turned toward Hallock.

"You have a gryphon."

Devon nodded earnestly. "Yes, sir. And he's hurt pretty badly. Birce is trying to stabilize him, but he can't do it in the rain. We need somewhere to put him and it looks like we don't have anywhere but in here. Would you—"

"I've been around gryphons before. Permission granted," he replied, before the spinning of his vision grew to be too much for him. He drifted again.

Lucidity became intermittent after that, but he was aware of much talking and activity. His cot was moved against the wall of the tent by at least four people, he could tell, and the susurration of rain against canvas lulled him into true sleep.

Hallock awoke to an awful throbbing in his head again, and a burning ache in his gut. He groaned and clutched at his belly. It seemed as if the wind from last night's rainstorm had moved into the tent with him, slowly but rhythmically changing in magnitude. Strange acrid and earthy smells struck his nose. When he opened his eyes, Birce was leaning over him. The Healer was dressed in a green tunic far cleaner than the last one he had been seen in, except for what looked like parallel rips and brush strokes of dark paint all down the front and sleeves. He was wiping his hands with a rag as he looked Hallock over. "Good morning, sir," he said gently. "Sir, just keep looking right at me. There was something that you said last night that I need to confirm with you. I need to be sure that it was not because of the influence of your medicine. You gave permission to share your tent with someone."

Hallock grunted the confirmation Birce wanted. The Healer nodded and remarked, "Not many people are brave enough to share their tent with a wounded gryphon." He laid aside his rag and offered his patient a cup of the dreadful but familiar drugged juice. "No one else wanted anything to do with him. Devon said you'd served with one before. In Haven."

Haven. Where Genni was, even now, not knowing at all that her husband had fallen. Genni with her bright smile and milky gauze scarves, always ready to help anyone she met—probably going about the market stalls hunting up a good length of dyed cloth for those crinkle-skirts she loved to make.

Hallock blinked himself free of his wife's memory and grunted once. "Haven. Collegium Guard. During the Storms, I was Master Levy's escort. There were two gryphons at Haven, with two of their young. They helped the Crown. Helped the Crown save us all. When Levy went to confer with them, I went along. Met them. They were like royalty. Dignified." After a pause, of luxuriating in the melting away of his worst pain, he added, "They aren't animals. I'm not afraid of them."

"Candidly, sir, everyone else is. No surprise. Devon and I wound up closing an even dozen lacerations and a pretty serious puncture just among the crew that unloaded him from the wagon."

Hallock rolled his head sideways to get a look past the Healer. What he saw was huge, as large as a horse, but in sorry shape. Flattened against the oiled canvas floor of the tent was what might have been a gryphon of the same species as the nobles at Valdemar's Court, though precious little looked intact. Stains, smears, and pools of unnamed dark substances showed all around his trembling body, even after the Healers' meticulous cleaning regimen. Broad patches of feathers were sheared away, revealing whipstitched gashes and a bulging packed wound in the gryphon's shoulder, with an exit wound in his upper back. Hemp rope had been cut and knotted in clearly improvised splinting made from tent poles and greenwood, interrupted by clumps of broken and skewed chestnut feathers down the length of the right wing, which stretched to fill the rest of the tent. The gryphon's eyes were covered with towels and more rope to hold them in place. His body heaved in a wheezing but labored rise and fall as he breathed.

Birce frowned, gazing at his bizarre patient. "He's been shot up, hacked at, lanced once, and I think he's been poisoned," the unhappy Healer continued, pausing to lick his lips. ". . . and . . . he won't be flying again. At least as far as I know. That right wing of his was turned all the way around, with bone showing, when I got him in here. I've tried irrigating, filling him up with nutrients and keeping him warm, but beyond that I am lost. His blood's alien to me. I don't know his anatomy. I couldn't do anything to help him except bind and stitch his more obvious wounds. He didn't offer any useful help when he was conscious. He's coming in and out, sometimes delirious or twitchy, other times wide awake. He claimed to be a leader of some kind, ally to Valdemar. I don't know much more than that, except his name. Kelvren."

"Fffirrresssong. He may be a peacock . . . but he can fixsss anything."

"Herrraldsss! Mussst know. Tell Herrraldsss . . . ssshow k'Valdemarrr I live."

"Hurrrtsss . . . Ssskandrranon would not crrry . . ."

"Why issss it ssso darrrrk . . . ?"

The candlemark after the Healer left on his rounds was punctuated by fitful starts, groans, and growls from the stricken gryphon, as well as scores of cryptic declarations. Hallock made it a practice to occupy his mind by piecing the rantings together, but could make little of it. The name "Firesong" he knew; that was the white-haired shaych Adept that he had escorted Master Levy to see numerous times, and "peacock" was accurate enough. If a Herald was anywhere to be found, they'd be told every word, but Hallock had yet to see any white cloth that wasn't a blood-stained rag.

The gryphon stank, and the insects were finding their way inside to him, despite the repelling quality of the lamp oil. It offended Hallock, but he mused that it spoke well of the painkiller Birce had him on, if something so minor was even an issue.

All the time that Hallock's mind was not on the meandering speech of the gryphon he shared the tent with, it was on Genni and her little habits. He could see her at his side now, bringing him medicines and sitting with her palm on his forehead, singing popular songs or telling stories of the neighborhood children. He could see her curly brown hair falling down her cheek and neck, catching the sunlight through their dormer window. He could see her curling a few strands of hair around her fingers as she spoke of her sewing circle and the ceramics her sister had presented to the Captain, hoping to catch the bachelor's eye.

Then the gryphon clacked his beak loudly and said with surprising clarity, "Am I prrrisssonerrr?"

Hallock blinked and glanced side to side without moving his head. The blinded gryphon flexed a foreleg, the uninjured right one, and popping sounds of torn floor canvas punctuated the question.

"No. You're a patient," Hallock ventured, and saw the gryphon's ears prick forward as far as the improvised hood would allow. "You're in Valdemar, in a Healer's tent. They say you were hurt defending the Crown's soldiers, and when you fell, they dragged you here."

"Hurrrrh. Feel morrre like drrrresssed game than patient," the gryphon hissed, not commenting on the rescue story. "Can barr-rely think. Need Healerrr. Trrrondi'irrrn. Darrr'ian needs to know I am herrre, and Brrreon and k'Valdemarrr . . . wherrre isss Herrald?" He raised his head and whimpered, dropping down again as the strain unsettled the lance wound, repeating, "Wher-rre isss Herrrald?"

"I'm sorry. We don't have one. No one knows when a Herald will arrive here, or a better Healer." Hallock winced at his own choice of words. "Another Healer. The ones here are doing their best, but it would take the Gift to save us." That choice of words was no better.

"Sssave usss," the gryphon hissed, apparently clear of mind enough to read the implications in the Guard's ill-advised comment. "Ssso you are asss clossse to death asss I. Hurrrh. I could Heal . . . ssstudied long at the Vale. But I am ssso exhaussssted . . . ssso much pain, makess it harrrd to think." The gryphon unstuck his foreclaws from the flooring canvas and tested his range of movement. Another whimper of pain and labored breathing revealed he could at least raise his head with evident effort. "Can block sssome of the pain . . . ssssimple charrrm. You sssoldierrr?"

"Hallock Stavern. Guard officer, Haven, Second of Sixteenth Regiment. I serve under the Captain," he explained, in case the gryphon didn't understand their command structure.

"And the Captain enjoysss you therrre, I am sssurrre," the gryphon wheezed, apparently trying to make a joke, but falling flat in the delivery. "I am Kelvrrren, of K'Valdemarrr. Wing-leaderrr . . . of all the grrryphons of the Vale." A spark of pride lit in his voice when proclaiming his title, but was snuffed out when he went on. "Sssscouting forrr Brrreon. I musssst rrreport beforrre it isss too late. Therrre isss no one elssse herrre to tell. You arrre a sssseniorrr offisssscerrr—you have a good memorrry? Or wrrrite?"

"Yes, but—you can't see. I could be an enemy soldier pretending so that I can find out what you know."

The gryphon tucked his head down against his filthy and blood-encrusted breastfeathers, to pick with his talons at the eye-blocking towels and ropes that were evidently annoying him. "You arrre Hallock Ssstaverrn. I can tell you sssspeak trrrue. Lisssten and rrrememberrr. Frrrom the forrrk of the white ssstrrream therrre is sssupply line, and camp of prrrisonerrrs to the eassst of the ssstand of black oak. Sssixty-two trrrroops have built an arrow-nessst therrre—but arrrc of firrre isss blocked by fallen oak to the norrrthwessst . . ."

Kelvren's report was exhaustive and apparently, exhausting. Winces of pain and pauses for deep, sucking breaths stopped the gryphon's forced speech every minute or two. Half a candlemark or more passed before he summoned up the last of his strength to finish the report. It was, indeed, crucial information, giving a literal overview of the insurgents' military might, ranges of influence and deployment, and unwatched vulnerabilities.

Hallock had always been an honest man, and now was no time to start lying. These reports the gryphon spoke of were important to Kelvren, and Hallock could not bear the thought of lying to the broken flyer. His pain was building up again, and the throbbing of his lacerated forehead ramped up steadily the more they talked. "It may not matter, Kelvren. I am dying. Gut wound killing me. They have me on strong medicine. No one can Heal a gut wound without serious magic. I'm isolated in here because they don't think I'll recover, and it's a bad idea to put the dying with the savable."

The gryphon snorted in obvious derision. "Valdemarrransss arrre ssso ssstrrange. We would put all the wounded togetherrr ssso they would heal each otherrrsss' painsss. If not of the body, then of the sssoul. Pain sssharred isss pain halved."

"It isn't that . . . it isn't my own pain I fear. It's that I won't see Haven again. Or Genni."

"Genni. Yourrr mate . . . ?"

"Mate, yes. Wife. We call a mate a wife. We were going to have a family . . . a big family. Genni . . . so beautiful. I wish you could see her, the way I see her. . . ."

"Ssso tell me . . . I have hearrd of Haven, wherrre the Great

Ones arrre. Grrreatessst explorrrerrs of ourrr time, Adept magesss, herrroesss. We sssurrrvive thisss, we ssshould see them togetherrr, yesss, Hallock Ssstaverrrn? They ssstay at the Palassce, in their own prrrivate Vale. And you can ssshow me Haven'sss bessst decadencccesss." The gryphon wheezed a chuckle, surprisingly humanlike. "Tell me what you love therrre. Tell me of yourrr mate. Yourrr wife."

Hallock smiled. The tragically, perhaps mortally wounded gryphon was so much in his humor like the two he had encountered in Haven. "Genni. She is so . . . so sweet. I don't know how to describe her, but I can tell you stories about her. I can tell you about why she makes me smile."

"Tell me, then. Ssshow me in wordsss . . . keep my mind on sssomething that won't hurrrt. Hurrrh, whoever put thisss on me will pay dearrrly!"

"Birce probably thought you were like a falcon, that if you were in the dark, you'd be calmer. He meant well." The gryphon replied with a growl but seemed at least a little mollified. "Haven, with Genni. There was a day off, just last month, before autumn had set in. Autumn in Haven is cool and breezy, and even though winter is coming, everything smells like newness. Late summer is when the hedges in the Collegium come into second bloom. Color is everywhere in little splashes, and the vines flower over every archway."

Hallock found himself smiling as he spoke, staring up at the canvas as it rippled lightly in the breezes outside. "Genni can make everything you do every day seem new, too. There was a carter who served the Guard houses, with meat pies and breads. I ate what he brought almost every day, when on duty, we all did. Not great food although not bad either, but it kept us filled. Well. Genni and I were out, and I was carrying bags for her, because we were going to walk all the markets in Haven together. She makes these skirts and shawls, you see, with ribbons on the edges. Really complex interlaces that make checkers, then fall in these long fringes." Hallock warmed to the subject, putting in details that, on some level, he knew the gryphon couldn't possibly care about—but he was talking about Genni. Nothing was unimportant about Genni. "Maybe out of habit, because she would stop in and visit me while I was on duty, we swung toward the Guard house. The carter was on his rounds, as usual, and Genni said, 'Let's get something to eat!' I must have looked like a toad spitting up a bug, the way she laughed! But she took my hand and pulled me there anyway.

"Genni walked right up and said, 'I want today's special,' and the fellow went behind the cart, opened up an oven and handed her a basket. A whole basket! With a wink, just like that, no money or anything. She had set me up, my Genni! I remember looking back at the carter, who was laughing so hard as to raise the dead, while Genni led me off. The Guards at the Collegium gates waved us through, and she took me there right into the grounds, through those flowering arches. Birds were all around, singing and swooping around. Skeins of geese went overhead, one after another, going south through that wide blue sky. She led me in to one of the side gardens next to the Bards' auditoriums, by the practice rooms. No one there but the groundsman. Then, the groundsman angled off toward us. Brought something to Genni in a brown cloth bundle, that was just dripping wet. Genni hid it from me, just giggling away. Well, see, I pulled the groundsman aside then, while she looked at whatever her prize was. Worked a deal with him, and off he went.

"Genni sat down in the grass, just like that, and opened up the basket. There was crockery inside, from our own cupboard! She'd planned this long in advance! There were no dried-out pasties and cornbread in there, oh, no. She laid out hot plates and roast duck, steamed carrots and sweet potatoes in honey glaze. She had sweetbreads and salted butter, and when she unwrapped the bundle from the groundsman, I almost cried right there. A cold bottle of wine, from who knows what cellar. Oh, I can taste it now. And then, right then . . . ?"

Hallock sniffled, and tears ran down his temples as he lay there. "And then, in the practice rooms, the chorus started. Bard's choral, practicing together . . . forty voices, if there was one of them, singing 'Light of Freedom's Majesty' in the old style. Genni poured the wine and the groundsman arrived then, with what I'd arranged . . . a bouquet of hibiscus, daisy, and bluebell from

Companion's Field. And he said, 'I'll make sure you aren't disturbed,' and went away to the entry of the garden, to work. Genni . . . oh, Genni. We drank the wine and ate, and listened to the singing of the chorus echo off the walls of the Collegium and surround us. We traded jokes, and we kissed, and fed each other sweetbreads. We were young and new again. It was a perfect day. A perfect day."

Hallock couldn't say anymore. His medicine had almost fully burned off. There was no rain outside, but a dull roar filled Hallock's perceptions like a storm raging. Before long, the sound of the gryphon's breathing, growls, and wheezing grunts as he worried at the improvised hood were drowned out by the rush of Hallock's pounding heartbeat in his ears. He looked imploringly toward the gryphon and made eye contact with the raptorial gaze at the moment the shreds of the hood were pulled free. He flinched when he heard the gryphon shriek—a word. A Valdemaran word, Hallock realized, before another wave of agony shattered his sensibilities.

"Healerrrr!" the gryphon shrieked.

The gryphon swung his head sideways and called the word again, extremely loudly. The huge predator's keening was impossibly loud. It made Hallock's head hurt so badly that a mace to the skull would have been a mercy to him. Pounding heartbeats passed beyond counting, and coherence left Hallock completely. This could be death, he thought. But wasn't death supposed to be peaceful?

Motes of orange starlight swum in the Guard's vision. A shadowy shape and disconcerting sounds of tortured crying and tearing cloth burst in on the crackle of red lightning taking over his vision and the pounding noise in his ears. Hallock closed his eyes, but they sprung open again of their own volition. The tent and lamps were spinning all around him, but seemed so distant as the sensation of falling manifested into tunnel vision. Spikes of pain wrenched him from oblivion. Something huge was pressing down on his belly, and his gut screamed agony anew. His head felt split open from so much pain, and yet strangely, warmth was spreading into him from his gut and forehead. There was the distant silhouette of a raptor's beak against shuddering, dancing lamp-light—his last vision before dying?

To die in Valdemar, in service of his nation, would be a good death. For Crown and Country, he would die as a hero, who had fallen defending his own. His name would be cast in bronze and added to the Honor Columns of the Guard house. A good death, if it was indeed his time.

He numbly realized there was a presence beside him, as the sunlike, spreading oblivion engulfed him, pushing out the darkness. It could be an angel of the divine, or a spirit to guide him to the Havens above.

But no matter who or what it might be, he wished with all his heart that it was Genni at his side.

Hallock couldn't see anything at all, but, like the last time he had found himself in this circumstance, the fact that he could think at all was proof that he was alive.

"The gryphon's resuscitated, Healer," he heard a woman say. "Soft tissue's mostly knitted, bone fractures are fused, over-pressures are alleviated. What a mess. He looked like he fell hard on a sword factory."

Devon's voice chimed in from nearby. "Should have seen him when they brought him in."

The woman snorted and continued. "He won't be flying for a long time. Wings and those other weird organs of his will take specialty work I can't do. I sure couldn't do anymore today any-way. The lance hit and the slashes weren't so bad, but the blood poisoning and bruising took a lot out of me."

Devon replied, "We're lucky the Skybolts came north as quickly as they did. We all feel a lot better knowing mages, Her-alds, and Gifted Healers are with us."

The woman yawned, agreeing. "Yeah. Lucky break all around. You did fine, though, and you were probably wise not to risk drugs with his metabolism. I can't imagine the agony he must have been in, just to move an inch, much less use spells. Glad I'm not an empath or you'd be hauling me out of here in a bucket."

There was a pause. "Listen, I have a concern. I'm going to check with our mages about it. The gryphon has no magic left in him that I can find."

Birce's voice replied to the unseen woman, from very near. "When I got here, he'd dragged himself to Stavern's side. I had to pull his claw off of Stavern's belly. I think he used all the magic he had left on whatever Healing spell he had."

"Could be. I know the tracework. The more precise a Healing spell, the less energy it needs, but that takes a lot of medical knowledge. A broad-use spell takes fifty times the energy as it tries all kinds of things to set a bad situation right. For all I know, he used a Summoning and got whatever spirit he brought here to Heal up your Guard."

There was a long pause in which no one said a word, as they mulled over the implications. In those moments, Hallock could hear the deep breathing of a gryphon somewhere nearby, steady and reliable. The woman finally said, "They live on magic—use it to fly—practically breathe it so far as I've heard. I don't know what a total depletion will do for his long-term health, but for now, I think he'll pull through."

The blurry image of a concerned Birce suddenly loomed in Hallock's vision as the cold compress that covered his eyes was lifted away. The senior Healers was at his side, and for once, was in a clean uniform. "Sir? You're going to be all right. You've received Healing by magic, for all your conditions. We'll feed you as soon as we can, and move you to another tent."

"No," Hallock croaked. "Thanks, but—no. Get me two company clerks and prop me up. I stay here. You just change the ribbon. I stay with Kelvren."

"Kelvren," he heard the woman say as she left the tent, still unseen. "Huh. Well. That explains it."

Candlemarks passed, during which Hallock had a bland but filling meal fed to him, got cleaned up, was changed into fresh bedclothes, and made complete reports for the Herald on station to peruse. Despite the weariness he felt, he still could not get to sleep, and his sleep medicine sat untouched at his bedside. Finally, he levered himself out of bed, stretching muscles that felt like they hadn't been used in years. Hunching down, then going to his knees beside the great beast's head, he spoke to the sleeping gryphon.

"Kelvren? Can you hear me?" He tried touching the feathered brow. It was the first time since Treyvan had brushed against him in Haven that he'd put palm to feathers on one of them.

A low growl came from the feathered hulk on the floor. "Rrrrh. Hussssh. You talk too much."

Hallock grinned, then sobered as he tried to find good enough words. He finally settled for the simplest.

"Kelvren . . . I owe you my life."

There was a long pause, and then the gryphon heaved a gusty sigh.

"Hurrrh. Had to be sssurrre . . . my rrreporrrt . . . got thrrrough."

Hallock responded gravely, "You could have used your Healing on your own wounds, then reported it yourself. You could have killed yourself just getting to me."

Kelvren lifted his head up with obvious effort and fixed his gaze on the human before him. His beak swayed, and his eyes dilated then focused again. They seemed somehow darker than before, but Hallock knew with a certainty deep inside that the risk of death had passed this noble soul by for now.

"Perrrhapsss. But yourrr life . . . would have ended. You have yourrr Genni. And in a life . . . no one sshould be alone . . . and no one sshould have . . ."

The gryphon laid his head down and dozed, contentedly, after murmuring four more words. ". . . only one . . . perfect day."

Irene Radford

There are many reasons why people write under names which are different from their given one. But in the case of Irene Radford we found ourselves faced with an unusual dilemma. I had read the manuscript for *The Glass Dragon,* and I knew I wanted to buy it. The only problem was that the author's name was Phyllis Karr. And there was already an author named Phyllis Karr who was an established writer in the genre. What to do? Well, thankfully Phyl/Irene had been graced with more than just a first and last name, and so we decided to make use of the Irene Radford part of her own identity for her writing career.

And it's just as well we did because "Irene" has a lot of stories to tell, not only in her popular *Dragon Nimbus* universe—which readers were introduced to with the publication of *The Glass Dragon* in December 1994—but in her historical fantasy series, *Merlin's Descendants,* as well.

I think it's especially appropriate that "Draconis Ex Machina," the tale Irene has written for this anniversary volume, reveals the story of how Prince Darville was trapped and transformed into the wolf we first meet him as in *The Glass Dragon.*

—SG

DRACONIS EX MACHINA
Irene Radford

"WE go on foot from here, Prince Darville," Lord Krej, my father's cousin, announced to me. A placid smile creased his broad face but did not reach his deep blue eyes.

He maintained the masked expression he wore at court.

Gratefully, I dismounted. After three days on steed back, hunting a rogue spotted saber cat, I needed to feel the Kardia beneath my feet for a time.

Eliminating an animal that had developed a taste for human flesh did not necessarily fall to the Crown Prince and the First Lord of the Council of Provinces. But I had taken Krej up on the offer of adventure for many reasons.

Our six guards dismounted with me. We'd left behind the pack of nobles and retainers a day and a half ago. Knowing Krej's need to preen before an audience made that decision suspect.

I left the heavily jeweled ceremonial sword my father insisted I carry as suitable to a man of my station in the saddle sheath. For this adventure I wanted something sturdier, stronger, and keener. Krej had too many secrets to trust him with only a useless weapon in my hand.

Instead, I belted on a serviceable blade I'd purloined from the palace armory.

"You three remain with the steeds," Krej ordered the guards. "Make camp."

They set about their business with unquestioning efficiency.

I needed to know what my cousin plotted. He'd not reveal himself in front of men sworn to my father. For that reason alone I did not question why the horses needed more than one guard, two at the most.

"You other three." Krej pointed to the remaining guards.

"Rest your steeds an hour, then return to the rest of the party. Send them home or bring them here. Whatever they choose." He shrugged as if disgusted with the lack of stamina among his cronies.

I suspected the nobles who had ridden out with us from the capital felt more loyalty to him than to me and my father. Possibly more loyalty to my cousin than to the kingdom of Coronnan.

Why else had they feasted on Krej's bounty the last night we were all together? Krej had wounded the deer, then run it nearly to death. While it lay panting in terror, he had cut the living heart out of it. His mad laughter as he performed the hideous deed still haunted me.

I'd caught a whiff of something strange in those terrible moments. Something worse than the smell of fear and sweat and blood and offal.

What?

I had not eaten any of the deer that night. But the nobles had. Nearly all of them had been sluggish and sick the next day. We left them behind.

Only Krej and I remained to hunt the elusive spotted saber cat. Reputedly, the beast had savaged one of Krej's villages, killing a child. I added a stout dagger to my sword belt.

Whether out of fear of the cat or of Krej, I could not tell at that moment.

While my steed stood between me and Krej, I checked my boot knives and the blades in the wrist sheaths.

The gang of city boys I had run with as an adolescent had taught me to fight for survival. I needed to wade into this fray with intent rather than honor. Rumors in the capital claimed that Krej knew nothing of honor in any of his dealings.

I slung a pack of provisions over my shoulder and stepped toward the path Krej indicated.

"We won't be gone long enough to need those," Krej said, pointing to my pack. He smiled again. His teeth gleamed in the winter sunlight like the predatory animal we hunted.

"The cat is that close?" I asked. The tracks we'd been following for days did not look fresh to me. I bent and placed my dominant left hand atop a clear print. It was nearly as broad as my palm. Stray leaves and twigs as well as dust had blown across it. It was not fresh. Still, I needed to keep up the pretense of ignorance and wits dulled by cold, if Krej were ever to reveal his plans to me. He loved to boast, but would not take unreasonable chances with men equal to him in strength and intelligence.

In a fight I had the advantage of longer reach and greater agility, as well as youth. My left-handed dominance often proved awkward to right-handed men. Krej had brute strength in his broad shoulders and sturdy legs.

He flung a cloak made from the pelt of a spotted saber cat around his shoulders. A new cloak I had not seen before. A cloak that would earn admiration and gasps of awe from the court. A man as vain as Krej could not resist wearing the garment before the audience he craved.

The fog-hazed colors glistened in the weak sunlight, nearly rippling with life and menace.

Every portion of my being froze. Krej did not need to hunt a cat that preyed upon his villages. He had already killed the beast.

Surreptitiously, I fished a talisman from my pack and stuffed it into my pocket. I remembered clearly my friends warning me that the magic in the amulet would not activate until I kissed it and placed it in a pouch around my neck. I had kept the thing only to please my friends. At the time I had scoffed. I did not need magical protection. I was a prince and a trained warrior.

Now I was not so certain.

Krej's cloak covered most of his magician-red hair.

Another rumor I needed to verify. Krej reputedly used magic to ensure the cooperation of the twelve lords on the Council of Provinces, and to coerce wealthy merchants to guarantee his debts. Debts he rarely, if ever, repaid.

Kings and their families were not allowed to possess magic in Coronnan.

In his youth Krej had studied at the University of Magicians. He'd inherited his talent from his outland mother. Neither of his two older brothers showed signs of magic.

Five strong men had stood between Krej and the throne—my

father, myself, Krej's father, and his two older brothers. He'd been allowed his magic.

But then, quite unexpectedly, all within the space of a few months, Krej's father and two older brothers had died of disease or accident.

Only two lives, mine and my father's, now stood between Krej and the throne.

Krej had renounced his magic and assumed his new responsibilities as lord of Faciar, cousin to the king, and leader of the Council of Provinces.

My magician friends questioned the accidents and suggested poison instead of disease in the death of Krej's relatives. I had not the courage to question until I saw what Krej did to the deer, and heard what he'd done to one of his peasants.

Had he really forsaken the practice of magic? I knew he could not get rid of his talent—even if bedding his new bride before he achieved master magician status was supposed to rob him of his powers.

I left my own cloak of wolf fur and oiled wool open across my left shoulder, keeping my sword arm free.

We stepped off the caravan road onto a steep trail leading up the mountain. The lucky charm bounced reassuringly in my pocket.

Not once did Krej pause to inspect the tracks I discerned occasionally along the trail. He did not bend to sniff the spoor. I knew he no longer hunted.

I worried that he no longer *pretended* to hunt.

But I had to know what he was up to. For my father's safety and that of our kingdom.

Two days before we began the hunt, word had reached me that one of Krej's villagers had tried to run away. Krej had run the man to death—never even trying to capture him, just kept him running and running until he could run no farther. When the man finally lay on the ground gasping for air, too spent to move aught but his lungs, and those only painfully, Krej had dismounted and kicked the man in the groin and the chest until he died.

The villager had fared little better than the deer.

And Krej had laughed as he murdered the man.

I could only wonder what cruelty on Krej's part had driven the commoner to run away.

Now I paced warily behind the most powerful lord in the land.

The higher we climbed the colder the air became. I smelled snow. The tree canopy obscured the sun. By the time we cleared the upland forest and moved onto the open slope of the mountain, clouds blocked the noon light and a fierce wind howled. I wanted to draw my cloak closer about me. But I needed my sword arm free.

Finally, I stopped. A broad ledge, about ten paces deep, cut across an open curve of mountain. Above us, the mountain soared to uncounted heights now lost in clouds. Below us, an old landslide dropped sharply to a stony valley. I did not want to be caught out in the open on that ledge.

"Why have you lured me here, Lord Krej?" I drawled the title with contempt, all pretense gone.

I fought the urge to pace. My habits demanded movement. I thought better while moving. Now, as I looked around, I realized we had been following the cliff edge for some time. My sense of space had been tricked by a gentler, rolling slope to my right. Now that it climbed thousands of feet, in a single glance I felt the danger of the drop to my left much more keenly. My safety depended upon staying away from the edge of the cliff. I glanced nervously toward the valley below, a long, long way below me.

I held my breath. I often dreamed of flying with dragons. The reality of the danger made me sidle closer to the solid security of the mountain.

"The time has come, dear cousin," Krej replied with a sneer— all trace of mild condescension vanished—"to end the charade of your father's reign over Coronnan. To end the de Draconis line and the myth of your dragon protectors."

"So soon?" My thoughts whirled. I lifted one eyebrow in an attempt to stall for time. "You have no son or grandson to succeed you. Only five daughters. I would think you would marry off at least one to get a male heir before attempting to displace the de Draconis line, a line of kings born of legend and worshiped along with the dragons." I kept my tone emotionless. "You should have put aside your wife years ago. You'd suffer a lot less frustration with a younger woman capable of producing a son."

The longed-for son must be the only reason he had waited nearly fifteen years to eliminate the last two men who stood between him and the throne. Fifteen years while he lulled Father and me with false words of loyalty and honor and—choke—love.

I clasped my hands behind my back instead of pacing. If only I dared move, I might keep my blood from freezing.

A piercing screech sounded above. I looked up. Saw nothing but a bright flash and dismissed it as the wind and storm.

Krej recoiled from the noise, shifting uneasily closer to the upper slope of the mountain.

No one had seen a dragon in generations. They truly were myths. My sword was the only reality, the only rescue I trusted.

I shifted my hands to the hilt of my weapon.

Krej swallowed deeply. Then he seemed to shrug off whatever had frightened him. He turned his piercing blue eyes on me.

I could not move. He seemed to drive a spear through my will with those eyes.

"Only I know how to tap Coronnan's greatness." Krej's voice took on the rhythm of a chant. He began to draw arcane symbols in the air. Red fire would follow his gestures, leaving the sigils in plain sight if I had enough magical talent to read them.

I struggled to free myself from his thrall. Sweat broke out on my back and brow despite the freezing wind.

"Your oath of loyalty . . ." I tried to stall while I fought for control of my sword arm. If I could speak, his spell over me was not complete.

"Loyalty to Coronnan is loyalty to me. Only I can bring our land into its true greatness," Krej replied in song.

His words chilled me more than the rising wind.

He blinked.

The thrall cracked. I reached for my sword. My cloak tangled around the hilt.

In a flash and a whirl of spotted fur cloak, Krej was behind me—between me and the return path.

Uphill, the faint trail narrowed sharply beneath an overhang and disappeared. Legend claimed that only dragons could climb higher upon the mountain.

No place to run.

I stepped forward. I needed to pressure Krej into keeping his distance.

He laughed and held his ground. I still could not get the sword free. He took up his chant again.

A flicker of movement caught my eye. A small brindled brown cat stalked us. It could not help me and might hinder me in my escape.

The cat had to be Krej's familiar. Why else would it be out in this weather?

Even a dragon would not be caught out in the blizzard to come.

The sharp smell that had haunted me since hunting the deer wafted across my senses again. An instant of dizziness and blurred vision.

(*Tambootie.*) The word came into my head without prompting. Poison.

Dragon salad.

The tool of rogue magicians.

"The de Draconis line is weak, Prince Darville," Krej continued in song. "You waste your time with women and drink; your father dreams away his days and nights with tales of past glories. I shall not allow you to taint the throne when your father dies." The wind grabbed his cloak. Lifted it. It did not swirl as mine had to block his eyes or hands.

I flung off my cloak rather than fight it. My sword came easily to my hand now. The wind picked up my garment and flung it in my face. I ducked it and lunged toward Krej.

He wasn't there.

I whirled. He faced me from the path above me. I plunged toward him. The sharp rise of the mountain on my right became an overhang. The path narrowed further.

Again Krej eluded me. Another giggle sounded that bordered on insanity.

My sword met only air.

He danced around me quickly. I barely saw him move.

The first flakes of snow rode the back of the wind. They whipped past us to plaster themselves against the slope. They showed no interest in melting.

I had to end this soon. I circled my blade, seeking an opening, a moment of distraction.

"Have you noticed, Prince Darville, how pale and ill your father has become of late?"

I had.

"Have you also noticed how the Council of Provinces listens to you less and less and to your father not at all?" Again he giggled.

I'd heard a man giggle like that once before. A condemned rogue magician who had eaten of the Tambootie tree to enhance his magic.

The poison in the tree sap had rotted his mind.

And I knew then, with desperate clarity, that Krej, too, had eaten of the tree of magic to enhance his powers.

Logic and argument meant nothing to him. Only power.

"Your father is weak," Krej cackled. "Growing weaker. At my command. He does not rule Coronnan. I do!" Krej punctuated the air with another sigil, larger and more intense than his previous gesture.

"You lie!" I snarled. I flipped one of my wrist blades at Krej's eyes. He ducked it easily.

Fear began to knot in my gut. "My father rules with the aid of the Council of Provinces." I said it quietly, logically, to reassure myself more than to convince Krej.

"And who leads the Council of Provinces, eh? Who makes decisions when your father is too sick or weak to choose aught but which tunic to wear?" Krej smiled, showing his teeth in a feral expression. The cat that watched us mimicked him.

I tried to run, to just plow through Krej and get back to the bottom of the hill and the guards who would witness my cousin's treason.

My feet refused to move. They felt frozen to the ground.

"The Council listens to me. They respect me," I asserted as I struggled to free my feet. Doubt crept into me along with the cold wind. Did the twelve lords of Coronnan truly listen to my advice, or did they just smile and nod and then go about their business as if I did not exist?

"But you are rarely in the capital, Prince Darville," Krej said through his gloating smile. His teeth remained clenched and his eyes glittered with malice, not mirth. "I see to that. I send you where you will dissipate yourself with wild escapades with your band of street boys, your women, and drink."

I tried to lift my sword. It seemed to weigh more than I did. My arms bunched and strained, but still it would not move.

"Calm down, boy," Krej laughed again. Insanity shone in his deep-set eyes. "This won't hurt a bit. And Coronnan will profit from my rule in ways you cannot yet imagine."

A sharp screech above the rolling clouds sounded again. Not the wind. A dragon?

"You are supposed to help me. Protect me!" I called back to the creature who patrolled the skies.

I thought I caught a glimpse of a translucent wing amidst the snow. Could a creature as large as a dragon do anything on this narrow mountain ledge?

The location for this confrontation had been chosen well.

My enemy began dancing in place while he drew more sigils in the air. I could see them now. I had no defense against the pulsing red and green magic. Soon they must lock tighter circles around me. I had to break free before he closed the spell.

If only I could move.

The dragon screeched again.

Suddenly the cat leaped to Krej's back. The creature's claws dug deep. Its teeth sought the great vein in his neck. Single-minded fury drove it.

Something deep within me knew the creature attacked its master at the prompting of the dragon.

The thrall that glued my arms to my sides faded.

I lifted my sword and freed the remaining wrist blade.

Krej batted away the cat like some annoying insect.

It twisted, reached out, and landed perfectly balanced. Like all of its kind, it prepared for a new attack almost before its paws touched the ground.

I lunged for my cousin. I hit an invisible wall. The shock vibrated up my arm to my shoulder. Hot pain lanced through to my heart.

Krej laughed loud and long.

A fresh wave of snow rushed toward us. I could not see my enemy through it. It must have met the same barrier as my sword, and it fell in a circle around me. A small circle—barely a pace in circumference—remained clear of the white stuff. The wind seemed not to penetrate the barrier either.

I was almost warm.

The cat leaped again to the magician's back. It slammed into a similar barrier and fell to the ground, stunned. It lay motionless. Confusion showed in its yellow eyes.

I lunged again. Once more I hit the invisible wall. This time with more force. My sword blazed golden fire. Heat lashed my hand. I dropped the weapon from nerveless fingers. My entire body trembled with the force of the magic.

Hot tingles became jolts, anchoring me in place. No matter how hard I tried, I could not move so much as a muscle even to blink my eyes.

Panic threatened to choke the breath from me.

With one last singsong stream of words and a wave of Krej's hand, the magic shot from his fingers into my eyes. It penetrated every hidden corner of my being.

I could do nothing to stop it.

The spell was complete.

My skin itched. I could not scratch it. Golden fur sprouted from my arms and legs. The torment of raw skin beneath the new growth increased. The hair bristled and stood on end. My ears stretched upward. I think I screamed at the pain. My own howl sounded strange, more intense and primitive than a human throat could utter. Tiny sounds pricked my hearing: rocks shifting under

Krej's feet; the wind sighing on several levels beneath the roar through the tops of the trees; the cat sobbing.

How? What?

My nose found new smells in the snow, the soil, Krej's sweat. Confusion muddled my thoughts.

Above us the dragon cried in anguish that echoed my own. The sound threatened to shatter my hearing.

Krej reeled away, hands clapped to his head, nearly doubled over in pain.

I wriggled and swayed, trying to break free.

Neither the dragon nor I could stop the transformation. I had only Krej and the little cat as witness to who I had been.

I think I sobbed.

My face ached sharply. I sensed my nose elongating into a muzzle. My jaw receded. I smelled my own fear, the pain in the cat, and triumph in my enemy.

Then my joints began to crack and bend at odd angles. I cried out at the pain. I collapsed. My clothing fell away, including the useless good luck charm in my pocket. Not even magic could hold me upright any more. Fire seemed to engulf me. The noises erupting from my throat sounded more like the howl of a wounded animal than a man.

Horror choked off the sounds. My heart beat wildly, and I despaired that I would ever see my father again. I wanted to cry and could not.

As I lay there, rolling about on the ground like Krej's wounded deer, my limbs contracted and bent. My bones grew heavy and dense.

Language deserted me.

My hands became paws without the useful thumb to grasp a weapon.

I had only instincts and anger left.

I panicked. I growled and leaped again. And bounced against the wall.

I opened my mouth, baring my fangs. I could not allow this man to corner me. I ran forward, lunged . . .

Krej shoved me backward with another wave of his hand.

I scrabbled for purchase. The unaccustomed shortness of my legs skewed my balance.

I slipped on loose rocks. Clothing tangled around my feet. I rolled sideways.

Krej reached a grasping fist for me.

I shied away from his touch.

The wind caught me.

Suddenly I flew. Only air stood between me and the bottom of the cliff.

Stargods help me!

I cringed and flailed for purchase before the collision with rocks and ground that would crush my bones and rip my flesh.

My hands/paws scrabbled against the rocks. After too many rapid heartbeats my claws found purchase on a protruding boulder.

The dragon above cried her mournful anguish.

Krej roared with laughter in answer. "No need to explain your transformation by a rogue magician now," he chortled. "I'll discredit the University of Magicians another way. But I shall have to forgo the pleasure of leashing you and keeping you subservient at my side."

The cat roused enough to scramble to the cliff edge and look over at me. It extended a paw as if offering me a hand up.

I had nothing to grip with. No help. Nothing between me and a very painful death at the bottom of a long fall.

"I think I will tell the court that you chased the spotted saber cat too vigorously and fell to your death. Wild and drunk as always. But they will find no body if they bother to search when the storm passes. Who will give the body of a dead wolf a second look?" He flicked his fingers in dismissal. "You will rot in this forgotten valley, as you justly deserve. And your father will crumble in his grief. I'll rule all of Coronnan uncontested before spring! I won't even have to kill the king. He'll just wither away to dust of his own volition."

He stomped about in his mad glee.

I lost my fragile hold. Fell. The ground rushed upward. No exultation. Only heart-stopping fear.

Then I crumpled on the stony valley several dragon lengths below.

A moment of shock. No breath. No thought.

"And now, just for fun, you shall join the princely wolf, cat. You deserve punishment for my wounds," Krej sneered above me. How did his words come to me so clearly?

Eerily, I heard the whoosh of air as he kicked out at the tiny creature that had tried to help me.

No sound of a heavy boot connecting with a furred body. Only the thump as Krej lost his balance and fell on his butt. Another time I might have laughed.

He picked himself up, cursing. "You shall pay for this, cat. I shall find you again and make certain you pay!"

The faint sound of tiny paws scampering over the edge of the cliff drifted toward me.

Krej's shouts followed the cat all the way down the cliff. Eventually his noise faded. He must have retreated from the storm.

The storm that would kill me.

Chill invaded my limbs.

Darkness crowded my vision.

Snow built up around me. My body warmth kept the flakes at bay for a time, but as I chilled even more, the snow would cling and bury me. No one would find me until spring.

I could not even tremble in fear or shake with the endless pain. Each breath became a new agony.

But I had to live. I had to stop Krej and his plans to rule Coronnan.

The cat crept closer to me, nose working.

I breathed. Snow moved in a different pattern in front of my nose.

The cat jumped back. Hissed. Crept forward once more.

I live, I tried to tell it. *Get help.*

My mind spun and drifted. Each time I blinked seemed to send me away for longer and longer.

Darkness calmed me. I welcomed death. Anything to relieve me of the pain and the cold.

Some time later, when hours and minutes had no meaning

anymore, I felt someone digging the snow away from my body. Someone breathed a gentle warmth across me. It eased one discomfort. Magnified others.

I looked up into the swirling circles of dragon eyes. The nearly invisible creature towered above me. I had to concentrate to see it. Very difficult. My hurts demanded my attention. And yet the dragon drew my gaze, challenged me to look closer. Each hair of its fur was a thread of crystal. Or an icicle.

Easier to look around it than at it.

It spread its all color/no color wings to shelter me from the snow and wind. A long spiral horn growing out of its forehead provided its primary tool to remove the accumulation of insulating snow from around me. Once more it blew a warming breath over my fur.

I watched the snow turn to steam around me.

Why did it protect me? My wolf body should have been a tempting meal for the giant predator.

You will be safe now, my prince, the dragon spoke directly into my mind. A feminine voice. A mother's concern for a pup. *Brevelan will guard you. Remember this day and remember me.*

Then the dragon launched herself into the sky. The downward thrust of her wings blew more warm air around me. I lost sight of her within an eye blink. Obscured by snow and her own camouflage.

A woman appeared out of the storm. She must be the Brevelan the dragon had called to me. A thick coat of oiled wool covered her from crown to toe. Within the shadows of her hood I detected a wisp of red hair and deep blue eyes. Krej's eyes.

I recoiled in fear, baring my teeth and growling.

She crouched before me, murmuring soothing words.

A sense of comfort and safety washed over me.

The brindled brown cat jumped from the woman's arms and pressed her nose against mine. I blinked in surprise.

"Golden-brown eyes to match his fur," Brevelan said quietly. "Why?" she asked, looking up into the air. "Why did you bring me out in this storm to save a wolf? You should have just eaten him."

I cringed away from the dragon's roaring reply.

The woman sank to her knees and covered her ears.

"All right!" she shouted back to the dragon. But it sounded more like a protest than acceptance.

A braver person than I to question a dragon.

"This is going to hurt, golden wolf," Brevelan murmured.

Her words invaded my mind, and I did not fear her or the pain I knew must come. Somehow she would make it all better.

Gently, agonizing inch by agonizing inch, she rolled me onto a blanket she had spread on the ground.

I tried not to cry out. A noble man did not show his pain. But I was no longer a man; noble, peasant, or prince. Pitiful whimpers escaped me.

Pain robbed me of breath. I went to a place deep within the core of me, beyond pain, beyond thought. I was still conscious, I think, aware and yet. . . .

Then—wrenching pain. Brevelan grunted and pulled with all of her might on one foreleg. She had planted her tiny foot on my shoulder joint.

I snapped my fangs. Bit only air.

Grind. Twist. Wrench.

My shoulder popped into place. Dull ache replaced sharp pain.

I retreated once more to that place where pain and memory of treachery could not reach me.

In later days I would remember what I saw on that long lonely trek. But I did not feel anything.

I think Brevelan and the cat dragged me some distance out of the valley, and up a hill or three. They paused often whenever a rocky overhang or the spreading branches of a tree offered a semblance of shelter. The woman's teeth chattered. She and the cat clung to each other for warmth. Once they even curled around me on the ground throwing a second blanket over all of us.

Perhaps we slept, tangled together for warmth and comfort.

Eventually we reached level ground. A tingle of magic rippled over me as we passed into a clearing. As a wolf, I had no problem crossing the invisible barrier. Was it like the one Krej built to imprison me before working his evil spell? Would the barrier be so accepting if I still walked upright as a man?

I might never know. Only the cat had seen my transformation. Brevelan saw me only as a wounded golden wolf. A new pet to gather close to her heart.

Across a snowy field stood a hut. It looked almost as if it grew out of the land, thatch nearly reaching the ground, weathered plank walls, a rough chimney spouting a trickle of smoke like steam rising from a dragon's breath.

That memory seemed very far away, though I knew it had happened only hours ago.

A little more fuss, and Brevelan dragged me inside. Heat from the glowing coals in the hearth blasted me. I jolted out of my reverie back into reality. The pains seemed worse as the warmth rooted out the numbing chill.

I think I whimpered again.

Immediately Brevelan crouched beside me. She stroked my ears and spoke in soothing tones. The words passed beyond my ability to understand.

The pains eased to a tolerable level.

I think in that moment I fell in love with Brevelan of the magic clearing.

She placed a bowl of fragrant broth before me. I studied it for long moments wondering how to drink it. I could not grasp the bowl with wolfen paws even if one of them were not broken or sprained and the other immobile from the dislocation.

The cat appeared before me. She bent to the bowl and lapped a few drops of the nourishment. My wolf instincts took over. My tongue darted out, curled, captured a little moisture, drew it back into my mouth.

Wonderful flavors and healing warmth coursed through me. I lay back exhausted after only a few mouthfuls. But the broth had already worked wonders on my body and my spirit.

My Brevelan held my face in her hands. She looked directly into my eyes. "Who are you that a dragon called me out into a storm to rescue you?"

I stared back at her, wishing her to read my mind, challenging her to read the cat's memories.

Eventually she looked away and shook her head.

"Now for the hard part, wolf. Don't snap at me because it hurts." Brevelan glared into my eyes.

I accepted her words for truth and gritted my teeth. A tiny growl escaped me without thought.

She was right. It did hurt. She splinted a break or two and bound my ribs so tightly I could barely breathe. She draped wet bandages around my shoulder and chest. As they dried, they hardened. I could not move that limb if I wanted to.

Once more I went into that place beyond pain. I wished only for the release of death. A prod to my mind broke my trance.

Remember. A voice came to me from a far distance.

Remember what?

Pain still existed within me. Much of it oozed out of me with a few more tonguefuls of broth.

Brevelan dragged me closer to the hearth and rolled me onto a dry blanket. She sat at my head, stroking my fur. Each time her hand touched my fur, I grew sleepier and more in love. She sang to me. The cat joined us, adding her rhythmic purr to my lady's song.

Blue light engulfed us, shutting out the storm, shutting out the pain. My world shrank to this hut, my lady, and her song.

Perhaps I drowsed. I awoke hungry again. The broth had cooled. I lapped it up anyway.

Full tummy. Warmth. A lady to love. Safety.

What about tomorrow? Would I remember who I was? I must remember that I was betrayed. The dragon had commanded it.

Tomorrow.

What is tomorrow?

I knew only now.

Warm.

Safe.

Not hungry.

Marjorie B. Kellogg

While I was still at Signet, I came across a manuscript by an aspiring author. The manuscript was a science fiction novel, *A Rumor of Angels,* and it was to be the first of several science fiction novels Marj Kellogg wrote for me at Signet.

After I moved to DAW, Marj continued to write science fiction for Signet, but we'd become good friends by then and kept in touch, and, naturally, when we got together we talked about writing and ideas for projects. Those conversations started Marj thinking about writing fantasy, but she didn't want to fall into the standard fantasy clichés. So she continued percolating ideas, even as she devoted the majority of her time to her first career as a set designer.

Eventually, her ideas crystallized into a vision that would become *The Dragon Quartet,* which began with *The Book of Earth* in February 1995. *The Dragon Quartet* is innovative in style and serious in intent, a cautionary tale of where our world could be going if we persist in ignoring the warning signs, preferring the greed and self-gratification of the moment to the preservation of our own planet.

"The Hamlet" melds both of Marjorie Kellogg's careers in a poignant and powerful tale that will remain with you long after the last word is read.

—SG

THE HAMLET
Marjorie B. Kellogg

W E stood at the edge where the road branched off, debating
the downward-heading, miserable little track as loudly as a
cluster of ravens at a midden. Not a cairn, not a signpost to be
seen. Raw mountains and too many miles behind us; before us,
the blank stretch of the island sea. So far, we'd resorted to no
more than the usual blame-tossing and invective, but it was only
a matter of time. This was not good country to be lost in.

"That's Clearwater?" Little Pete brushed frost from his two-
day beard and spat into the frozen mud. "Not on your life."

"No? Why not?" Sofie shook out the excuse for a map that
the blacksmith back in Westering had scrawled on a shred of her
kerchief. "We turned right by that old wall, like he said we
should . . ."

"Obviously he was wrong," I replied, more harshly than I'd
intended. "Or we'd have been there yesterday."

"It's not Clearwater." Stephen advanced three heroic paces
along the main road. Three. It was always three. Meaning you'd
better stand aside if he was headed in your direction. "I say we
go on."

Bella nodded, Stephen's faithful echo. But she held her place
beside us. I could hear her teeth chattering. By nature childlike in
her optimism, even Bella had been shaken by the past few weeks.

I jerked a thumb at the black roil of cloud shoving past the
snowy summits of the mountains. Worse than wolves or bandits,
I feared the storm that had us in its sights. The first stiff gusts
were already arguing with our packs and cloaks and clothing.
"I'm from the north country. I know about snow. All we need
now is to get caught in a blizzard."

"But it's just around the bend, I tell you!" Stephen gestured along the frigid coast. "Marcus is expecting us! We'll run lines for the new piece as we go."

"No, Jamie's right," said Little Pete. "Snow would not be good. Marcus can wait."

Marcus was our advance man. Little Pete didn't much like him, or the new piece. "Overblown" and "melodramatic" were the kindest of the objections he'd raised. Stephen had written it in the "old style," which required a more straightforward narrative than our usual fare. It was intended as a crowd pleaser, but Stephen was no populist, so it did not showcase Pete's considerable (and crowd-pleasing) comic talents to advantage.

"Her voice is going." I was keeper of the purse. I should be stern with them. Instead, I heard myself pleading, and felt humiliated. "Another night on the ground and you can kiss the next week's bookings good-bye."

"She'll perk up once she hears the applause."

"Stephen, the new piece won't draw if she can't appear in it."

"Pooh! They'll be cheering us in Clearwater by dinnertime!" Stephen spread his arms to embrace the darkening zenith, and I tried not to despise him for believing that an adoring public was the only proper goal in life. Once I might have agreed, but not now, now that I'd seen how truly fickle their adoration could be.

"Especially if we get Act Three down letter-perfect," Stephen concluded.

Sofie flexed her skinny knees and drew one yellow-clad leg up beside her ear. "I'd remember my lines better if I had a few more of them."

"Did someone say dinner?" Little Pete gazed mournfully down the snow-flecked trail to where it dropped sharply into the elbow of the cove. A few small, unpainted boats bobbed on the gray water. A few blue slate roofs poked up through wind-scoured scrub. A solitary stone chimney gave up a slim curl of pallid smoke. "I remember dinner. We might actually get some, down there."

"Oh, spare me!" Stephen swept to the brow of the slope and posed while the icy wind battled in the violet fullness of his cloak.

"If the entire sorry populace of that flea-bit hamlet can gather three pennies in a jar, I'll eat my doublet."

"You may have to," I murmured, relishing the image.

Sofie giggled in her dazed way, and turned her map upside down. Bella, even faithful Bella, expelled her little breathy laugh and mimed perishing of starvation in a snowdrift.

"A show for a meal, then," determined Little Pete. "Why not? Other people do it."

Stephen glared. "We are not 'other people.' We do that, and soon every town we come to will be expecting a freebie!"

"Word does get around," I agreed, much as it pained me ever to find myself on Stephen's side.

Pete crooked his bristled chin at me, and for a moment I feared he was going to bring up the Forbidden Subject, right out there in the open. "It's not free if they feed you," he said instead.

And then the Diva's wagon clattered up behind us, and the bickering abruptly ceased. We four stood there feigning innocence, while Stephen resumed stalking about hopefully and conspicuously in the icy road ahead. The mules stamped and blew. Sofie leaned against the wagon and traced its bold lettering with a fond and fretful finger, while I tried to ignore the racking cough coming from inside the cab. Up on the driver's perch, Joanie fixed a skeptical eye on the steep and slippery trail to the village.

"This is the place?"

"Um . . . I'm pretty sure it isn't." I shrugged my cloak tighter. The muffled coughing raked along my spine. "But there's a mean blow at our backs."

Joanie pursed her lips at the visible if not very recent wheel ruts. The last show's eye pencil blurred on her plucked brows. "I dunno. We might get her in there, but I wouldn't bet on getting her back out again."

"Dinner, Joanie . . ." Little Pete wooed. "Perhaps a mug of ale . . ."

"A hot bath, a dry pallet . . ." I stopped, squeezed my eyes shut. I was pleading again.

"I don't think . . ." called Stephen from ahead in the road.

The wagon creaked, and the coughing ceased. The painted

curtain shielding the side window crinkled aside. "Is there a problem, darlings?"

"Not at all!" Stephen's shout was shrill after the low and smoky music from inside the cab. Even roughened by chill and exhaustion, the Diva's voice stirred souls. At least, it still did mine. And my guilt as well. She needed help, and I could offer none. At least, not the sort she needed.

"We're lost!" Sofie flashed her coquette's grin. For a mad instant, I suspected her of irony, and wondered how she could have so long hidden such complexity.

"Not lost!" Stephen strode back to us. "We're just not there yet!"

"Bad map," growled Little Pete.

"Sssshhhh!" hissed Bella. This was one of her most expressive sounds.

The Diva's dark eyes, so black, so knowing within the folds of her hood—how could a human eye show less light than the sky at night?—swept us all and settled on me. "Is there a problem, Jamie?"

Such sadness, such profound world-weariness and self-contempt, all expressed in five mundane little words! A tiny sob rose in my throat. "Uh . . ." I began, and cursed myself. Six years in the Diva's Company and still unable to face her without stumbling over my wretched, worshipful tongue. "Well, yes, I guess there is . . . seems to be."

Silence. Only the wind's deepening snarl and the snorting of the mules. Yes, we were lost in bad country with a storm bearing down on us, but we all knew what the real problem was: six sore and hungry people, teetering on the edge of a cliff in a stiff wind, unable to reach a consensus. The worry that had been swirling around us like a flood had risen and finally incapacitated us. Worry like dread, like a canker, unrelieved and unexpressed because even to mention it was to admit to the reality of its cause.

The Diva's tar-pit eyes moved from me to the downward track. Lashes thicker than the falsies the rest of us wore dipped heavily, then rose. We didn't need to explain a thing. "I'm not helpless, you know. I can walk down."

"You mustn't!" cried Stephen.

His gasp drowned out my own sigh of relief. I hadn't expected such easy acquiescence to the idea of stopping in an out-of-the-way place. So naturally, and because the idea was mine, I began to question the wisdom of it.

But Joanie knew how to play to advantage. She leaped from her perch, crimson ringlets slashing across her cheeks, and grabbed the lead mule's bridle. "That's the spirit, boss! You wrap up nice and warm, and I'll take the boys down first, in case the wheels slip a rut or something."

"I really must object!" Stephen loomed at the wagon door. For a moment, he actually pressed against it as the Diva tried to ease it open. "Bad enough stopping here when we're so overdue for our next booking. But for you to go in on foot, Josepha? Into that scruffy village, like any daily player?" He paused, too horrified to continue.

All but the Diva's wide lips and pale, tragic cheekbones were lost in the wagon's dark interior. What was visible, we studied as our text, for mood and meaning, for a sign. I longed so to see her smile again. Instead, her mild regard was like a sigh of regret.

"Daily players," she mused. "Perhaps, Stephen, that's just what we need to be right now."

"But we're mere inches from Clearwater! Marcus will have your likeness all over the neighborhood, and there'll be none but us to protect you! All those dirty hands and staring faces? Wanting? Demanding? Touching? You know how you abhor that!"

"Abhor is a strong word, Stephen."

Had he ever won a single of these reckless skirmishes? I would never have tried, and wondered why he persisted. In more generous moments, I admired Stephen's self-immolating passion, knowing it was beyond my reach. Of all of us, only Stephen called the Diva by her first name. Each time, I was surprised she let him get away with it. Now I could hear her gathering up her outer robes. Silken voice, silken rustle, from the darkness, and our course of action was at last decided. I told myself that a little danger and exercise would do her good. And even if she was recognized, in a remote village like this one, how bad could the danger really be?

"It'll be a small mob, most likely," Little Pete observed dryly. "Tiny. The town is. You said it yourself, Stevie."

Nearly hysterical with defeat and disapproval, Stephen bellowed, "Then why are we going there?"

The rest of us stared at him. Wasn't it obvious?

Our fame and fortune required both a clamoring multitude and the Diva's safety. However pampered, she was bound to beat at the walls of her prison every once in a while, and Little Pete encouraged her every whiff of rebellion. I was just glad that my own personal goal—keeping the Diva warm, dry, and fed—for once coincided with her own.

So while Stephen ground his teeth like a pantomimic villain, Sofie did pirouettes, her dervish arms twined above her head and her rainbow cloak a bright swirl against the chill and fading light. "A tiny mob, a tiny mob, a teeny tiny mob!"

I shrugged, stepping up to my favorite role as the only sane one. "You know, uhmm, nothing we can't deal with."

Joanie prized Stephen's hand from the door handle, then stowed it companionably beneath her arm. "Come on, dearie, don't be an old pisspot now. A hot meal would be a blessing. We'll pull the tarp over the wagon, turn our cloaks inside out, and go in like civilians."

"But we're not!" Stephen wailed. "And we never can be!"

But he didn't pull away, and we dutifully exposed our shivering limbs to the elements long enough to reverse our colorful players' plumage to its drabber inner linings.

The Diva unfolded her tall muscular frame from the wagon's cramped cab. She stretched, slowly and thoroughly, until she could move without limping, then tightened her hood against the wind and public scrutiny, and down we went.

The Diva, as you may have guessed, is not your ordinary performer.

For instance, I'm a fairly stolid sort. I'd never have left my tranquil youth behind to chase after anything less than a walking miracle. So, in case you think our precautions extreme, here's how it goes each time we come to the next village.

First, there's always a troop of quick lads staked out along the road, eager to sprint ahead and be the first to announce the Diva's approach. In the smaller towns, Marcus has been known to slip them pennies enough to speed their step. Farther on, the men in the fields toss down their hoes to stand smoking and grinning along the verges, while the farm wives coo from their gateposts, their broods all lined up for a wave and a blessing. If they've never seen the Diva work her wonders, an aunt or a neighbor has, or a traveler's tales have enlivened a winter tavern or fireside.

By the time we haul into town, there's a big crowd already waiting, kids and grown-ups and grannies, thronging both sides of the main drag if they're orderly, or pushing, shoving, and clamoring if they're not. Marcus usually puts on a little extra local security, but even with the orderly crowds, the Diva rides in hooded majesty, only her strong, long-fingered hand signaling her greetings from the window, while the rest of us close ranks around the wagon. After all, a good mystery lures even the most hardened skeptic.

But the real reason for all the caution is this: everyone in every crowd has an agenda, and every one of them is convinced that the Diva is whom they should take it to. After all the cheers and applauding come the demands. Most are banal and innocent: a dream needing interpretation, a sickness needing curing, a reluctant lover needing to be convinced. But the folk are like sheep. When one makes a move, they all do, and next thing you know, we've got a stampede. Even when they don't come with a problem, it never occurs to them that the Diva might prefer a little personal space to their unsolicited company. We're all gifted performers, even me, it turns out. But the Diva would draw crowds without the theatrical window dressing we provide. Basically, we're there to fend them off.

But it's not the ordinary fan that keeps all six of us armed to the teeth. The Diva disapproves of weaponry—Art should not be held hostage, she harumphs—and I'm never comfortable with the hard chill of a blade strapped to my thigh. But Joanie insists, and too many close calls have proved her right.

For there are those out there whom passion rules beyond all reason: the furious husband (or father) from a previous town who's convinced that his wife (or daughter) has run off with the baker (or miller or shoemaker) because of something the Diva did or said. Or the man in whom meager talents and overweening ambition have combined to produce a fatal poison, the man whose delusions tell him that the void left by the death of the Diva is one only he will be called upon to fill.

At least, that's how it used to be, not so very long ago, before the Diva lost her Power. And there you have it: the Forbidden Subject.

So the crowds had been leaner in recent weeks. Like I said, word gets around. But just for the record, this lack of any advance welcome at all was unprecedented.

"The folks must be all out fishing, huh?" Little Pete liked to think he understood what went on in towns, though he hadn't actually lived in one since he was a child. Several paces ahead, the Diva picked her way along as if mere walking required all her concentration. Stephen followed watchfully, his ear being badly bent by Sofie's latest proposal for an expanded dance number in Act Two. I doubted anything was audible over her enthusiastic trilling of the music she'd written. If the town hadn't known we were coming, they'd know it now. But Pete kept his voice down anyway, in case it should sound like he was making some sort of point about the sparse turnout. "Or maybe they're at dinner," he added hopefully.

"Joanie did say to go in as civilians," I pointed out, as the wind flung its first sleety salvo in our faces.

"Hey, I'm as modest as the next person, but there are limits."

"Maybe they're waiting for us in town."

"Nah, I'll tell you what: that fuck Marcus went straight to Clearwater and never left the first tavern he went into!"

Little Pete carried on with his old bitch-and-grumble, crowding me precariously on the narrow path though his lithe little clown's body could have danced safely over every snowy rut and boulder at a dead run. Plumper by far and less sure of my footing, I listened with half an ear. I was sick of the arguing, and I was hungry and my feet hurt. Besides, though I'd never been much given to sight-seeing, I found my attention oddly drawn to the landscape —not out of boredom or to escape Pete's litany of complaints, but as if the rugged, pine-dotted slope itself demanded my particular scrutiny. Individual details stood out to me as still lives, even in a cold driving rain, when any sensible being would keep his head down and his eyes glued to the precipitous path. I noticed how the wind eased as we descended into the lee of the hill. How the trees farther down relaxed out of the tortured poses of those caught in the cross drafts at the cliff top. How the gray water in the cove below was as still as a mirror, while just outside the harbor, the inland sea raged with whitecaps. The sea. Its gray vastness riveted me. I was keeping the books for a dry goods store in the forest town of my birth when the Diva's company happened by and swept me up in its wake. I'd never in my life seen so much water in one place.

"Nice little spot," I remarked, mostly to myself.

Pete peered up at me. I was never much good at satire, as he was fond of pointing out, but he clearly suspected me now of some feeble attempt.

"It's warmer. Don't you think?"

He rolled his eyes. "Warmer. Right."

"Well, it's stopped sleeting."

"Hummp. So it has."

The trail switchbacked down the rocky, brush-pocked slope into the moderating shelter of a thin wood of birch sapling, ash, and pine. Casual piles of kindling and hewn logs marked the first outskirts of the village, then a broken scrawl of stone wall along the seaward edge of the path, as if someone with the best civic intentions had begun the barrier but was soon distracted toward some more pressing project. Still no sign of welcome. I wondered how the Diva was taking it.

Finally a house appeared among the trees, also of stone, a bit more barn than dwelling. Its paddock held tucked against the hill-side a damp pair of lop-eared mules and a cud-chewing spotted cow. From a square window beneath deeply protruding eaves, a young girl peered out at us. Sofie grinned up at her and waved. Polite more than curious, the girl waved back, as if bands of cloaked strangers accompanying shrouded wagons were a common sight along this road. Already, Stephen was scowling. Astonishing that he could complain so bitterly about the crowds and yet long for them so desperately. But I knew by then that I could never comprehend Stephen. I could only learn to live with him.

Soon the population of quiet barnyards and homes thickened into the cramped and cobbled streets of a village, woven by its braided stones and slate roofs into the very rock of the hillside. Soon after, the villagers themselves appeared, sweeping snow from their stoops or loading barrels of salt fish onto carts. But little fuss was made over our arrival. A nod here, a smile there, a brief "good even." Nothing further.

It was hard to keep from looking behind us for the usual entourage of fans and petitioners. But we did, or we'd have looked pretty silly. No one was there. Only an old black boat dog nosing lazily along our trail.

"Eyes front," advised Joanie. "Don't want them to think we've someone after us."

None of this boded well for the evening's purse, once we did reveal ourselves as players. Oddly, I felt myself breathing easier. It was even possible that my feet hurt less. I found the quiet town and our sudden anonymity rather novel and interesting. But there, however, opinions diverged.

"That fuck Marcus," muttered Little Pete. "He'll hear a thing or two when we haul him out of whatever dive he's holed up in!"

I couldn't blame Marcus for being loath to advertise what he could no longer make good on. I'd be drinking, too.

"They fancy us mere peddlers!" Stephen owned a rich stock of such phrases, culled from roles he adored and nobody else would play.

"No," said Joanie significantly. "Civilians."

"Be careful what you wish for," I joked, encouraged by the

softening angle of the Diva's broad shoulders, which reminded me of a smile. And I'd noticed that despite the knee-jerk complaints, our habitually close ranks had eased apart, and our hands had relaxed away from our hidden weaponry.

We went along into the middle of town, easy to find, as the road led right into it, then right out again, to climb back toward the cliff top. Still no waiting crowd. The Diva's posture relaxed a few notches more, no less erect than was her habit, but more fluid, like an ice-chocked river thawing into a stately current. I had an inkling suddenly of how much effort that heroic posture must be to maintain. Were we simply working her too hard?

A central market plaza fronted on the harbor at the head of the cove, cozy-seeming despite the damp and chill. The docks defined one long side, a row of inky wooden tongues lapping the still, reflective water, comfortably pressed left and right by small but sturdy fishing vessels. Past their faded canvas canopies and the dark traceries of rigging, the rocky arms of the shore curled around to stop just short of meeting. In the narrow gap, the waves of the inland ocean crashed and foamed like lions in a cage. Their roar rolled toward us over the smoothing inlet as an audible fog. The Diva moved dreamily past the halted wagon as if drawn by a tightening cord. At the edge of the quay, she stood inhaling deeply and gazing out to sea.

Stephen stared around the nearly deserted square as if he mistrusted his eyes. "Are they in bed already? Is there a plague? Has war been declared?"

"Hush!" scolded Joanie. "It's a chance for a night off!"

The plaza wasn't entirely deserted. Low warehouses formed the short sides of the rectangle, and in one open doorway, two merchants in leather and fur concluded their business with the driver of a slat-sided poultry wagon. Two rows of canvas stalls crouched in the center of the square, most already closed or closing for the day, but here and there, still some activity—a last minute casual choice, a final minor purchase. I watched the Diva watch the villagers, absorbing their ordinariness as avidly as Pete thought about his dinner. This was how people led their lives when nobody famous was around.

The fourth side of the plaza, facing the harbor, was a stubby civic building, recognizable by its insistent blandness. Its blocky columns supported the slate roof of a portico, raised a step or two above the level of the pavement.

"That'll make us a perfect stage," I observed, without adding the obvious: if we can gather up any sort of an audience. I saw no potion-sellers among the tented stalls. No games of chance, no dream-readers, not even the usual local charm merchant. "Wonder what these folks do for entertainment?"

"This burg is dead as ashes," retorted Pete.

"They're probably just home eating."

Which all of us wanted to do sometime very soon, so Joanie set the brake on the wagon and tied up the mules, and we set about searching up a suitable inn. There proved to be two, one farther along the docks, facing the harbor and unmarked but for a weathered board in the shape of an ale keg. The other was on the wide street leading back out of town. It boasted a walled yard with a stout gate that sported a brightly lettered sign: The Quiet Woman. Its glazed windows tossed warm rectangles of light onto the cobbled pavement. Instinctively, we all chose literacy and the light, as more likely to be the polite sort of place where we could both walk into without being mobbed, and find a paying audience. But the Diva called us back.

"Darlings, what do you say to the other?"

Stephen peered around willingly enough. "Is there a third?"

"No, I mean that one, by the water. Couldn't you just devour a hot bowl of seaman's chowder and a mug of grog?"

Stephen's eyes rounded in horror. "G . . . grog?"

I'd have been inclined to agree, but a dim memory prodded me: hadn't the Diva hailed originally from the seacoast? I squinted toward the harborside establishment. It seemed a dreary place, hunkered down on the wharf like a slumbering walrus, grim in the graying dusk. Its two-story facade was nearly obscured by haphazard stacks of crab traps and salt boxes, or lumpish mounts of fishnet. It looked tough and dark and unpredictable. The Diva's fit of nostalgia could get us into serious trouble in such a place.

I said, "I guess . . . If you think it's . . . it'll sure be cheaper."

The Diva laughed, deep and throaty, like I hadn't heard in weeks. "Jamie, Jamie! Where's your spirit of adventure? Just smell that salt air! Ah!" She turned as if inspired, and the folds of her cloak flared around her and lifted, allowing me several rhythmic glances of the robe beneath. I started, blinked, and thought, *No, it can't be. I'm only seeing what I hope for.* But echoing Bella's soft intake of breath, Pete's elbow gouged my ribs.

"Hey! You see that?"

"Yes!" If three of us had seen it, perhaps it wasn't just a trick of the fading light. Perhaps there had indeed been a pale and evanescent shimmer, revealed then concealed by the darker, heavier silk of the outer garment. After long weeks in quiescence, was the old Robe at last stirring to new life?

Meanwhile, there was the Diva, striding alone and unprotected across a darkened public square, her gloom and languor apparently forgotten.

"After her!" Stephen cried, and whatever we'd seen or thought we'd seen, it was no longer in evidence by the time we'd caught up with her at the dockside tavern's door. At least she'd had the courtesy to wait for us before entering.

"Josepha!" Stephen panted. "Have you gone entirely mad?"

Stephen was tall, but standing fully erect, the Diva towered over him. "Not that I know of. Why do you ask?" While Stephen sputtered, the Diva counted heads. "All present, my darlings?" Stunned by her sudden energy, we nodded like obedient ducklings, and she turned once more to the squalid door.

"Wait!" Stephen actually grabbed her by the arm.

She shook him off abruptly and her white teeth were a phosphorescent crescent inside the shadow of her hood. Little Pete's elbow raked my ribs a second time. The Diva waved her hands in front of us like the country fair magician she claimed not to be. "Remember, darlings: Joanie said to go in as civilians, and so we shall. Bend your talents to the task! I require your finest performances!"

"In the worst dump in town?"

"Ah, look at it, Stephen! Look at it! See how kindly and

demurely it sits in the landscape! How natural it seems. Surely not everything has to be about props and costumes and attitude?"

Of course, for us lately, that's all it had been about, and it was Stephen who saw to it that the less successful were the Diva's Transformations, the more elaborate was the entertainment that bracketed them, or more recently, replaced them entirely. And, as always, he felt compelled to meet implication with argument. "No, Josepha, but I think it helps. An audience loves a little glitter and fancy clothes."

"Glitter I can no longer provide, you mean."

Suckered, Stephen glanced away. "No, I . . ."

"Ah. Perhaps you think I am withholding on purpose?"

"Of course not!"

"Do we have to do this now?" Sofie danced a little jig of beseeching, while Bella mimed heartfelt support.

"Well, ummm . . ." I agreed that the stoop of the local tavern was an unfortunate spot to begin airing the company's dirty linen. Still, any step taken toward discussing the matter would be a forward one.

"It has to come from here!" the Diva insisted, one palm softly striking her robed chest, though it could have been in self-reproach as easily as in emphasis. "There has to be need, Stephen! True need! You think hauling just anyone up out of the audience is all that's required!"

"No, I . . ."

"Do we have to do this here?" Joanie demanded.

The Diva inhaled hugely from her diaphragm, then let out the very longest of sighs. "No. Let's eat."

When the door finally opened on the dim and unprepossessing interior, we all piled in, hooded but casual, offering just the right mix of exhaustion, boisterous relief, and eager appetite, seasoned with due respect for the local folk already well into their chowders and grog. We nodded to the barkeep, and headed for a back corner veiled by the sooty haze and away from the prying blaze in the stone hearth that squatted in the center of the low-ceilinged room. The table had seen better days, and was in need of a serious mopping up. While I dabbed at it ineffectually, the Diva leaned over and swiped at it broadly with her sleeve. I would have paid anything for a glimpse of the face that went with Stephen's strangled gasp, but he'd turned it away to the wall. Joanie surreptitiously snuffed the single candle guttering in a broken saucer, but because not to do so would attract more scrutiny, most of us doffed our hoods. The Diva shook hers back a bit, then drew a thick silver braid from behind to drape across her chest like a lopsided necklace. She slouched into her chair and grinned around at each of us.

"Stop glaring into the shadows, Stephen! We're perfectly safe here."

Little Pete rose, swallowing a guffaw. "Okay, what'll it be? Chowder and grog all around?"

"Let's hear the menu," said the Diva. "Call the girl to the table."

Pete lifted an eyebrow, but dutifully went in search of her.

An ambivalent silence settled over the table. It was buoying to see the Diva so cheerful and vigorous, but the rest of us reckoned that our rare chance for a night off would be immediately compromised by the arrival of a serving maid. Close up, even in near darkness, the Diva would surely be recognized. So we tensed a bit when Pete reappeared through the smoke and shadows with a lank young woman in tow. Her manner was subdued, her eyes downcast, and her gait listless, but she stood where Pete placed her and recited the choices in a thin but audible monotone.

"Capon stew or beef pie."

We waited until it became obvious that she'd said all she had to say, or perhaps all that she could manage.

"That's it?" Sofie mourned. "That's all there is?"

"That's all, m'am." The girl brightened, or maybe it was just that she'd reached to the next table for a candle to relight ours. "Tomorrow there'll be lamb shank."

"Hmmmnah," said Pete. "Well, while we're struggling with this very difficult decision, we'll start with a hot jar of grog for the table."

"Ale, sir."

"Huh?"

"Ale's all we got."

"Ale, then." Pete shrugged and shook his head. "All around."

"Yessir." The girl turned to go.

"Just a moment . . ."

"Sir?" The girl slouched back, offering Stephen a dispirited glower. When he looked blank, she turned the same exhausted look on Little Pete, and then on me, the look of one whom the world is sucking dry. I recognized that look. I'd seen the Diva wearing it herself of late.

"Umm . . ." I searched for an appropriate expression of sympathy.

"It was I who spoke," said the Diva from beneath her now scarcely concealing cloak.

"Oh, no," Sofie whispered, drawing up her shoulders tortoise-like as if to avoid whatever was about to happen. Joanie and I glanced left and right, gauging the actual extent of our privacy. Sometimes the Diva needed reminding where her own safety lay.

"I was just wondering about that chowder . . ."

Joanie tried to head her off. "They have no chowder, dearie."

"That's right, ma'm. No chowder."

"But surely you have some milk about the kitchen?"

"Oh, yessum, we have that, all right."

"And some onions, perhaps?"

"How 'bout some ale?" Little Pete slid his chair back, then halted abruptly as if by a hand clamped heavily on his thigh.

The Diva leaned forward, allowing the renewed candle flare to invade the dark cavern of her hood. The light drew a pale outline around her strong, square jaw and glinted in the close-cropped silk of her beard. "And potatoes?"

"Yessum . . . er . . . sss . . . yes, we got all that."

The Diva shifted to lean the black weight of her glance against the discomfited girl's face. "Perhaps you could even scare up a carrot or two."

"Um, mm . . . sss . . . can't really say."

"Can't really say . . . no. Right?" The Diva smiled.

The girl squinted as if caught in a sudden burst of sun, then returned a confused sort of smile, as if not at all sure why, or if she should. "I guess, um, there must be a carrot or two around somewhere."

"Excellent! Now, tell me this, my girl . . ." The Diva hiked forward on one elbow, as if prepared to share the most intimate information. The hood slid backward across a sleek crown of silver braids and collapsed in conspiratorial folds about large-lobed ears. In the left lobe sparkled the blue Eye of Albin.

The rest of us readied ourselves. Even silent Bella let out a faint hiss of alarm. But the serving maid merely nodded hip-slung and folded her scrawny arms, to show she was well used to windy customers; in fact, as it was a slow night, she had all the time in the world. I offered Little Pete an oversized shrug. The silly girl had no idea who she was talking to.

"Tell me," the Diva continued, all heavy lids and hush-hush. "Where in this lovely harbor town might one procure a fish?"

In her innocence, the girl would also not realize the implication of the Diva's "tell me." But it perked my ears up all right.

"A fish, mmm, uh, sir? . . . why, anyone here can get you a fish!"

The Diva clapped both hands delightedly. "Oh, marvelous! Then we can have our chowder after all, if its parts are all right here to hand!"

The girl stuck her tongue into her sallow cheek, mildly vexed to have been snared by simple logic. "I suppose you could, if you could talk Mr. Harry into fixing it for you."

"But I don't need to, do I, when I have you, darling girl, to do it for me?"

"I dunno . . ."

"I know you can manage it! Tell me, what's your name?"

Yes, to make it work, the Diva would need the name. I could sense now where things were headed. More than chowder was going to be at stake here, and I wasn't sure it was a good idea. Of course, the Diva shouldn't give up trying, but I worried that each disappointment would be the final blow. What if it got half-way and then failed? How would the girl feel, afterward? The poor thing couldn't have avoided mirrors all her life. But I didn't want to stick my nose in. There was always the chance that the Diva would succeed.

"My name?" the girl repeated, as if no one had ever asked. "Lucy, sir."

The Diva nodded encouragingly. "Well, Lucy, surely a pretty wench shouldn't mind employing her wiles in the service of a starving patron?"

Stephen snorted audibly, but at last the girl's wan mouth showed some life of its own, just the faintest upward curl, and I knew the hook was set.

"Starving, sir? Wouldn't know it to look at you."

"Ah, but appearances are deceiving, are they not? So, starving I am. Believe it, Lucy! Starving for the taste of my lost childhood." The Diva sat upright and shook off the last of the hood's confining folds. They resettled in a dark frame that revealed the high collar of the robe beneath: luminous blue chased with the same silver glimmer as the beard and braided hair, and brows as pale as moonlight rising above the nighttime valleys of the Diva's eyes. "Will you do this for me, Lucy?"

Around the table, we were silent as the grave, poised between incurable hope and pragmatic dread.

The girl bobbed her head as if compelled, and found resolve. "I'll sure try, sir." Off she went through the shadows, toward a faint glow that might have been the kitchen. The Diva smiled after her, and soon the smile turned inward and thoughtful.

The rest of us exchanged uneasy glances, but heedless Stephen spoke up before anyone could stop him. "Are you sure this is wise, Joseph? I mean, to attempt this here?"

"Where better?" replied the Diva darkly.

Referring, I assumed, to the convenient absence of a paying audience. I thought I might inquire if we were planning to look for one that evening, and so distract them both. But as I never could gather the presence of mind to look the Diva straight in the eye, I missed the flare of bitterness and determination that made Stephen sit back a bit and blink.

"Um, well . . ." I began, and then the girl was back at Pete's elbow with a tray full of brimming pints, her step a world more sprightly than before. She leaned over the table to set the first dripping mug between the Diva's clenched fists, which promptly relaxed into cupped palms of welcome.

"Mr. Harry says he'll do it, can you believe it, sir, seeing as he's made up a pot for his own supper tonight. But you mustn't let on to the other customers. He says to make you promise."

The Diva laid hand on heart. "Not a word, dear girl."

Beside me, Little Pete chuckled and reached for his pint.

The ale was bright and clear and bracing. A sigh went around the table, and I gave up all sour thoughts about our earnings as we followed the Diva's example by offering our next long swig in toast to Lucy, our savior. The girl giggled, and leaned against the wall beside Little Pete's chair. I thought there was better color in her drawn face now, though that might have been due to exertion, or the heat of the kitchen. *True need?* I mused. This girl is the very definition of it. Casually, I shifted my seat around. I wanted to be able to watch her.

She hooked thin strings of hair around her ears and regarded the Diva sidelong, the sort of glance we all give when we first realize we're interested. "You're not from around here."

Little Pete sucked foam from his mustache. "What was your first clue?"

"Not of late," replied the Diva with pointed grace. "But forever ago, I was born on the Inland Sea, a week's hard travel south of here. It's marvelous to breathe the salt wind again and hear the roar of the surf."

News to me that the Diva ever had a clue where we were geographically, or was even interested. But I'd long suspected that the famous vague frailty that we all indulged was her passive revolt against the strictures of our care. Of course, the frailer the Diva seemed, the more closely we guarded. I rolled ale around on my tongue and pondered a solution.

Lucy saw no frailty now. "You travel a lot, looks like."

The Diva nodded. "Travel we do, to our detriment."

Next the girl would likely inquire after our occupation, and then our idyll would be at an end. Instead, she sighed, as forlornly as a tragic heroine. "I never do. I've never been anywhere, 'cept to the next town, once or twice. That's Clearwater, y'know. Are you going there? Oooh, that's a lovely town."

"Then I look forward to it," said the Diva gravely.

Over the top of my ale, I noted Bella's gaping yawn. Little Pete plopped down his empty mug more heartily than was necessary. "How 'bout another round before dinner?"

Lucy's palms flew to her cheeks. "Oh! So sorry! Right away! And I'll check on the chowder while I'm at it!"

As she scurried away, a starved mouse fleeing for the baseboard, the Diva frowned gently into the smoky air above the table.

"Well, we came in here to eat, didn't we?" groused Little Pete.

"Tch, tch," the Diva chided.

I almost mustered the nerve to say that I agreed.

"Oh, come now," smirked Stephen. "A little local travelogue? Hardly the most scintillating conversation ever."

"Ah, but you, Stephen, any one of you, can have unscintillating conversations anytime. You can walk down snowy hillsides and into strange villages on your own two feet, whenever you like."

A familiar argument, and none of us could deny it. Such was the price of fame, one that Stephen and Sofie and maybe even Little Pete would gladly have paid. As for myself, I was tiring of the road, though I hadn't known it until that moment, when I suddenly realized that I could see the Diva's point.

Which had been delivered this time with particular vehemence. But Stephen moved through life enclosed in an invisible reflective bubble that mirrored only his own opinions back to him. So he said flippantly, "If you're going to risk our one chance for peace and quiet, Joseph, you could at least find an interesting subject."

The Diva rounded on him, those black eyes fired by hot points that had to be more than candlelight. "You'll never be a great actor, Stephen, if you never learn to study from life!"

Stephen stared. Then, gut-shot, he wilted. Rarely did the Diva level so personal a reprimand.

"And when fame no longer allows you the opportunity," the

Diva continued, "that might be the right moment to pack it all in."

Silence. Then because he was incapable of seeing that he was not, nor ever, the real target, Stephen muttered something about finding a privy, and stalked off to lick his wounds.

"Um . . ." I said, my favorite conversational opener, but once again, Lucy appeared, bearing a fresh round of drinks.

"Lucy, my darling!" exclaimed the Diva extravagantly. "Come to me!"

Briskly passing around the mugs, Lucy blushed, then let a smile bloom hesitantly over her shoulder as she darted away again. "Your soup is warming, Mr. Harry says. I'll be back with it in a moment."

"Feeling peckish, boss?" Joanie remarked when Lucy had retreated. "Drink up. It might improve your manners."

"Mine? What about his?"

"He's never had any. Why expect it now?"

"Because, dearest Joan, diminished expectations are precisely the root of our troubles. Mine of you, and yours of me."

Silence again. The Forbidden Subject hovered once more. But maybe this time was different. I wanted to ask if anyone else had noticed the change in little Lucy, but I knew that premature scrutiny might jinx a still fragile charm. So I entertained myself by worrying about how we were going to pay for our dinner. Whereupon, the chowder appeared.

The girl had lugged the broad iron kettle all the way from the kitchen, its handle looped over one outstretched, shaking arm, a stack of clay bowls clutched under the other, and a wooden ladle clamped between her teeth.

She seemed to be managing, but because my woodlands mother brought me up right, I sprang up to help lift the heavy, soot-encrusted pot onto the tabletop. Lucy flicked me a surprised and grateful smile over the clenched ladle, and I saw that her eyes were a particularly interesting shade of sea blue. The dim light or smoky air must have prevented my noticing this until she stood a little closer. She set the bowls down, stuck the ladle into the pot to stir up the bottom, and from that black and scabrous vessel arose the most divine odor imaginable.

When the bowls were filled, the Diva claimed the nearest and inhaled its rising steam. "Lucy! Bide with us a while, my girl. Tell us about the town."

Lucy's cheeks shone like polished apples. "Oh, sir, I mustn't!" But she slid into Stephen's abandoned chair eagerly enough. "What would you want to know about a nothing old town like this?"

"No town is nothing, child."

"This one is."

Spooning in milky-fragrant chunks of fish and vegetables, the Diva murmured, "Tell us of your life, then."

The girl took a breath, saw we were all waiting, blushed again, and to our astonishment, plunged right in. A mere half hour before, she'd hardly been willing to offer two words in a row. Suddenly she was voluble, a veritable mistress of narrative, as if telling the story of it gave her life more substance and color, more . . . reality. She sat up straight and shapely. Her blue eyes flashed, her apple cheeks glowed, and her mousy hair escaped its bindings at her neck to decorate her animated face with lovelocks of purest shining gold.

I caught myself leaning openmouthed over my empty bowl, and sat back, chagrined. I sensed stirrings in my heart and groin, places I'd thought gone dead of disillusion and disappointment. I recalled the sensations right enough, but the memory was a pale and dim one compared to this. The future seemed suddenly more open and possible. Lucy seemed possible. I wondered if I'd had too much ale. I looked to the others, but their noses were all buried in their bowls.

Across the table, the Diva downed a last swallow of chowder, setting aside spoon and bowl with an air of inner purpose and precision. In his left ear, the blue Eye of Albin glimmered. He turned his head a careful fraction, just so, and the jewel sparked incandescent shards of light that slammed into my eyes, exploded in my brain. I reeled and shuddered, less from pain than revelation.

Flattening both palms on the scarred tabletop, I tried not to suck in air, as if I was drowning. Though, in fact, I was.

The true need had not been Lucy's, but my own.

The Diva's smile flashed into the corners of my soul like sunlight off rippled water. "A thousand thanks, Jamie lad."

I became aware just then, as in a particularly vivid dream, of the tavern's warmth and homeliness, of the humble strength of its stones and sooty beams and whitewashed walls, of the peaceful murmur of its inhabitants, of the scent of fish and garlic.

"But what will I do here?" I knew but was not yet convinced. In my mind's ear, I heard the roll of the sea and the cry of the harbor gulls. I saw Lucy, bright-faced in a garden.

The Diva's frown grasped at stern impatience, but managed only wistfulness. "Live. Raise a family. Have a life."

Behind us, a cheerful commotion erupted at the door. Stephen rushed up breathlessly. He flicked a contemptuous glance at the servant girl discovered sitting in his chair, then looked right through her.

"Stephen!" I cried. "Guess wh . . ."

The Diva reached to lay a hand upon my arm. "He'll never see what you see."

And, of course, Stephen wasn't listening at all. He whipped off his cloak and turned its purple richness right-side out. "Joseph, our luck is changing! There's a late stage arrived from Clearwater, and two fancy carriages driven down off the high road by the storm! The inn is full to bursting! One of the swells spotted our wagon, and the search is on! They're clamoring for you!"

Sofie cheered, and threw off her own cloak. Gauzy scallops of yellow and orange, lime, lilac, and magenta danced in the candlelight. "A show tonight after all!"

"A life," I repeated stupidly, pinned to my seat by the Diva's eye. I would miss them all, of course, even the impossible Stephen, and the Diva most of all. But my time with them was finished. "What sort of a life?"

The Diva shrugged, rubbed his beard. "You'll know what to do better than any of us would. Who knows? Maybe you'll start a theater company."

We both laughed, but the Diva's laugh was hollow. The rowdiness across the room blew up into a loud chorus of discovery, and headed our way. We rose from the table as one, Joanie reaching swiftly for the Diva's hood to snug it tight.

He caught her fist and kissed it, then shed his outer layer and, laughing, tossed it into her arms. The Robe shone forth blue and radiant silver, the moon on a rising tide, illuminating the darkest corners of the room. Joanie's answering grin was brighter still.

Stephen whooped for joy. Little Pete leaped straight up, turned a perfect somersault and landed in the center of the table, arms outstretched. The diners and drinkers shouted for more.

"We'll head for the yard at the Quiet Woman!" Stephen crowed, not caring an iota that the romantic lead would not be his tonight.

As the others closed around the Diva, moving toward the door, Lucy stared after him, forgotten. "What? I never . . . can it be? Of course! I should have known!"

I drew her away and into the curve of my arm. Her lovely face was bewildered and bereft, and I accepted that it would be a while before I ceased to be anything but a substitute and a disappointment. The crowd surged around us, calling, pushing, pleading, snatching at the Diva's cloak, or any cloak within reach. The Company rode the hubbub like dolphins on a cresting wave, but this time, the Diva led the way. Once outside, he'd no doubt vault onto the lead mule's back and drive team and wagon hell-bent into the inn yard. Then he'd vanish into the cab to emerge beribboned, bejeweled, and begowned. And each person watching would see what they most wished to see. The greatest spectacle Stephen could devise was no match for the Diva when the Power was on her.

At the door, I held back, wondering if my friends would even notice my absence. Or the true magic that the Diva had wrought.

But it didn't matter.

I had my Lucy, and the Diva could take care of herself.

Jane S. Fancher

I first met Jane S. Fancher when she was illustrating the graphic novel of C. J. Cherryh's *Gate of Ivrel.* I never realized that she was also a writer until her first science fiction novel from another publisher came out to glowing reviews.

Her fantasy series for DAW, which began with *Ring of Lightning* in 1995, follows the literary tradition of gender-bending in science fiction and fantasy which was pioneered by Ursula K. LeGuin's groundbreaking novel *The Left Hand of Darkness.* While LeGuin wrote about aliens with the power to alter their sex, Fancher writes about an ancient race of human-like people who are true hermaphrodites. In Jane's *Dance of the Rings* series these people face self-hatred, xenophobia, racism and oppression. They are rarely celebrated for their magical talents, and try not to disclose their true nature, even to those closest to them. Her story in this volume is about one of these magical people. It has been decades since the publication of *The Left Hand of Darkness,* and many authors in our genre, including Marion Zimmer Bradley and Mercedes Lackey, have since broached the subject of alternate sexuality in their fiction, whether by inventing a new race of people, or simply by making a character gay.

As long as homophobia exists in our culture these portrayals will always be not only poignant, but important. And if even one life is improved or one person's viewpoint enlightened by reading about a heroic gay character, these books will always be worth publishing.

—BW

MOONLOVER AND THE FOUNTAIN OF BLOOD
Jane S. Fancher

I DON'T remember the day I was born, but the moment of my death is seared into memory.

I'd been riding with my lovers—too many lovers, Mother would say, and not enough friends, but that's another story. . . .

Or, perhaps not. As to that, only time will tell.

But I get ahead of myself.

As I say, I was riding. Upon returning, I'd sent my lovers on to the house ahead of me, wanting time in my garden, and my garden being that one, hidden part of my Self that I shared with no one: lover, friend . . . or enemy.

I recall the scent of the roses. Even then, with senses no better than any other human's, I could close my eyes as I walked and know where I was in the maze by the scent of the nearest rose. As the essence of sun-warmed raspberries filled my nostrils, I paused, opening my eyes upon my current favorite, a rose that radiated the color of the glowing sun at its center, shading to the deepest of mountain berries along the edges of the petals. I remember noting that it thrived while its neighbors wasted— perhaps because it *was* my favorite. I felt guilty that in loving one more than the others I'd caused suffering.

I knelt beside the nearest of those distressed plants and thrust my fingers deep into the soil, seeking the flow of lifeblood from the Fountain. As I'd suspected, the sunberry was getting more than its share, the patterns flowing deep beneath the neighboring plants, rising again to touch the roots of the sunberry.

I sternly redirected the flow, then stood watch as the wilted leaves plumped, and the heads of the valiant buds lifted.

Tomorrow there would be blooms.

Assured the flow had stabilized in the new pattern, I sent a silent apology to those I'd neglected and moved on, working my way inward toward the Fountain that glittered with rainbow colors in the sunlight. Weaker colors than was my preference, as the lifeblood's scent had been weak, hence my determined march on the center of the maze.

In the pool at its base, those colors swirled, eddied as I passed my hand through them. I thought of my lovers, and the liquid calmed, turned mirrorlike, reflecting those thoughts, not my own face.

As I knew they would, they'd retired to the rejuvenating pools deep in the mountain beneath the tower, basking in the soothing liquid, doing what lovers did.

I blew their reflections a kiss and silently wished them joy. Perhaps I'd join them later.

And perhaps not. It depended on how hungry the Fountain was today.

I drew my knife, set the point to my wrist and jabbed quickly, cleanly, severing only skin and the artery that was my target.

Blood streamed across the pool, dissipating quickly. Too quickly: the Fountain was starving. I held my hand steady, resisting the instinctive urge to thrust it into the pool, feeding the Fountain until at last the mirror on my lovers turned deep, rich red.

Finally, weak with blood loss, I lowered my hand into the mirror, scattering my lovers into the Fountain's red spray. I closed my eyes, sent my inner awareness to the wound, waiting only long enough for the Fountain to heal the artery before pulling free.

My knees gave way, and I sank to the ground beside the pool. Leaning my back to the stone edge, I drew my legs up, rested my arm in my lap, and waited for the skin to heal. The Fountain's blood-touched water evaporated quickly in the dry summer air, leaving the job undone. I dipped a single fingertip into the pool and dabbed the red spot, keeping it moist, using only enough of the lifeblood to heal the wound.

For the rest, dinner, a good night's sleep—alone, I remember thinking, though reluctantly—and breakfast and I'd be ready to feed the Fountain again. In the meantime, I drifted in the sunlight, gathering its warmth.

"Well, that was rather foolish, now, wasn't it?"

"Hello, Mother," I said, without opening my eyes. She was the only one I allowed here. Of course, since it was her garden before it was mine, I couldn't very well keep her out.

"Child, you must stop this. You spread yourself too thin, the garden is too greedy."

"My garden isn't greedy. It takes only what it needs."

"And the blooms grow fat as you grow thin. Greedy, I say, as these leeches you bring into my house are greedy."

Mother never thought much of my choice of lovers. "They aren't leeches."

"They want only the things you give them, the beautiful home, the good food and fine clothes—"

"The hot baths." I laughed aloud. "But, Mother, I don't care. In return, they give me what I want."

"Cheap, uncomplicated sex?"

I lifted my head defiantly.

"Child, you grow tiresome—and old. You must give me an heir, before the garden and the leeches eat you alive."

"I'll have no woman beneath my roof."

"Your problem isn't with women, it's with yourself."

I said nothing.

"There are other ways," she persisted.

"Not for me. Go find yourself an heir the way you found me."

"I didn't find you, I simply lost you for a time. You were conceived in this house, in love, but her parents came and took you away before you were born. When the women of the village expelled you, the earth led me to you, and I brought you home."

That was news. I remembered my mother and the village, but nothing of my father. "Was my father owner of this house?"

She shrugged. As usual, Mother's moments of enlightenment were as short-lived as her arguments were persistent.

"The point is, my lazy darling, the heir to this house and this Fountain must be born of love, and love is receiving as well as giving. You *give* too much . . . to the Fountain, to your leeches. You must learn to accept in return."

"I'm doing fine, thank you."

"Rabbit piss. You're killing yourself, inside and out. Your body rejuvenates your blood, but what rejuvenates your spirit?"

"Love."

"You don't know the meaning of the word. Won't so long as you surround yourself with these sycophants."

"Speak from experience, do you, Mother?"

"Yes."

I hadn't been expecting so plain an answer, wasn't accustomed to the cold, determined expression on her face.

"Were they to see you as you truly are—" she began, but I interrupted:

"They won't."

"If they loved you, it wouldn't matter to them."

"No one can love that—creature."

"Nonsense. *I* do."

A ludicrous comment which deserved no answer.

"You get in there now and tell those leeches to leave, or—"

"Or?"

"Or I will."

I laughed, knowing it for an empty threat. My lovers never saw my blessed Mother. I pulled and pushed myself to my feet, then leaned over to kiss her cheek—carefully, I was still dizzy.

She hissed annoyance, but cupped my face between her clawed hands, matching us lips to lips, and exhaled into my mouth. I didn't resist, felt, as I knew I would, the weakness evaporate from my knees, and the vitality elsewhere returning.

Mother didn't need the Fountain. She drew her strength from deep within the earth itself. Hers was a magic well beyond my understanding, let alone my ability, and I was sincerely grateful for the gift.

I wrapped my arms around her scaled shoulders and held her close, whispered, *"Thank you,"* and bounded for the house.

The last call I recall clearly from that day was her voice in my head as I left the garden: *Don't thank me too soon.*

The rest of that day is awash—murky—with sensations. Sight, sound, smell . . . my very sense of the lifeblood soared beyond human ken.

I remember running all the way to the baths beneath the ancient tower, rushing to my lovers, so full of energy, I wanted to have them all at once. I recall my poor servants jumping out of my way, clearing the halls before me.

I remember flashes of glowing stalactities, the small streams that crisscrossed the path, the exhilarating rush as I dived, head-first, into the glowing pool among the smooth, beautiful bodies.

I recall coming up for air.

I recall the horror on their faces.

The fear.

The disgust.

I recall the way they pulled away, pressing themselves to the edges of the pool, and how the cousins, Jhemin and Jharl, leaped out and disappeared up the pathway, screaming for help.

"Cal?" I asked the nearest, oldest and best of my current lovers, and I reached to catch his arm as he, too, pulled away. But my voice was not my own, and my hand, my fingers, my . . . claws . . . bit into his arm, scoring deeply before I realized those claws belonged to me and let him go. "Cal, it's me, Tammerlindh." I struggled, forcing the words past a throat that seemed too stiff to make the sounds, but Cal heard, or saw, something that made him pause, at least long enough to look more deeply, past the scales, the claws . . . the fangs I felt pressing my lower lip.

By now, the pool was empty, leaving only Cal, and . . . whatever I had become.

"God of lightning, is it you, Tam?"

I nodded, afraid to open my mouth lest he flee as well.

"Wha—what happened to . . ." Cal was shaking. I remember how he sank into the pool, seeking its warmth. I remember sensing the flow of the lifeblood to the wounds on his arms and how my own soaring energy drained as the pool sought to heal the deep gouges.

Gouges *I* had made.

"I don't *know*—"

Cal winced, and I closed my mouth on the unnatural sounds.

"What happened?" Mother's voice, a voice very like mine had become, finished for me. The words echoed in the cavern. "Nothing *happened*, Calwern of Tandoshin, worshiper of . . . *lightning*." And Mother herself appeared—for the first time to one of my lovers—standing on the edge of the pool, her tail whipping from side to side, her scales glimmering in the light from the pool. "This is *my* child, Tammerlindh."

"Mother, no!" I cried in protest, but it was too late, and I was condemned by my own words. Cal stared at me in horror. "Cal, this isn't . . . I'm *human*, Cal, as human as you. I was born in Kheroshin. Bastard, yes, but human. My mother hid me for years, but the village women discovered me, stole me from her hut, and left me, naked and bound in the woods. Mother found me, yes. Raised me, *yes*. But this—" I raised my hands between us. "This is *not* me! She's done this—" And turning to Mother, I begged an answer. "Why?"

"For truth, child. For love. *True* love will break the spell."

"Cal loves me. —Don't you, Cal?"

But the horror remained on Cal's handsome face, and the distance between us grew steadily.

"Cal?" I held out my hands, pleading, and something in my eyes must have reached Cal at last, because almost, I swear, he lifted his hand to meet mine.

But at his movement, the pool rippled, sending out waves of light.

The scales on my fingers glittered.

Cal jerked back, shook his head as I reached desperately for him, shook his head again as he stumbled out of the pool and up through the tunnel.

"The garden is dying."

Mother's words: the first sounds I recall from the days following my death.

"So am I."

But in truth, I was already dead, my sleek, scaled form nothing but a mobile tomb.

"Rabbit piss. Get back up there and tend your roses."

My answer was to slither farther into the utter darkness of the cavern depths. Somewhere in that time following my death, I'd left behind the rejuvenating pools. Lack of food and water made my reptilian shell ever smaller, allowing for deeper and deeper penetration into oblivion.

But one day I made one crawl too many. Before me, then around me, the glow returned.

Too easy, child. Mother's voice in my head, and in the next moment, sunlight blinded me.

Well, not permanently: Mother wasn't a total fool. She transported me into the shadows beneath an arbor, but it took many long minutes for my long-unused vision to return. When it did, I wished for the darkness back.

The garden was, indeed, dying.

I tried to stand, but my body had forgotten how to walk. I crawled slowly to the heart of the garden, where the Fountain ran clear and cold as mountain ice-melt, its lifeblood totally consumed.

I had no knife, my clothing was gone with my skin, but I had the weapons of my new form. I aimed a sharp claw above my wrist, plunged it deep . . .

But there was no blood.

Frantically, I tried again.

"That won't work." Mother's voice, and Mother herself, perched on the side of the pool.

"What . . ." My voice was little more than a hiss. "What, then, can I do?"

"Tend them. Love them."

"The soil has no life. Without the lifeblood, the water is impotent. *Your* truth, Mother, not mine."

"Leave, then. Find Love. Assume your true form and return to feed the Fountain."

"And in the meantime, the garden dies."

"Perhaps."

"And perhaps I'll remain here and die with it."

"A compromise. I give you the night. You shall have your true form back, but only at night. And you will have no more substance than the greater moon. When it is new, you will be nothing but shadow. As the moon increases, so shall you. Only when the moon is full will you be solid flesh. Only then can you feed the Fountain."

"The roses will die."

"Not if you control the lifeblood's flow more carefully. The roses need little merely to survive. You were profligate with the Fountain's essence with your glamours and your parties, your gifts to your lovers. Conserve. Wait. Find love for you, not your gifts."

"You ask the impossible. No human, man or woman, could love what I've become. What *you* have made me."

"And that, child, is where you do me an injustice."

"How?"

"One day, you'll understand."

My life became a morbid dance of hope and disappointment. Travelers passed through my gates, took advantage of my shelter and my generosity . . . then left, never to return. I tried, oh, how I tried, to be the gracious host, but my form was frightening, even to myself. I banished all mirrors from the house, and ultimately all objects with a polished surface. I avoided looking at myself . . . I didn't have to, I saw Mother's truth in the eyes of the travelers.

Finally, I shut my gates. Not all Mother's insults could make me reopen them. Without my tapping the Fountain for human comforts, the garden did well enough. I survived off the woods. I became more and more a *creature.*

And thus did I exist, growing darker and more bitter with each passing breath . . . until *he* came into my garden.

But again, I skip too far. It was the merchant, first. The merchant and his servant boy.

I saw them first in the woods. The merchant was in the cart, the servant at the donkey's head when the wolves attacked. The boy tried to ward them off with his puny stick. The merchant wielded a heavy whip that hit the boy as much as the wolves.

It was obvious who would win that fight. I turned my back, content in the knowledge that had I not been there, they'd have died anyway.

But the boy's cry proved my undoing: I looked back. He was down, with the pack leader's teeth reaching for his throat.

I *was* there, and because I was there, I couldn't pretend otherwise. Before I thought again, my claws were digging into the pack leader's scruff. I pulled him off the boy and thrust him into the woods, hissing and snapping my teeth. The pack leader challenged; I threw him back again.

In my hunting, I'd grown wise in the strengths of my inhuman form. I used those strengths to liberate the merchant and the boy, and knew satisfaction for the first time, as the pack slunk off into the shadows.

I turned back . . . to an all too familiar fear on the merchant's face.

I approached the cart, slowly, palms upturned, so as not to frighten. The donkey had a laming wound in its hindquarters, the boy lay still on the ground.

I thought to help.

The bite of the merchant's whip ended any such inclination.

Without a word, I escaped into the woods, glad to see the last of this ungrateful pair. I ran through the woods that day, ran and ran, trying to escape the face of the servant boy, the fear and the pain that changed, or so I wanted to believe, to hope and gratitude as I freed him from the pack leader's weight.

Night fell. A clear but moonless night, and so I became shadow.

It was, perhaps, the strangest of my forms to comprehend. I existed. I saw, I thought, I moved through the landscape. But I could not touch or speak.

I returned home . . .

To find it invaded. The merchant was there, eating—*gorging* himself on food I hadn't created. *Mother's doing*, I thought, though I hadn't seen her since I closed my gates.

But the boy was not in my house, not gorging on Mother's food. I thought myself through the door and into the courtyard, where I found the cart, but no donkey, no servant boy. Traces, a veritable trail of blood led through the maze and into my garden, all the way to the Fountain.

I found the servant collapsed on the ground beside the donkey, a bloodied rag in his hand. The ugly wound I'd seen on the donkey's hindquarters at the last was half-healed. The boy leaked a steady stream into the thirsty soil.

Dying. Trying to help the beast while his master stuffed his face inside.

I knew if I could get him into the Fountain, he would not die, but I had no substance. I couldn't so much as dip fingers into the pool.

I could, however, direct the flow of the lifeblood. *That* was a feat of will, not of substance. I sank my insubstantial fingers through the boy's body and into the soil. I sensed the flow. I called it to me, drew it up and into the body, to that wound in his side.

I knew, when the long-lashed eyelids flickered, that I had succeeded. I kept drawing, feeding the slender body, restoring the lifeblood lost.

It was, Mother would say, profligate spending of the Fountain. But I knew the limits of the Fountain now, understood the needs of the garden. The roses would suffer, but they wouldn't die.

The boy shuddered to life, curled into a ball, shivering in his thin tunic.

Cold, but he would live. There was nothing more I could do for him.

Dawn approached. Soon, I would resume my reptilian form. I returned to the house . . . where I found the merchant awake and stealing jewelry.

Not that I particularly minded: the jewels had been gifts to my lovers. The merchant had slept in one of the rooms vacated in that last hurried exodus. I didn't mind the theft, but somehow, the ingratitude overwhelmed me. Anger flared with the dawn, and I descended on him in fury, as my claws and scales glittered into substance in the light from the window.

The merchant cowered, dropped to the floor, pleading innocence. I called him liar and coward, and thinking of that boy left to die, raised a hand to even the score.

"Stop! Please!" A voice from the doorway stayed my hand. A deeper, richer voice than I'd expected the boy to have. But not a boy, seen on his feet and in dawn's light. A young man. A young man covered in blood and dirt, his long hair in tangles about his face, but with a dignity utterly lacking in his master.

A sigh heaved beneath the dirty tunics as I lowered my hand.

"Thank you." The young man stepped into the room and moved toward me, carefully avoiding the carpet with his filthy feet. "He didn't mean to hit you yesterday, my lord. He was frightened. If he'd understood, he'd have thanked you. I'm certain of it."

"Thanked me. And is stealing another way he . . . shows his gratitude? Is leaving you outside to die while he feeds his overstuffed face?"

"He was very hungry, my lord. It's been days since we ate a real meal. He came in to find help. I imagine he was . . . distracted."

"You make excuses."

"Do I? Forgive me. If you won't accept his gratitude, will you at least accept mine? You saved us yesterday . . . you also saved me last night, in the garden, didn't you?"

His gratitude disturbed me. "Corpses lying about upset my gardener."

A knowing smile lit his face.

"It still doesn't excuse the theft," I persisted, resisting the lure of this proud young man, who defied my anger and who showed no fear of my fangs and my claws.

"I'm certain it was for his wife, my lord. He's a merchant who lost all on this venture. She's expecting a gift, and she's . . . very demanding."

"Then perhaps she should find herself a more prudent husband."

"It wasn't my fault!" the merchant protested, even as he tried to rise.

I pushed him back down with a flick of my tail.

"But it's the truth, my lord." The servant touched my arm, not shrinking from the texture so foreign to human fingertips. "The failure was not his, but mine. I brought the wrath of his trading partners down on his head."

"And how did you do that?"

Another faint smile. "I flooded their cargo."

"And why did you do that?"

"Seemed like a good idea at the time?"

I laughed aloud for the first time since my form change. It was a strange, hissing sound. The merchant cowered. The servant joined me. I felt . . . human for the first time in countless seasons.

I couldn't let this young man leave. Not yet.

"Fault or not, thief or not, he's insulted my hospitality. He will remain here until he convinces me of his penitence."

"But, my great lord." The noise arose from beneath my tail. "I'm *most* sorry! I do regret my hasty, ill-thought actions. I'll never—"

"Oh, shut up. While you're in this humble mood, however, try apologizing to this loyal young man you've so wrongly treated."

"Never!"

Any stray thought of forgiveness vanished.

"Very well." I waved a hand—very grandiose gesture and utterly meaningless—and the room transformed into a dark cell. "Good-bye. Come, lad, I'll find you a bath."

"Wait!"

I turned to the merchant.

"You *can't* leave me here."

"Can't I?"

I was out the door before I realized the young man hadn't followed, but was beside the merchant, helping him to rise, being cursed and cuffed for his efforts.

"Boy?"

Eyes lifted to mine, eyes brimming with unshed tears.

I held out my hand, but the young man shook his head, though he winced from the fingers biting deep into his flesh as the merchant used his arm to gain his feet. He ducked his head under the older man's elbow, holding him upright, steadying his steps to the pallet of a bed I'd left him. He eased the merchant onto the pallet, covered him with the blanket, then straightened, his back pressed to the cold stone wall.

"I—I can't, my lord."

"Why not? *You've* done nothing. If you fear your master's wrath—"

"He's not my master, my lord. He's my father."

There was nothing for it, then. I had to let them go.

A month passed. The garden blossomed, a final burst of brilliance before winter set in. Fall colors filled the woods.

And I had a visitor.

"Why'd you come back?" I asked the young man, whose name, he said, was Khendar.

"I owe you my life. I've come to repay you."

"And how much is life worth these days?"

"You mock me."

"I tease you, lad. My own life is quite cheap, I assure you. Now, what are you offering?"

"Not money, since I have none." Khendar went to the window, stared out across the maze to the garden beyond. "I've come to offer you the life you salvaged."

"Doing what?"

Khendar shivered, then turned, his eyes wide but unwavering. "Anything."

"Anything."

A quick nod.

"Tell me, Khendar, why *did* you flood that cargo?"

"I objected to the price they demanded."

"That price being?"

Lips tightened. The proud chin lifted. "Me."

"I thought as much." I watched him a moment, judging, then: "Truth, sir: you aren't here of your own accord, are you?"

Lips tightened. "I wanted to come, yes."

That surprised me, but what followed surprised me even more.

"Truth, my lord? Truth is, my father discovered my desire to repay you, somehow. He fostered those desires, and now the entire plan is tainted. I hoped to serve you, to tend your garden, perhaps help with your estate's books—I'm good with numbers. And I'd keep your confidences, despite what my father—"

He broke off and turned away, tension in every line of his body. Clean, with an obviously new set of clothing, his fine dark hair a shining veil about his face and down his back. I'd scarcely recognized him when he arrived at the newly repaired gate.

But I'd known the proud stance, the expressive mouth.

Of a sudden, he struck the wall with his fist. "Dammit, I won't do it!" He spun to face me. "He wants me to steal from you, too. Not your things, but your knowledge. He wants to know who you do business with. He wants to know the source of those jewels he found. He wants to know your finances and the secrets of your magical home. But I won't do it, I tell you! I won't!"

I blinked. The thought of estates and balancing books so foreign to my experience I had to laugh.

Khendar glowered.

"Oh, lad, I'm not laughing at you. Forgive me. If it's trading knowledge your father seeks, perhaps we can give that to him, but we'll have to look for it, or make it up. I'm no merchant."

Khendar blinked. Charmingly confused.

"I'm no merchant, but I am lonely. Bored, too, if truth be known. I'm tired of my own company. I'll have no servant, but if you'd care to guest here, you may consider the house yours for as long as you care to stay."

Another confused blink.

I smiled and headed for the door, not sure which of us I tormented more with that offer.

The following months were dreamlike in their splendor. Khendar *did* have his ideas about the markets his father dealt in and began feeding his father advice based (supposedly) on my nonexistent ledgers. His father's business prospered, and Khendar at least seemed content.

But if Khendar ever received thanks from that ungrateful wretch who had sired him, I never heard about it.

For me, as the cold white of winter descended around us, I cared for nothing but the smile on Khendar's face when I materialized each morning.

Of course, he didn't *know* I materialized. He didn't know anything about his monstrous benefactor. But he smiled and welcomed me, and for a time, I felt less monstrous than ever in my life.

At night, I'd call up his image from the pool, the bed in which he lay in the room he'd chosen, which was my room, though he didn't know that. I'd call up his image and watch him sleep. Sometimes I'd enter the room itself, moonshadow that I was, and insubstantial as the moon. But as the moon waxed, so did my substance and I longed to touch him, to lie next to him, to feel the wonder of human hands on human skin.

On those nights, I watched from the Fountain.

And on the night of the full moon, I fed the Fountain, draining myself to oblivion to keep myself from crawling into that bed beside him and taking advantage of a nature I knew would refuse me nothing.

And would never again look on me with that welcoming smile, should I ever give in to that desire.

The Fountain glowed now with color. The garden, dormant for the winter beneath its snowy blanket, required little more than enough warmth and damp to keep the small roots from dying in their sleep, and Khendar was blessedly easy to keep, laughing when I tried to give him jewelry and clothing, asking rather that I teach him to read and write, that he might enjoy the books in the library.

With numbers, he was beyond my comprehension, but his father had never allowed him to learn his letters, except as symbols representing companies. What he knew of markets, he held in his head, the "letters" he sent his father no more than coded advice on what to buy and what to sell and for how much.

He was an eager student and learned quickly, and thus we spent the winter sitting beside the fire made of wood Khendar gathered, working our way through the library built and stocked by my predecessors in this house, a library I myself hadn't touched since I'd discovered lovers.

The house had been the place I lived after Mother found me. The garden was my passion, the Fountain my responsibility.

That winter, Khendar and I made it a home.

We found a book, a journal that the earliest owners of the house had kept, folk of the valley, not the hills as were Khendar and I. They'd built the tower to defend against invaders from the East, and when the battle was won, they'd returned to their distant villages.

Or so I'd heard. Those were ancient times, not our times, and the journals were in a language I didn't understand.

But the old book raised questions. Paging absently through its aged leaves, Khendar asked me about my father, and about the house and about my predecessors, and I fled when I realized I had no answers.

The next day, I returned . . . to a quietly penitent Khendar, who asked no more questions.

But when I took him at last to the caverns, to the rejuvenating pools I'd shunned since the day I died, it was Khendar who had answers.

"Tamshi," he whispered, running his fingers along the glowing rock, and as he slid in beside me, those fingers traced my scaled arm with the same fascination. "That's what you are, isn't it, Tam?"

I just stared at him, lost in my ignorance of my own existence.

"Why don't you answer him?" Mother, whom I hadn't seen since before Khendar had entered my life, was sitting there on the edge of the pool.

Terrified of a repetition of my last visit here, I lunged for her. But she stopped me effortlessly, twisted me about in her hold, forced me to face . . .

But the pool wasn't empty. Khendar was drifting closer, watching with that wide-eyed curiosity I'd learned to treasure.

"I didn't know Tamshirin came in pairs." Khendar said, and above my head, Mother hissed.

"We don't. This is my child. He's very lonely. Do you like him?"

"Very much."

"Rather silly looking, don't you think? Scary, perhaps?"

Khendar laughed, that wonderful, ringing sound that filled the air with joy. "You're baiting me, mother-of-the-ley. You know he's beautiful, as are you. Frightening . . . yes, if I were a wolf. I'm very glad I was not. I'm also very glad he was there to frighten wolves and save a foolish traveler."

"Sensible lad."

She kissed the top of my scaled head, and then she was gone.

I fell back against the stone, filling the spot she'd vacated, staring at Khendar, waiting for him to speak, mesmerized by his look of wonder.

But I didn't want wonder. I wasn't what he'd called me. Mother was, perhaps, but not I. I was human. I *needed* to be human again. I was lost and getting farther away with every passing moment.

I could stand it no longer. I bolted from the pool and up the tunnel to the surface, hoping Khendar would find his own way safely, trusting his good sense.

I was freezing. I wrapped myself in blankets, hiding the scaled glitter from myself, burrowing, waiting for nightfall. I'd be shadow, but I'd be human, too. Warped and twisted beyond words to describe, but human.

And for the first time since I died, I cried.

When I awoke, I was no longer alone. Night had fallen, and I was a crescent-moon shadow, the blankets had begun to drift through me, my substance sufficient to slow their progress, but not to stop them altogether. Under the blanket, drooping somewhere around my shadow heart, was a strong, human arm.

Khendar had sought me out, had joined me in my burrow, comforting, as Khendar would.

I winced as he stirred and pulled his arm and the blanket too fast through me. But I held steady as he settled again, his arm and the blanket atop me rather than within me. For the moment. I dared not move but rather had to wait while arm and blanket once again sank through me. And when I was free, I darted away, leaving my sweet friend to his dreams.

"Tell me about the Tamshi?" I asked the next day as we settled near the fire with our current book, and Khendar looked at me, then closed the book and set it aside.

We hadn't spoken about Mother or the pool or last night, but Khendar's large, curious eyes had followed me all morning.

"You really don't know?" he asked, and I nodded, looking away, ashamed of my ignorance.

He held out his arms; I stared at them, not understanding. Touches had been brief between us, last night's invasion of my blanket unprecedented.

"All I know are children's stories. Being held is part of the telling."

I frowned and shook my head.

"They get pretty scary if you don't have arms around you." He lifted his hands a degree farther. "Come, my gentle host. Indulge me."

I edged over, reluctantly, though it was not onto his lap. We sat on the floor, a fur rug beneath us, the fire before us. With my back to him, I draped my tail over my legs, and leaned against his chest. His arms closed around me, and I acknowledged my Khendar's wisdom as his voice drifted magically overhead.

He told me of wondrous beings, shape-changers, lightning-dancers, and of the source of their great magic, the ley-touched water, the caverns filled with the purest of the magical ley. I sensed Mother in these stories, and our rejuvenating pools, but not me, not even in the changelings, though that had been the judgment cast upon me by the village women who left me to die in the woods.

Khendar's changelings were normal human children taken and raised by the Tamshi, returning to their villages having gained wondrous powers. While my Fountain might bear some resemblance to Khendar's ley-touched springs, and while Mother had certainly taught me to use its lifeblood to feed and to clothe me, there all resemblance ended.

Besides, it was not what I'd become under Mother's tutelage, but rather what I was beneath it all that made me different. Human, but so warped my own mother had hidden me, and the village women had set me out to die.

As Kendar's stories grew ever more fantastical, I began simply to drift on the sound of his voice, to think more of the touch of his arm against mine than any connection I might have to any of his tales.

"You aren't listening."

It was a moment before I realized he was speaking to me, not for one of the creatures he'd brought to life for me.

"I'm sorry," I murmured and the words came more easily than they should. Dismayed, I looked to the window.

Night was coming. Soon, I'd be shadow once more.

"I must go." I shifted my weight and with a final, lingering caress of his arm, I deserted him and the nest we'd made beside the fireplace.

"I've bored you," he said, and the color rose in his cheeks.

I envied him that heat.

"I just have to leave."

"Stay. Please?"

I shook my head. I saw the pain my rejection caused, saw the burning desire to question these nightly disappearances, but I felt myself changing, fading, and I had to escape.

"I'm sorry . . ." I whispered, and ran from the room.

I tried not to hear his calls, begging me to return.

But my determination had been undermined. I could no more stay away from his room, *my* bed, than I could cease to feed the

Fountain. I lay next to him, atop the covers until the moon waxed sufficient for me to slip beneath them. Not solid, but enough to touch, however lightly, and beneath that touch, Khendar sighed and twisted, asleep, but not. It was an invasion of his dreams, and in his dreams, he reached for me, grasping with fingers that slid painfully through my insubstantial flesh.

I wept, not for the pain but for want of that touch.

During the day, he looked on me with lustful eyes, but what he saw, what he *wanted* was no more me than the me my other lovers had welcomed into their beds. He was a lover of the fanciful. He told his stories with the awe and delight of a true believer. He felt he had one of his mystical Tamshi in his thrall, or he was in its, and he was ready, eager, even, to sacrifice himself on that altar of fantasy.

And yet, a part of me asked, what could this be, but love? Khendar wanted me, human or not. I ached for him, wanted no one but him. But if this was true love, Mother's curse should be broken, and I should be returned . . .

To that warped human form. And seeing me thus, would not Khendar leave me as quickly as those others had? I'd survived their departure; I am not at all certain I could survive his. . . .

* * *

The journal entry ended there.

Khendar closed the ancient tome and sat, hands crossed on the well-worn leather cover.

His eyes misted; he blinked them clear.

So many questions answered, so many more asked.

He shouldn't have read it, shouldn't have invaded Tammerlindh's privacy, but— Oh, to have the answers to those sweet, searing, impossibly real dreams he'd begun to have. In his heart, he'd known Tam was responsible, but the blunt-nailed, oh-so-human touch had not belonged to the Tamshi lover of his waking fantasies.

But the curse . . . he knew even if Tam avoided the truth, why Tam hadn't been set free. The Fountain needed an heir. He and

Tam together could never, not with all their wishing for it to be otherwise, give that gift to the mother-of-the-ley.

And so the answer was simple: he must leave.

* * *

Something happened last night.

Ink sprayed. Tammerlindh set the pen down, gripped his hands together until he had his shaking under control and dipped the pen once more.

The moon was full . . .

. . . and yet I couldn't stop myself from entering his room. He'd announced that morning that the thaws had come and he must go home, for all that the thought brought him no joy.

I hid my pain, and told him he was welcome to return, but I knew he would not.

This was his final night in the home he'd created, and I wanted only to kiss him, to feel, once, the firm flesh beneath my lips. But as I leaned over, his still form came to life. He reached up and pulled me down, bathing me in sweet kisses.

He called me Tam, though I swear I'd never given him my name.

I protested, but my heart was not in my objections . . . until his eager kisses reached my waist and traveled lower.

And stopped.

I looked down, saw those wide, wondering eyes staring at what he'd found, there in the moonlight.

Terror filled me. I had no glamour, not even Mother's magic now, to hide my hideous deformity. Unable to bear his revulsion—worse, his pity—I thrust him aside and ran from the room and from the house, out into the awakening garden. I reached the Fountain, sought the knife I kept there, and slashed both wrists deeply, not caring now for nerves and tendons, seeking only release from the world.

Let Mother find another.

Red blood gushed black in the moonlight. Within heartbeats, my knees went weak and I slipped to the ground. I braced my arms on the stone edge, buried my face in my arms, all to keep my wrists from falling into the pool when I lost consciousness.

But release was not to come from death.

"Tammerlindh!"

Beloved voice through the buzzing in my ears, as the scent that filled the air around me was dearer to me now than my roses' perfume. Hands grabbed my arms above those wounds, forced them into the pool.

"Stop!"

Mother's voice, and Khendar's hands left me.

I jerked my arms free of the healing pool.

"Well, child," Mother said, "which is it to be? Love? Or death?"

"M-monster," I whispered, watching the steady drip of lifeblood. The arteries had healed in the brief contact, but blood still ran.

I willed it to run faster.

"This bright lad doesn't think you're a monster. Do you, child?"

"Scaled, moonshadow, or flesh, he's Tammerlindh, and Tammerlindh is no monster."

"You can s–say that—" The words came with increasing difficulty, breath and blood deserting me equally. "After seeing . . . what you've seen tonight?"

"What are you talking about? Mother? What's he mean?"

"I'm certain I don't know. He's an idiot."

"Damn you, Mother," I gasped. "How can anyone love something which is neither man nor woman?"

A long silence during which, despite my efforts, my wrists continued to heal, the lifeblood maddeningly slow to evaporate in the damp night air.

"Is *that* what all the fuss is about?" Khendar asked.

"You mock me. Damn you both, let me go. Mother, find another. I'm done."

"The *hell* you're done." Khendar's hands gripped my shoulders, lifted me, forced me to look at him. "So you're a child of Rakshi? *So what?* All that means is we—*we*—can provide the ley-mother with her heir. *I* don't have to leave now!" His arms slipped around my shoulders, forcing me to face Mother. "Lift the curse! Lift it now!"

"You don't understand. Neither of you has ever understood. The curse is not of my making, but his own. I but loaned him the power to achieve his desires. Until he accepts what he is, *loves* what he is, true love can't touch him. *By his choice.*"

"Then I'll *make* him accept it. I'll change his damn mind!" Defying Mother's orders, he thrust my hands into the pool, kept them there as he whispered another tale in my ear, the tale of Rakshi, a human child given to the forest at birth—because it was neither male or female, but equal parts of both.

Reared without human contact and without human morals, Rakshi was kept alive by the ley-mother, but grew wild as the mountain itself. S/he danced to the forest melodies, hearing rhythms no normal human could imagine. And Rakshi loved— oh, how Rakshi loved. Male, female, all were drawn to the wild, beautiful creature who danced like the wind and the clouds. Women who knew Rakshi had beautiful, equally ambiguous children; men who loved Rakshi found such children left on their hearths in the middle of the night.

"And when at last Rakshi died," Khendar's voice whispered in my ear, "the ley-mother sent him to join the ley. He filled the mountain itself with his joyful, wild essence. Now, when we love, when we dance, when we laugh, we join with Rakshi." He drew my hands from the pool. The cuts were gone, healed even to the weakness. He pressed his lips to the invisible wounds, first to one, then the other, then looked me in the eyes. "And you, my wonderful, beautiful love, are one of his children. You were born to love and laugh." His lips pressed mine. "Come home and laugh with me?"

I was still unconvinced, but I followed him, mesmerized, to the room we'd shared in so many ways. In the remaining hours we had, I opened myself to him, and in opening, began to discover myself.

We fell asleep, tangled in each other's arms. And when dawn touched the Eastern window

Arms curled around Tammerlindh's neck, crossed on her chest, and teased the tiny nubs.

"Put the pen down, and come back to bed," Khendar's voice whispered, and Tammerlindh, not the least reluctant, obeyed.

She cleaned the pen, closed the journal, and set her hand, pale-skinned and blunt-nailed in the golden morning light, into her lover's.

Michelle West

One of my earliest memories of Michelle West is seeing her sitting at Elsie's feet during some convention party, ready to leap up and get Elsie anything she might desire. How could I not immediately like Michelle. Oddly, when I first got to know Michelle it was as a bookseller. For Michelle worked at Bakka Bookstore in Toronto, and Bakka is probably one of the best places in the city to go to if you are trying to find a science fiction or fantasy title.

Tanya Huff also worked at Bakka, and she and Michelle were good friends. I think I first became aware that Michelle was a writer when Tanya told me that Michelle was jealous of the cover copy on Tanya's own books and wanted to know if I could write her cover copy, too, even though she was being published by a rival house.

When I told Tanya to let Michelle know that if she wanted me to write her cover copy, she'd have to be a DAW author, she sent in a proposal along with several of her books so I could see what her writing was like.

Interestingly, some of the first ideas she sent me have yet to see print. But in October 1995, Michelle got her wish when her first DAW book, *Hunter's Oath,* was published.

Michelle is an incredibly good short story writer, which those of you who are only familiar with her rather lengthy novels may find hard to credit. Although, it is also true that, over the years, her short stories have grown in length as well. "The Memory of Stone" is certainly the longest piece by far in this volume. It is fully deserving of its length, however, as the story it tells demands it. If you have not yet read any of the novels in *The Sun Sword* series, this tale of Guildmaster Gilafas and the young Artisan Cessaly will offer you a spellbinding glimpse into this extremely rich universe.

—SG

THE MEMORY OF STONE
Michelle West

THE Guildmaster Gilafas ADelios, commonly acknowledged by The Ten houses to be the most powerful man in *Averalaan*, stood in front of the long window by which he might survey the eastern half of *Averalaan Aramarelas*. He had no throne, no place in the Hall of Wise Counsel, no direct route to the ears of the Kings, the two men who ruled the breadth of the Empire of Essalieyan. But money counted for much in the Empire; what The Ten owned in the political realm, he rivaled by the simple expedient of wealth.

He was not a young man, nor a particularly tall one, and his hair, on those days when he had no onerous public duties, fell in a white plume down the back of his head.

On this particular day, it was a solid braid.

He glanced out of the window, his eyes skimming the surface of the ocean beyond the seawall. Light sparkled there, in a pattern the makers of the east tower were doubtless attempting to capture. It reached his eyes but no more; he looked away.

The ocean's voice was strong. The strongest of the voices that he heard.

"Master Gilafas."

Certainly the most welcome voice. Gilafas was an Artisan. But in truth, he was only barely that; the weakest, the most insignificant of the Artisans the guild had produced in centuries. It galled him when he thought on it, and he was a maker; he could dwell upon any fact, without pause to eat or drink—or sleep, for that matter—for a full three days.

Duvari, the man who had spoken, knew it.

He was called the Lord of the Compact, the leader of the Astari, the men who served in the shadows the Kings cast. Although the

Lord of the Compact understood Artisans as well as any not
maker-born could, he was not by nature a patient man. Nor was
he a man that anyone angered without reason, and that, only a
good one.

Gilafas ADelios turned. He did not bow; Duvari's rank did not
demand such a gesture of respect. Indeed, his presence today almost demanded otherwise.

"Master Duvari."

"Duvari."

"Duvari, then. How may I help you?"

The insincerity of the question was not lost upon the Astari,
but it brought a cold smile to his lips, his austere face.

"You may help me by tendering to the Kings their due."

"You've become a tax collector, have you?" Testy, testy words.
The door opened. Sanfred, Gilafas's assistant, and a Master in his
own right, froze beneath the steepled wooden frame, his robes
swirling at his feet. Clearly he had run the length of the hall.

He had the brains to bow instantly. "Guildmaster."

"I am afraid, Sanfred, that we will begin the testing late today.
Tell the adjudicators to stand ready."

Sanfred was not a subtle man. He hesitated. But he was not an
Artisan either; the only madness that possessed him possessed
him when he made, and none of the makers worked without the
leave of the Guildmaster during the testing. "There are—"

"Not now, Sanfred."

"Yes, Guildmaster."

The doors swung shut. Gilafas turned to face the man who
ruled the Astari. "The applicants are waiting in the city streets."

"Indeed."

"The adjudicators will not begin without me."

"Then I will be brief."

"Good."

Again, the winter of Duvari's smile crept up his face. Gilafas
wondered idly if Duvari had a smile that did not make his expression colder and grimmer. The Guildmaster was not, however, a
simple noble, to be intimidated by a mere expression. "The Astari

had heard that you were to personally oversee these applicants. A highly unusual step for a man of your rank, is it not?"

"Your business, Duvari. Please."

"It is my business."

"You overstep yourself. It is guild business; an entirely internal matter."

"May I remind you, Guildmaster Gilafas ADelios, that in the history of the Guild of the Makers annals, the Guildmaster has only presided over the testing when he has had reason to suspect that among the applicants, he will find someone . . . unusual?"

Gilafas shrugged, and considered, briefly, the folly of giving himself over to the ocean's song. As Artisan, he could almost do so without giving offense. Frowning, he lifted his hands; they were shaking. He had not expected that. "A moment," he said, more curtly than he had intended. He reached out and gripped the edge of curtains heavy with the fall of chain links. They snapped shut audibly at the force of his pull.

"Guildmaster, is there any chance that you seek your successor among the applicants?"

Gilafas chuckled. "No chance whatsoever, Duvari. Is that all?"

Duvari did not move.

They stood a moment, two men assured by their successes in life of their rank, their power.

To Gilafas' surprise, it was Duvari who spoke first.

"I was sent to tell you," he said stiffly, "that the Orb in the Rod is now white."

Ah. Gilafas closed his eyes. Were he any other man, he might pretend that the words had no significance; he might ask, in a pleasant, modulated tone, *What rod, what orb?* But that game was not a game he could play. Not against Duvari; Duvari served the Kings.

Behind the shell of closed lids, he could see not the Kings, but the hands of Kings, and in them, the items gifted their line by an Artisan centuries ago: the Rod and the Sword. Wisdom. Justice. Weapons for the oldest of the Empire's many wars, and the most important: the war that was its founding. Magic lay within them and upon them, bound to the blood of the god-born.

He had never touched either Rod or Sword. Had prayed that he never would. He could not say what force they summoned, what spell they contained, but he knew them for more than simple ornament. They were weapons against old magic, old darkness, old wars.

And they had slept for centuries.

When he opened his eyes again, Duvari was closer; had closed the distance between them without making a sound. "You expected this," he said softly. It was the first accusation he had made.

"Aye, we expected it," Gilafas replied, weary. Why now? Why today? He brushed nonexistent hair from his eyes. Yes, his hands were shaking; the pull of the ocean was stronger than it had been in weeks, and he would have to take care.

"What of the Sword, Duvari?"

"The Sword?"

"The gem in the sword hilt."

"It is as it has always been."

"And the runes upon the blade itself?"

"The King has had no cause to draw the Sword."

"He has cause," Gilafas said, forcing strength into words that wanted to come out in a whisper. "Tell him—ask him—to draw the blade. Read what is written there. Return with word of what it says."

"I suspect, from your demeanor, that you already know." Duvari held his gaze, and that, too, was a threat. "Very well. I will return with your answer." He walked away then, and only when he reached the doors did he turn and proffer the most perfunctory of bows.

Gilafas waited until he left, and then he made his way to the grand desk that served as this great room's foundation. There he paused, running his hands over the surface of a very simple box. It was a deep, deep red, and the carvings across its face were not up to the standards of the least of the guild's makers.

But he had been told what lay within.

Cessaly stood between the twin pillars of her mother and her grandmother, her knuckles white as the alabaster statues in the distance.

Distance was a tricky thing to measure. There were men who could do it; they could tell you things by the length of cast shadows, the rise of buildings beneath the fall of sunlight some arcane measure of the shape of the land. Or so her father had once said. He had stayed in the Free Town of Durant. Said his good-byes at the edge of the fields that had yet to be tilled and planted, his face dark, his eyes squinting against the light. Except that the sun had been at the back of his head, a shining glint over the brim of his weathered hat.

Her brothers, Bryan and Dell, had hugged her tight, lifting her in the twirl and spin of much younger years. They hadn't said good-bye. Instead, they had offered her the blessing of *Kalliaris*, asking for the Lady's smile, and not her terrible frown.

She had offered them gifts. Wood carvings, things made from the blunt edge of chisel and knife. *To remember me by*, she'd said. *In case I don't come back.*

A bird. A butterfly. Nothing useful.

But in those two things, some quickness of captured motion: tail feathers spread for flight, beak open in silent song; wings, thin and fine, veined and open, devoid only of the color that might have lent them the appearance of life.

Dell had handled the butterfly as carefully as he might had it been alive; his clumsy, heavy hands, callused by the tools of their father's trade, hovering like wings above wings, membrane of wings, afraid that his grip might damage the insect's flight.

Her father had taught them that, each in their turn, and butterflies sometimes sat on the perch of their steady fingers, wings closed to edge, feelers testing wind. Birds had been less trusting, of course, and they were predators in their fashion, beaks snapping the skein of butterfly wings in a darting hunt for sustenance.

Cessaly loved them, hunter and hunted, because they were small and delicate when in flight. She had never been large.

Her brothers took after their father; they were broad of shoulder, silent, slow to move. But they put their backs into the labor that had been chosen for them, taking comfort in the Mother's season.

Cessaly had tried to do the same, she a farmer's daughter. But the hoes and the spades, the standing blades of the scythes, often spoke to her in ways that had nothing to do with the Mother. She might be found carving mounds of dirt, or fallen stalks of wheat, into shapes: great fortresses, sprawling manors, even small castles— although the poverty of her splendor had become apparent only when she had reached the outskirts of Averalaan.

They thought her clever then.

Her father would often cry out her mother's name, and the deep baritone of his voice, cracked by the dry air of the flat plains, returned to her. *Cecilia, come see what your daughter has made!*

Even her mother's habitually dour expression would ease into something akin to a smile when she came at her husband's call, and they would stand, like a family of leisure, for moments at a time, oohing and aahing.

She had loved those moments.

But those moments had led to this one.

"How long?" her grandmother said, when the man in robes came out from the distant building and walked down the streets, a pitcher of water in hands as callused as her father's. She asked it again when he was ten feet away, repeated it when he was before them.

His face was lined with shadow, eyes dark; his chin was bereft of beard. But he smiled, and if the smile was curt—and it was—it was also friendly. "I fear, good lady, that it will be some hours yet. You are not at the halfway mark."

"You're sure that they'll see us all?"

Again, he offered her a curt smile. "Indeed."

"We've brought some of her work," her grandmother said. "If you'd like to see it."

"I would, indeed." His tone of voice conveyed no such desire. "But I fear that my opinion, and the opinion of the guildmasters, do not have equal standing here."

Her grandmother frowned and nodded, allowing him to pass.

There were others in the line who were just as thirsty as they were, after all, and if she was anxious, she wasn't selfish.

"Cessaly, stand straight, girl."

I was, she thought sullenly, but she found an extra inch or two in the line of her shoulder, and used it to blunt her grandmother's nervous edge.

Her mother had not spoken a word.

The halls of the guild's upper remove were unlike the simple, unadorned stone that graced its lower walkways. They were also unlike the halls in which the makers worked, for those stone walls were decorated, from floor to vaulted ceiling, with the paintings and tapestries, the statues, the interior gargoyles, that were proof of the superiority of the artists that had guild sanction.

No; in the halls of Fabril's reach, the walls were of worked stone. These contours, these rough surfaces, these smooth domes, took on the shape of trees, of cathedrals, of Lords and Ladies, of gods themselves; they began a story, if one knew how to read it. There were very few who could, in the history of the Guild of the Makers, for such a reading could not be taught; it could be gleaned if one had the ability and the time.

No, Gilafas thought, with a trace of bitterness. It was the ability that mattered; time was what the inferior could add, if they lacked ability in greater measure.

Guildmaster Gilafas, to his shame, was only barely an Artisan. No Artisans had survived in the generation that preceded him in the guild, and no men remained who might have seen the spark of his talent in time to kindle it, to bring it to fruition.

Or so he had told himself. It was not his fault; it was not his failing. And on the day that he had been completely overtaken by the voice of the ocean, on the day that he made, out of crystal, a decanter that returned to the waters of that great body the clarity and the purity of its essential nature, the acting guildmaster had cried tears of joy.

There is magic here, Gilafas. Look. He had lifted the decanter to the eye of the sun. *The waters placed in this vessel can safely be drunk. Do you understand? You are not a simple maker—you are an Artisan.*

The old man had, with great ceremony, ordered the opening of the upper remove, and installed the young man within its stone folds. *What you need to learn, you will learn here. Or so our history says.*

Aye, history.

That old man had been dead twenty years. Dead, a year and twelve months after the day he had made his joyful discovery. Gilafas had attended him for the two weeks he lingered abed with a fever that he could not shake. Healers had been sent for, and healers had been turned away; the guildmaster would have none of them.

"I'm an old man," he had said, "And close to death, and I'll not drag a healer there and back for the scant benefit of a few more months of life." His hair across the pillows was his shroud, his chosen shroud. "And I'm happy to go, Gilafas. You're here. You're Artisan. You will guide our guild."

"The Artisans," he had said, "all went mad, Nefem."

"Not all."

"All of them."

"Not Fabril."

"I'm not Fabril, Nefem."

"No. But you *will* be guildmaster. You are an answer to the only prayer I have ever made. I give you the responsibility of the guild, and its makers. They are fractious. You've seen that. But fractious or no, there is no greater power in the Empire." He lifted a hand. "Say what you will. The mages can kill men; they can raise them to power. But they cannot accomplish what we have built here."

"The Kings—"

"Even the Kings, when they choose to come here, come as suppliants. Be the guildmaster, Gilafas. While you are alive, the guild will have no other. Listen to the halls in the upper remove; hear the voices that we *cannot* hear. You have the ability." His cheeks were wet. "Protect what *I* have built."

The maker's cry. "Protect what I have created." Never "protect
me."

Gilafas had become a maker without parallel, and in the streets
of the city, in the streets of the Holy Isle, that counted. But here,
within the stretch of the great hall in which the Artisans had lived
and worked since the founding of the guild, he was almost incon-
sequential. The walls spoke to him seldom, and when they did,
they spoke in a language that was almost entirely foreign. Until
the day the demon voices had filled the Old City with the cries of
the dying.

The halls had been dark as thunder-clad sky when he had come
to them, gasping for air, desperate now for the answers that his
meager talent denied him. He had starved himself of all sustenance: company, food, and water. For three days, while the moon
rode high in the harvest sky, while the winter waxed with the
bright, jeweled ghosts of the Blood Barons and their legacy of in-
dulgence and death, he had had for company, for clothing, for
sound, nothing but the walls themselves.

The walls. He had traced their passage from one end of the hall
to another, over and over, creating a maze of his movements.
Closed eyes, open eyes, breath creaking through the passage of a
tight, dry, throat, he had lost his way. Become lost in his home of
decades. Lost to stonework. Lost to the hand of the Artisan.

And lost now, absolved of all dignity, of all power granted him
by the accolades of other men, he had come at last to the altar.

It was in a room that did not exist. Sanity knew: sanity had
denied him entrance. Some part of his mind, stubborn, sane, anchored to the world of his compatriots, could not be dislodged,
but it had been shaken so thoroughly he had at last his proof of
the truth of his existence.

The halls had opened the way, for him, and he had walked it.

And he wept, to think of it now; wept bright tears, salt tears.
Ocean tears.

For he had come across the broken body of a young woman,
her pale, pretty face scarred in three places by the kiss of blade's
edge—her only kisses, he thought, the only ones she had been

permitted. Hands bleeding and blistered by some unseen fire, she was the sacrifice.

Demon altar. Dark altar.

And upon it, across the naked skin of her pale, upturned breasts, she clutched them, broken, the Rod and the Sword of Kings.

He heard laughter; could not think that it could be hers, she was so still. This was a monument the Barons would have been proud to own.

When Sanfred and Jordan found him again, wandering naked, bleeding, skeletal, they had taken him in silence to the lower halls, and he had made good his escape.

But in escape, he carried knowledge: the Rod and the Sword would fail. The orb would be shattered, and the runes on the blade would speak in the tongue of an accusation he understood well: they were hollow vessels, their metal and their finery too superficial for the task at hand.

The line stretched on forever. Grandmother, mother, and daughter, they faced it like a family faces drought: grimly, silently. Cessaly was uncomfortable in the present, and she was young, adept in ways that her elders, too slow and rigid, could no longer be. She sought past. Found it.

Cessaly's father, his pride contained in the scarcity of his words, had taken some of the things she had made to market when the merchants began their spring passage through the Free Towns on their way to the Western Kingdoms, those lands made distant and mythical because she would never set eyes upon them.

She had been younger, then; a good five years younger, and still prone to be mistaken for a boy whenever she traveled in the company of her brothers. But she had gone with her da when he took the wagons into the common, and she had stood by his side while he offered the merchants—at some great cost—the fruits of her half-forbidden, half-encouraged labor.

She had made horses, that year. Horses fleet of foot and gleam-

ing with sunlight, manes flying, feet unfettered by the shod
hooves that the merchants prized.

"You made these?" the merchant said, lifting the first of the
horses.

Her father had shrugged.

"These are Southern horses. You've seen action, then?"

He said nothing. The Free Towners knew that her father had
been born on the coast; knew that he had survived the border
skirmishes that were so common between the North and the
South. They also knew better than to ask about them.

"You've a good hand," the merchant continued, eyes narrowing slightly. "What do you want for them?"

Her father had named a price.

The merchant's brows rose in that mockery of shock that was
familiar to any Towner who had cause to treat with him.

They had bickered, argued, insulted each other's birthplace,
parents, heritage. And then they had parted with what they valued: her father with the small horses, the merchant with his
money.

It might have ended that way, but Cessaly, impatient and
bursting with pride and worry, had said, "What'll you do with
'em?"

The merchant raised a brow. "Sell them, of course."

"To who?"

"To a little girl's parents in the West. Or in the East. They are
. . . very good. Perhaps if you had paint," he had added, speaking
again to her father. "For a price—a good price—I might be able
to supply that."

"You wouldn't know a good price if it bit you," her father replied, mock angry.

"We want the paint," she'd answered.

And he turned to look at her, at her eager eyes, her serious
face.

"What will you do with paint, child?"

She smiled. "I don't know."

And then he frowned. "Did *you* make these?"

"Yes."

"By yourself?"

"Yes."

"And who taught you this, child?"

Her turn to frown, as if it were part of the conversation. She shrugged.

The merchant went away. But when he came back, he handed her—her and not her father—a small leather satchel. "You can keep these," he told her, "if you promise that I will have first pick of anything you make with them."

"If the price is right," her father told the man. "If we don't like the price, we're free to take them elsewhere."

"Done."

To find sunlight again was a blessing. Master Gilafas paused at the foot of the steps and bowed. Sanfred was at his side before his stiff spine had once again straightened. He felt the younger man's solid hand in the crook of his elbow, and was grateful for it: the memories of that early passage through Fabril's reach had teeth, fangs, gravity. To struggle free of them today was almost more than he was capable of.

Once, that would have pleased him. And perhaps, if he were honest, it pleased him in some fashion today. But triumph gave way to horror, and horror sent him scuttling away like insect evading boot.

He cleared his throat. "The applicants?"

"Waiting, Guildmaster."

"Good."

Sanfred had never once asked him why he had chosen to oversee this testing. No one had.

By unspoken consent, the makers, fractious as only the creative can be, granted him the privacy of their admiration. What he could make—in theory—no one among them could ever hope to make.

A mage could, he thought, irritable. *A mage of lesser talent and no ambition.* But he had too great a love for his authority to speak the words aloud.

"Take me."

"Yes, Master."

"And bring the box on that desk. I do not need to remind you to handle it with care."

After that day, Cessaly's size was no longer a problem. Her father spent some part of the summer building a small addition to his barn, and he placed her tools, her paints, the pieces of wood that he found for her use, beneath its flat roof. He had no money for glass, but the doors themselves opened toward the sun's light, and Cessaly worked from the moment it crossed the threshold of the room, ceasing when it faded.

The merchant returned three times in the year, bringing different tools, different materials, different paints. He asked if she had ever seen metal worked, and when she shook her head, he offered to take her to a jeweler in the largest of the Free Towns. It was an offer that was flatly rejected by both her father and her mother.

They were very surprised when, two years later, that jeweler made the trek at the merchant's side when the caravan returned.

"This had better not be a waste of my time," he said curtly to the merchant.

"I'm paying for your time," the merchant had replied, with a very small smile. "But I know my business."

"Where is your young paragon of creativity, Gerrald?"

"In front of you."

"What, this girl?"

"The very one."

The jeweler frowned. He was balding, and the dome of his skull seemed to glow. "How old are you, child?"

"Twelve."

The frown deepened. "Twelve. And you've never apprenticed to anyone?"

She shook her head.

"Well. I'm not sure that I can offer you such a position—I've heard that your parents won't hear of you traveling, and this town is not my home. But Gerrald has offered me much money to teach you for the summer, and I admit that the offer itself is unusual enough to have piqued my curiosity. If you are willing, I would teach you some small amount of my craft."

He brought with him gold and silver, sparkling gems and glossy pearls, opals and ebony, a small dragon's hoard.

But he brought something better, something infinitely more alluring: fire. Fire, in the heart of the rooms her father had built.

She had waited for her father's permission, and her father had granted it.

The man in robes came again, three times, the water jug heavy in his hands. She watched his shadow against the cobbled stones, and her hands ached. Her grandmother's hands ached as well— but she blamed that ache on the ocean Cessaly could taste when her tongue touched her lips.

Cessaly had not yet seen the ocean; she had seen buildings, horses, and streets that went on for as far as the eye could see. There were white birds in the air above, birds with angry, raucous cries; there were insects beneath her feet among mice and rats; there were cats sleek and slender, and dogs of all shapes, all sizes.

There was no workshop; she had been forbidden all of her tools. When traveling along the road, she had been permitted to idly carve the pieces of wood she had taken from the farm; they were gone now.

She wanted them.

There was no dirt beneath her feet; there were stones, smooth and flat, longer than she was and at least three times as wide. There were fences, too, things of black iron or bronze. Nothing that she could work with.

She plaited her hair instead, until her mother caught her at it, and grabbed both her hands, stilling them.

"Not here," she had said severely. "Not here."

Her hands began to ache; her eyes began to burn. She could not wait forever.

The jeweler stayed in Durant for four years. He bought a house for himself, very near the common; he built his workshop, sent for his apprentices, and brought his business to the town. He also made a room for Cessaly, and her mother brought her to it, and took her from it, every day except for the Mother's day.

Cessaly worked with gold, with silver, with platinum. She handled his diamonds, his emeralds, his rubies, the blinking eyes of curved sapphires, the crisp edges of amethyst and firestone. He had begun by telling her what he wished her to achieve, and had ended, quickly, by simply giving her material to work with.

He often watched as she worked; often worked by her side, making the settings upon which he might place the results of her labor. He was not a man who was given to praise, and indeed, he offered little of it—but his silence was like a song, and his expression in the frame of that silence, a gift. Cessaly liked him.

And because of that, she decided that she would make something for him. Not for the merchant to whom all of her work eventually went, but for Master Sivold himself.

Because she wished the gift to be entirely hers, she chose wood to work with; wood was something that she could easily afford on her own. The merchants came in the spring, and when they did, she asked if they might bring her something suitable. But she did not ask for soft wood; did not choose the oak that came from the forests a few miles outside of the village. She requested instead a red, hard wood, something riven from the heart of a giant tree.

She was so excited when the merchant placed it in her hands; she was absorbed by the tang of wood, its rough grain, the depth of its unstained color. She wanted to rush back to the workshop, to begin to work *right away*.

But she heard its voice, wood's voice, and it bade her *wait*.

Voice? No, not voice, for the words it spoke were not quite words, and the wood offered her no more than that; she could not speak to it, could ask it no question and receive no answer of use. But she could feel it in the palms of her hands as if it were a living heart; could see it move, shrinking in size until the truth of its shape was revealed.

She waited.

Four days later, at the height of summer, during the longest day of the year, she began to carve. To cut. To burn. She worked until the sun had begun to touch the colors of the sky; worked until the first of the stars was bright.

And when she was finished, she saw that her mother was asleep in the great chair in the corner; that the lamp had been lit and rested on the table beside that chair; that the workshop itself was empty.

She was very, very tired, but she tucked the box away, hiding it beneath the heavy cloths that protected the gems and the metals from sawdust and insects. Then she woke her mother and together they went home.

The next day was the day that changed her life.

She came to the workshop later than she usually did; her mother had had a great deal of difficulty waking her, and was concerned that she might have fetched ill. But Cessaly wasn't running a fever; she didn't cough or sneeze, didn't shake much, didn't throw up—and in the end, her mother had relented and accompanied her to the jeweler's house.

There, shaking off lethargy, Cessaly ran inside, ran to her workbench, and grabbed the box she had made. It was simple, perhaps too simple for a man like Master Sivold. But it was not without adornment; she had carved a pattern around the lip of the lid that made the join between lid and box almost invisible. Only with care could she see it herself.

"What's that, then, Cessaly?" he said, as she approached him.

"Last month you said that you'd run out of space for the things—the things that you can't bear to part with."

"Did I?"

She nodded. "And I—you've done so much for me here, you've shown me so many new things, you've let me make what I—what I have to. I—"

His brow rose. "Is this for me?"

"Yes. I made it. For you. Only for you," she added. "It's not for Gerrald. And anyway, it doesn't matter if he does see it. It won't do him—or anyone else—any good."

He smiled and held out his hand. "It's very elegant, but a little too plain for Gerrald's taste. Or for his customers." He lifted it, examining the carving around its side. "Cessaly, what is this?"

His fingers brushed the trailing strokes of letters, letters hidden in the movement of leaves, the trailing fall of their branches.

"Your name," she told him.

"My name?" He frowned. And the frown deepened. "Why do you say that, child? It does not say Sivold."

"It doesn't?" Her eyes widened then, with panic and fear. She reached for the box, and he must have seen the horror on her face, for his frown eased. But he did not return it to her hands.

"My eyes are not nearly as good as they once were, and your work here is so delicate, child. Perhaps I am misreading." He shook himself, and the smile returned to his face. "I didn't know that you knew how to spell or write."

She didn't. She said nothing.

After a moment, he lifted the lid from the box, and then his eyes grew wide, and wider still; his lashes seemed fixed to his brows.

"Master Sivold?"

He continued to stare.

"Master Sivold?"

And when he finally blinked, his eyes teared almost instantly. He closed the lid of the box with great care, and set it down on the workbench. "When did you make this, Cessaly?"

"Yesterday."

"Yesterday?"

"Yesterday. And a little bit of the night."

He raised his hands to his face. "I knew we were doing you a disservice, child," he said, when he at last chose to lower them. "But I thought that your parents would be happier if you—if you worked in the Free Towns." He shook his head. "You must send for your parents, child. Tell them I need to speak with them. Tell them it is urgent."

And so she had.

They had come to speak with Master Sivold, and the closed

door came between her understanding and their adult words—but she had waited just beyond the reach of the door's swing, and when it opened, it opened upon her pale face, her wide eyes.

Master Sivold was angry. Her father was angry. Her mother, grim and silent, stood between them, hands curved in fists, knuckles white as the bone beneath stretched skin.

She knew better than to ask what had been said. It was obvious that their anger had had no good place to go, and she wasn't about to provide one.

But Master Sivold's anger was pointed, directed; when he turned toward her, it smoothed itself away from the lines of his face. She almost wished it hadn't; he looked old as it left him.

"Cessaly, I want to ask you a question."

She gazed sideways at her father; his glance spared her nothing, but his nod was permission.

"How did you make the box?"

"How?"

He nodded. Gentle, that nod, as if she were a babe. She didn't like it. "Same as I make anything else."

"Tell me," he said again. "Take as long as you like."

"I chose that piece of wood," she said, "because it was the right wood. It took a little while."

"How did you know what to carve?"

"Wood knows," she said quietly. She never talked about her work, and it made her nervous to speak now. She wasn't sure why. "I wanted to make it for you," she added. "And I started the minute I got the wood home, but it told me to wait. It told me to wait for the longest day."

"And how did you know what day that was?"

"I didn't," she said again. "The *wood knew.*"

Master Sivold turned to look at her father. Her father, whose shoulders seemed smaller somehow.

"And the sun knew," she continued, thinking about it, feeling the wood in her hand, the warmth of that sun on the back of her neck, her head, its light on the dark streaks of grain.

"Tell us what the sun said," Master Sivold told her.

She looked at his face for a moment, seeing in the lines around his eyes and lips the movement of wood grain. She reached out, unthinking, to touch him, to feel the surface of that skin, that grain.

And when she opened her mouth, when she began to speak, she left bruises there, around his lips, where her fingers grazed flesh. There, and in the dark of his eyes.

They kept her until the harvest's end, and then they traveled east, east to the Empire of Essalieyan. Her father and mother had argued three days—and nights, tucked in the battleground of their bed, their voices loud and rumbling, their words muted by log walls—and in the end, her mother had won, as she often did. Her brothers were to stay; she was to travel with the caravan until she reached the city, and from there she was to seek the Guild of the Makers.

"But—but, Da—"

"It's your mother's decision, not mine. I don't send my kin to—"

"Father," her mother had said, clipping both ends of the words between tight teeth.

Cessaly wanted to be happy. Or she wanted him to be happy. She wasn't sure. "But if I'm a maker—we'll be rich. We'll be *rich*, Da."

"You'll be rich," he said gruffly. "And we'll be farmers, here, in Durant."

"I don't have to live there."

He looked at his wife. His wife said nothing.

She did what any sensible girl would do. She went in search of Dell. Bryan was older, and minded his father's commands.

"Dell?"

"Aye, Cessaly."

"Why can't I live here?"

"They think you're maker-born," he said.

"But all of the makers don't live in the Empire."

"No."

"Then why do I have to?"

"Because you made that damn box, is why."

She wanted to tell him to burn the box, then, but she couldn't quite say the words. Wasn't certain why. "I did bad?"

"You did too good," he told her, when he heard the tone of her voice. "And now they're all afeared. Master Sivold—"

"What?"

He shook his head. "It's nothing. They think you'll go crazy, Cessaly."

"Then why are they sending me?"

He shrugged. "Because all the crazy people live in the Empire?"

So she hit him. Lots. He wasn't supposed to hit her back.

The crowds wavered like a heat mirage in Gilafas' vision. The great doors had been rolled back, and light skittered off the sheen of marble and brass, abjuring its smoky green, its black, its curling grays. Beyond the open doors, the grapple of a thousand people moved and twisted like the ocean's voice; he could make out no words because he could hear them all so clearly.

"Master Gilafas?"

He lifted a hand. "I think—I think, Sanfred, that I will have my pipe. Now."

"Your—ah. That one. Yes, Guildmaster." He hesitated for just a moment, and then he waved another maker over and relinquished his grip on Gilafas' elbow, forgotten until that moment.

Everyone hovered. It was annoying. Their shadows against the floor, the fall of their feet, the drifting haze of their cloudy beards, made him think of the storm. He waved them away. *Ocean voice,* he thought. *What am I to do today? It is not the time.*

Sanity. That was his curse. He listened to confusion dispassionately, refusing, as he had always done, to allow it reign. His brief dalliance with insanity had given him no cause to regret that decision.

The pipe came, and he lit it carefully, inhaling bitter smoke. It was not to his taste, and not to his liking, and it would be less to his liking on the morrow when he woke to the taste of something dead and stale on his tongue. But the alternative was less appealing.

"Send them, then."

"Yes, Master."

Hours passed. Of the many hundreds of hopeful applicants, Guildmaster Gilafas found two he was certain belonged within the guild walls. He treated them not only with the respect of their future rank, but with the affection reserved for kin, no matter how distant, who have found their way home against almost insurmountable odds. It was not an act. There was a brotherhood among the men and women who were, by nature of birth and some quirky, divine providence, driven to these strange acts of creation.

That brotherhood buoyed him, although he was not entirely certain that some part of that warmth was not caused by the contents of his pipe. It had been some hours since he had filled it, and he hesitated, hand over pouch, to do so again.

Looking up, he realized how costly that hesitation had been. He had never walked so close to the edge without realizing it; somehow he had stepped across it.

Had he the voice for it, he would have cried out in fear or horror. It was the only thing in the long day that he would be grateful for later; his dignity was spared.

For the doors *were* there, they were open; the makers *were* in attendance; he was not in Fabril's hall, and the visions of that complicated, terrible place did not hold him in their painful grip.

Only memory did, but memory was enough, more than enough. He handed his pipe to Sanfred, hands shaking so much he feared to drop it before it held what he required.

And he tried to smile at the young woman who walked toward him.

In the privacy of his thoughts, he was still a coward, had always been a coward; he told himself that he was mistaken, old, befuddled, that the voices of the ocean and the voices of the Maker had grown strong because he had done too little, these past few days, to still them. He tried to tell himself that what he remembered could not be real.

But cowardice provided no shelter: he recognized the girl's face.

She had lain upon a bloodied altar in a hidden room that he had never tried to find again.

When Cessaly saw the man who sat behind a table that was larger than any she had ever seen—including Master Sivold's workbench—she froze.

"Cessaly," her mother said, impatient, fearful, angry.

But for once, her mother's voice was almost beneath her notice.

As if he were wood, or silver, or gold, the man caught the whole of her attention, diverting daylight, the vast rise of ceiling, the width and breadth of wall. Only the ocean's taste grew stronger as she met his eyes, and the inside of her mouth was dry as salt.

She should have remembered that when she approached wood, or gold, or silver, she approached first with ax, chisel, knife, fire; that the only voice allowed these things that waited transformation was hers.

She said to him, before she could think—and this, too, was akin to her movements with wood, with silver, with gold—"You make things."

It lacked manners, which would have been a crime in a different place; lacked them in the presence of a man of obvious import.

But it spoke to the heart of the matter.

"Yes," he said gravely. "I make things." His hand reached out, and out again, as if he would touch her; it stopped inches short of her face, and fell.

She had seen glass in windows, although her family's home had had none until the third year of her work with Master Sivold, and she understood that the one that stood between them now was closed.

You make things.

"Yes. Yes, I make things."

She lifted a hand.

"I do, too."

He would never hear the ocean again, not as he had. A man's mind had room for only so much madness, and Gilafas' less than any Artisan before him.

"Sanfred," he said, rising, pipe somehow no longer a danger.

"Master Gilafas?"

"I am done for the day. This girl is maker-born; ask her— mother?—for the information we require, draw up those forms that you deem necessary, do what needs be done." He rose. Picked up the box he had ordered carried to this table with such care.

"This was once yours," he said.

She looked at it, and her expression twisted. "It was never mine," she told him solemnly. "I made it for Master Sivold." She frowned when she said it, and her face lost some of its luster, some of its terrible lure. "Are you upset about it, too?"

He nodded. Before he could catch himself—if he would ever be able to catch himself—his chin fell and rose in a sharp, jerky dip. "But for a different reason. I have not seen the inside of the box. I could not open it."

"Would you like me to open it for you?"

"If you would."

She took the box carefully, placing the left palm firmly beneath the center of its flat, legless bottom. And when she opened it, Sanfred understood what Gilafas had not yet said, because he was standing just to his right, and he was human enough to be curious.

The inside of the box itself was longer than the table at which the Makers now sat; it was as deep as a man's arm from palm to shoulder.

"He needed more room," she told him gravely, "for the things that I made. Will you give it back to him?"

"Yes," he told her gently. He knew how important the answer was; she was maker-born, after all.

It took some hours to settle not the girl, but her mother. She would not leave without speaking to the Guildmaster—a sure sign of her ignorance of the workings of the Guild of Makers.

Therefore, Gilafas, exhausted and on the edge of compulsion, drove himself for a second time from the confines of his quarters in Fabril's reach. Sanfred was nowhere to be seen; neither was the girl, although he had been quite specific.

It was only when he reached the visitor's lounge that he realized that hours had not, in fact, passed; the sun was wrong for it—it was still in the sky. He steadied himself against this dislocation as Sanfred appeared. Sanfred who could hide mortal concern behind a placid, workman's expression.

He sat in front of this dour woman, and she beside an older, dourer one. They formed the sides of a triangle; Sanfred, attending, was simple shadow, and moved like a trick of the light.

Master Gilafas had only one desire when confronted with this woman, and it was strong, terrible, as visceral as any need to make, or make again, had ever been.

Take your girl, take her as far away from this place as you can, and still live. Go North, to the barbarians; go South to the slavery of the Southern Courts; go West, to the kingdoms of which I know so little. Leave her anywhere but here.

But he did not.

"Will you take care of her?" the woman asked. She was fidgeting now.

"I assure you, there is not another place in all of the Empire where she will be—"

"Because she's always been a bit odd." The woman, having said the words, lost half a foot of height. Her hair, dark with streaks of gray, seemed to frame a face too pale to carry it. "She's more than a bit odd now. We're her kin, we know what she means when she speaks; we know there's no harm in her wild ways. She's a good girl. She's an honest girl."

He started to speak, but she had not yet finished.

"She won't thieve, mind, not for herself. But she takes a fancy to things she sees—bits of wood or stone, mostly—and she'll pick 'em up."

"We understand that, here."

"And she'll work funny hours, if you don't stop her. It's hard, but she needs to eat." Care had worn lines deeply into the material of her face. "Don't forget it: she needs to eat. And drink. And sleep. She's got to be reminded; we let her work once, thinking she would stop in her own time. Waited to see how long that was." Hands were clenched now.

He stared at her. To his surprise, he wanted to offer her comfort. "She will be treasured here in a way that you cannot envision. Sanfred, the man who is hovering, was trained to do two things: he is a painter, here, one of a very few. And he is a . . . baby-sitter. We *all* work the hours that your child would work, unminded. And we have learned to watch out for each other. She will not go hungry; she will not go thirsty. Sleep is harder to dictate."

She wasn't satisfied. He could see it.

He said simply, "There are things that she is beginning to learn that she should not learn on her own. The box—you saw it—is only the first sign of that. There are others things she might have made. In our histories, a boy much her age walked into the blacksmith's forge shortly after a bandit raid. The raids that year were fierce and terrible, for most of the land had seen little rain, and the fields would not take.

"He made a sword. It killed. That was all it did. It was his rage and his desire; he wielded it. It sang. He carried it to the bandit's home, and he had his revenge, and it was bright and bloody.

"But he had had *no* sword skills, and he was not a large lad; the sword itself contained both the desire to kill and the ability. In the end, the bandits themselves were not enough to slake its thirst, and he wandered into the village he had loved. Hundreds perished before the sheath that would hold that sword was created."

She was pale, now, pale as light on his beloved ocean. But she asked, simply, "What happened to the boy?"

A mother's question.

"He was mad," he replied. "And he remained so."

"They didn't kill him?"

He hesitated. "No," he said at last, and gently, "they did not kill him. They gave him, instead, to *our* keeping."

Before she could speak, he raised a hand. "And in our keeping, in the safety of these walls, or in the stewardship of those best suited to such a task, he made such things as Kings wield, and his work helped to change the face of the lands we now call the Empire. He was honored, he was revered. In his fashion, he was loved."

She closed her eyes. Opened them. "I can't take her home," she said, the statement a question.

"No."

She rose then. "Let me say my good-byes, and I'll not trouble you further."

But she would. He could see it in the lines of her face, the depth of her concern. She would go home, to Durant, and the fate of her daughter would draw her out, again and again, to this vast, intimidating place. She would see a stranger in this daughter, and the daughter—he was not certain what the daughter would see.

Because he was sane. Because he had always been blind, that way. He rose and offered the woman his hand; she accepted it as if it were an anchor on a short chain.

To be a failure was something Gilafas had contemplated for the better part of his adult life. But he had contemplated it in the temple makers made of quarters an accident of birth had granted him. To do penance for his failure, he had strengthened the Guild of the Makers immeasurably, giving it the steady guidance that a madman could never have conceived of. This he did for the old man whose joy he had not the strength to live up to.

If he could not increase the mystery of the guild, if he could not add to the grandeur of its legends, he could at least do that.

And he had thought himself an honest man, had thought acceptance of his paltry ability had been his for the better part of a decade.

Now, it was unbearable.

The girl—Cessaly—had been moved to Fabril's reach the moment her mother had left. He might have assigned the duty of settling her to Sanfred, or another of the makers who served him directly, but cowardice prevented it, presenting him with the first of many menial tasks he was to adopt.

Because Sanfred could not fail to see in the girl what Gilafas himself lacked. How could he?

So it was that Guildmaster Gilafas ADelios led her to the winding tower stairs that led to Fabril's reach.

She had taken the steps timidly at first, her hands faltering upon the fine rails beneath the grand sweep of open tower, the fading light. She had no experience of this world, save in story—if that— and her fear made her precious to him, for he had no children.

But the fear itself was fleeting.

The light in her eyes was not; it was fire, of a sort, the fire of a forge, the fire of one maker-born who sees into the world of mages. Or gods. He could not himself say, although he had walked that path.

But he knew the moment that she lost fear to wonder; he could see it in her. Could hear it, in the whisper of moving strands of her hair, taken by a breeze that did not—and had never—touched him.

She carved birds; he remembered that the grandmother had mentioned it to Sanfred. Birds, butterflies, creatures not bound to the earth. And he? He worked water, and whales, dolphins, things of the deep that might break the bounds of their element in fleeting steps, with will and joy.

So she flew. Up, up, and up. She knew where the doors were. Were she not small, were her step not contained by the reach of short legs, she might have evaded him utterly. He could not let her do it. He could not let her make herself at home in Fabril's reach.

Was ashamed of the inability.

We are not judged by what we create; we create. Maker's motto. And what use that motto now? It was a lie.

Vanity had its use.

Cessaly stopped two thirds of the way up the stairs and placed her hand gently upon the wall. A recess in the smooth stone caught the shape of her palm, molding itself to her fingers as if the stone were liquid.

He heard the ocean's voice then. A roar, a roar of water breaking stone and wood, rending cloth, burying men. She opened a door that he had never found.

And turned to stare at him, her eyes wide, her brows lost beneath the edge of poorly cut hair. Honey eyes, he thought, a shade too brown to be the eyes of a child of the gods. "Master Gilafas?"

He shook his head, lifting a hand to clear his vision. "I hear the ocean," he told her bitterly. "Only the ocean."

"Can you hear me?"

He stopped then, turned the full of his attention upon her, upon the question she had asked. She was a child. By age, she could be counted among adults, but there was nothing of that in her expression; she was made of curiosity, insecurity, joy, and fear.

"Yes, Cessaly. I can hear you."

His answer was important. Because she could hear him. She could hear the ocean in his voice, could see it in his eyes, her first glimpse of the blue surface against which sun scudded. She smiled, her hand against something soft and warm. "I can hear stone," she whispered. "I can hear wood growing. I can hear wind in the leaves, and the rain dance. I can hear the birds, seabirds, great birds. I can hear the sun's voice."

She had heard these things before, in the dells of Durant, in the furrows of her father's fields, in the quiet of log and peat and moss yards from the river's edge, where the water pooled before resuming its passage.

"I can hear silver," she told him. "And gold. And the voices of rubies and diamonds. Sapphires are quiet." She stopped. She had never said so much before.

"But I hear the voices. There, past the door. Other voices."

"Open the door, then, Cessaly."

She started to. Started, and then stopped. She felt the cold in the cracks between stone. The voices she knew fell silent, one after the other; the cold remained, and she began to understand that it had a voice of its own.

Death. Death there. The death of all things.

She drew back. Shook her head, although it was hard; all of her was shaking.

"Cessaly?"

Her hand fell away from the wall. "No," she told him sadly. "The cold will kill us." She turned to look at him, and she saw the shadows that the walls contained, straining for freedom, for something that might have looked like flight to a person who had never seen birds. Never made them, inch by inch, never carved the length of their flight feathers, the stretch of their pinions.

It was dark now. The world was dark.

But Master Gilafas was still in it.

He caught her hand; it was blue.

"Come," he said gently. "We are not yet there, and there is no cold in Fabril's reach."

"Where is Fabril's reach?"

"Up," he told her gently. "Up these steps."

"I can't see them."

"No. Sometimes they are hard to see." The lights in the wall sockets were bright and steady; they had never failed, and he was certain they never would. Fabril had made them himself, had made this tower, the reach.

"Will you take me there?"

"Yes, Cessaly. Can you feel my hand?"

She appeared to be thinking, as if thought were her only vision. He waited.

"I can feel it."

"Good. You have never made hands," he said. "But when we arrive, I will bring you wood and tools, and you must try."

"Just hands?"

"For now, Cessaly. Just hands." Speaking, he began to walk, the steps as solid and real as the fading light of day, the passage of time, the Holy Isle.

After she had made her way up the stairs—and in his estimation it took some two hours—she had to face the gauntlet of the great hall.

It was in the great hall that his envy, his bitterness, his resentment gave way to something more visceral: fear.

She screamed.

She screamed, and pulled away from him. Pulled back, turned to flee. He lost her, then. The hall swallowed her whole. She was gone.

He cursed as he had not done in years, the reserve and distance of age swallowed whole by the intensity of emotion.

She heard the voice of stone. The voice of mountains, old as the world; the voice of the molten rock in the heart of its ancient volcanoes; the voice, insistent, of its cracking, sliding fall. All the voices she had heard in her life were made small and insignificant; she lifted hands to capture them, and they came up empty.

She had no tools. No way to speak to stone with stone's voice, no way to soothe it.

But that didn't stop her from trying.

Trying, now, clawing at things too heavy and solid, her arms aching with effort, hands bleeding.

Past midnight, the fear left him, sudden as it had come. He was drained of it, like a shattered vessel of liquid, and what remained was the residue that had haunted his adult life.

Think. Think, Gilafas.

What a maker heard—if a maker heard what an Artisan heard at all—did not destroy the world; it did not unmake a reality. Fabril's reach, in all its frustrating, distant glory, was there before him. And he knew that the girl had come with him, slowly and hesitantly, eyes wandering across the face of its carved, misshapen walls.

And what of the door, Gilafas? What of the door that did not exist until she placed hand against wall?

It did exist. It always existed. I never found it. I never thought to look. I knew what the shape of the tower was—and is—I knew that such a door at that place could not exist.

Think.

He ran to the closed doors of his workrooms, those vast, open spaces in which light dwelled when there was any light at all. He opened drawers and cupboards, looking for chisels, for the knives which woodworkers used; wood was not his medium, but all makers of note often dabbled.

When he dropped a drawer on his foot, when the slender tubes made for blowing glass shattered about him, he paused long enough to avoid its splinters. Just that.

He did not think to call Sanfred, and would wonder why later. For now, he continued to search until he found the oldest of his supplies; blocks of wood as long as his forearm.

Thus armed, he paused again. *Think, Gilafas. Think.*

No. Not think.

Listen.

By dawn, he found her, and in finding her, he found a room that he had never seen.

It lay behind the stonework on the west wall, between the arch made of the raised arms of two men whose likenesses were said to be perfect: the first Kings of Essalieyan. They were not overly tall, and the space between them just large enough to fit a small girl with ease. A large man would not have been able to follow that passage, and if he had never felt cause to be thankful for his lack of stature before, he was grateful now.

The passageway was narrow and poorly lit; it was cold with lack of light, and almost silent; his breath was captured by folds of cloth, muted.

He could not have said why he chose to follow this path. But having begun, he heard her, and hearing her, saw her clearly, small, fine-boned, clear-eyed. He thought of what she might be, robbed of color and lent the clarity of glass or crystal, and this helped; he could imagine the fires, the glass, the workroom, the movement of hands and lip, the changing contours of a medium that was fluid, as close to the ocean in texture as anything solid could be.

He had never had to work so hard just to walk in Fabril's reach.

Fabril's reach will teach you everything you need to know.

For the first time in years, he turned those words over in his mind's eye, blending them with Cessaly until they were a part of her, a part of his making. *What, Master Nefem, do I need to know? And if this is a part of it, why do I need to know it?*

The hall ended; it opened into a room that had windows for a ceiling, a dome of fractured light. Crystal cut its fall into brilliant hues that traced the sun's progress.

She huddled in their center, her hands scratching the surface of the floor. She did not see him; could not see him. What she saw, he could not say, but he knew that she would see it until she found some release from it, until it was exorcised.

He could see what she could not: blood, dried and crusted upon the palms of her flailing hands.

He did not touch her. Instead, he knelt by her side and placed those tools he had found into the hands that were so ineffectual.

For the first time since he had entered the room, her focus changed. He placed the wood before her, but above the flat, smooth surface of stone.

He would take her from this room, in time. But that time was not yet come.

"Cessaly," he said, although he was certain she wouldn't hear him, "make what you must; I will return."

She loved the sound of Master Gilafas' voice.

No one had ever had a voice like his, and she marveled at it, for there was a texture beneath the surface of his words and his emotions that moved her to listen. She had thought to miss home; to miss her da and her mother; to long for Bryan and Dell, the two people who had brought her close to flight in the days of her childhood.

She forgot that longing quickly. The soles of her feet forgot the earth and the tall grass; forgot the slender silver stream; forgot the soft mosses, the heavy leaves of undergrowth. The stone spoke to her in a voice that was so close to her own she felt it as a part of her. To lose that would kill her.

And the only person with whom she could share this strange homecoming was Master Gilafas. His friends, Sanfred and Jordan, were as deaf as the man who had helped to birth her.

Master Gilafas understood her. He came to her with bits of wood, smooth stone, raw gems; he gave her room in his workshop, and brought to her the glass that he loved. She did not love it, but she listened to its voice as it spoke to him, and sometimes, when the world was quiet and her hands could be still, she would sing a harmony to its quiet voice.

But at other times, the stones would lead her to rooms that Master Gilafas could not find on his own. She was afraid of the stone, then; afraid of being alone. She hated the darkness that lingered at its edges; it hurt her, and it promised to hurt her more.

She knew it. Because she heard what the stones said to *him* when he walked by her side. She would glance anxiously at his face when the stones spoke in their sharp, cold voices.

Sometimes she would ask him about the voices.

And he would take her hands in his and smile gently. "Yes," he would say, "I hear them. But they are only words, Cessaly. Pay them no heed."

And she would see her death in these stones, but his words and his voice were stronger.

He was reduced, he thought, to being a baby-sitter.

He had, in that first month, attempted to foist that duty upon

Sanfred's broad shoulders, and Sanfred was more than willing to accept it.

But the greatness of the talent that all but consumed Cessaly was denied in its entirety to Sanfred. He could not hear what she heard. He could not see what she saw. Instead, he heard madness, and only madness.

The stories were there, of course. Every apprentice, every young journeyman, every man who desired to be called Master— and there were not a few of those in the guild—knew the stories.

The Artisans were mad. Gloriously, dangerously, mad.

Only madness could conceive of a small jeweled box in which the whole of a room might be contained. Only madness could create Fabril's reach, bending the fabric of the real and the solid to the vision of its maker. Only madness, yes.

But madness had created more, much more.

And Gilafas was doomed to understand it. To see what he could not be; to almost touch what he could not acheive. His curse.

Sanfred lost Cessaly for two days. He came to Gilafas, ashen and terrified, and all but fell in a groveling heap at the Guild-master's feet, weeping. Two days, Gilafas searched; two days, he listened.

He found her at last in a room he had visited once in night-mare, standing before the effigy of altar upon which her naked body lay, cradling rod and sword. What he found in search of Cessaly, he was never allowed to lose again. It waited, that room.

He had carried her from it with care and difficulty; she had in her hands the softest of stones, and powder flew from it as she carved and polished its face, her eyes unseeing, her ears bleeding.

Two days later, she had begged him for gold. He had brought that, and more besides: gemstones, large as eyes. She was thin as a bird; lifting her, he could believe that her bones were hollow. She said, "I'm flying, Master Gilafas. You've made me fly!" And laughed, delirious. Insane.

He loved the sound of that laugh, and he understood, when he called Sanfred again, that Sanfred not only did not love it, but in fact, was terrified by it.

The fear galled Gilafas; the pity and horror that Sanfred could not hide when he next saw Cessaly enraged him. He had not expected that. Had he, he might have been more temperate.

More cautious.

"Do you not understand what you have witnessed?"

Sanfred was mute in the face of his words.

"The guild has not been graced by a talent as pure as hers since its founding. Do you not understand the significance of her presence?"

An ill display indeed, for he knew the answer. No. How could he?

"You . . . are not . . . as she is."

"No, Sanfred, I am not. To my profound sorrow, I am not. Get out. Get out; I will tend her myself."

He was her captive. He came to understand that. The whole of his life, his authority, his stature meant nothing to her. And where was the justice in that? For his life revolved around her. The hours of his rising, the hours in which he might sleep, were dictated by hers, and she slept the way a newborn does: unaware of the strictures of day and night, light and darkness.

She took food at her whim, and when that whim was weak, at his; she drank because he demanded it. Sometimes, when he was exhausted beyond all measure, he went to the apothecary and fed her bitter brew; it dulled her for some hours while he slept.

Sanfred, unable to champion Cessaly, became in all things Gilafas' ears and eyes; only upon royal command did Gilafas choose to leave Fabril's reach. He had lost Cessaly for two days; he did not intend to do so again.

Captivity breeds either hostility or resignation, and in Gilafas it bred both.

He was surprised, then, to find that in the stretch of the days from summer to Henden, he had learned to love the cage.

He discovered it thus: Duvari came to visit.

It had been months since their first meeting in the heights of

Fabril's reach; the Astari had sent no word, and by its lack, Gilafas understood that the Sword at least was whole.

But when Duvari appeared in the doorway of his workroom, he knew that the lull had ended. Cessaly was in the corner, by the cooling glass. She had, in her fashion, been singing, and together they had blown a bubble in which one of her butterflies was encased, its lines brought out by light. They had learned to work together in this fashion, Gilafas the hands behind their mutual will.

"Remember, Cessaly, not to touch it yet. It will burn your hands, and you will not be able to make until they are healed."

She nodded, too absorbed to look up.

Trusting her, then, he stepped away.

He was not dressed for an audience; indeed, he wore the oldest of aprons, the most worn of gloves. The glass that protected his eyes sat upon his head like a wayward helm; he almost lowered it when he saw Duvari. The threat in his presence was palpable.

But he did not do it. Cessaly was sensitive to gesture this close to making's end, and she was always sensitive to the tone, the texture, of his voice.

"I would speak a moment in private," Duvari said quietly.

In that, they were of a mind. Gilafas nodded politely. "I . . . would prefer . . . to remain in sight of her."

"It was not a request. The matter is of a sensitive nature."

"As is she," Gilafas replied evenly.

Duvari frowned. The frown was unlike the one that normally adorned his features, and Gilafas instantly regretted his words.

"Very well, Guildmaster. King Reymalyn has sent me with a message."

"And that?"

"The Sword," he said softly, "was drawn this morning."

Heart's blow. He lifted a feeble hand to ward it, but it was far too late.

"I confess that I could not read what was writ in the runnels, although the words were clear to me. King Reymalyn labored under no such handicap."

"The sword was forged by Fabril," Gilafas said, the words

leeched of the pride that once might have lodged within them. "If I was to guess, I would say that no one but the King Reymalyn—with the possible exception of the King Cormalyn—might read what is written there."

"You are correct."

"Why have you come?"

"If you must play at ignorance, I will indulge you. I came—"

"Gilafas, look!"

Cessaly had run from the room's corner, her eyes bright. She reached out and caught his apron, tugging at it insistently. "Come, look, look!"

He followed her, aware that he risked Duvari's wrath. Like a shadow, the Astari followed, dogging his steps. Gilafas, mindful of this, pried her fingers free, replacing cloth with the palm of gloveless hand.

In the circular globe, the butterfly hovered, wings flapping. They brushed the concave sides of the glass, and the glass trembled in response.

Duvari said quietly, as if there had been no interruption, "The Sword must be reforged, the Rod remade. They were meant to stand against the Barons; they were not created to stand against the darkness."

"Then you are doomed," he said, but without hope, "for the man who made those emblems of the Kings' power is long dead."

"Indeed. But it is not by his hands that they must be remade."

Gilafas stiffened. He was surprised, but he shouldn't have been. The Lord of the Compact, it seemed, made all secrets, all hidden histories, his business. "I had thought it might be by yours, Guildmaster." He bowed, and when he rose from the bow, his face was as smooth as the surface of the glass that now contained the floating butterfly.

Gilafas had a moment of clarity, then, standing before the most feared man in the Empire. He saw the pity in Duvari's face; the pity and the ruthlessness.

"It is trapped," Duvari said, speaking for the first time to Cessaly.

"Oh, no," she said, eyes round, face serious. "It is *safe.*" And

then she frowned. "I have something for you," she told him.
"Can you wait here?"

He nodded gently. He, who had never done a gentle thing in
his life.

Cessaly floated from the room, bouncing and skittering around
the benches, her arms flapping.

"Understand," Duvari said quietly, when she had vanished,
"that the Kings have no choice in this. The darkness has risen,
and it is gathering. The Kings cannot go unarmed into that battle,
and they *will* go."

"She is a child," Gilafas replied.

"She is an Artisan, and if I understand the hidden histories
well enough, she is the Artisan for whom Fabril built the reach.
What she needs to learn, she must learn here, and she must learn
it quickly."

The Guildmaster closed his eyes.

"Because if I am not mistaken, she will not survive long."

"She is not the power that Fabril was."

"She does not have his knowledge," Duvari replied, "nor the
allies with whom he worked so long and so secretly. But the
power?" Again, something akin to pity distorted his features.
"Affection is a dangerous burden, Guildmaster. We go, in the
end, to war, and the chance of victory is so slight we can afford to
spare nothing."

"It is not in my hands," he said stiffly.

That was his truth. It was not, it had never been in his hands.

"Is it not?"

She came then, before he could frame an answer, and her
hands, so often spread wide to touch the surfaces of the world
around her, were clenched in loose fists. Sunlight caught the
edges of gold, the brilliant flash of diamond.

She walked up to Duvari without even a trace of her usual caution. "These are for you," she told him gravely.

"For me?"

"Well, maybe for the Kings."

He held out his palms very slowly, as if she were a wild creature. She placed in them two pendants. They were eagles, the

guildmaster thought, wings spread in flight, flight feathers trailing light. At their heart, large as cat's eyes, sapphires. To Gilafas' eyes, they glowed.

"These will help," she told him quietly. "With the shadows."

"The shadows, Cessaly?"

She nodded. "We have them here, and I *don't like them*. I made one for me, too. When I wear it, I don't hear shadow voices. Only the other ones. The stones," she added, by way of explanation. "The wood, and the gold—the sapphires are quiet, but you need the quiet—and Master Gilafas."

"You hear the shadows here?"

"Don't ask her that!" Gilafas cried out.

But her face had turned, from Duvari, from him. Skin pale, her eyes darted along the workroom's walls. Here, the voices of nightmare were weakest; this *was* Gilafas' space.

But the nightmares had been growing stronger; there was now not a single moment in which she could safely be left alone without some sort of work in her hands. She jerked twice, as if struck, and then turned and fled the room.

Gilafas, prepared in some fashion for these episodes, ran to the workbench and swept up the satchel in which the most portable of her tools were contained.

"Guildmaster," Duvari began.

"Not *now*, Duvari."

He did not expect argument; he did not receive it. But he was angry enough that he could not stop himself from speaking as he strode to the door. "If I have lost her again, you will pay. One day, she will go someplace where she *cannot* be found; she will be beyond us, working until she starves. If that day is today, I swear to you—and to the Kings you protect—that the Guild of the Makers will never again serve at your command."

He did not wait for the reply.

And perhaps he would have been surprised to know that none was made.

Cessaly did not run far.

Had she been afraid of Duvari, she would have, but she found herself liking the man; he was very quiet. He wasn't cruel, but he wasn't kind; he was almost like the stonework on the walls: made of a single piece, and finished. He needed nothing from her.

The shadows were not afraid of him either. The moment he mentioned their voices, she heard them clearly, and they were some part of his. But although they touched him, he somehow did not touch *them*.

Important, that he never heard their voices.

She had used sapphires to capture quiet, and diamonds to capture light; the eagle was simply the ferocity of a flight that did not necessarily mean departure. She had made those in the round room because she had been afraid. But she had made *three*. One, she wore; because she wore it, she could now find her way up—and down—the winding stairs that led to the below.

But two she had simply held, and when she had seen Duvari—when he appeared at her side as the butterfly began its flight—she knew why: they were for him.

But she didn't like his "thank you" very much, and she wasn't certain if she wanted to see him again.

Maybe. Maybe she wanted to be able to see *him*.

She frowned. Things she had not tried now suggested themselves in the brilliant hues of the floor of the round room. She had her stone, of course, and she carved while she paced the floor, a hollow feeling in throat and stomach. She would ask Gilafas for what she needed. He always gave her what she needed.

He found her almost instantly, which should have stilled his anger; it did not. She was working, although not in a frenzy, and when he entered the chamber—her workroom, as she often called it—she offered him a smile at home in the deep, soft rainbows cast by sun.

"Master Gilafas," she said, as he bent a moment and set his knees against those colors, "could you bring me a loom?"

"Yes. Yes, Cessaly. After lunch, I will bring you a loom." He did not tell her that such an undertaking would take more than a single morning, and did not ask her where the loom should be set;

he did not speak to her of cost, the responsibility of expenses, the things that had always balanced his momentary, frenzied desires.

She did not care; could not.

And in truth, neither did he.

The loom should have been foreign to her; the working of metal was a gift that had been taught over the course of months. But he was not surprised to hear the clacking of the great, wooden monstrosity that now occupied some part of his workroom. There were no other rooms that could house it in Fabril's reach—at least none that he was aware of, and if Cessaly knew otherwise, she did not choose to enlighten him.

He considered her carefully as he worked, and he *did* work; the voices were upon him, and they rode him unmercifully. He no longer knew if ocean's voice drove his hands, or if hers did—or worse, if his own now moved him, with its anger and its self-contempt. Not good, and he knew it; not good to be driven by that last voice. Men died for less, grabbing in a frenzy at those things that might still it—and not only the maker-born; all men with hollow power.

But it drove him.

Glass was before him, broken, colored, and around it a skein of lead; the things he knew better than he knew himself.

The loom was racked with the passage of her hands. It seemed fitting that they should work in this fashion. He was surprised that he was aware of her at all, for he knew by the feel of the glass in his hands that he should have been beyond her.

He failed in his duty, this day; he forgot to feed Cessaly. Forgot to feed himself.

Was not aware, until Sanfred forcibly removed his hands from his tools, of what he was making.

But Sanfred, having wrested the cutters from his hands paused, frozen, in front of his mosaic.

For the first time, Gilafas permitted himself to see what the glass contained.

Cessaly.

Cessaly, who, in bleeding hands, carried two things: a Rod with a crystal Orb that must deny all hint, all taint, of darkness, and a Sword whose edge glittered like the diamond wings of her eagles.

And he looked at the sky, red and dark, sun bleeding into the night of the horizon. Three days, for three more days, the light would wane early, the night sustain itself. The heart of the month of Henden would arrive, and with it, the longest night.

Duvari returned two days after his first visit with Cessaly. He came without warning, which was wise; had he offered warning, the Guildmaster would have forbidden him entrance, and personally would have dismissed anyone who disobeyed that order.

But he offered no such introduction; worse, he did not come alone. The companion he had chosen to bring to the Guildhall had caused concern and quiet outrage long before the two men had mounted the stairs that led to Fabril's reach.

Gilafas understood why the instant he laid eyes on the second man. His hair was long and white; it fell across his shoulders like the drape of an expensive cape. He had not chosen to bind it, which was unusual; Gilafas had never seen that hair escape the length of formal braids.

"Guildmaster," the man said.

"Member APhaniel," he replied coolly. "To what do I owe this . . . singular . . . honor?"

"To the busy schedule of Sigurne Mellifas, alas. The Council of the Magi occupies all of her waking time at the moment."

"I had heard there was some difficulty."

Meralonne APhaniel shrugged broadly. "Among mages, there is *always* difficulty."

"Among makers, the same can be said." But only grudgingly. "Although I confess that I have seldom had cause to resent the difficulties that keep Member Mellifas away, I resent them this day."

A pale brow rose in a face that was entirely too perfect on a man of Meralonne's age.

"It is understood. Sigurne is better at handling difficulties of this nature. In all ways. But perhaps I am not entirely truthful."

Gilafas snorted. "Of a certainty, you are not entirely truthful."

"No? Ah, well, perhaps my reputation precedes me." A glimmer of a smile then. "And one day, when we both have time, you must tell what that reputation *is*. The dour and incommunicative Duvari cedes not even the most paltry of rumors to the mageborn. He is significantly less . . . suspicious of the maker-born."

"Not, apparently, of their guildmaster."

"Well, no, of course not. The Guildmaster actually possesses power."

"Gentlemen," Duvari said coldly, "may I remind you of the scarcity—and therefore the value—of our time?"

Meralonne reached into his robes and drew from it a long-stemmed pipe. "May I?"

"Of course."

"You might join me, Guildmaster."

Gilafas started to say that he did not smoke, and thought better of it. He did, and he guessed that the mage-born member of the Order of Knowledge knew exactly what it was that burned in his pipe when he chose to bring it to his lips. He reached for pipe and box, and bitter, bitter weed. Spread dry leaf in the flat bowl of his pipe.

"I have seen the work of your apprentice," Meralonne said, when smoke lingered in the air. "The two pendants."

"And they?"

"You must guess at what they do, Guildmaster."

"I confess that I have not the resources—nor the desire—to test them. They are effective in some measure against the—against our enemies?"

"Yes." Meralonne's cheeks grew concave as he inhaled. "I had not thought to see their like again, not newly made. But yes." He turned, then, to the corner of the room in which Cessaly lay sleeping. In sleep she was much like a cat; she found it as it came, and took it where she sat, stretching out against floor or chair.

"She is young," he said at last.

"She is."

"Do you understand what it is that is asked of her?"

He could not find the words, but for once, he didn't need to. He turned to his bench, and lifted the gauze he had placed across his work, setting it aside with care; he wanted no dust, no wood shavings, no metallic slivers caught in its threads. Then he lifted the glasswork, the mosaic of transparent color, and he turned its bitter accusation toward the magi.

Through the wild skein of her hair, he saw the golden skin of Meralonne APhaniel.

"I see," the magi said quietly, "that she is not the only Artisan to busy herself in Fabril's reach."

"I have always worked in Fabril's reach," Gilafas said dryly.

"Oh, indeed. But you have only twice created something that blends the skill of the maker with the deeper, wilder magicks. Ah, I stand corrected; this is the third, and if I were to guess, the most subtle, the most powerful, of the three."

Gilafas' turn to be surprised. "Is it?"

"The most powerful?"

"A work."

"Do you not know?"

He said nothing.

"Magic—such as mine—is not sanctioned within these halls, Guildmaster, but were it, I am not certain it would divine the purpose behind your creation. Certainly it will not tell me more than you yourself know. But I will say this, and perhaps I say too much. I am not Duvari. I am aware of what is asked, of both you and your apprentice. Duvari accepts all cost and accrues all debt in the cause of the Kings. I? I do not believe that debt ever goes unpaid, and I am loath to accumulate it.

"And I believe your apprentice is waking."

Gilafas frowned; he had heard nothing. But he did not doubt the Magi. He turned to see that Cessaly had taken to her feet. She was smiling shyly.

"Have you come to see my work?"

"I have," Meralonne replied. "And I have come to bring you something. Which would you have me do first?"

"My work." Her smile was unfettered by such things as caution or suspicion. She walked over to the closet Gilafas had emptied for her use, and drew from it three bundles of cloth. One was as blue as cloudless sky, one as dark as midnight, and one the color of light seen through the fog of cloud. "I made these," she said, as if it were not obvious.

"Did you make them for anyone?"

"I don't know. But I made them. They are all too large for me. The loom moves quickly and the cloth chatters."

She handed him the darkest of the three, and as he unfolded it, Gilafas saw that it had a hood. A cloak, he thought.

"Put it on." Her little, imperious voice was the only one in the room.

Meralonne did not hesitate. He laid a hand against the weave of the cloth, and ran his fingers across it, his eyes wide. "Child," he said softly. Just that. But there was no mistaking the longing—and the wonder—in the single word. "You remind me of my youth." He caught the cloak by its upper edge, and twirled it backward until it fell over his back, obscuring the length of his hair.

He raised the hood, and then, with a smile, fastened the silver clasps that hung at his collar. Gilafas was not surprised to see him vanish.

Cessaly clapped her hands in glee.

The hood fell, and the man reappeared. "My lady," he said, and he fell to one knee before her laughing face. "We have come to beg a boon of you."

"Member APhaniel—"

"We have brought, for your inspection, two things." He gestured. *Magic,* the Guildmaster thought.

"I have the Kings' writ," Duvari said evenly, before Gilafas could voice even token outrage.

A bundle appeared in Duvari's outstretched arms. He brought it to Meralonne APhaniel, and the magi unwrapped it with care, until he was left with two things.

Gilafas bore witness; he could not bring himself to move.

She came to Meralonne as if she could no longer see him; as if she had eyes only for what he held. Bright, her eyes, like liquid, like the ocean in summer. And dark, like its depths.

She took them from his arms and did not even notice their weight, although she buckled beneath it. She brought her knees to the ground, as if in obeisance, and touched the dull white of the broken Orb, the black and gold of the Sword's scabbard. Her lips opened and closed, and Gilafas knew a moment of pride, for he could hear her voice, and he was certain the others could not. After a moment, she raised her head, and she looked at Mera-lonne APhaniel, all joy in the lesser creation gone.

She said, "You should not have brought these here."

"We had no choice, Lady."

She rose, staggering; she would not allow him to touch their plain surface. "But the demons will come now."

"Yes."

She woke in the dark of the night, in her bed, alone. She had gone to sleep there, her hands absorbed with the beads she had asked for, the strings upon which to place them almost full. Her fingers were stiff with the damp and the cold; she knew that she had worked them while she slept. Master Gilafas would worry. She knew it.

It was why she had forced herself to walk the halls, to come to this room, to let sleep take her while he watched. He only left her when she slept, and only when she was here.

But she had work to do; she knew it. The days. The days had gone; the nights had slowly devoured them. They waited above her head and beneath her feet, gathering the shadows and the darkness. All the voices were strong.

And steel's voice strongest of all.

She slid her feet out of bed; the floors were cold, but she dare not wear shoes. She wanted no light, nothing to see by, and without it, her feet were her eyes; they knew the halls at least as well as her eyes did.

Beneath her bed, she found the Sword; found the Rod. Her hands knew them by more than their weight, but it was their weight that troubled her, for the Sword was so long it *would* drag on the floor, the metal of its sheath creating sparks and noise.

She struggled alone.

She understood, dimly, that she was not a simple child, but the child in her was often the only element that could survive the arduous task of making. The understanding clung to her as she struggled: she was not a child. She had come to Fabril's reach *because* she was not a child, and she had remained because no one— not even her beloved Master Gilafas—could hear the voices of the wild as well as she.

But she was grateful; had she been at home, had she been in Durant, she was certain the town would have perished this eve. The longest night.

She was not dour by nature; not grim. Master Gilafas, haunted and tired, was both of these things, but she understood that he had come to love her, and because of it, she knew she must leave him. Because she understood the whole of Fabril's intent, and had, from the moment she had found the room Master Gilafas so hated.

The Rod and the Sword were vessels; they were vessels, and those vessels had long lain empty.

She had listened to the ocean in Master Gilafas' voice. She understood vessels, and what they contained, or could contain, because of that distant voice.

She was not so old that she had forgotten fear. In the dark of her room, she armed herself: she fastened the clasp of the pendant she had made, cold sapphire resting against the hollow between her collarbones. She drew cloak from an armoire that was otherwise empty, and ring from the box at her desk. She took no gloves, and paused a moment before the silver sheen of dark mirror.

In the dark, she drew the blade. She was not a swordsman; it was an awkward action. But she must do it; she must leave the sheath here. The blade, the Rod, they must go where she traveled.

The moon was high. Fabril had loved light, and if gold was the color of day, silver shone now, radiant and cool. Enough light to see by, but she did not need it; she could see in the shadows.

She hesitated for just a moment, on the edge of the master's workroom. And there she laid down her burden, and ran lightly across the darkened threshold. Moonlight came through glass in all its muted color; she passed it by, again and again, until she reached the delicate globe of blown glass Gilafas had given her.

Inside, floating and fluttering, the butterfly.

She pursed her lips, touched the cool glass, and with a simple word, she set the butterfly free. It broke the meniscus of glass surface as if it were liquid and passed above her, circling her head three times.

She let it go and turned again to her task.

The Rod and the Sword had been forged and quenched in the whole of a single day. She knew it, by touch; understood what not even the cold man understood: that Fabril had made these in the light of the longest day, a measure of, and containment for, the summer. It was, as her simple jewelry box had been, an act of affection, a desire to help those loved and respected. And in summer's season, the Rod had served the son of Wisdom, and the Sword the son of Justice: the Twin Kings who had, for centuries, given their lives to the Empire of Essalieyan.

But all things living know time and its passage, and all things living know the shifting of seasons. Summer had passed, the season so long that winter had been forgotten.

Aiee, she hated the shadows, the sibilance of their terrible whisper.

But what was forged in the grim stillness of winter, what lived in its ice and its blankets of pure, cold snow, was strong in a way that the summer itself was not strong, and that strength, cold and terrible, existed *outside of* the shadows.

Terrible power, scouring and lonely.

She had heard of men who had died steps from their homes when the blizzards had come; they could not see their way to safety, and what love and hope they carried as they struggled ended there.

Kalliaris, she thought, for the first time since she had come to Fabril's reach. *Kalliaris, smile.*

She walked the long hall, seeing the frozen stone about her, fitting company, and silent, for this last voyage. She was afraid of only one thing: That she would finish what she had been born to finish, that she would remake the Rod and the Sword that would be so necessary to the Twin Kings upon whom the Empire depended, and that there would be no one to bring them home.

Other fears would come later, to keep her company and ease her loneliness, but this fear was the wisest and the strongest.

She could not make anything while she walked, and she felt the gnawing hunger take her hands, felt this scrap of reasoned fear, this almost adult comprehension, fray about the edges, pulled like the loose thread in a weaving from her loom. So she cradled the blade with care against the cloak that protected her from the sight of men, and she ran her fingers, over and over, across the surface of what was writ in its runnels.

She began to descend the stairs, and it was hard: the floor was cold, and the steps steep. The lights that existed against the walls were dim; they did not speak a language that her eyes understood. But she did not need them; she knew where she walked, and when she reached the halfway mark, she set her hand against the wall and waited.

The door opened.

The door opened into the Scarran night, and the Winter Road wound from its step into the hollows of the ancient, wild way.

Gilafas could not say what woke him, not at first.

He sat up in bed as if struck, the full face of the moon framed in the windows of his chambers. The night was silent; he listened a moment and heard the distant thrum of ocean voice. It was not insistent.

He rose, clenching fists, and cried out in shock and pain; his left hand burned.

He spoke a word and the light flooded his vision, forcing his lids down; when they rose again, he stared at the open mound of his hand, his left hand.

In it, in the light, were shards of delicate glass, the broken form of butterfly wings above crescent pools of blood.

He listened, and he heard the ocean, and only the ocean, and then he understood.

He dressed like a madman, taking the time to don jacket over his sleeping robes. He grabbed a dagger, although it was futile; tore a light from the wall and clutched it in his bleeding fist.

He took no care to be silent; silence was not his friend, and the noise was a distraction, a welcome one. He ran to his workroom, commanded light, banished moon. There, on the farthest reach of his personal bench, he saw what he had dreaded: the globe in which he had encased Cessaly's butterfly. This was their only common work, and it was empty now; what she built, he had in the carelessness of sleep destroyed.

What night? What night, he thought, frenzied. *Was this the longest night? Or was it past him, was it gone?*

But no: for once the darkness was blessed, for it lingered, deep and forbidding.

He began to search for Cessaly.

The first place he looked was her room, but it was empty; there was no trace of her presence in it at all, although the sheets were turned back and her cupboard door swung open as he approached.

The halls were long. He knew all of her rooms, for once she had opened the ways, they could not be closed. And he knew his own: the room in which her death was carved in stone, the obscenity of it stronger every time he chanced upon it.

He visited them all. All of them, and he found her in none, although his own horror waited around every doorway and every corner.

He had left her. In his exhaustion, he had chosen to leave her. If he found her, he promised whatever capricious god might be listening he would never leave her again.

No, Gilafas, fool. No. *Think.*

But thought eluded him, deluded him, sent him in circles that ended, always, with the workroom.

But the last time, the last circuit, had finished him; in agony, he retreated into the moonlight, his hands shaking.

The lights were dim; he could not remember dimming them. He started to speak, and lost the words as he turned to the great windows that formed a casement for the moon. No; not the moon, but some light that was much like it: radiant and cool.

In its heart, standing in robes the color of night, stood a ghost, a demon. He had brought the wind with him, and it was a foreign wind, devoid of the taste of salt.

He turned, and the light turned with him, and when at last this intruder faced Gilafas, he saw two things that he recognized.

The first, the least, Meralonne APhaniel, shorn of the emblem of the magi, the decorations of mage-born rank. His hair was white and long, his eyes the color of new steel; he wore no sword, no shield, no armor, but he was dressed for war.

The second, the source of the room's light: the mosaic he had made; the likeness of Cessaly. Golden hair, honey eyes now shaded to the green that was either trick of light or whisper of power, blue dress, and red, red blood, these burned in his vision. The lead that held the glass was grown insubstantial and weightless, or perhaps it was fluid; he could not see it clearly. Did not try.

"You asked," Meralonne APhaniel said softly, "what purpose this Work served, and I believe I have divined it. It is of glass for a reason, Guildmaster.

"It is a window."

A window. He stepped toward it, and faltered in the glow of its light. "Why did you come?"

"I told you. I am not Duvari."

"You are not truthful."

"Not entirely, no. This is Fabril's reach. Fabril was not seer-born; that was not his gift. But it is myth that he created the whole of this wing; he made it his own, but he chose it for a reason.

"For the summer, Guildmaster, and for the winter." His eyes were unblinking. "You do not hear the summer voice; you do not hear the winter. That is both your gift and your curse. What Fabril wrought does not speak to you. But it speaks to her, to your apprentice, and this is the longest night, the Scarran night.

"And I believe that *she* speaks to you."

Truth, Gilafas thought, but not enough of the truth.

"Why did you come here, mage?"

He was silent a moment, and then he said, "I believe that she will be drawn to the Winter Road, and if she enters into a great Work upon it, she may never return.

"But her Work *must* return. Do you understand?"

Gilafas said nothing.

"Guildmaster."

Silence.

"The Guild of the Makers has been waiting for longer than you can imagine, guardians against this age. It has waited so long, there have been those among you who have come, over time, to believe the wait has been in vain, a thing of child's story. But you know now. And I, and the Kings. Open the window. Open it, Guildmaster, for I cannot."

He cursed his gift for the first time in his adult life. Cursed himself for a fool for creating this window so small, although it was the gift itself that had guided the making. His hands shook as he approached her, trapped in glass, circled by lead. Her eyes were now closed.

They had not been closed when he had made her, for the width of her eyes was, among the many things about her, the one that he had come to love best.

He cried out in fear and reached for the glass, and his hands passed through it as if it were mist, or smoke, or veil.

The winds tore past him, then, and in their folds, they carried the screams of the dying, thin high ululation, the keening of the damned.

His eyes teared at once, and his cheeks froze; the wind was dry and cold, and it allowed for no liquid. Ocean voice denied him, then, and just as well. He saw darkness, felt it across the length of his arms. Frost formed in the folds of his jacket; flakes gathered against cloth and found purchase there.

Bodies lay aground, some writhing, most still. He saw an arm, a jerking hand, a fallen blade; saw a broken bow, its curve shattered, saw the spill of hair across snow, white upon white, with the thinning pink of spreading blood beneath it.

He could not count them all; he did not try. Once, in the whirl of the angry wind, he saw the pale skin of an upturned face, its eyes wide, lashes made of snowflakes. *Too beautiful,* he thought, although clearly the man was dead. Too beautiful to be a demon.

He moved, although he could not say how; he knew that the window itself was too small a passage for a man of his size. Could not regret it either.

Until he saw her.

He knew her at once, although he could not see her face, for her hair was short and golden; not even the snow that clung there could obscure its color. He knew the bent shape of her shoulders, the moving jerk of elbows at play; he knew the shape of her back, even seen now, without cloth to obscure it. He knew the soles of her feet, for in the vastness of Fabril's reach, she never wore shoes.

Had not, he saw, worn them now. She would freeze to death, she would freeze in the wailing storm, and he thought her unaware of it, for the madness was upon her.

He could hear it so clearly he almost forgot himself.

But she was not alone in that clearing; the trees themselves, like wrought-iron fences, surrounded her, and in their shadows a shadow rose, tall and slender and perfect.

It made a poverty of any beauty he had ever seen, and in the Guildhall, he had seen much of it. He was humbled, instantly, by the presence of this stranger, this Winter Queen.

She looked up then, and she smiled, and although she was beautiful, and the smile a gift, he was chilled by it in a way that not even the slaughter had chilled him.

"Yes," she said softly, "I am the Winter Queen, and you are bold, to come here on this night."

He could not speak; his legs would not hold his weight and he felt himself begin to bend so that he might place his life where it properly belonged: at her feet. Or beneath them.

But something held him up, something sharp and sudden.

"I do not walk the Winter Road," he told her, the words flowing through him as if they belonged to another. "I have placed no foot upon it, and I have taken nothing, touched nothing that belongs to the Queen who rules it."

Her smile deepened, and it was chilling; there was no pleasure in it. "You are wise, who appear to be a simple, mortal fool."

"I am not wise, Lady, or I would not be here, witness to winter; the mortal seasons are not your seasons."

"No, indeed they are not, and mortals themselves are so fleeting." And her gaze, the gaze he coveted and feared, slid from his face to the shuddering back of Cessaly. "But not all that is mortal is beneath my interest. You have come for the girl."

"I have."

"Ah. But she has not your wisdom; she has set foot, unencumbered foot, upon my path, and she has taken the lives of those who serve me." She stepped toward Cessaly, and Gilafas followed. Somehow he followed.

He wanted to shout, to give warning, to raise alarm; he was mute. The words that were not his words failed him.

The Winter Queen laughed in the wake of his silence, and her laughter was almost genuine.

She turned to him then. "Has it come to pass, little mortal? Have the gates been opened, and the Covenant shattered? Does the darkness stride the face of the mortal world once more?"

He was mute. Mute, still.

"Leave," she said. "Leave while I am amused and may know mercy."

"It is not for your mercy that I have come."

"Oh?"

"What the child carries belongs in the hands of the god-born; no other might wield or claim them."

"The hands of the god-born do not trouble them now," she replied, but amusement had left her face, and her lips were thinner. "And they have been made, remade, in *my* realm."

"They have been made and remade in the wild realm, Lady."

"And the wild realm knows no law but power."

"The wild realm knows no law but yours, it is true. But your vow is law in the realm, be your oath ancient, so ancient that it is forgotten upon this plane. You cannot lay claim to the Rod or the Sword until those vows are fulfilled, and, Lady—if you seek to retain even one, they will never be fulfilled, and your power will be diminished by the binding."

Her hair swept past her face; the gale had returned in the clearing.

"Perhaps," she said, one hand falling to the hilt of the sword she carried, and the other to the horn. "But so, too, will yours, and the mortal kingdom will surely fail. The Sword and the Rod came to me."

"Indeed."

"And they might lie here, unclaimed, until the seasons turn."

He fell silent again, the words stemmed.

And then she smiled. "I sense another presence, mortal. And perhaps this means that you do not understand what it is that you risk. What do you desire?"

His mouth opened. Closed.

Her eyes, her dark and golden eyes, flared; he felt a trickle of fire along his cheek, a caress that would leave a scar. "Speak," she said again. "And speak freely."

"I want the girl," he said. His words now. His own.

"Let me grant you a gift," she said coldly, "a gift of vision." She lifted her arms, one to either side; in the wake of the moon's light across the fine, fine mesh of chain shirt, the world darkened.

Dark, he knew it: it was his own. He saw the spires of the three cathedrals, raised higher than even *Avantari*, the palace of the Kings. They burned; circled in air by winged beasts and their riders, besieged by wind and shadow. They were empty, he thought; empty, he prayed. Beneath them, in the streets below, the flash of magic, the clash of armies.

Small armies, pockets of futile resistance.

The vision shifted as the wind changed; he flew over the dying city to the fields of Averalaan, and there he froze, for there he saw what they did not name.

Lord of Darkness.

It is not possible. It cannot be possible.

"Look well," she told him softly, "for you will see no Kings upon the field, and few armies. All of the bodies are yours; the Lord of the Hells has risen.

"I cannot say that the Kings would triumph had they the Rod and the Sword for which so much has been offered. But you have not even the hope of that: the Kings perished in *Avantari*, bereft of the power granted them by the artifacts of Fabril. Yes, even with her hand upon them, they are his."

She lowered her arms slowly, and the smile returned to her face. "I understand some small measure of mortality, Gilafas ADelios. It amuses me, and in this long, long winter, very little does.

"So I will give you what I have given few: a choice. You may take the child, or you may take the artifacts. But you may not take both. Choose," she said softly. "Choose; I will not intervene as long as you take only one thing when you return. Either—she, or they—will be of interest to me."

Gilafas was consumed by the winter, the winter's chill.

"The dawn is coming," the Winter Queen told him. "In your world, in the world in which you now stand, the sun will soon rise. Delay, Gilafas, and you will have neither."

He reached out to touch Cessaly; his hand gripped her shoulder. He had thought she would not notice, for she often didn't.

But she turned to him, turned at once, snow spilling from her lap. Her hands were dark with blood, but he could see, as she lifted her palms, that that blood was not her own. She had never been so still, in all the time he had known her. In all the brief time.

"Cessaly?"

Her face was a young woman's face, her eyes round and dark with exhaustion and fear. She lifted her chin, and met his eyes, and he realized that she had poured so much of herself into *this* making that she could at last, for a moment, know sanity.

It was terrible.

I will not do this, he thought. *She is Fabril's equal. She is his superior. What Fabril made, she can make again, and better. If we have her. If only we have her.*

But he did not believe it. Desired belief more than he had desired anything, even the mantle of Fabril's legacy.

Cessaly touched his hands, pulling them from her shoulder.

She was so cold he would not have thought her living had she not moved; her lips were blue.

And her eyes. Blue, he thought, and reddened.

"You can only take one thing," she said softly. She raised the Rod; its orb was whole and glowing with fractured, colored light, a dance of fire, a thing not of this Winter place, although it had been born to it. "These."

"Or you," he said, and the words cut him. Guildmaster. Keeper of Fabril's legacy. If she were gone, he would again be the only Artisan to grace the guildhall.

She said, "I have made these. They are your responsibility and mine. Protect what I have made, Gilafas. Protect my making."

Maker's words. Maker's ferocity, in her sanity.

He shook his head. He knew; he knew what must be done. The Winter Queen had shown him the truth of that need.

"No. No," he whispered. "Cessaly—"

She smiled, her jaw shuddering with the effort of maintaining that expression. "Thank you," she told him softly. "I know what has to be done . . . but . . . thank you."

Then, before he could speak, she placed the Rod and the Sword into his arms, and she rose, quick and catlike, and she *pushed*.

Meralonne APhaniel was not Duvari, as he had promised. He restrained Gilafas when the Guildmaster almost threw himself into the window again; he forced him—as gently as one could a man made wild and frenzied with grief—to see that the window had closed: he had a mosaic, some proof of the existence of a girl he had foolishly learned to care for, and that was all. To run at it would simply shatter it.

At the time, that would not have been a loss.

"You have what you want," he had said. "Get out!"

But the magi had carried the stained glass to the window, and he had gestured there a moment, and when he had stepped back, it rested securely against the greater glass.

"This will not comfort you now," he said softly, "and perhaps it never will. But I will say to you that the Winter Queen has always had an interest in the Artisans; that their madness in the end is proof against the madness she would cause." He bowed. "I am sorry, Guildmaster."

He looked up. "What did she mean?" he asked, dully. "When she spoke of the turn of seasons, what did she mean?"

"Nothing," Meralonne replied. "For she speaks of the Summer Road, and it has been forbidden her for so long, I do not know if it will ever return."

"And Cessaly?"

"She will never return."

He was required to come up with a story that might explain a young girl's disappearance, and he did, but Duvari judged the explanation itself unwise, and in the end, in disgust, he accepted the Lord of the Compact's version of events and burdened Sanfred with its spread.

He labored in Fabril's reach in a fruitless search for a door, or a window, into the winter world, and the days passed, spring becoming summer, summer fading into fall, and from there, the rain and the shadows of Henden. He counted them, and lost count of them as he toiled; he spoke with the wise, and when the wise gently turned him—and his money—away, he at last surrendered.

He did not accept her loss.

And perhaps because he could not accept it, could not accept the terrible silence of the absence of her voice, it was a full year before he chose to leave the guildhall, to take the road that led to the Free Town of Durant. This was not his penance; it was his duty.

To the mother, he carried word of her daughter's greatest act of making, but the mother had no desire for the comfort of the accolade. Hero was a hollow word.

"You promised," she said.

And he had bowed his head, old now, and shamed beyond the simple use of words.

"How long?" she had said, her voice rising, the tone fierce and terrible. "How long have you known?"

He could not answer.

"Why did you not come sooner?"

Why?

Because to come here, to make this pilgrimage, to stand before her just and terrible fury, her keening loss, was to acknowledge what he had so desperately refused to acknowledge. Cessaly was gone. Cessaly would never return.

"She is not dead," he told her.

"How can you know that?"

He met her eyes, her wide, reddened eyes, and he bowed his head. "I know it," he said bitterly. "And I had hoped that you might know it as well. She was your daughter."

Fabril's reach was no longer a cage. It was his home, the place from which he ruled the guild in the splendor due his rank. Empty splendor, as it had always been, but empty now in a different way. He heard the ocean, and only the ocean, and sometimes, in anger and desperation, he gave himself to its voice. More often, he gave himself to the numb detachment of bitterweed, and the business, the empty, hollow business, of the Guild of the Makers.

And then, one quiet morning, he felt it: something familiar, some hint of strangeness in the tower walls. He rose slowly and dressed, and then he walked the hall, fingers trailing the rounded surface of stone until he reached his workroom.

He opened the door, and as he did, something darted past him and down the hall. Had he been in any other place, he might have thought it a bat; in the heights, they were common.

But its flight was too delicate, too much the drunkard's spin, and he frowned as he stepped through the door.

Froze there, in wonder. The upper reaches of his room were thick with butterflies. Butterflies of glass, blown in every conceivable color; butterflies of silver and sapphire, of gold and ruby, of wood and stone. Among them, smaller than life, were birds, and the birds, too, were the hatchlings not of egg and warmth, but of the things that Cessaly had loved to work with.

He turned to the window, to the stained glass, and his smile, in this room, was the first that had not been tainted by bitterness in a decade. He lifted his hand to touch it; felt glass, and only glass, beneath his palm.

But the butterflies landed upon his shoulders, his head, his arms; they rested lightly upon the back of his hands, and they spoke to him, and each of their voices held some echo of hers.

Fiona Patton

When you first meet Fiona Patton, before you've had a chance to get to know her, you're likely to assume she's a shy and quiet person. You'd be wrong. Of course, if you've read any of her novels you'll know that she revels in warfare and mayhem, mixed in with sensitive often misunderstood characters who far too often have had greatness they really don't desire thrust upon them.

Getting Fiona to submit her first novel, *The Stone Prince,* to DAW was no easy task. In a two-writer household the thought of sharing the same publisher seemed to be a cause for concern. But when I made it clear that there'd be a lot more to worry about if I were not the first editor to read Fiona's novel, she quickly saw the light.

And I don't think Fe would contradict me when I say that it's worked out just fine. She found a second home in the DAW family, and we added another talented author to our list.

"The Huntsman" introduces us to a new land and a culture far different from that in her *Branion Realm,* but one that is equally compelling.

—SG

THE HUNTSMAN
Fiona Patton

THE sea sparkled invitingly in the late autumn sun, belying the thin lines of whitecaps that hinted at its true nature, but the old woman who crouched on the nearby escarpment was not fooled. She had bathed her feet in the surf that morning and knew just how cold and wild the waves had become. Ordinarily she would have sought her portents in the clouds and on the wind—she was too old to go fishing for the future in autumn—but the Gotri, the ancient enemy of her people, would be making one final attack before winter. She had Seen it. They would come from the sea, using its own restless power to shield their movements, and she must be ready to catch the earliest hint of their approach or all would be lost.

Turning, she glanced through a copse of birch trees at the gray defensive walls of Ruthgreen. As the most accessible of the coastal Asti villages, it was no stranger to attacks and raids from both the landward and the seaward sides, but this time the enemy drove powerful magics before them, raised by powerful Gods. It would take more than mere walls to stop them. It would take blood and loss willingly embraced and, even then, it might not be enough.

Rising, she made her way back along the winding path. On the edge of the village she glanced through the trees at the outline of a half completed labyrinth just visible in the center of an open meadow. It would take more than those walls as well, she thought, whatever the Master Builder believed. They were as tied to blood as the walls of Ruthgreen, and the blood had not yet quickened, if it ever would.

The wind, dancing through her hair, sent the long white strands whipping about her face in a complicated forecast, and she

snapped her shawl over her head with an irritated flick. She'd
made her prophecies; it was up to the Huntsman and His Chosen
to fulfill them. If they ignored her words, it was no concern of
hers. *She'd* survive the coming attack whatever else happened.
She'd Seen that.

A man's presence, tinged with a bitterness that made her Sight
twitch, whispered through her mind, and she clucked her tongue
in annoyance. In her view, the Huntsman had less sense than the
prey He hunted. Erik Blackthorn had been His most powerful
Captain in a hundred years; with his guidance Ruthgreen might
have flourished, but now they'd be lucky to survive the season.
Shaking her head, she glared at a blackbird who regarded her with
one bright eye from high in a nearby tree.

"There's more to a man than the strength in his arms," she
told it sourly, "but try telling that to any of them."

Especially Erik. If he didn't figure it out soon, though, they'd
all pay the price of it. She'd Seen *that* as well. Twitching the edge
of her shawl away from a greedy pine bough, Ruthgreen's Oracle
stumped on down the path, chewing over the past and the future
with equal vehemence.

In the meadow, a small, greenish-brown house snake paused to
taste the old woman's scent on the breeze before continuing its
journey over a large jumble of stones piled just west of the labyrinth. It had no interest in the past or future, only the present,
and in the present the midday sun was warm and inviting. Resisting the instinct to curl up on the very top of the pile and sleep, it
stopped before a fist-sized piece of granite and raised its head,
waited for the man whose power kept it awake to notice it.

Feeling the weight of its expectation, Erik Blackthorn brought
his shadowed gaze to bear on the tiny serpent.

"Is that the one?"

The snake fanned its delicate, red tongue at him, but otherwise
remained motionless. Wrapping his fingers about the rock, Erik
felt the latent power tingling through his palm before carefully
lifting it away with both hands. They weren't good for much else,

but they could still feel the Touch of the Goddess even if they couldn't respond. Noting the round indentation on one side and the scattering of fossil remains across the top, he nodded.

"That's an entrance piece."

He laid it carefully to one side, then reached out. The snake slid along the back of one weakened hand, around his wrist, and up to his shoulder, gently pressing its smooth, blunt muzzle against the crooked scar which ran along his jawline, then settled loosely about his neck. He glanced up.

"Berne?"

The barking of two dogs in the distance was his only answer.

Closing his eyes, Erik sent his thoughts out on the afternoon breeze, searching for his younger brother's presence. He tasted leaves and newly harvested grain, salt water and raw earthworks, but no Berne. His brows drew in. He didn't like the boy going off alone even if he was with Erik's two hunting dogs. The Oracle had said the Gotri would attack within the month but could not specify the day. Until they were defeated and driven back, no one was safe.

His mind traveled over the newly repaired walls of Ruthgreen, still searching. Since the Oracle's prophecy, the village had been a hive of activity as everyone, young and old, had scrambled to bring in the harvest and strengthen their defenses. So far no one had fled farther inland, yet, and that was because of Bri Jensen.

Turning, Erik glanced toward the man crouched in the center of the labyrinth, a large, flat piece of shale in one hand and a pendulum of pointed amber swinging from a finely braided chain in the other. The amber moved gently back and forth against the breeze; when it began to weave a complicated figure eight, he set the rock carefully down between two others, then reached for another. His gaze was drawn inward to a design only he could see, and Erik could sense his power cast over the entire creation like a giant net.

He blinked deliberately, and the vision disappeared.

The labyrinths were the Asti's answer to the continued threat from the Gotri and other seafaring raiders. Bri had built five, linking the three largest inland villages with their neighbors on the coast. Ruthgreen was the sixth and final link in a chain of mystical defenses which, when activated, would band the Asti together, able to invoke their Goddess with one, strong voice to aid them against the enemy. Bri had promised them She would respond; the Oracle wasn't so sure.

Erik didn't particularly care. The process of drawing out the most powerful stones from the pile the villagers brought each morning was healing. It made him forget the weakness in his hands and the pain of his other injuries for a time. As the autumn waned and the rest of Ruthgreen had turned their attention to the harvest and the defense of the village itself, he and Bri had fallen into a smooth pattern of choosing and placing each stone, aided only by Berne and one or two of the other village youths. But progress was slow and Erik was beginning to believe the Oracle was right. They would not be ready in time. The other Asti villages would cower behind their own walls as they always had and Ruthgreen would face the Gotri alone.

"Berne!"

Two huge dogs came bounding through the trees; a tall, gangly boy of twelve, black hair tumbling into his eyes, loping along behind them.

"Where have you been?"

Berne held up a brace of rabbits in explanation. "Supper."

"A good catch. Did you call for them?"

"Tracked 'em."

"Still, you might want to show them to Pieter."

His brother's eyes, so like Erik's, darkened slightly.

"They're not for Pieter; they're for us and for Bri."

"And one for the Oracle?"

"If she needs it, but Pieter took the Chosen out this morning. They downed a big buck east of the inlet, so she should be well looked after." Setting his bow against a tree, Berne tied the rabbits to a high branch where the dogs couldn't reach them, then glanced at the smaller pile of rocks.

"That's a lot today. You must be feeling stronger."

Erik's eyes darkened much as Berne's had.

"Snake helped," he said simply.

"Still. Snake didn't pile them up."

"No."

Stroking the serpent along its pale, yellow throat, Berne took in his brother's gray pallor and the faint tremors in his hands before indicating the pile. "I'm finished now. Did you want help carrying these over?"

"Could do." Erik began to slowly fill the sling about his shoulder with the smaller rocks while Berne collected the larger ones, careful not to take too many in case it hurt his older brother's feelings. Erik just shook his head with a smile.

Ever since their parents had died in the Gotri attack two years ago, he'd struggled to care for his younger brother, but, in truth, with the injuries taken in that same attack hampering even the simplest of tasks, it had been Berne who'd done most of the caring. He'd say by Erik's bedside for weeks while the Goddess decided which world he belonged in, then spent another two years helping him along the path to partial recovery. He'd grown into a strong, responsible young man who, at nearly thirteen, was more than ready to set out on his own path, but he'd lingered, unwilling to leave Erik to his own melancholy devices. Ruthgreen's elders, especially Pieter, wanted him to follow the Huntsman—he was as powerful as Erik had been at his age—but Berne, showing a flash of uncharacteristic anger, had flatly refused. The Huntsman had allowed the Gotri to destroy his home and murder his parents, then abandoned his older brother when He might have used him to save them all. He would not give the Huntsman the chance to do it again. Not even the Oracle had been able to change his mind, and Erik had no wish to. Berne would make his own choices when he was ready to, but, right now, he needed him to carry rocks.

Together, the two brothers made their way to the labyrinth, pausing to pile their load by the entrance while the dogs chased each other along beside them. Bri had made it to the first path's west turn, and he accepted the stone Erik held out with a smile.

"That's a fine one. It will anchor the left side." He passed his hand over the rest. "These feel farther in. Will you take them to the center, please, Berne?"

The boy eyed the pile with glum resignation. "You could have asked before I dropped them," he observed in mild reproach as he began to fill Erik's sling again.

"I wasn't sure of their position until they touched the ground."

"Uh-huh." Heading for the entrance, Berne paused to smile mischievously at his older brother who frowned back at him.

"Don't cut across the path."

"Who said I was going to?"

"You did. You practically shouted it."

Berne eyed the much shorter distance between the entrance and the center, then cast his brother another sly glance. "The labyrinth isn't even finished yet," he pointed out, knowing Erik's response before he voiced it.

"It doesn't matter. You don't cut across the paths. It's disrespectful."

"It's rocks and meadow grasses."

"It's the womb of the Goddess made physical. You pass in, are transformed, and pass out again in the way She prescribed, third path first, then second, first, fourth, sixth, and finally fifth. To do it any other way is contrary to Her desire and very, very dangerous, you know that."

"I should, you remind me every second day. But Bri cuts across the paths all the time, *you* know that."

The Master Builder turned an amused glance in their direction, waiting to see how Erik would respond to this logical bit of heretical teasing.

"It's his labyrinth. When you build, one you can cut across the paths, too."

"I would, but by then my feet will have worn off."

"It's good for you. Teaches you to control your talent instead of just letting it run wild wherever it fancies. Jake! Spike!"

The two dogs came bounding from the north woods, cutting straight across the low line of stones which marked off each of the labyrinth's paths. Berne turned a withering look on his older brother, who just shrugged.

"Dogs are special."

Glancing over to where the larger of the two animals had paused to rub his muzzle into the remains of a dead bird, Berne's face twisted in disgust. "Even Jake?"

"Especially Jake. Black dogs belong to the Huntsman who is beloved of the Goddess."

"Well, I'm beloved of the Goddess, too. The Oracle said I was born in Her regard."

"She said you were born in the *light* of Her regard. That's not the same thing."

Berne dismissed the difference with a simple flick of one hand. "Either way, She still loves me."

"Either way, don't cut across the paths, or She might give you a smack you won't soon forget, love or no love."

Berne just laughed at him. Hefting the sling over his shoulder, he whistled for the dogs.

"Don't forget to bow at the entrance."

"I won't."

"And, this close to completion, you should invoke Her presence and meditate on your task while you walk the paths," Bri added.

"I know. You told me this morning."

"And don't run!"

The two men watched as the boy sprinted for the entrance despite his load, took two steps inside, then shook his head and retreated to the entrance stone to bow, then carry on at a half-walk, half-trot. The power of the labyrinth rose up around him like fine dust.

Bri chuckled. "He has talent."

Setting the house snake down on the entrance stone, Erik nodded. Berne did have talent, talent to feel the birds in the trees and the animals in the thickets—Pieter was right, he'd make a powerful Chosen—but Berne could also see the shape of an object in wood or clay, sense a storm coming from miles out to sea, and know if an arrow would hit its mark or miss. And the labyrinth wrapped about him like a cloak whenever he walked the paths. Erik had been serious when he told him he might build his own someday. Berne had the talent to turn his hand to whatever he chose, regardless of what the elders wanted.

If he survives the coming attack, that is, Erik's mind amended caustically. If any of us do.

Something—a chill along the back of his neck like a whisper of approaching danger—made him glance up as an errant cloud touched the west side of the sun. The sky began to darken. The wind picked up, tossed a few leaves over the labyrinth, and momentarily obscured the sight of his brother.

"Berne?"

He stood. The boy was pelting along the third path, both dogs in full pursuit.

"Don't run!"

As Berne turned sharply toward the first path, Jake suddenly swerved, leaping over the fourth path and knocking against his legs. The boy went flying over the rocks, to land sprawled in the entrance just as the sun passed behind the cloud.

"Berne!"

Erik made the labyrinth in half a heartbeat as his brother picked himself up, both knees scored and bloody.

"Are you all right?"

"I'm fine. Jake, go away!" The boy shoved the dog back as Erik knelt beside him.

"Don't scold him."

"He knocked me down."

"You were running." Erik tried a smile despite the fear suddenly wrapped around his heart. "Maybe he thought you were a deer."

"Very funny."

"Well, next time . . ."

"I know, I know, don't run. I start out walking, mostly. It's just hard. The labyrinth makes me all . . . I don't know, twitchy."

"All the more reason to move slowly, then."

"I know."

"Is he all right?"

Both brothers looked up. They hadn't hear Bri approach, but

then they never did. The Master Builder crouched down to lay one finger on Berne's bloody knee.

"You should see Collyn."

Berne ducked his head in embarrassment.

"It's just a scrape. I don't need a Healer."

Bri turned the boy's hands up to reveal the bloodstained dirt and gravel embedded in the palms. "See the Healer anyway. Blood left to flow unheeded is an open doorway to the Gods, and even incomplete the labyrinth calls to them."

Something in Bri's tone made Erik glance over at him. "Take the dogs with you, Berne."

"Yeah, all right."

"And bring the Oracle back when you're done," Bri added. "It's time to begin the labyrinth's consecration."

Berne nodded and limped off, the two dogs in tow. When he was out of earshot, Erik turned to the other man with a questioning frown.

"I thought we were at least a week away from consecration?"

"We were." Bri crouched, pointing at the smear of blood across the right entrance anchor stone. "It's formed the shape of a ship, Erik. You know what the Oracle will say."

"That the Gotri are coming by sea and from the west. We already know this. They always come from the west."

"Right, within the month, but I'd say looking at this, within the week is more likely."

"You said we'd be finished in time."

Watching Berne's blood slowly dry in the rising breeze, Bri shook his head. "I was wrong."

They caught up with the boy quickly and, after leaving him at the Healer's, went in search of the Oracle themselves. They found her crouched on the escarpment, staring out to sea. The waves were dark and wild, crashing against the cliffs and scattering spray across her face and hair. She ignored it, turning eyes as gray and fathomless as the water below, toward them as they came up.

"They'll come on a clear night," she said, her voice deep and throaty.

Erik glanced up at the now cloudless sky, the power in her voice causing the hairs on the back of his neck to rise.

"And on a cold one."

The wind had already begun to grow chill, now it whistled past the cliffs with a new pitch and urgency as if the words themselves had called it into being.

"On the full moon."

Bri glanced toward the south where the moon was already rising in the afternoon sky.

"It's the full moon tonight, Oracle."

"Then it will be tonight."

"Tonight?" Erik stared at the waves in disbelief. "They'll never make it."

She stood. "Their Gods drive the storm before them. It will reach the coast first; they'll come after. They'll come in force . . ." Her eyes widened and, as she whirled about to stare into the trees, her faced grew suddenly pale.

The men turned with her. "What . . . ?"

She threw up one hand to forestall the question, then her eyes cleared.

"It's a feint. They've come overland as well."

"*What?*"

"They're already here."

"Where?"

"At the village."

Erik and Bri locked stares.

"Berne!"

Together, they ran for the path.

By the time they cleared the trees, the storm and the attack were already well underway. Fire had broken out inside the walls, and, as they crested the hill east of the village, they could see flames begin to lick greedily at the grain stores. At the gate, Pieter was leading the defense, but as they watched, he fell, taken by an arrow in the throat.

With an incoherent shout, Erik flung himself down the hill.

Bri caught up with him at the bottom.

"You can't go down there!" he shouted above the wildly blowing wind. "You've no weapons. You'll be killed!"

"Berne's down there!"

Half a dozen arrows zipped past them as their movement attracted notice from the enemy, and Bri jerked him down into a crouch. "Seek him through your blood-link!"

His eyes rolling wildly in his head, Erik forced himself to take a deep breath, then reached out. Contact with Berne had him nearly faint with relief.

"He's safe," he gasped. "He's heading this way."

"Smart boy. Come on." Together, they sprinted back up the hill and, supporting the Oracle between them, made for the other side.

The sun had dropped below the trees when they finally found Berne. The storm tearing at his clothes and hair, Erik caught his brother up in a desperate embrace.

"You're safe!" he shouted.

The boy nodded. "After I left Collyn's, I felt something dangerous on the wind. I tracked it south and saw them coming through the forest pass from Tarluth! They must have attacked it first. There are hundreds more than last time, Erik! What are we going to do? The whole village will be overrun!"

"I don't know!"

"Invoke the Goddess."

They both turned to stare at the Oracle. She hadn't raised her voice, but her words echoed through the forest.

Ducking a wildly swinging pine bough, Bri shook his head. "We can't, the labyrinth's not finished yet!"

"We can."

Erik tasted saltwater and blood on his lips as a scattering of small pebbles scored against his face.

"How?"

She caught him in a powerful stare, her eyes glowing with green fire. "Walk the paths and call on Her to send the Hutsman to save the village."

His own eyes went dark. "Are you addled?" he grated, using his own power to cut through the howling wind. "The Huntsman's feral. He's as likely to kill us all as save us. Only His Captain has a hope of controlling Him in full manifestation."

"Then be His Captain again."

"I'm crippled. He won't use me."

"Then let Him use me."

Erik whirled about to stare into his brother's strained, young face. He was about to forbid it outright, but Bri began nodding emphatically.

"He's beloved of the Goddess, Erik, he said so himself! He can do this!"

"No."

The wind tore a sapling from the ground and sent it spinning toward them. Berne caught Erik around the chest, flinging them both to the ground just as it whipped by over their heads.

"I don't like this any more than you do," he shouted, "but one of us has to do something before we're all killed! I can See it!"

"If a Blackthorn does not invoke the Goddess this night," the Oracle intoned, "Ruthgreen will fall."

Erik continued to stare searchingly at his younger brother, seeing their mother's eyes in their father's face, then slumped. "All right."

The storm fought them every step of the way, but once they made it through the trees, the meadow was hushed as if the enemy had yet to penetrate the sanctity of Bri's working. They headed for the center at a run and, as the labyrinth came into view, Berne caught Erik by the arm and pointed. All around, the ground writhed as hundreds of snakes, both domestic and wild, flowed from the forest to take up position by each of the directional stones. Erik couldn't see his own snake, but he knew it was somewhere among them. A dozen dogs also stood guard before the entrance; as they ran up, Jake and Spike came out to meet them, their eyes glowing red in the moonlight. The Oracle climbed to the top of the entrance stone, and Bri caught up Berne's bow, fitting an arrow to the string before jerking his head at them.

"Go."

The two brothers ran for the entrance. The center stood out clearly, and Berne licked his lips, the urge to run straight across obvious on his face. Erik caught him by the shoulders.

"Now remember," he said vehemently, "even though it may not seem like it, the paths of the labyrinth are laid out in a non-linear pattern for a reason, with each path representing a separate aspect of ritual and each one building on the last. You'll feel the power grow, both yours and the labyrinth's, and they'll start to merge. That's good, that's what you want to happen. You can control it just like you can control the Huntsman. It's in your blood and well within your abilities if you stay calm and focused, understand?"

Berne nodded, but Erik could sense his heart beating wildly.

"Believe that you're Captain and you will be. That's half the secret."

"And the other half?"

Erik made himself smile. "Well, He has to believe it, too. But He will," he added as Berne opened his mouth to protest. "You're beloved of the Goddess, remember. Born in the light of Her regard."

"I am."

"Then trust in Her protection and walk."

Armed figures suddenly broke from trees.

"Go. We'll hold them. Jake, Spike!" As Berne bowed to the entrance stone, and took his first two steps inside, Erik threw his arm out toward the enemy. "Sic 'em!"

The dogs leaped forward.

Time seemed to slow. As Erik led the dogs' attack, he could sense Berne making the first turn onto the third path with stiff, deliberate steps. As the wind began to rise, more figures poured into the meadow. The dogs drove them back, but others followed only to be met by a barrage of green fire from the Oracle's outstretched hands. Those that fell were quickly overrun by snakes. They did not rise again. Throughout, Berne kept his focus locked on his feet. Erik sent as much of his own power to aid him as he could spare and felt his brother's resolve grow stronger. As he rounded the third path and began the ritual with thought, calling on the Goddess to aid him as the Captain of Her Beloved, the power of the labyrinth began to rise around him.

The wind whipped about the meadow, bringing the smell of burning homes and burning flesh. Berne stumbled, but righted himself and made the turn onto the second path, sending out his feelings as he did so, forming his fear and his need into a great ball of power, shooting it through the barriers between this world and the next.

The labyrinth began to glow.

More Gotri appeared at the edge of the meadow, but now they were met by the survivors of Ruthgreen who flung themselves at the enemy with a rage born of desperation as Berne reached the end of the second path. As he turned onto the first and outermost path, Erik could see his eyes widen with both fear and the growing power that almost obscured him altogether. He reached out, locking their minds and talents together around the blood-link and, with the extra power, Berne brought the physical into his invocation, weaving his wildly beating heart and shallow breathing into the call as he took step after deliberate step. This was the longest path and the hardest on which to maintain focus. He seemed to take forever, and Erik's own legs ached with tension as he resisted the urge to press him into moving faster.

A thread of amusement trickled through the link as Berne recognized the thought before he brought his attention back to the ritual. He reached the turn for the fourth path, and Erik let out a great breath of relief. But Berne made the turn as if he were forcing his feet through heavy clay, and suddenly Erik realized that someone else was hampering his efforts. He turned and saw a man with wildly flowing hair and blazing gray eyes leap onto the west cornerstone, scattering the guardian snakes as he went.

The Oracle spotted him at the same time. Without a word, she launched a bolt of green fire at him. He met it with a wall of burning fog that quickly settled over everything it touched, but it stopped just short of the labyrinth and could go no farther as Bri Jensen brought his own considerable power into the fray to protect his working. The meadow grasses began to smolder, then the ground around the enemy burst apart as a dozen serpents flung themselves into the air. He fell, his muffled screams cut short almost immediately.

Freed from the enemy's attack, Berne headed a bit too quickly up the fourth path, then made himself slow, weaving his faith and his own personal oaths into the ritual. A dozen steps, a dozen more. Erik found himself counting each one and forced his mind to still, setting Jake and Spike on yet another enemy. One dog took the man low, the other high, snapping at his throat as the first tore at his hamstring. As he went down screaming into a nest of spitting, striking snakes, Erik returned his attention to Berne. His brother was already on the seventh path, his unshakable trust in Her love shimmering around him like a green mist. Resisting the urge to glance hopefully at the center, he turned his back on it and made the turn onto the sixth path, the paradox of the labyrinth sending him both one step farther from and closer to his goal.

The wind began to tear leaves and limbs from the trees as the storm entered the meadow in full fury. Trees were uprooted and the piles of rocks so diligently gathered by the villagers of Ruthgreen became deadly missiles that struck friend and foe alike. Most of the smaller snakes fled underground, their tiny powers unable to withstand the wrath of a God-induced wind, but the larger ones stayed to fight beside their human and canine counterparts and slowly the tide of battle began to turn their way.

Now on the sixth path, Berne formed the invocation into one clear image of the Huntsman trampling his enemies underfoot. Beneath his own feet the ground began to shift. The power of the Goddess rose in the center of the labyrinth and with it something else, something wild and dangerously chaotic. The sharp scent of musk filled the air and in the meadow, Asti and Gotri alike found new reserves of strength and aggression. A heartbeat more and Berne made the turn onto the fifth path, once again one path farther from his goal yet closer since the fifth path would eventually lead to the center. By now the power of the Goddess was so strong that only the blood-link kept Erik in contact with his brother at all. He could feel Her press against the barriers between the worlds as Berne made the final turn and set one foot inside the center. Slowly, very slowly, the figure of a huge man in hunting greens began to overlay his features as the Goddess pushed the Huntsman into the world.

The arrow came from the forest. It caught Berne in the chest, and the Huntsman leaped free as he crumpled to the ground.

Erik screamed his brother's name. He leaped for the labyrinth just as another arrow streaked out to catch him behind the left knee. It felled him like a tree inside the entrance and, as his hand scraped across the anchor stone smeared with his brother's blood, the force of it sent his mind slamming into Berne's. Unbound, the Huntsman towered above him, growing larger and larger with every second. A rain of arrows scattered harmlessly across His legs and He reached into the trees to scoop up the archers and dash their heads against the ground. Then with a wild laugh, He turned toward the forest but came up short as a man, blood streaming from his leg, rose up to bar his way.

Erik Blackthorn had followed the Huntsman since childhood. The Oracle had passed a stage horn over his cradle when he'd first leaned to focus his gaze, predicting that he would be a talented Chosen, and he'd trained and fought and risen to be the most powerful Captain in a hundred years, but when the Gotri had attacked the village, ambushing the Chosen, and leaving him bleeding out his life on the ground, the Huntsman had turned his feral gaze away from his broken Captain and melted back into the forest. Erik would not allow Him to do the same to Berne. Screaming out the ritual words, he flung his crippled hands wide and caught the Huntsman in a vast green net of power.

"Jake! Spike!"

The dogs responded immediately to his ragged call, leaping to his side. Gripping them both by the scruff of the neck with a strength he hadn't possessed for two years, he turned toward the labyrinth. He began to run, green God-fire outlining the arrow still embedded in his knee, the dogs keeping pace behind him. As he reached the crossed walls which separated the entrance from the center, he leaped.

Power coursed through his body, outlining every scar and every injury, old and new, as the Huntsman struggled to free Himself from his damaged Captain. Erik landed hard, losing his grip on the dogs but not on his prize. Snatching his brother up in his arms, he screamed out his demand and slammed the Huntsman into the boy's abilities with one great bolt of fury. The Goddess caught him as he fell, and then the Huntsman burst into full manifestation, held tightly under the control of Berne Blackthorn. The blood-link exploded.

In the meadow, the force of the Huntsman's passage knocked Bri off his feet. He saw the Oracle flung from the entrance stone and dragged himself to her side as Berne's and the Huntsman's towering figure strode from the center of the labyrinth, chest burning hotly around what should have been a killing wound. The Huntsman reached down and caught up four of the Gotri invaders at once, squeezing their bodies into a bloody pulp. Three more were crushed as He brought one great foot down on top of them and two more died instantly as He kicked them from His path.

Bri was nearly killed by the Huntsman's next step, but managed to throw himself and the Oracle behind the west directional stone just in time. The Huntsman swept the meadow clear of enemies, then gave a great whistle. With every surviving dog scrambling along behind, He headed for the village. Bri stuffed his jacket under the Oracle's head, then followed as quickly as he dared.

By the time he reached what was left of the walls, the Gotri force was either dead or had fled into the forest. The Chosen had rallied to pursue them, and the screams and war cries quickly faded into the distance. Bri continued down the Huntsman's destructive path all the way to the inlet. He made the escarpment just in time to see Him smash His huge fist into the side of the invader's flagship. The rest of the fleet followed the first to the bottom of the sea, then, as the great figure threw back His head to laugh, the water grew calm. The attack was over.

The Huntsman beat the waves for a long time before turning to the escarpment. He stared up at the Master Builder with Berne's wide, dark eyes, then just as quickly as He'd come, He vanished. Berne slowly crumpled to the rocky beach.

Somehow, Bri made it down the escarpment in one piece. He dragged the boy free of the surf, then collapsed beside him, one arm wrapped about the pulsing wound in his chest. It was the last thing he remembered for a long time.

He awoke to Spike licking his face. Shoving the dog's head aside, he sat up carefully and looked around. Bodies lay scattered across the rocks. Berne lay as he'd left him, and Bri knew a moment of panic before he saw the boy's chest rise and fall. The injury that had nearly ended his life was now a faint, pink scar formed into the shape of a ship and, breathing out a quick prayer of thanks, he took him up in his arms and headed back toward the village.

In the dawn light there wasn't much left of it. People huddled together looking dazed and lost, most either bloody or bruised. The Headwoman turned a blank gaze on him as he approached, indicating the burned-out buildings with a weary gesture.

"The grain stores are all gone," she said woodenly.

"The inland villages will send more," he promised. "We can call them now that the labyrinth's been fully consecrated."

"Yes."

Bri moved on, still carrying Berne. Many of the survivors reached out to touch the boy on the arm or hand, murmuring

praise and thanks as they passed. Bri followed the path of uprooted trees and ragged ground and finally came to his working
still set firmly in the nearly destroyed meadow. The Oracle was
seated in the center, a bloody rag pressed against the side of her
face, Erik's body cradled in one arm. Crossing the paths, Bri laid
Berne down beside them.

"Is he . . . ?"

"Yes. The Goddess took him up as the Huntsman left the labyrinth."

"And Berne?"

She peered down at him. "He'll awake eventually." She
sighed. "Well, the blood quickened, and just in time, too. I was
half afraid it wouldn't."

Bri passed one weary hand over his chin, scratching at a glob
of dried blood imbedded in the stubble.

"Was it worth it?"

She shrugged. "Erik gave up his life and power so that Berne
might save the village. The village is saved—what's left of it—so
I'd say yes. Still, it was quite a price," she amended. "If you ask
me, we'd be better off with a less violent Patron, but nobody
does."

"What do we do now?"

"Rebuild, of course, what else can we do? Care for our
wounded and grieve for our dead and rebuild."

"And if the Gotri return?"

She turned a toothy smile in his direction. "I think they'll find
a new Captain quite strong enough to send them packing, don't
you?"

"Yes, I suppose they will."

"And a Master Builder able to turn his hand to both physical
and metaphysical walls."

"Are you asking me to stay?"

She shook her head. "No. I'm telling you to. Berne will need
you, so will Ruthgreen."

"You've Seen that?"

With a snort, she got stiffly to her feet. "Don't ask idiotic questions. Now, help me get the boy to Collyn. This lying about on the cold ground can't be good for him."

"What about Erik?"

"Spike and Jake will wait with him until he can be prepared for burial." She rose with a groan, and together, Ruthgreen's Oracle and Master Builder carried Berne from the labyrinth, leaving two hunting dogs and a small greenish-brown house snake to stand guard over the body of the Huntsman's greatest Captain in a hundred years lying in the center of his Goddess' womb.

Kristen Britain

An editor often has an author who she considers to be her "new baby." At this moment in time, my new baby is Kristen Britain. Kristen's first novel, *Green Rider,* published in hardcover at the end of 1998, was an incredible find; a vivid fantasy adventure with a stubborn, feisty heroine, and dark undercurrents of danger both real and magical. *Green Rider* met with resounding success. Kristen's writing has a harder edge of reality than that of many writers, and that's not surprising, because Kristen is a genuine outdoors person. As a national park ranger, Kristen spends her life protecting wild animals and the environment from the dangers of marauding tourists. Her home address includes the line: "second log cabin on the left." There aren't too many addresses like that left in America today.

Personally, I owe Kristen an enormous debt of gratitude. In the summer of 2001, Kristen came to New York to meet me for the first time. She stayed at my loft in lower Manhattan, and the day before she left we went up to the top of the World Trade Center. It was a beautiful clear day, and because there was no wind, visitors were allowed onto the roof of the tower. We stood outside in the sun, one hundred and ten floors above the street, and New York harbor lay before us like an illustration in an art book. For twenty-six years I had lived seventeen blocks from the Trades, but I had never been up to the top. Six weeks later the buildings were destroyed. Thanks to Kristen, I saw something that I never would have seen, and that no one will ever be able to see again.

—BW

LINKED, ON THE LAKE OF SOULS

Kristen Britain

FAR in the northern reaches of Anglas Herad, an eagle perched high in a towering pine watched as a boat drifted on the lake below. He had seen plenty of boats before on other lakes where the humans engaged in fishing, an activity to which he could relate.

Never before, however, had he seen a boat on *this* lake, a lake even waterfowl had the wits to shun. The eagle cocked his head and blinked his golden eyes, his curiosity piqued.

The pair, he decided, were unlike the fishers he was accustomed to seeing. They dropped no netting over the side of the boat, and carried no bait. Nor did they dip paddles into the lake to propel themselves along, for they had none.

Curiouser, and curiouser, the eagle thought.

The gleam of metal caught his eye and he dropped down a few branches to get a better look. One of the females was clad in a shirt of metal, but that was not all. They sat in the bottom of the boat, bound back-to-back by heavy chains, while individual sets of manacles clasped their ankles and wrists.

If all of this was not odd enough, one of the boat's occupants appeared intent on capsizing it, which would surely bring about undesired results for both.

The eagle ruffled his feathers and preened. He despaired of humankind ever using the intelligence it was gifted with at birth. The antics of the two in the boat only seemed to confirm his low opinion of the species.

Then one of the humans cried out. The eagle paused in his preening and refocused his eyes on the boat. The cry had been a warning tinged with panic.

*"**M**yrene!"*

The boat lurched as the warrior shifted to peer over its side. Of course, any move Myrene made, Tiphane was forced to make as well.

"What? I just want to see how deep the water is."

"Trust me," Tiphane said, "it is quite deep. Deep and icy cold."

Myrene grunted, unconvinced.

Had they not been chained together back-to-back in the bottom of the boat, Tiphane would have seen Myrene's scowl. But Tiphane did not need to see it to know it was there, for the two had been working together for nearly three years now and had grown to know one another well. Too well, it sometimes seemed.

Myrene leaned even farther over the boat's edge, hauling her chain-bound partner with her. The boat listed at an alarming angle.

"You'll capsize us!" Tiphane cried.

"I just want to find out if I can see the bottom."

"You'll see it when we overturn and that lovely mail shirt you're so fond of, along with these chains, drag us under."

Their boat, a tiny, unstable coracle, floated on silken, calm water that reflected the bright autumnal colors cloaking the rounded mountains that ringed the lake. The lake was vast, and as Tiphane said, icy cold, for it had once been a part of the great ice sheet that still lingered in the wastes beyond the mountains. And there was more waiting in the lake's depths than Myrene could ever imagine.

"I don't intend to sink us," Myrene said. "If we aren't deep, maybe we can—"

When the coracle heeled enough for icy water to leak over its rim, Tiphane said, "Believe me, you don't want to see what's in the lake. There are—"

Myrene uttered a sudden, strangled cry and jerked away from the edge with such force that the flat bottom of the coracle slapped the surface of the lake. She slumped against Tiphane, her breathing ragged.

Tiphane was rather rattled herself from being wrenched around by her larger and stronger companion, and by a nightmarish vision that had flashed through her mind of the coracle capsizing and the two of them sinking inexorably downward into the lake's depths where phantom arms were outstretched to receive them. . . . Perspiration glided down her temple.

"Damnation, Tiph," Myrene whispered, when finally she caught hold of herself. "Why didn't you tell me?"

Tiphane could feel Myrene trembling against her back. "I was about to tell you. I was going to tell you there is a reason it's called Lake of Souls."

The lake was crystal clear, though in the very middle, where it was said to be hundreds of feet deep, the sun penetrated only so far before it gave way to the dark. Even there, however, *they* could be seen; pale hair swirling around bloodless, cadaverous faces; dark eyes staring up, mouths gaping, arms of white flesh always reaching, reaching as if to haul the unwary into the depths with them. There were thousands of them.

"What are they?" Myrene asked.

"No one knows exactly," Tiphane said. "Perhaps they lived here before the ice. Perhaps they are lost souls seeking the company of the living. I do not know."

Myrene, not one to spook easily, shivered. She had seen more than her share of carnage on battlefields, Tiphane knew, but what this deceptively beautiful lake concealed beneath its sun dappled surface was another thing entirely.

A silence fell between them as the coracle, really nothing more than an oversized basket of woven willow boughs with a hide stretched over it, bobbed down the middle of the lake, tracking southward with the current.

"Are you sure you can't get the manacles off?" Myrene asked.

"I'm no lockpick," Tiphane said. "I'm a weaver of light and wind and rain. Besides, you heard what Sedir said, and you've the runny nose to prove it."

"You've no idea how I long to wipe it." Myrene rattled her chains in frustration.

Their captor, the wizard Veidan Sedir of the Drakdorn Order, cursed be his name, had gone to great extent to ensure their torment. The coracle was held together not with the ancient boat building craft of fishermen who netted salmon on the rivers, but with magic. The moment Tiphane attempted to touch her own gifts, even for the slightest of breezes to skim them to shore, the coracle would unravel and they would sink into the waiting arms of the souls beneath the water. A cold finger of fear slithered down her spine.

They knew Sedir had not lied about the nature of the magic that held the coracle together, for Myrene reacted to the casting of magical spells with sneezing fits. Her nose had started running the moment they were forced into the little boat.

It was a rather odd affliction Myrene suffered from, considering her constant companion, Tiphane, was a priestess who used magic as a matter of course. But it was also useful in its own way, warning them when magic other than Tiphane's was afoot. Or, it could be a liability, as in this instance, for Myrene's sneeze had given them away to Sedir as they spied upon him in his hideout.

"We're drifting to the south end," Myrene said. "I wonder what awaits us there."

"A waterfall."

"A . . ." Myrene was clearly too stunned to go on.

"It's the outlet of the lake. It's not a particularly big waterfall."

Myrene groaned. "That's just fine and good—a *small* water-fall."

Myrene was not known for her subtlety, and Tiphane knew her comrade blamed her for their current predicament. It was Tiphane who had insisted they follow the trail of deaths made by Veidan Sedir, leading to his hideout in the mountains.

Sedir and his adherents practiced magic that went against the laws of nature and Givean Herself. He was no favorite of Myrene's either, but she had preferred the option of lying low in the valley until winter forced Sedir from the mountains. It was safer, she argued, than tracking him into his own territory.

And here we are, Tiphane thought, *because I couldn't wait.* She supposed Myrene had the right of it, but she just couldn't have lived with herself if she'd allowed Sedir to run amok among the innocents who sheltered in tiny villages in the shadow of the mountains.

"We can't let Sedir wander the countryside doing blood magic at his leisure," Tiphane murmured more to herself than to her partner. "It goes against all our precepts."

"*Your* precepts. You're the Givean priestess."

"And you are my sworn Shield. Therefore you must uphold the same principles as I."

Myrene grumbled something unintelligible and sneezed, sending rings rippling outward from their coracle. Had they not been bound in chains, and had they not been floating on the Lake of Souls, it might have been an enjoyable excursion, for the scenery was breathtaking and the air, with the bite of oncoming winter in it, was exhilarating. An eagle soared through the clear sky above and screeched. Tiphane ached for its freedom.

Myrene abruptly straightened, rocking the boat.

"Can't you sit still?" Tiphane asked. Myrene tended to be all action and little thought, and it grated on more than her nerves, especially considering they were currently attached.

"I thought I saw something moving along the shore."

Tiphane craned her neck and scanned the shoreline. It was jumbled with talus from some long ago rockslide and thick with low-growing shrubbery. Some spindly evergreens grew up between the rocks.

"I don't see anything."

"By the big boulder."

Tiphane rolled her eyes. There were hundreds of huge rocks, some the size of a shepherd's cot. "*Which* big boulder?"

"The one . . . The one . . . Damnation. I've lost it now."

Tiphane sighed in irritation, and as they drifted, she thought about how many tight spots she and Myrene had gotten themselves into over the years, ever since her mentor Radmiran had brought them together. They'd met the night she had taken the Oath of Givean, which had occurred after ten years of study and prayer. She had relinquished her family, friends, and all worldly goods to serve Givean.

The world was a dangerous place, and every priestess who chose the path of wanderer was paired with a protector. When Tiphane was in her last year of study, Myrene, a warrior who had been sold by her family to a mercenary company at a tender age, had been found among the dead after a terrible battle. Broken, bloody, and unconscious, she had been mistaken for a corpse until one of the gravediggers noticed her shallow breathing. She was brought to the Order for healing, a healing that almost failed because of her odd response to the use of magic. The priestesses had to depend mostly on conventional methods to save her.

While Myrene healed, she learned much about the good works of Givean. That, coupled with her brush with death, moved something deep within her mercenary spirit, and she changed her course in life to help others as she herself had been helped. By swearing to protect Tiphane, she swore herself to Givean.

It was understandable their tempers flared from time to time. Myrene, a woman of action, was helpless in her fetters. There was no constructive way to direct her rage, no way to lift a sword and cut down the bastard who had put them in this position; the same bastard who left the broken and shriveled bodies of people—men, women, children; the young and old alike—in his wake to foster his own powers and pay homage to Drakdorn, the god of unraveling and chaos.

Tiphane was likewise fettered, unable to touch her own magic for fear of drowning them. Of course, sooner or later, the water would take them, either in the clear, cold depths of the lake, or in the churning, whirling water pounding at the base of the waterfall.

"There it is again," Myrene said, chains clinking as she leaned forward. Water sloshed about the coracle at her sudden movement.

Tiphane scanned the distant shore, and this time she, too, saw something—someone—moving about the gigantic boulders.

"No doubt it's Sedir coming to watch us die," she muttered. "It is his kind of entertainment, us becoming one of his sacrifices."

"I would like to sacrifice *him*," Myrene said.

"You do have truly violent urges, don't you?"

"Yes," Myrene said, her voice filled with conviction.

Tiphane kept her eyes to the shore, watching for more movement. "That is not a very Givean attitude. Perhaps you should meditate on it, for Givean is the force of life, not death." Which was what made Sedir's depredations all the more loathsome to her and her Order.

Myrene snorted. "Since when has meditation saved you from bandits wielding clubs and swords on the road, hmm? I don't think meditation is going to unlock these manacles either." She rattled the chains for emphasis.

"It has occurred to me that violent urges are not helping—"

"Look," Myrene said, cutting her off. "There are three of them."

Tiphane saw them then, a flash of bright white, which could only be Sedir's robes, followed by two darker figures, one of which seemed to be struggling.

"One of the others must be Cha'korth," Myrene said. Cha'-korth was her own counterpart—Sedir's Shield.

"How much would you wager the third is another sacrifice?" Tiphane said. "It would be a good day for Sedir, you know, tormenting us by holding the sacrifice in front of us, before we die ourselves. He wants us to feel as helpless as possible."

As if to affirm their suspicions, Veidan Sedir called to them, his voice carrying easily across the water.

"Greetings, ladies! Such a lovely afternoon for boating, is it not? I thought, perhaps, I might offer you a diversion from your own forthcoming deaths."

There was scuffling along the shore and the flash of a blade, and a scream that resounded off the mountains. When it faded, Sedir continued, "A first offering of blood to give Drakdorn a taste of what is to follow."

Myrene snarled.

"The victim looks small to me," Tiphane said, narrowing her eyes against the glare of the sun on the water. "A young boy." The boy was putting up quite a fight despite whatever injury Cha'korth had inflicted upon him. "I can't simply sit here while they commit blood magic right in front of me, and we drift to our deaths."

"Have you a plan?"

"No," Tiphane admitted. "You?"

"Maybe, and maybe not." Myrene fell into a long spell of silence before she spoke again. "We are drifting in a current which is taking us to the waterfall, correct?"

"Correct."

"What if we got out of the current, or at least tried to get out of the direct path of the waterfall?"

Tiphane watched as Sedir, his Shield, and his victim picked their way toward the lake's outlet. Preventing their own dive over its edge would solve one problem.

"What do you propose we do?" Tiphane asked.

"If we seesaw the coracle—"

"We'll swamp it."

"Not if we're careful."

"All right," Tiphane said, "and what happens if we make it to shore?"

"You're the one with the magic."

"Hmm. I was afraid you'd say that."

She sighed, noting that their current moved more swiftly now. Sedir paused by the lip of the waterfall, looking over the area as if to decide which rock would best serve as a sacrificial altar. Myrene's idea, she decided, was better than doing nothing and helplessly awaiting their fate.

"Let's try it," she said.

Myrene and Tiphane started rocking back and forth, slowly building up momentum. Tiphane sweated with the effort, and Myrene's mail shirt abraded her back. They banged heads more than once, but they kept at it. They succeeded in splashing a lot of water about, and very nearly did swamp the boat. They gave up after that, realizing their course remained unchanged.

Tiphane grimaced as cold water soaked into the seat of her trousers.

Sedir's laughter bounced off the mountains. "Good try, ladies."

It appeared he had found his altar—a big, flat rock. Cha'korth was securing the victim to it, and Sedir was unrolling the cloth in which he stored his ritual knives. He glanced up at them, and now Tiphane could clearly see his sharp features as they drew closer.

"My robes shall be dyed in blood before I'm done," he yelled to them. Then he set about laying out his knives. Different knives for different parts of the body.

The bile roiled in Tiphane's throat. She growled in memory of the lives of the innocents Cha'korth and Sedir had cut short, and at the cruel wound the Shield had given Myrene that almost took her life a year ago.

"We need to try something else," Myrene said.

Tiphane envied Myrene her seemingly boundless determination. Maybe it was all those years she served in the mercenary company, where there was no choice but to fight or die. Tiphane, in contrast, knew they were doomed, doomed to ride over the edge of the waterfall only to be dashed on the rocks below.

Then the boat jolted and lurched without warning, and Tiphane jammed into Myrene's back with a cry, her end of the coracle rising skyward.

"What . . . ?" A hundred impolite words rushed through her mind, but she couldn't sputter a one for the fear that enveloped her.

"I'm using my feet," Myrene explained matter-of-factly. "Don't move or we'll both end up in the water." There was a loud splash, and Tiphane pictured Myrene's feet, ankle manacles and all, plunging into the lake. She whimpered, feeling certain the boat would flip over.

There was a lot of splashing as Myrene kicked, her efforts to move the boat far more effective than their previous attempt.

"Ick!" Myrene cried. "My feet! Help me get in—they're grabbing my feet!"

Tiphane didn't need to ask *who* was doing the grabbing. She knew. They scooched and wriggled until Myrene's feet were safely in the boat.

"You did it," Tiphane said, both amazed and grateful they weren't on the lake's bottom.

Thanks to Myrene's efforts, the little coracle slipped away from the main current and spun into the eddies along its edge. By now they could hear the roar of the waterfall, but the lake had grown considerably shallower. Just yards away, grasses and boulders poked up through the lake's glassy surface.

A glimpse toward shore revealed Sedir blessing his knives one by one, now focused on his ritual. Cha'korth stood over the victim with his arms folded, his ugly, scarred face even more contorted with a grin as he watched them.

The coracle bumped into a rock, impeding further progress.

"What now?" Tiphane asked. "Water's still over our heads."

"Do some magic."

"Do— Are you mad? The boat will—"

The wizard was immersed in inscribing fire runes into the air, and a glassy cloak of magic shimmered about him. He closed his eyes, falling into a deep magic weaver's trance.

"I can't," Tiphane said. "He's wrapped in a cloak and it will deflect anything I do."

"Then inflict something on Cha'korth, and hurry."

Cha'korth's amusement at their plight had changed to suspicion, and now he drew his sword.

"Hurry," Myrene said, "do something to him. Hurt him if you can."

"I can't use Givean magic to hurt someone," Tiphane said. Doing so, even to Cha'korth, would pervert all she believed in.

"Well, do something—anything." Myrene's voice was pitched a note higher with urgency.

Cha'korth stalked to the water's edge. He glared menacingly at them.

Tiphane searched her scattered thoughts for an idea. A rainstorm would just drench everyone, and it would take too much energy besides. She could focus the sun on him, but he'd simply walk away with an impressive tan. No, it had to be something else, and she thought of the more spiritual side of her Order, and the words she and Myrene had exchanged about meditation.

She closed her eyes and blocked out the sound of Sedir chanting his blasphemous incantations to Drakdorn. She did not think about the glinting blade he held aloft as he stood enraptured by the dark ecstasy of his magic. Tiphane drifted deeper into her trance, feeling her own sense of joy as she sought her gift.

She delved into the deepest part of herself, to the wellspring of her spirit. It was a secluded place—deep and mysterious and tranquil. She felt no shackles about her, nor did she even feel Myrene against her back, at least not in a physical sense. Instead she found her partner's energy and life within her, like a bright burning flame. This was the link that had been forged between them when they were brought together before Givean, the night she had taken her oath.

Myrene is a part of me, she thought, *as I am a part of her.*

From this peaceful place, she wove together positive strands of fire, life, energy, balance, and love until they formed a net, which she could see only in her mind's eye, shimmering and glowing. She mentally "tossed" it at Cha'korth.

Tiphane opened her eyes. It had all taken mere seconds. Cha'-korth stood stock-still, his mouth gaping, his eyes wide. His sword slipped from his hand and clattered to the ground. A burnished golden glow shone about him, and one could almost hear the harmonious flourish of harp strings. . . .

And even as the glow surrounded him, Myrene sneezed lustily. "Damnation, Tiph, you cast a spell of ecstasy on him?"

Tiphane had no time to reply for the coracle disintegrated beneath them and they plunged into the freezing lake. She was unprepared and inhaled lungfuls of water. She fought to break the water's surface, but they kept sinking. Myrene struggled, too, twisting, writhing, jerking, sinking.

The water-pale faces of the lake's souls turned up to them. As they sank into a tangle of soft, pale limbs, dead fingers groped at them. A scream welled up within Tiphane that emerged as a cloud of bubbles. She was drowning, suffocating, and the souls of the lake would have them. She kicked their hands away.

Their feet met the lake bottom and they came face-to-face with the horrors. Tiphane closed her eyes and turned her face away. She felt Myrene gather herself, then launch them upward. They broke the surface sputtering and coughing, only to sink again.

When they touched bottom this time, Myrene lunged upward at an angle toward the shallows. When Tiphane realized what Myrene intended, she added her ebbing strength to her comrade's. Sink, push off, and sink again, all the while fighting the grasp of the lake's souls. Soon they no longer submerged after each lunge, and stood in water only up to their waists.

Tiphane, miserable and weak, coughed up what seemed to her to be half the lake.

"Next time you tell me to trust you," she croaked, wheezing and shivering, "remind me not to." A pale hand grabbed at her ankle. She stomped on it, almost retching again at how squishy it felt beneath her foot.

Myrene did not hear her comment. "Look," she said, "I think Sedir is starting to come out of his trance."

Tiphane's back was to the shore. "I can't see."

Myrene twisted around, almost knocking Tiphane off her feet.

"Myrene!"

"Hush, now look."

Sedir was murmuring more incantations, but his eyes were losing their glazed appearance. His magical cloak shimmered about him, and he kissed the sacrificial knife. The boy bound to the rock beneath him sobbed in fear.

"We've got to keep going," Myrene said, sniffling. "We can't let him kill that boy."

"I'm afraid I won't be much help." The use of magic exhausted Tiphane, as if she had used up much of her life force. Being half-drowned did *not* help.

"You did your part with Cha'korth," Myrene said, "now let me do mine."

Before Tiphane could utter a single word, Myrene used their chains for leverage and hoisted her onto her back. She then waded through the shallows in a crouched position, Tiphane's legs dangling over her buttocks.

Tiphane craned her neck, but could see little beyond the sky, treetops, and mountain summits. She knew Myrene was strong, but . . .

"What are you going to do?" she asked.

"Don't know," Myrene grunted. "Sedir's 'bout out of his trance now."

Myrene's ankle chains clattered across rock as she staggered onto shore. Tiphane twisted her head, pressing her cheek against the back of Myrene's head, so she could see better. They passed Cha'korth who still stood enveloped in the spell of ecstasy, drool sliding down his chin. She brimmed with pride at a job well done.

"What's happening here?" It was Sedir, apparently fully out of his trance and much surprised by the turn of events. "You're ruining the ritual. Cha'korth! Cha'korth, to me!"

"Myrene," Tiphane said, "you've got to strike now while Sedir's between energies. If you wait, it'll be only moments before he regains his strength enough to use his powers against us."

"Hold on," Myrene said, gasping.

Tiphane gritted her teeth as Myrene's lopsided gait increased in speed. "Do I have a choice?" She prayed to Givean that Myrene wouldn't trip over her chains.

"Stick your feet out. He's coming at us with a knife."

"Wha—?"

"Do it!"

Tiphane obeyed and straightened out her legs. The warrior half-loped at the best pace she could manage, chains ringing, Tiphane bouncing. The priestess thought her teeth might rattle out of her head. The next thing she knew, she was spinning, her surroundings a blur of granite, evergreen, and sky. She glimpsed Sedir briefly, his expression frozen in astonishment, before her feet connected with his wrist and sent the sacrificial knife flying out of his hand in a glittering arc.

They stopped abruptly, but it seemed the world spun for a breathless, dizzying moment. Myrene panted raggedly.

"Uh-oh," she said.

"What? What?" Tiphane twisted her head this way and that, but she still couldn't see what was going on.

"He looks unhappy."

"Unhappy? How unhappy?"

"*Very* unhappy. He's holding his hands out, and there is a bluish, grayish glow floating above them."

"Put me down," Tiphane said. "I need to see what he's doing."

Myrene straightened, and Tiphane slid down the accursed mail shirt. When her feet met the ground, her legs were wobbly, but they didn't fail. The two shuffled around so she could see Sedir.

Indeed, Sedir was recovering rapidly, and the spell he was weaving had a sickly cast to it. Myrene sneezed violently.

"Now what?" she asked.

Tiphane thought hard. She could not attack him directly—it would go against her beliefs, and she couldn't get around his protective cloak anyway. Not that she had much energy left for spell weaving, but there was a little reservoir perhaps, and she had Myrene oozing with all her violent urges.

Sedir's incantations reached a crescendo as the cloud of blue-gray vapor enlarged.

"Myrene," Tiphane said, "it's your turn to trust me."

"I always have," her partner said in a quiet voice. "Always."

Tiphane was touched by this admission, and wished she had not seemed to doubt Myrene in return, for she depended on her brave partner—no, not just partner, but *friend*—a great deal more than she liked to admit.

"We need to get closer to Sedir."

Without comment, they shuffled within feet of the vengeful wizard. He was so involved in his spell that he could do little to stop them. It was such times as this that a magic weaver was most vulnerable and depended on his Shield for protection. Sedir's Shield still stood on the lakeshore drooling.

"I want you to face him," Tiphane said.

Myrene's shoulders tightened, but she faced Sedir without argument. She was, after all, the Shield, and putting Tiphane's life before hers was a matter of course, and of honor. Still, it humbled Tiphane.

"Now what?" Myrene asked, her voice catching on a sneeze.

"I'm going to make a little spell. I think I have the necessary energy."

"Do it quickly then!" Myrene replied.

Tiphane was already deep within herself, shaping a globe of blue fire, calling up a gust of wind, or at the very least, a slight breeze. She molded it into the globe. Then she found that spark of light and energy belonging to Myrene, and touched it with the globe.

Myrene sneezed so explosively the two of them toppled over onto the stony ground. The gust of wind, born of Tiphane's magic and channeled through Myrene's sneeze, blew Sedir's cloudy spell back into his face. He screamed, clawing at his eyes. Red, oozing boils spread instantaneously across his flesh. He whimpered and ran knee-deep into the lake, splashing water onto his face.

Myrene clucked. "Not a good move. You would think he'd know better."

Half-wedged beneath Myrene, Tiphane wriggled around so that she might see better. Sedir paused in his splashing, looked into the water, and screamed again. Something jerked on his leg.

The surface erupted and boiled around him. White deathly hands reached out to clutch at him and drag him under. The struggle was brief.

"Sedir had the key to the lock," Myrene said ruefully, "and I'm not going in after it."

They sat on the "sacrificial altar," still chained back-to-back. They had managed to use one of Sedir's knives to cut the ropes binding the boy who had been the intended sacrifice. He had then run on ahead to his village to tell family and friends the news of his rescue and the demise of Veidan Sedir in the Lake of Souls.

"The boy said his uncle was a blacksmith," Tiphane said, "and would break the chains."

"Do you think he'll remember to send him?" Myrene asked.

"I doubt it. They'll be celebrating all night."

Already, the autumn sun was making its westward descent. The Lake of Souls darkened in the shadows of the mountains.

"I'm cold," Tiphane said, "and hungry."

"Let's go before all the feasting is over."

"That village is five miles away, and over a mountain path, no less."

"Then we'd better get started."

Tiphane groaned.

They stood up, accustomed by now to coordinating their efforts.

"What about Cha'korth?" Myrene asked.

Tiphane glanced at the warrior still caught in the rapture of the ecstasy spell. "The spell will wear off in a day or so. Exposure to the harmony of Givean will undoubtedly give him a new perspective on the way he leads his life. Like it did for you."

Myrene snorted.

The two women sidled and shuffled along the trail that skirted the lake. It was slow going.

"There is one positive thing that has come out of this," Myrene said.

Tiphane, of course, knew it was not only the demise of Veidan Sedir that made this a good day, but the reaffirmation of their friendship. So it surprised her when Myrene sniffed and said with great joy, "My head has never felt so clear!"

The eagle soared above the lake anxious to tell his brothers and sisters all he had witnessed. Never before had he seen such sport, and he wondered what folly the winds held next for the two females. Whatever it was, it was sure to be entertaining.

Maybe, the eagle decided, he would stick around and find out.

Lynn Abbey

I first met Lynn Abbey in the heyday of her famous Thieves World™ anthology series. We were introduced at a professional science fiction function, but didn't really get to know one another.

It wasn't until years later that she approached me about a fantasy novel she was writing. In 1999 DAW published *Jerlayne*, a dark fantasy about an elfin woman trying to unlock the forbidden secrets of her world.

Lynn is a native New Yorker now living in the south. The following story is her first piece of fiction set in her new home. She says that it is her way of making peace with central Florida—a place she thought was "too weird for fantasy" for the first four years she lived there.

Too weird for fantasy? Is that possible?

—BW

IT'S ABOUT SQUIRRELS . . .

Lynn Abbey

"SQUIRRELS?" Nic repeated.

"Yes, ma'am," the utility company spokeswoman replied, unaware of, or completely ignoring, Nic's sarcasm.

Nic abandoned subtlety. "I lost power at nine A.M. this morning, at nine A.M. yesterday, at the same time the day before yesterday, and the day before that, too. After four days, my computer's dead as a doornail. I'm wondering if it's safe to replace my hardware, and you're telling me that my problem is *squirrels?*"

"Yes, ma'am. From what you've said, your problem is squirrels."

"*Florida* squirrels read clocks?"

"No, ma'am," the utility representative replied, steadfastly polite.

Like so many others, Nic was a transplant to the Sunshine State, and a recent one at that. Six months ago, Thursday mornings would have found her in an urban office, sipping coffee while she dreamed up new ways to seduce consumers onto the Internet. Now she was just another dot-bomb survivor with a stagnant resumé and an endangered checking account. She'd sold most of her furniture, put the rest into storage, and retreated to a one-bedroom trailer at the end of an unpaved road somewhere between the middle of nowhere and the warmer levels of Dante's Hell. Worse than that, her parents—comfortably ensconced in a nearby retirement community—were footing her rent. But worst of all, Nic's computer—her lifeline to civilization—had fallen victim to *squirrels.*

"All right, I don't understand. What makes you so certain I've got a squirrel problem?"

"You've lost power four days in a row, each time at the same time, ma'am. That sounds like squirrels. Squirrels aren't loners. They do the same things—together—day after day. They take turns chasing and following, but if the squirrel that's leading makes a mistake and falls in a pole transformer—"

"It gets fried and I lose power?" Nic cut to the chase.

"Yes, ma'am, except you didn't really lose power; your voltage fell. I'd be surprised if the drop even affected your microwave clock—"

The spokeswoman was right: Nic's microwave clock, the canary among household appliances, hadn't faltered.

"When *it* happens, there's a little hiccup as the transformer drops off the grid just long enough to reset itself," she continued. "The whole process takes a lot less than a second. You wouldn't have noticed at all, if you weren't close to the transformer."

"And then the follower-squirrels come back the next day to make the same mistake?"

"Yes, ma'am—that's exactly what happens. They keep doing what the dead squirrel did until another squirrel takes over . . . or until the whole group's dead. It's like their needle's stuck. Our engineers even have a name for them: pallbearer squirrels. It's a real problem here in Florida."

Only in Florida, Nic thought before asking: "How serious a problem? My computer's already lost its hard drive to these hiccups. How long will squirrels be committing serial suicide in my vicinity?"

"Usually it stops after three or four days, ma'am, but they had one up near Tallahassee that went on for nineteen days. If you've got one of those fancy batteries, you shouldn't have any problems. Those stick surge protectors they sell in Wal*mart won't help you against squirrels and ospreys—"

Without knowing the cause of her problem, Nic had anticipated its solution. Along with a replacement hard drive, UPS had just delivered fifteen pounds of continuously recharged, uninterruptible battery power. She could safely resurrect her computer—assuming there wasn't something Floridian that went after batteries the way squirrels went after hard drives. Determined not to be caught blind again, Nic asked—

"Ospreys?"

"Birds, ma'am. Some call them fish-eagles. They're endangered because people've cut down all the snag trees around the lakes. Sushine Power built nesting platforms on top of our poles near the lakes. The ospreys think our poles are as good as pine trees. Around this time of year, they bring fish back to the nests for their babies. They carry the fish in their claws and have to drop them in the nest before they can land. But sometimes they miss and the fish fall into the pole transformers. They don't usually miss twice, though, so when a transformer hiccups two days running, and at the same time, we think squirrels."

Nic wondered why Sunshine Power didn't put lids on their transformers but didn't ask the question, and the conversation died a natural death. She had her day's work cut out for her. Even with the best backups—which Nic didn't have—resurrecting a computer took hours. It was well past midnight before she left the kitchen table that had replaced her ergonomic desk. Since her hard drive's manufacturer replaced its warrantied products, no questions asked, in exchange for the defunct hardware, Nic's last acts of a long day were wrapping the hard drive in antistatic plastic and boxing it for the post office.

Her eyes were closed before her head hit the pillow. For a few moments, she cursed the slings and arrows of outrageous fortune that had her sleeping in a secondhand bed, but the wounds were too familiar to keep her awake.

Florida wasn't called the Sunshine State by accident. The dawning sky brightened quickly and even if it hadn't, there was a Chevrolet dealership at the other end of the dirt road which opened, noisily, at seven. Nic made coffee and stuck close to her resurrected computer, waiting for the witching—squirreling— hour. At 9:08 the battery's LEDs flickered from green to red and back again while somewhere in its heavy depths a switch clicked twice.

Another squirrel was transformer bouillabaisse, but Nic's computer had survived. She collected the sealed box, headed for her car and the post office. Her neighbor—one RJ Walker, according to the letters shakily painted across his mailbox—had done a worse-than-usual job of parking his pickup truck last night. Nic couldn't get her Honda around its bright-red rear end without running through mud. Though the Honda could probably handle the risk, Nic couldn't. She considered tucking a nasty note under RJ's wipers, but his truck was plastered with Deep-South decals in praise of guns, NASCAR, and the University of Florida Gators; prudent Yankee that she was, Nic knew better than to roil *those* waters.

Other than the Chevy dealership, there weren't many buildings within walking distance of Nic's trailer, but one of them, barely, was a post office. There were no sidewalks, of course, and traffic was surprisingly thick for a road in the middle of nowhere. Nic treated it with respect, paying more attention to what was hurtling along the asphalt than what else might be walking beside it. She didn't realize she wasn't alone until a man warned:

"Don't do it!"

The dead center of Florida wasn't the state's most prosperous region. As near as Nic could tell, it rated near the wrong end of just about every county standard, but full-blown derelicts weren't common, even along a road once known as the Hobo's Highway.

The man wasn't criminally scary. He didn't look strong or steady enough to wield a weapon. Nic didn't doubt she could outrun him—and she wasn't a runner. His clothes were long, loose, layered, and literally ragged. Whatever their original colors, they'd faded in the sun and seemed covered by grayish dust. His hair matched his clothes: faded, dusted with gray, limp, and shoulder-length. Nic lowered her eyes as the distance between them shrank.

"Don't send it away. Don't! Take it home. Get him out of the box!"

Nic stretched her eyes and wished she hadn't. The man's stare was dark, wild, and riveted to the box she carried. She clutched it tight and held her breath as they passed.

"Keep it! Keep it. He belongs *here!*"

He—the derelict had definitely muttered the word *he.*

She dared a backward glance: grass, sand, the usual roadside debris, and the Chevrolet dealership in the background, but no derelict, not even a shadow of one. No screeching brakes or battered bodies in the road, either, or footprints in the sand. The faded man had simply vanished.

Heaven knew the Florida sun got brutal enough to fry human brains, but not in the season the natives called winter, so Nic called the derelict a waking dream, a brain-cramp—the sort of mistake anyone could make and no reason not to finish her trek to the post office. But she returned to the trailer instead.

RJ Walker had removed his pickup; Nic could have driven her Honda. There was a squirrel sitting on the hood, twitching its tail, the way squirrels did. Another squirrel perched above the trailer's door while a third raced along an overhead wire, headed for a transformer pole. Her heart skipped when the squirrel leaped safely for thicker wires where it paused, twitching and scolding.

Nic climbed the aluminum steps to her front door. The drive's manufacturer gave her a whole month to return the hard drive before it debited her hemorrhaging credit card. She poured cold coffee into a rinsed cup and sent an e-mail to a close, yet distant, friend who lived not far from her stored furniture—

Hi, Sara. Sorry I've been out of touch. This places gets weirder all the time. Monday I lost a hard drive to suicidal squirrels— pallbearer squirrels, according to Sunshine Power, and they should know, I guess. Today I thought a saw a hobo's ghost out on the highway. I'm still sending out resumés by the score and hearing nothing back. Unless it's my folks, I'm lucky if I say two words to another human being in a day—I wound up complaining to Sunshine Power just to have someone to talk to. It's them or the squirrels. I keep telling myself this is only temporary, that I'll be out of here in a month, so there's no need to get my stuff out of storage up north—as if I could afford to bring it down here.

Miss you. Miss winter. Miss everything I ever complained about.

All for now . . . Nic.

Nic was catching a nap in the bedroom between rounds of boredom and e-mailing resumés when someone banged loudly on the door. There was no good reason for anyone to come knocking on her door, but a bunch of bad ones. The first bad reason to form fully in Nic's imagination was her parents, who were in good health but *retired* now and *getting old.*

Never mind that bad news usually traveled by phone; once the idea had occurred to Nic, it filled her entire imagination. She had hospitals on the brain before opening the door.

Nic heard the twangy drawl of the natives: "Afternoon, ma'am. Bobby Walker, ma'am—"

He was too old to be a Bobby. No one over the age of eighteen should be a Bobby, unless he was a professional athlete and Bobby Walker, though not grossly out of shape, was long past eighteen. His face was more weathered than tan beneath unruly hair that had started to recede. He squinted as though he needed glasses—which might account for his parking habits.

But Bobby Walker—RJ Walker, in all probability—had all his teeth, at least all the ones that showed when he talked. Nic hadn't gotten used to seeing people her own age with missing teeth. Snaggle-tooth grins were a constant reminder of how fundamentally *different* life was in dead-center Florida.

Bobby Walker stuck out his hand. She clasped it barely long enough to say—

"Nicole Larsens."

"I don't mean to bother you, ma'am, but you've got to quit feeding the squirrels."

"I'm not feeding them," Nic replied, feeling very un-ma'am-like in her jeans and nap-wrinkled T-shirt.

"Maybe you don't think you're feeding them, ma'am, but they wouldn't be here like this, if they weren't finding food."

Nic blinked and realized that between Bobby and his red pickup, there'd been a squirrel explosion. The animals were agitated. She couldn't count more than a few without losing track. There were at least a dozen and more when she looked right or left.

"I'm not feeding them. I'm not doing anything to attract them."

"Well, ma'am, then maybe they've got a colony under your trailer. In winter they like to find someplace warm—"

A colony of squirrels under the sagging bedroom floor? The image conjured up countless bad movies, and Nic's thoughts must have shown on her face because Bobby Walker quickly said—

"I could check underneath, ma'am. Set a few traps—?"

Spring-loaded rings of rusty, serrated metal added themselves to Nic's imagination without improving her sense of security.

"*Live* traps, ma'am," Bobby Walker added, accurately guessing the reason for Nic's silence. "I'll empty 'em down the road. I'll look for holes, too. You don't want to go under there, ma'am."

Southern hospitality. Southern charm. And every bit as effective as Northern sarcasm. Whatever Nic saw when she looked at Bobby Walker, what *he* saw was another damn Yankee without the sense God gave ants. On the other hand, he was absolutely right: Nic didn't want to crawl around under the trailer. She could waste time begging the park owner or accept Bobby Walker's offer.

The choice was clear, but before Bobby Walker went off to get his traps, Nic asked, "Have you heard of pallbearer squirrels?"

He gave her a doubting glance. "No, ma'am, can't say that I have."

So she told him, in quick sentences, about the power problems, her call to the utility company, and the explanation she'd received.

"Huh," Bobby Walker concluded. "They do get into habits, but so do people. Never heard anything about them following leaders—" He caught himself, changed his mind. "My momma used to say that when squirrels got crazy, it was because they were chasing brownies. My momma said things like that; she was Scottish."

Nic took note of the past tense and said nothing about Mrs. Walker's opinions of ancestry.

For the next hour, Mrs. Walker's son thumped and cursed beneath her rented trailer on his way to deciding that the crawlspace wasn't squirrel-infested.

"There's a hole or two they might fit through, but there's no scat, no nothing to say they've set up housekeeping. Looks like they've just got a fascination for your front door—"

They both took a moment to study the squirrels. Nic couldn't say that there were more now than when Bobby first knocked on her door, but certainly there were no less.

"If you're not feeding them, I can't imagine why they're doing that, but once a few of them get trapped, the rest will get the idea that there's nothing here for them." Bobby had set his traps beneath the steps and beneath a holly bush midway between the steps and Nic's car. "You might hear something as they're sprung," he warned Nic.

Nic forced a smile and thanked Bobby Walker for his help. He lingered at the foot of the aluminum stairs as if he expected an invitation. She gave him a question instead.

"What happens next, if the traps work?"

"Oh, they'll work, ma'am," Bobby Walker replied, lapsing into Southern formality. "I've got 'em baited with more peanuts and corn than any squirrel can resist. Might not trap them all, but there'll be a mess of squirrels in those traps when I check them tomorrow morning."

"So, you'll be checking them? I don't have to?"

"No, ma'am. I'll take care of everything on my way to work."

"Good," Nic said. "I really appreciate that."

She closed the door and closed the curtains, too. Twice during the long evening, Nic thought she heard the sounds of squirrels succumbing to corn and peanuts. She stifled her curiosity and stayed away from the curtains. The local news had finished and there was no reason not to go to bed.

Darkness did wonders for Nic's imagination. Never mind that she was reasonably certain that squirrels weren't active at night, she could hear their little claws scratching the roof. Nic tensed, expecting to hear the traps clanging, and stayed that way. A green-glowing midnight became one A.M., then one-thirty.

Finally, noise happened: not the expected *clang*, but a duller *thud*; and not outside the trailer, but inside.

Nic kept a broom handle between the mattress and the box spring—a souvenir from an urban survival class. With it grasped in her fist, she slid silently out of bed. Aside from glowing clocks, the trailer was dark—or it should have been. There was a steady, soft light at the end of the corridor connecting the bedroom. By that light Nic saw that both the curtains and the front door were still closed, exactly as she remembered leaving them.

Fear and curiosity battled for Nic's mind. Curiosity won—because, with the door and curtains undisturbed, she expected an annoying explanation for the light. Striding to the living room, Nic's only concession to caution came when she sidestepped along the kitchen counter rather than walk straight into the light.

Nic was fortunate that the counter was behind her when she beheld a gray-clad, self-luminous woman kneeling in front of the door: it kept her upright when she reeled and knocked unwashed silverware to the floor. The clatter—the loudest noise Nic had ever heard—surprised the kneeling woman who flung herself at the closed door.

The whole trailer should have rocked on its wheeled foundations, Nic thought with the slow clarity of panic; it hadn't. There should have been noise as the gray-clad woman pounded her fists against the door; there wasn't. The woman should have known that beating the door wouldn't help, that she needed to release the bolt and turn the doorknob.

Any full-grown woman knew that.

Then again, any full-grown woman didn't glow with her own silvery light, and most people had rounder, fleshier faces than that turned toward Nic.

"Wha—?" Nic croaked. She inhaled and tried again. "Who are you? What are you doing in my living room?"

The woman heard Nic's questions; that much showed in her reactions, but she didn't answer, just pushed herself away from the door and toward the curtains which didn't move when she touched them.

Nic wondered if she might be dreaming and willed herself to wake up. Nothing changed, then the retreating woman's gown-like clothes withdrew across a box—the box Nic hadn't gotten to the post office. It was upside down and on the floor; Nic guessed what had awakened her.

The other woman raised her hands to her face when she saw the box. Nic imagined a horrified gasp, but heard nothing.

"What do you want?" Nic demanded, though the answer to that was obvious and the wiser question would have been, *Why do you want a dead hard drive?*

The woman didn't—or couldn't—answer. She reached for the box, tears glistening on her luminous cheeks. To Nic's eyes, the woman's fingers touched the box but failed to grasp it. The pieces came together in Nic's mind; their pattern was irrational, but clear.

"You want what's on the drive," Nic murmured. "You want what's *trapped* on the drive."

The weeping woman met Nic's eyes with silent eloquence. Her mouth opened, shaped a word Nic couldn't hear, then she vanished, leaving Nic with the impression of a streak of light drilling through the wall.

Blinded by the dark, Nic stayed put, balanced on the cusp between fear and curiosity. Once again, curiosity won. She opened the refrigerator and by its light retrieved the cardboard box. One corner had been slightly crushed by its fall and there seemed to be a faint odor of ozone around the front door, though that dissipated quickly. Nic threw the bolt and opened the door to moonlight.

Nothing—no footprints, not even a squirrel or a glass slipper.

Back inside, Nic closed the refrigerator, turned on a brighter light, and opened the box. Like every hard drive meant to be installed in a personal computer, Nic's dead drive was a factory-sealed slab of metal and plastic, plastered with warranty warnings. Inside the slab were magnetic disks so sensitive that microscopic specks of dust would ruin them. Nic considered breaking the seal, but she couldn't afford to void the warranty. By 100-watt light, her curiosity soured. She turned out all the lights and made her way to the bedroom where sleep came in fitful naps and broken dreams about a luminous woman who opened a hard drive.

Nic was still in bed when Bobby Walker knocked on her door. Wrapping herself quickly in a bathrobe, she faced him at the top of the steps. He'd already loaded his two traps, each seething with frightened squirrels, into his pickup truck.

"Didn't get 'em all," he admitted, "but we got enough. Look around—" He opened his arms to the yard where not a single squirrel chattered or twitched.

"Thanks."

"Ma'am?" Clearly he expected greater enthusiasm. "Ma'am, are you okay?"

Nic nodded. "I haven't had my coffee yet . . . didn't sleep too well either."

"Traps must've been snapping all night."

She could have said yes and ended the conversation, but Nic needed coffee before she could lie effectively. "No, I never heard them. It was something else—"

Nic watched the squirrels tumbling over one another. Echoing memories of computer crashes, pallbearer squirrels, a strange man warning her to take the box home, and a stranger woman crouched by the door blurred her vision. She blinked and focused on Bobby Walker's face.

"Did your mother say what a brownie looked like?"

"Ma'am?"

"Yesterday you said your mother told you that squirrels chased brownies. Did she ever say what one looked like?"

He shrugged. "Can't say as I remember. Little fellows, I guess. Couldn't be very big, could they, if the squirrels chased them."

"Not tall, then? Not tall and thin and silvery—or maybe dusty?"

Bobby Walker gave Nic a slow, sidelong stare. "You see something like that?"

"Not exactly." Nic couldn't lie, but she could evade.

A squirrel ran along the utility wires. It jumped from the wires into a pine tree's dense branches and a heartbeat later dropped to the roof of Nic's car where it gave her another version of Bobby Walker's sidelong stare.

Nic said, "They're back."

"They were never here, ma'am."

"The squirrels." She pointed at her car.

"Damn. Thought we'd scared them off."

"They're the pallbearers."

Bobby Walker didn't know what to make of Nic's remark. He stood silent on the porch while a second and third squirrel took position on Nic's car.

"I better get rid of these and reset the traps—" Bobby's voice rose, as though he were asking permission.

"Did your mother ever say anything about brownies, except that squirrels chased them? Like were there special ways to catch them or—or set them free?"

Bobby shrugged. "Only that they were lucky and they'd clean house for you if you set out a bowl of milk and soaking bread for them. I think she was hoping for miracles. She had me and my brothers and my father to clean up after. It was a lot of work, if you know what I mean, and we maybe didn't make it easy for her. She went home to Scotland when I was twelve . . . said it was a vacation, but she never came back."

"I'm sorry," Nic said without hesitation.

"She didn't like the weather here either. Missed the rocks and hills and all those cold, dreary days."

"And the tall, thin ghosts?"

Another shrug. "Not ghosts. Fairies—not cute, cartoon fairies, but the nasty kind, one step removed from devils." He glanced at his pickup. "I gotta get to work—"

He paused, as if expecting a similar revelation from Nic. When she said nothing, he promised to reset the traps when he got home. There were four squirrels chasing one another around Nic's car by then and dozens more when he returned in the late afternoon. Nic caught Bobby peeking at her door and windows as he reset the traps.

While Nic watched and fretted, Bobby Walker tucked his second trap under the stairs to her front door and, after a vigorous shake of his head, walk back to his own home without knocking on her door. Try as she might, Nic couldn't blame him. He had a job . . . a life. Nic's hands trembled as she typed an e-mail to Sara—

. . . It's worse than weird, Sara. Ever since I replaced the hard

*drive, I've been surrounded by obsessed squirrels. No kidding.
They're all over this place. I've got a neighbor who's trapping
them and carting them away by the dozens. He thinks I'm feeding them. I'm not, of course; I'm too busy sending out resumés
to be feeding squirrels. He's got to think I'm a slug, not that I've
seen a slug around here, but every time he knocks on the door,
I'm just waking up. I didn't sleep well last night. I dreamed there
was someone in the trailer with me—a woman all dressed in
glowing, silvery gray. In my dream—I'm telling myself it had to
be a dream—the fairy woman was trying to steal the dead hard
drive because there was a brownie trapped on it because squirrels
had chased it into a transformer. My dream made sense, but
nothing makes sense now, except that I'm losing it . . . fast.*

Nic checked her e-mail throughout the evening. She picked up
the phone more than once, but her per-minute long-distance rate
was too high for commiseration, even on a night when she found
herself more depressed than she'd been when she'd first lost her
job. When midnight came and went without communication
from the civilized world, Nic shuffled into the kitchen, ready to
wolf down some unhealthy snack on her way to bed. Her hand
was inches away from a box of generic cookies when she spotted
a can of evaporated milk she didn't remember purchasing.

A bowl of milk, Bobby Walker had said: bread soaking in a
bowl of milk for brownies, luck, and a clean kitchen. The formula
hadn't worked for Mrs. Walker, but Nic was willing to give it a
try. She shredded slices of bread into a milk-filled cereal bowl.
Then, because she couldn't feel any more foolish, Nic set the bowl
beside the dead hard drive.

It was still there, lumpy, scummy, and utterly unappetizing,
when she awoke hours later. So were the squirrels, both in the
woven-wire traps and racing free around the trailer. They'd
grown destructive overnight. Several of the rodents squatted on
the car's hood, stripping away her windshield wipers as though
the black rubber were licorice candy. Nic slapped the picture window in a futile attempt to scatter them.

The sound snared the attention of a squirrel perched on the narrow banister beside the door. It launched itself at the window and hung there a moment before sliding down. Another squirrel hit the window hard enough to make Nic jump away with surprise. This second squirrel, more determined than the first, fought the pull of gravity. Its dark claws squealed frantically against the glass before it, too, fell from sight.

When a third squirrel leaped from an overhead branch, Nic had had enough. Grabbing a dish towel, she burst out the door, flailing cloth and shouting. The squirrels scattered, but not far. When Nic turned around, one of them was at the top of the steps, scratching at the door which was closed, but not completely shut. She whirled the towel above her head and charged.

"Whoa!"

The voice came out of nowhere, along with an opposite pull on the towel. Nic let go of the cloth. She spun around and found herself perilously close to Bobby Walker.

"One more step, and you'd have landed on the ones we already caught."

Nic looked down at the writhing trap inches from her foot. She didn't know what to say, but was spared the need for words when a squirrel flung itself at the window.

Bobby Walker whistled his astonishment. "Never seen a squirrel do that before."

"They're pallbearer squirrels."

"Didn't you say that had something to do with transformers and blowing out your computer?"

She nodded.

"But these fellows are jumping at your windows."

Nic nodded again. "I lost a hard drive when the transformer first blew. It's sitting out on the table by the window. They've spotted it and are trying to get to it."

There was a squirrel—maybe the same squirrel, maybe a different one—scratching at the front door. Bobby clapped his hands. It scampered a few yards, then sat up on its haunches, twitching its tail and poised for another leap at the door.

"Is that something squirrels do?" he asked. "Doesn't seem

right to me. It's not like there's anything for them to eat in a computer."

Nic took a breath before explaining. "There's something on the hard drive—something that got trapped there when the hard drive failed. Now, instead of just a few squirrels stuck in a rut, it's attracting more and more of them."

Bobby Walker opened his mouth, but shut it without saying a word as another squirrel leaped at the window. The glass shuddered in sunlight.

"Maybe you should hide that hard drive where the squirrels can't see it. Too bad it's attracting squirrels. If it was turkeys or deer you'd really have something going during hunting season—"

Nic's imagination took a Hitchcockian turn as she imagined Thanksgiving-sized birds hurling themselves at the trailer.

"Or you could just bing it out here and give the little beggars what they want. I'd like to see what they'd do with a worthless hard drive."

"It's broken, not worthless. If I don't get it back to the manufacturer, I've got to pay for the new one."

"Then take it to the post office. Let them worry about the damned squirrels."

Nic sighed and told Bobby Walker about the disappearing man she'd encountered on her way to the post office.

"Just some crazy old man—"

She told him about the luminous woman with silver tears.

"A dream—"

"Not a dream," Nic insisted. "I wished it were a dream. I even tried to wish myself awake, but I wasn't asleep to begin with." She saw disbelief in Bobby Walker's eyes. "You must think I'm the one who's crazy."

"Not crazy. Someone who doesn't want to be here and would give anything to be anywhere else. It's too bad—"

Before Bobby could share the rest of his insight, they were both startled by two squirrels striking the window in quick succession.

"I better hide that hard drive."

Nic bounded up the stairs and didn't object when Bobby Walker followed her. The hard drive was in plain sight on the table. So was the bowl of milk-soaked bread. Nic grabbed it first, but not quickly enough.

"There's where you've made your mistake," he said flatly.

"Where?"

"Well, ma'am—I told you, bread in a bowl of milk won't work. That's for Scottish brownies. What we've got around here are *suth'run* brownies. You want to catch a *suth'run* brownie, ma'am, you've got to set out beer and a dish of pork rinds, or some of those little hot dogs in a can—"

Nic froze.

"That was a *joke*," Bobby Walker insisted. "You've got to laugh at yourself, Nicole Larsens, or whatever's eating at you *is* gonna make you crazy."

"I don't belong here."

"Nobody belongs *here*." He opened his arms to include the whole trailer park. "We're just passing through on our way up, or down."

"Which way do you think I'm going?"

"Can't tell yet."

"And you?"

"Can't tell that either. Up, I hope."

Nic offered to make coffee and washed the incriminating evidence out of the cereal bowl while the elixir filtered into the pot. She returned the hard drive to its antistatic pouch and stuffed the pouch into the cardboard box which, after a moment's thought, she put in the oven.

"It doesn't work," she explained. "And it's so dirty, I wouldn't use it, even if it did."

"Why not just take the box to the post office?"

"Because today's Saturday and the post office isn't open at this hour on Saturdays; and, besides, I'm going to try the beer thing."

"Do you believe in Santa Claus and the Easter Bunny, too?"

Sarcasm sounded different with a mid-Florida drawl, but no less biting when wielded by an obvious expert. Nic had underestimated Bobby Walker and his bright-red pickup.

"There are squirrels knocking themselves silly against my window—"

But the twitchy multitude was fast departing. Only one squirrel chewed rubber on the hood of Nic's car, another pair circled the traps that held their siblings or cousins, the rest had scattered.

"Out of sight, out of mind," Nic and Bobby Walker said together, then fell silent together, wondering if something significant had taken place.

"Can I borrow a can of beer?" Nic asked to break the silence.

"You could, if I had any. Never got a liking for the stuff. Tastes like horse piss. Wouldn't do you any good right now, even if I did. According to my momma, brownies are nocturnal. 'Course, what did my momma know? She never caught one, not in Scotland or Florida. Could be our Florida brownies like their beer in the morning or, could be, they spend the whole day racing squirrels and don't get thirsty till the squirrels go to bed. My daddy's kind of like that."

Nic would have asked a few polite questions about the Walker family if she'd gotten the change, but with coffee still dripping into the pot, Bobby Walker got restless.

"I'd better load those squirrels into my truck and take them out to the woods—it's cruel to leave them trapped up. You going to want me to set 'em out again later today, or do you think the beer will do the trick?"

"Better set them out," Nic decided and knew in a dark corner of her heart that the reason had nothing to do with squirrels.

"You gonna put the beer in the oven with the box or put 'em both where the squirrels can see them?" Bobby asked, with his hand poised about the doorknob.

"I don't know, Nic admitted. "I'll decide tonight and tell you tomorrow."

Bobby Walker drove off with the squirrel traps and was still gone when Nic went shopping for a single can of beer and another of Vienna-style sausages. His pickup was back in its usual place— partly blocking Nic's end of the dirt road—when she returned. She thought about knocking on his door for a change, but the traps were already set, and she locked herself in for the night.

After a day's contemplation, Nic had rejected both the oven
and the table for her Florida-brownie trap, choosing instead to
build herself a tower of beer-filled plastic cups, sausage-bearing
plates, and noisy silverware on the seat of a warm rocking chair
with the naked hard drive tied securely to the back. If anything
happened overnight—not that anything possibly *could* happen—
the Rube-Goldberg construction insured that Nic wouldn't sleep
through it.

And she didn't. When the tower collapsed somewhere between
midnight and dawn, she was sitting bolt upright in bed before the
last fork clattered to the linoleum floor. There were no follow-up
sounds, but there *was* light! Grabbing her broom handle, Nic
raced down the corridor in time to see something dark and cat-
sized dart behind the refrigerator. The scuttling shadow didn't
hold Nic's attention long. The light was in the living room—two
lights: one feminine and familiar, the other masculine and also
familiar, but more aristocratic now than he'd been in sunlight.

The man's dark eyes shone with an unfriendly temper. He
tossed a flowing cape over one shoulder and stalked *through* the
front door. The woman gathered her skirts but hestitated, watching the refrigerator as closely as she watched Nic.

"I set him free," Nic reminded her glowing guest. "Or her. I
think that's what you wanted, and if it was, I think I'm entitled
to an explanation. What happened? How did he, or she, wind up
on a hard drive? What's with the squirrels? And, last but not
least, what are *you*?"

"I am myself," the woman replied without moving her lips.
Her voice was whisper-soft in Nic's ears, yet easily understood.
"As you are yourself and the little ones—the *brownies*—" She
made it plain that the label was not one she preferred to use. "Are
themselves. They know better—" She cast a mother's stare
toward the refrigerator. "But the *ee-lek-trece-ity*—" Another
word that did not come easily to the glowing woman, "Is so sweet
and their minds are so small. When they play, they cannot always
remember the danger."

Darkness surrounded by dust bunnies emerged from beneath
the refrigerator. Nic got an impression of spindly limbs and a

leathery, sharp-featured face before it was gone—*through* the door—and only the dust bunnies remained, settling to the doormat.

"And they wind up trapped on a hard drive until you rescue them?" Nic asked.

The woman—the fairy queen, Titania?—shook her head. "Usually," she uttered a birdlike musical sound, "this happening is rare, very rare. We hear them suffering, but rescue is difficult —impossible."

"Without the help of something more irresistible than electricity, something like beer?"

Titania nodded. "There will be great celebration—and fear, too, that they will forget everything and think because one was rescued, there is no longer any danger. This happening was chance, not plan."

Nic heard more fear than celebration in Titania's voice. "If there's ever anything I can do . . . set out another round of beer and sausages . . . ?"

Titania raised her arm and Nic felt a brush of warm velvet against her cheek and the faintest scent of ozone, like dew-fresh air after a thunderstorm. Nic closed her eyes as the velvety touch passed over them. When she reopened them, she was alone.

Hey, Sara—Sorry I've been such a lousy correspondent. It's been so hectic these last two weeks! Would you believe I got a job right here in Central Florida and I've signed a lease on a house—a real house with a porch and garden? I'm going to fly up to rent a van and bring my furniture home. And it looks like I might not be alone when I do. . . .

DAW:sf
BOOKS